DRIVE-BY
CANNIBALISM
IN THE
BAROQUE
TRADITION

DRIVE-BY CANNIBALISM

IN THE

BAROQUE TRADITION

OR, THE BOOK OF BEING SICK OF IT ALL:
IT ALL IT ALL IT ALL,
MULTIPLIED BY INFINITY

AUTHOR'S CUT

AMIR PARSA

P.O. Box 200340
Brooklyn, NY 11220
www.upsetpress.org

Established in 2000, UpSet Press is an independent press based in Brooklyn. The original impetus of the press was to upset the status quo through literature. UpSet Press has expanded its mission to promote new work by new authors; the first works, or complete works, of established authors—placing a special emphasis on restoring to print new editions of exceptional texts; and first-time translations of works into English. Overall, UpSet Press endeavors to advance authors' innovative visions, and works that engender new directions in literature.

Book design by Wendy Lee / wendyleedesign.com

Library of Congress Control Number: 2014916017

ISBN 9781937357931
Printed in the United States of America

PUBLISHER'S NOTE

I knew I had to read this book after hearing its title, and I knew UpSet Press had to re-issue it after reading it. I didn't know its re-release would eerily coincide with current events: uprisings in various parts of the world, revolutionary movements in full swing, shifting tribal and national affiliations, and a rash of beheadings in the news.

This book was written in early 2000's, and originally published by Non Serviam Press in 2006. UpSet Press began the task of re-publication with Parsa in 2012. These are important dates because they inform how the text should be read, that is, they offer context. They illuminate the prescient nature of the work. They caution the reader to not consider the work as spin-off of sensationalized media. They confirm the timelessness, and timeliness, of the story.

Parsa's satirical depiction is remarkably true to the framework of revolution, from initial upheaval to internal discord, to the "disappearance" of confidants, to civil war, to the ultimate (albeit impermanent) emergence of an unforeseen, ruling party. Parsa conjures scenes of extreme violence in serene, suburban settings. The violence serves as parable for the madness we are capable of. It's so ridiculous it succeeds in detaching the impetus for revolution from the monstrous acts of revolution, thus allowing the reader unbiased entrance as witness. As readers, we are safe because we are neutral, detached. We don't know which side we're on. We can't see ourselves on either side. And we're not asked to. I'm thankful to Parsa for this avail, this access. It's what allows the text to be experienced universally.

Where else could revolution happen and no one notice? The suburbs are microcosms of ignored rebellions. Drivers run through stop signs, turn right on red, speed, pass on the right, partake in road-rage, drink and drive (bars are situated off highways), drive more on sidewalks (to enter/exit parking lots) than walk on them. It's a wasteland of garage apartments and shopping malls. But even here, there is insurgence. Martyrs are exalted and eulogized on weekends. Poetry is composed and sung in basements. Dismemberment is planned and carried out in parking lots, off exit ramps. Traffic is transcendent.

I confess *Drive-by Cannibalism in the Baroque Tradition* makes me giddy. I find it, in all its despicable hilariousness and imagistic excesses, exhilarating. I've read this book multiple times, and once I start, I can't put it down. "Ostrich in a Cadillac!" This could be any cry, any expletive. But it's not. This could be based on a true story. But it's not. This could be inconceivable. But it's not. This could be the chorus of our times. But it's not. This could be drug-induced babel. But it's not. This could be one book you absolutely have to read. It may just save your life.

— Robert Booras,
   April 2015

For all those who have lived in the 'burbs
And all those who have not

Yékee bood yékee nabood
Zeeré gonbadé kabood

'Ostrich in a Cadillac! Ostrich in a Cadillac!'
The call like a cuckoo's metronomic exactitude (a tick and a tock, a tick, a tock) spews from the inner reaches of our cantankerous comrade's throat. Like a cock's dawnish cue rises from deep within as he stands proudly and alone upon a raised patch of dirt (O how solitary he seems, so nostalgically *treeest*—French for sad) and crows! Like a crocodile's (the swamp, the muddied waters surrounding his imaginary hovel), tears stream down his visage. Like a... Well, it would serve the reader enough to learn that the crooning does get somewhere, what with the coup de grace given by the swerving before him of a car, seemingly out of nowhere. Certain about the seemingly? I am—although it appeared as if, literally from some dreamland or daze, it had stumbled upon the confines of the tale.

'There, there!' crows still crestfallen the cockeyed creep. 'An ostrich! In a Cadillac!'

The vehicle has come to a halt in the emergency lane, right before the exit ramp where our hero, our panicked hero, has been jumping up and down. His finger is now pointing to the site of the unusual scene, hoping that the newly arrived will be capable of offering some form of assistance.

The door on the driver's side of the car is now opening, slowly—inviting, almost, out of this slowness, to the netherworld whence it seemed to have originated. A tall gentleman swerves out, immaculately dressed, and with a cowboy hat that he immediately places on his head as he straightens the torso. Bottom of jacket pulled down too—a crisp tug—and the collar is fixed, splashingly. He speaks not however, walks simply to the other side of the car, on the curb, next to the hero, looking down.

'There! There!' thunders again the man, pointing to the bottom of the hill. 'An ostrich in a Cadillac!'

The lanky guy looks down. He still hasn't said a word, but there, indeed, no doubt, none whatsoever, he spots the rear end of a white Cadillac, at the bottom of the hill, its front end hidden by the thick foliage of a tree it seemed to a) have been deliberately parked under (but how and why, if that indeed were the case), b) have skidded to by accident.

He turns his head back to the crooner, no sooner has stopped half-way and like a brooder turned around again, that he checks out the improbable event, then turns again, uttering, thinkingly:

'An ostrich? Are you sure?'

Staccato, the query. With gusto and gumption, yet not aggressive. Surprised yet without sentiment. Curious, yet uncaring—at the same time. Wondering, and somehow… oblivious.

'Yes, yes!' the hero says urgently. 'There is an ostrich in that Cadillac. An ostrich I tell you, in the Cadillac!'

Pause of the driver. Quick glance down, quick glance back. He wants to say, Well what the hell is an ostrich doing down in that Caddy and what in the hey are you doing up here yelling if you know it, but he says: 'But the whole ostrich? I mean, shouldn't it be just the head, isn't that what ostriches…' He trails off, uncertain and muted, beset, basically, by further doubts. (Not his fault, that's how we're taught… Not his fault/That's how we're taught/Not to doubt/Just to shout/ That's our lot/Do your part/Or be shot/Not necessarily/Just metaphorically/Either—sings hiphopishly, spokenwordishly, with bent fingers distorted extended fragmented, in all directions on hands gesturing with contortions on arms flowing in gyrations, the narrator in the midst of the tale…)

The current hero of this beginning of our story is frustrated. The nerve of this fellow! 'What do you mean?!' blathers he. 'I'm not believed! I'm offended! Of course the whole damn ostrich is in there, if I'm telling you!'

O vagaries of chance! O despicable cruelties perpetrated by the weary, the wicked, the demoniacally devious among us! O senseless tragedies spun from group dynamics! O irresolvable dilemmas of humanhood! Shall the laws governing the fragile fabric of our firmament rear once more their ugly heads? Shall we bear witness to another in the gory annals of rebellions, power-grabbing schemes, power-sharing arrangements, manipulation and control of inhabitants, subsequent betrayals, assassinations, coups, overthrows, civil wars, consolidations of powers, new laws and games and names and the labeling of people as undesirables of some kind? And then another revolution? (Maybe.) Reader, are you willing? Shall you avail yourself? Or have I given away too much already?

The driver, still staring down at the back of the Caddy, is hesitant, yet somehow believes that doing a good deed is worth it and that, besides, what's the risk, what would happen at the bottom of a hill in or around a Cadillac off the exit ramp of a, granted, not so oft traveled expressway but not some far-flung deserted nowheresville either, with a panicked dude who surely has better things to do than just stand by the ramp and jump

up and down and shout Ostrich in a Cadillac Ostrich in a Cadillac if there were not some real, legitimate, defensible, desirable, reason—and besides, besides: what would he be planning
anyway, some voodoo version of a rebellion, a takeover, some
grotesque, grossed-out, homegrown version of nausea-inspir-
ing, monstrous, goonish cannibalism? Yeah, right…

'Let's rock 'n' roll then, shall we?' he says cheerfully, quite
the able-bodied volunteer, and quite forthright and forthcoming (and almost frothing at the mouth) in his desire to help the
considerably shorter shouter (a whole foot maybe, the lanky
dude measuring oh… six-four, five-ish, and the current main
character somewhere around, say, five-six-ish). 'Let's go on
down and take a look!'

He notices, however, that his counterpart is hesitating, and
offers, yes, solace. 'Are you all right?' says he, lending even an
arm to the other's shoulder (the shoulder-for-head exchange
not appropriate yet given the short time of acquaintance).

'Fine, fine!' the other says. 'Just that…' (It's a fake hesitation, cowboy, watch out: the concocted and contorted slide of
the neck sideways, that's not what a real man would do, even if
he were worried! Or scared! There's no hesitation there, there's
no fear! He's setting you up guy, look: the sly, invisible smile,
the I-don't-really-wanna-go-but-yeah-let's-go that's actually a
gotcha sucka of the worse kind… The Pause, before peering
down… The pointed Glance… Don't go down, I tell you,
don't do it, don't fall for it, I mean, I know, trust me, I *know*…)

'It'll be fine, really,' the tall driver says. 'We'll just see what's
up and be back—or, do you prefer that I go alone?'

'Well,' hesitates the hero, 'I guess it'll be all right.' (Set up!
Set up!)

The driver thinks of informing himself a bit more, might
be helpful after all, useful (go ahead, ask him the logical ques-

tion, Is that your car down there and did you get into an accident…), potentially revealing and lending itself to a solution, or a resolution, or… but—

'Let me just lock this thing up all right?' he says as he walks to the driver's side of the car again, looks inside, opens door, takes out a small bag, closes, locks with his remote on his keys (alarm sounds, good to go), and, 'Allllready'—he extends the ahhh—'All set. Do you…'

'I'm fine, let me just'—hands in pockets, pretension of looking for something in jacket—'All right, fine…'

The two stand at the top of the hill peering down.

Should they just walk down the hill? Is there some sort of path? How did the car get down there anyway?

'Is that your car?' the driver asks (finally). 'Did you get into an accident or…'

'No no, not my car, no… I was… I saw the ostrich run into it is all, right from under the trees. No idea what's going on down there…'

'So should we just—'

'I don't think there's a path or anything.'

'Has the Caddy been down there for a while? I mean—'

'Yeah, yeah. It's been there for a while actually. Myself, I don't live too far, and, pretty much, you know, it's like, the Cadillac, all right, but the ostrich, that's sort of the question you know.'

'Got it, got it!' the driver says. 'Let's go then, no use standing around, I'll just…'

There he is, the courageous cowboy, taking one step down the hill, then another, his right arm shooting up as he slides slightly and tries to balance himself—O mister acrobat, slippin' and a-slidin' down the hill, with the Caddy under the tree, and the ostrich in the seats—singing, *ings, the silence of The Great Risk, the silence that accompanies the rush of adrenaline or of the rollicking good times, the silence that dawns after the messy noisefulness and the busyness that are just ways of staying away from The Grand Undertaking—in these many silences in fact, as he begins his descent, Steve's mind goes back to the Next Exit sign that he'd just seen, and how even though it had actually indicated how many miles away it was, he could only recall that it was far, had only recorded the sensation of its farawayness, far away, very far away... And then the images flash in his mind's eye, again he's sitting behind the steering wheel leaning back in his Corvette, his shades on, nothing but open highway in front of him, wide open space of his boyhood dreams and fantasies, the open highway of his melancholies, the open highway of the nostalgic mindmaps, American tapestry, this he'd always known, how proud he was too, the highway quiltwork that constituted the grand visage, lo, the patchwork soul of this his great land: how the treetops' branches in wintertime merge with the blue of the sky, and the cold that impregnates the air, and the sudden rush of the birds swooping in and through, the lampposts and the branches crisscrossing on the canvas that is the backdrop, the high wires, passing by, swooping by, through the tinted glass, the wires and the posts and the small branches and the clouds and the shadows of cars on the road, the shadows that appear and vanish, the oncoming headlights of the cars in the opposite direction, at night, among the dark all of these machines, worshipped machines of the age, sudden points of lights disappearing into othernights, into the vastness of the highway that extends, into the horizon, lines along the roads traversed, rhythmically how they appear and slide underneath the vehicles, rushing through the geometric grids, with the open sky, and the reflections on the mirrors, and the reflections on the windows, and the body's fragmented limbs as if torn and unconnected, flying maybe, to otherplaces and otherworlds, carousing down in the dark, with all the signs and billboards and the letters and the colors and the lines and, how free you feel, and yet not, enclosed, entrapped, alive, unencumbered liberty, no borders no frontiers... And along the way, Steve thinks—although think is the wrong word, images rather, they are, still invading his being, invading his mind, a flash, a moment, eternity enclosed within, all rushing through—there is only despair, only sadness, only the silent gaze of the muted, how all these places are unreal, not real, the places, the actions taken within, his stopping and going into the Maryland house and walking by the masses and the fatsos holding their children's hands, and the girls with their ponytails and their guy-talks, and the old men and women soulless cleaning the areas around the concession stands and the tables and the garbage, crushed by the overwhelming misery, and the businessmen on their trips with their families, and the migrants working in the restrooms cleaning the stalls and mopping the floor and wiping around the sink areas, wordless, and the signs in the stalls, for a great blowjob call three zero one... And the video machines in the back, with the images flickering on their screens, rushing towards the viewer, except that no one sits on the chairs, no one spins the wheels wildly, no excited teens are manipulating or twisting or contorting their bodies, and so the aloneness of the joint, how alone one feels, how alone, in the back, in the dark of the alcove, with unmanned video machines in all their frenzy pointing to the solitude, how it all seems not of this world, Steve thinks, even his stopping at a gas station and waiting in line behind the other cars because there's just one open and you can only go in one direction, and his sitting with his window open now, his elbow on the windowsill, blank gaze fleeing into the night, how all on the highway is quiet, how a stillness now reigns, with the dark, and the silent cortege of the passing cars, the majestic ballet of the traffic flow, its glow, the unique rhythm, this uncanny dance, unrecognized dance, the cars in the traffic flow,*

O mesmerizing traffic flow, seen from the driver's side, while he is sitting and waiting in line for gas, how it always happens and now again as he takes a few steps down the hill how it always happens that when images from the traffic flow and of his waiting in line at the gas station at night invade his being, the song again comes to mind, he's not sure why, the association, had he heard it once when waiting in line at the gas station, or somehow the song had awakened in him those images and now eternally they were linked, he did not know why, but it did so happen, that at each such occasion, the words and the rhythm, the beat and the inner scream, the guttural cry, of the teens hit him—and hard—sitting in the seat waiting, his neck turned, watching the cars pass by on the highway, in the dark, tree branches and lampposts and high wires in their embraces in the purple dark sky, in this unreality, the cars that pass by, their rhythmic getaways, into unknown worlds, so many strangers that pass you by, so many heads and lives that pass you by, once and never more, along these purple highways, and how then he begins to murmur his song, he begins to murmur, the lyrics to:

Teenager in the Basement
(Rock ballad/opera with hard riffs, incorporating fake head-banging motion of musicians swaying back and forth, intensely involved, holding air guitars and strumming, with long motions of the arms that go all the way up, and suddenly crash doooooooowwwwwn...)

O teenager in the basement
O teenager in the basement
Wake up from your slumber
O teenager in the basement
Think about your predicament!

21

Get your chin off the pavement
Get your soul out the gutter
Get your mind off the stripper
Get up and make a statement!

I am, I am, I am—
A teenager in the basement!
Sick—and tired!—of strumming my lonely guitar!
Sick—and tired!—of dad's old beat-up car!
Sick—and tired!—of staring at blank walls!
Sick and tired, sick and tired, sick and tired
(More hard-nosed riffs with head-surging motions)
Of fakin' all my higgggggghhhhhhssss...
And passin' out on the
Cheap-ass
(This and next expressions in staccato rhythms accen-
tuating each syllable with accompanying movements
of heads back and forth)
Devil-red
Old-style
Lazy-chairish
Motha-fuckin'
Beeeeeeeaaaaaaaaaan baaaaaaaaaaaaaaaaaag!

And his recollection, of how on the first of his many impromptu
singings of the tune, a young teen seeing him in the car with his
glasses on walking by with a girl around his arm, had blurted out:
'Dude, cool specs!')

Anyway: setting is set, as it should be. There is, however, a
twist in the plot, and that always helps. Characters? Check.

(And so our beloved litcrits' holy trinity is covered.) Indeed, unexpectedly, not quite midway down the hill (yes, all of that hadn't even brought them to the midway point), but, say, one third down, a sudden light-bulb (picture the picture) goes on in Steve's head. He has an idea and although he seems like quite the amicable and amenable fella, he can be quite insistent too, for he is doing just that. What's he insisting upon? Glad you asked. He's insisting now that they go *back up* the hill, that he's got something in the trunk he wants to show A., quite the surprise, Make our way down and have some fun, says he, and easy too. A. in turn is insisting, Really, we should be going, but Steve, stubborn Steve, is not only not relenting, he's already turned around and is making his way back up, all huffy and puffy too. This is going to throw some dent in A.'s plans no doubt, unsettle the whole operation as luck (or is it chance? or fate?) would have it, but does he really have much of a choice now, much of a say in the matter, no matter how badly or violently or horribly things turn out? Is there, an option?! (Is the question/I must say/No hesitation/As the centerpiece for aaaaaaaaaall deliberation!)

If he insists or panics, A. thinks, Steve could become suspicious, perhaps revisit his own engagement, and that would really, *really*, suck! And then who knows what else. Who thought this would ever get so complicated! A slight push, a last nudge, a belated pleading, none could hurt though, and so A., forceful yet somehow hesitant, attempts: 'You know Steve, we should really get down there! I mean, you never know...' Steve, on his way up (as previously noted) and as he takes his strides, lets out that, 'Yes yes, we will, believe you me, we'll get down there even faster, that's just the point, just you wait and see...' He trails off again, suggesting a sort of request to just get on with it, go ahead and follow him, got a good surprise for you type of thing, fret not kind of thought. A., unfortunately falling into the eternal trap of expecting from others what he himself has to offer (in the arena of human behavior) is immediately worried. Worse, semi-panicky. Is Steve, somehow, on to me, he wonders. Somehow Steve knows. Did he see something, feel something, that's bothering him, that's making him go back? (Repeat the word 'something' several times as an indication of vagueness of A.'s state of mind.) What kind of surprise would he have in store? Something Steve systematically sets up as a surprise surprise sort of song? (Alliteration in 's', gratuitously.) Surprise of getting me back probably! (Panic taking over.) He probably has a gun in the car! (Image of violence, strategical-ly—guns and more guns, always sells, good.) That's what he means! Shoots me and rolls my corpse down the hill! More fun! Shooting Steve (as in, Steve, shooting—like (grammat-ically speaking, only) 'flying saucers' or 'marauding hordes')! That's what he means. And faster! This is just... How can I be falling for this? This is... I gotta do something—can't just walk into the trap—walk right into my own murder—gotta—'Lis-ten Steve,' he blurts out suddenly, stopping as they are nearing the top of the hill, him still behind Steve by about three steps, 'I really don't know about this. Serious.'

Pleadings of the panicked, no doubt. What good could this last stand do anyway? It's too late, and he knows it. Steve has not even bothered to answer and, after a prolonged pause, A. has hung his head in the manner of the defeated and has resigned himself to his fate. What a turnaround though, he's thinking privately, what a pathetic turn of events! How ironic! Payback, A., for teasing those kids when you were in high school? You always did wonder how true the 'What goes around comes around' saying was, and you even attempted some unscientific experiments, remember? Not your fault, you always reasoned, they teased you, didn't they, when you were in elementary school, all bloated up on candy and sweets and juice and mind-bogglingly mind-controlling video games (flashback: years ago, A. as a chubby nine-year-old in front of the tube handling the sticks of the video game). You were the fat one then, they all mocked you, you even walked all by yourself, overweight and alone, at the back of the line, when you walked to the lunch room. You didn't take the high road no, later on in life, you turned it all around and bulked up with the football players, here a humph there a humph everywhere a grunt grunt, in the gym, where was anybody when you were sweating it out ey, that's what you liked to say and how you liked to justify your latter-day cruelty, even then getting teased by the already bulked-up lads, but then slowly, O so slowly, gaining their respect, becoming if not one of them, at least on par, muscle-bound and square and all goofy-looking with big arms and torso and neckless but still with your skinny legs, you weren't on the team but that didn't really matter, good enough you thought, or, did you, were there unarticulated in-securities or what, you figured you'd just turn it around, turn it around and give it back to the current crop of fat kids—who'd done nothing to you mind you... Or is this payback for when you saw your old buddy Pencoal Phark cleaning toilets, after a jock's life full of intimidation and humiliation of fellow class-mates in high school? You weren't part of the gang no, but you took a certain pleasure didn't you, when you saw his face as he suddenly turned around bent on his knees actually scrubbing the toilet, in the bathroom of Frenchies' Fried, you'll never forget that one, how you suddenly burst into laughter, paused, looked at him in the eye, smiled again, and just said, Sorry, and walked out, not feeling remorse, strangely, not even feeling bad for the guy, knowing too, he'd recognized you, knowing, you'd recognized him, knowing, how the untidy actions of our lives come back to haunt us. How ironic indeed! Is it all coming to a crash, here that repentance must kick in, here that it all comes back and, how shall I put it, bites you in the ass?!

Steve is standing behind his car now and A. has made his way up. Last step and—he's on the asphalt of the emergency lane: bends over, hands on knees, deep breath, and slowly straightens. Go ahead, he's thinking, make it short (strange, the acquiescence to one's doom)—and no excessive suffering if you will. A. even thinks of a sudden sprint away he does, there was time after all, to save his life, if he were uncertain, but that's just the thing, there was a chance that it wasn't what he was thinking, not the gruesome end he was envisioning, and then, how would that look, running away! How would he explain that one!

Steve takes the keys out of his pockets, shuffles, opens like a deck of cards, finds the right one, proceeds to bend slightly and place the key in the trunk's lock. Bends slightly more. A. is standing around, quietly to the side, watching, like a nice boy. (Good boy, stand right there until Stevie pulls out his gun and shoots you, he thinks, sarcastically mocking his own deficiencies as a human being, and the psychological barriers erected through his traumatic childhood experiences: goooood boy!)

Steve's body lunges into the trunk and momentarily disappears. This is it, A. is thinking, this is it, seriously it, can't be anything else, he's going to take his gun out and shoot me point blank. O thy father's soul in heaven, forgive me and all my sins, I never really meant to do all those horrible things I did, honest, peer pressure always, even in the worst of cases, or some unpopular stance I took (political, social, social-political), of which I was never convinced anyway. I'll harm no one from this very moment on, I promise, if you'll just, I promise, a righteous and good-deeded path is all mine, just this once, serious, thy father in heaven, not my time!

As Steve is slowly bending out from the trunk, A. closes his eyes. He's even contemplating slowly raising his arms (autom- atism of sorts, I guess) but quietly catches himself, what the hell after all, he's not under arrest or surrendering or being caught or—

'I was just gonna tell you to close your eyes, you devil you!'

That's Steve there a-hollerin', blurting out his folksy sen- tence, all good-humored still. 'Go ahead, you can open up now, you knew you wanted a surprise huh! Come on, open up!'

A. slowly opens the right, and… fully open now, then the left, and then, tenseness disappearing, eyes are wide open— and A., finally, at ease…

'I toldja you'd like it, see!' Steve blurts out. 'And there you are, all worried and complaining!' Steve imitates A.'s voice on the hill, squeamish and all, 'No Steve, seriously, we gotta get down there, fast, serious!' Switch back to his own voice: 'Well, whaddaya say ey! We're goin' down and goin' down fast now ain't we! Look at you, all smiles and all!'

'Tis true: A. was all smiles now, but less for the forthcoming adventure Steve was planning than out of sheer and absolute relief. Even questioned how he could have allowed himself the absurd visions that had completely invaded his mind, body and soul (to take a classical subdivision of our selfhood). How ridiculous! Propounded more by the fact that Steve was still standing, big smiles and all, still holding up, one in each hand, a set of, yes, electric scooters, one long handlebar and two tires each, with enough space for a full-grown man on the board.

'They ride like crazy,' he says. 'Now that is how we should

be going down!'

Steve sets both electric scooters down and rolls one to A. He goes back and closes the door of the trunk.

'Well?' he says again, standing by the door, A. holding the scooter by the long handlebar, examining it childlike and with a certain, how shall we say, degree of glamorous glee. 'What do you think?'

'Where do you get these things anyway,' A. asks.

'Got these babies online,' Steve says. 'In fact, all you gotta do, you put in 'electric scooter' and bam—you got a whole load of 'em.'

Steve begins to expound, with increasing passion and wild gestures accompanying his narrative. A prophet he seems almost, a car salesman, a homeless dude putting together found objects in peculiarly promising ways on a street corner because he refuses to play the art-world's silly games, showingly, a savior of the people, needing to be saved, a man of the cloth, lying again (now now, men of various cloths…), a visionary, on top of some hill or another, somewhere close to a desert (requisite element for godseekings of all sorts), his arm extended, his brow sweaty, in deep thrall, ecstatic almost, not yet whirling, but that'll come too…

He tells of the tires, how sturdy they are, how their grip on the asphalt is otherworldly…

He tells of the handlebars, how you can manipulate them and they don't ever snap off or break or what have you…

He tells of the body: 'Aluminum, reworked. Can't get it at any cheap-ass store. They even let you have a say in parts. Custom scooters!'

He tells of the intangibles: 'Some go faster while others provide more control, it's a trade-off you know, can't have your cake and eat it too. We're not talking Porsches here.'

He stops and says: 'Serious, they're a hoot. I take 'em sometimes on the weekend and down to the river and ride 'em all
the way across the bridge.'

So…

'You wanna ride *these* down the hill?' (Emphasis added by
present scribe, on behalf of A.)

'Well, why not? Breaks are pretty reliable.'

'Pretty?!'

'They're reliable, okay! Trust me, we'll be fine!'

Our hero A. is not thinking of the 'fineness' of their condition, just the inconvenience is all. What will he do with the
scooters afterwards? Trunk of the Caddy? It's bound to become
quite the depository anyway…

'All right then,' says A., thinking that any more hesitation
or negation might undermine the primary mission. 'Let's go,
but… I really mean it, let's GO!'

'Let's,' Steve says, countering A.'s rising impatience and anxiety with a delicate calm. He then takes his scooter and brings
it to the edge of the hill. A., hesitant, walks with the scooter in
his hand to the edge. The hill, this time, appears much steeper.

'Wanna take some practice runs?' Steve asks without the
slightest dash of condescension or irony. 'It might not hurt.'

Our hero A. is thinking that, heck yes, but, well, where…

'Where though?' he blurts out, accordingly.

'Right here!' Steve responds. 'Take a couple of runs on the
ramp. Cars are fine. Besides, not too many going by…'

Our hero A. steps on the scooter with one foot, hesitantly
puts other foot on and tries to get a sense of the balance. Not
quite the rough ride he was expecting. Not that smooth either.
Having never ridden any type of scooter, let alone an electric
one—in fact, never having put his body in motion with anything under his feet other than tight-fitting shoes (no roller

blades, skates, skateboards, skis, or other exotic machines for this stiff fellow)—he finds it a peculiar task to balance himself and move at the same time. It does get easier and easier though, after a few practice runs. A bit. He goes about thirty yards, steps down, turns around and begins again, Steve clapping and cheering him on and supporting him all the while. Hip hip hooray, Steve sings, ever the encouraging bloke,

Hip hip hooray, look at A.
He's ridin' high all the way
Ridin' on a scootay
Ridin' on his merry way...

(It is at this point that your obliging narrator, quite the timid scribe, must pause and in essence break the flow of the tale. For what follows in this tragic story of a revolution gone awry (don't they all?) before it even got off the ground, is cruel and grotesque beyond even this particular account's quite generous standards. A riot might be unleashed, not to mention a host of potential arrests and misunderstandings... Let it be said that Steve continued to cheer the good soldier A. on as he rode back and forth with increasing confidence and control on his scooter. Which makes everything even more gruesome and intolerable. For, shortly after the practice runs and the pointers given by Steve had prepared A. for his descent, the two did indeed shake hands, embrace, and promise to meet each other down by the Caddy, given the fact that there was no way for them to ascertain that they could ride down simultaneously, given the difference in skill level. So then, yes, they both go down at their pace, with various degrees of pleasure and fear: Steve hollering and laughing and screaming as if riding a monster roller coaster, A. hesitant, cautious, sweating, making sure he'd make it down. And then... Well... It's hard, I... This is where it gets hard, and I... Well, I do choke up... I just can't... What follows... The Caddy and all... O the beast within us all... O the venomous impetuous scourge of our ambitions... What happened at the bottom of the hill was this: Steve is a-relaxin' while A. struggles down all sweaty and anxious and finally rolls all the way into Steve's arms, who catches him, fatherlyly, and helps him stand up holding him from his underarms as the poor bloke stumbles with his scooter slipping from under him, the speed of the vehicle allowing him to ride it down on top but giving way as the hill flattens. 'Way to go,' Steve hollers as A. stands before him and dusts off. 'My man! Not so bad after all ey?!' Then he adds: 'Come on, relax, take a deep breath.' So then A. does take a deep breath, composes himself and asks Steve if he'd taken a look inside, upon which query he was informed that No, I haven't, waiting for you, upon which A., Great, thanks, so let's now, upon which he insists that Steve walk to the Caddy first (thirty or so yards away). Steve says, So you want me to go ahead? A. says, Absolutely! Steve says, No problem, glad to help, and then he adds, Let's go carefully though. Then... then: Steve on tippitoes and A. behind him, although then A. slips away, but Steve doesn't see him, keeps moving forward thinking A. is still behind him, even more careful now, even whispers, 'Be careful now' to no one (how sad that is, to be so well-intentioned as to utter such whispers to a void, summoning images of absence and loneliness and abandonment, all in one, while the intended target has moved away, who knows with what devious intentions), walks up, ever more cautiously, crouched, silent, and then jumps up, right at the Caddy, holding the door closed, a back door, just in case the ostrich was inside, then screams, Got it, then peeks into the vehicle, sees nothing, and no one, still hasn't turned around, holding the backdoor handle peeks through the front window, still nothing, then finally turns around and begins, 'I don't see any—' but cuts off, looking around since he doesn't see A., looks left again, right again, begins to call out, 'A… A.-heyyy… Yoohoo, A… Hello, A… Helloh-ohh…' and as he's spinning around and looking left and right and calling out, finally sees his buddy a step away, under the tree. 'Ah! There you are!' he says, and as he approaches, attempts the explanation: 'So I didn't…' but he trails off again (not exactly trail off, or cut off, but that strange line somewhere in-between, where time itself becomes suspended, almost irrelevant, almost non-existent, as a legitimate concept anyway, floating in the surreal space of ethereal inexistence), as A., cold stare that renders him unrecognizable to Steve, from behind him (his hands, indeed, had been behind his back), suddenly:

brandishes:

a machete—that:

swiftly hacks at Steve's neck, decapitating him in one, single, cruel, undeserving, instant.

The head rolls away, a last breath is taken, A. stands, still, under the tree, with the Caddy, empty.

'Ostrich in a Cadillac,' A. murmurs the cruel, sadistic, incomprehensible murmur, 'Ostrich in a Cadillac, Ostrich in a Cadillac…'

Then, this: he cuts up the body into pieces, buries parts, leaves small pieces on the ground and lets out several opossums and raccoons from two bags in the backseat of the Caddy so they can feast a little, collects rest in a bag, and places machete back where it was hidden (reader shall not be privy to that location). Brings the opossums and raccoons back in bag in the Caddy's backseat, closes and locks doors, throws bag on his shoulder, and… shit, the scooters! Puts bag back down, thinks, opens trunk of Caddy and places the scooters in the back, closes again and picks up bag, throws over shoulder, and, is off.

Let it be said also: there is no suggestion, repeat, NO suggestion, as in none, zip, zero, that any reader stand by ramps of exits and trick displaced cowboys down a hill and then proceed to kill, chop and (later) eat them. Litcrits, cultural observers, pundits, watchdog orgz, listen to me, and real good: no one should drag Texan cowboys riding Corvettes selling stuff stopped on exit ramps by one ruse or another to their deaths. That is not the point here. Nor is it a dark fantasy of the author's. Believe you moi. The point is not destruction, and cannibalism is not suggested, not even in coded language. Cowboys are safe, on freeways as well as all small alleys of the city or the 'burbs. No killing, promise, no eating and chewing. For real. (Although… now that one thinks about it… if you seriously weigh the proposal… but—))

2

Pause. Red traffic light in the distance flashing nostalgically. A Toyota Camry slows down, breaks, stops (the jerk forward is felt, however minimal), driver looks left, right, left right (double check), presses again on gas pedal to launch forward the automobile I will certainly not see again, disappearing into the horizon formed by the boulevard and the skyline, rolling toward the towers in the distance with the rhythmic, slow, coming in and going out, never fully either, in or out, of the red warning light, atop...

A man named Jose, name-tagged worker working at auto body I'd seen earlier, in the small deli, puts cream in his sugar, goes to cash register, head down, resigned... Two men, one in a baseball cap, open the trunk of a car in a parking lot and take out a small briefcase while two moms fully settled into migranthood cross the street with kids, one holding the hand of a young boy, with a new haircut, one with a little girl and a stroller in front, walking only midway through as they sense the traffic coming... An animated man on a pay phone with long shorts and sandals... Through the doors of a salon, a young girl plays around as several women are getting their hair dried under blowers... Two boys, one with red t-shirt, the other yellow, cross the median on their scooters, one leg rhythmically to the ground to push off with the foot... Around the baseball field, a middle-aged man jogs, slowly, trying to get rid of the belly that somehow formed on his body all these years. He jogs and breathes hard and awkwardly holds his head up, the fence behind home plate his reference point, where he turns, and turns again, to fulfill his own mandate, of at least a couple of miles jogged per day, so save him… Jerry sits in a coffee shop and stares straight ahead and watches the passersby. He works as an accountant during the day and now is trying to relax. He does not read a newspaper or a book or scribble notes or chat with a neighbor or work on any type of device. He's finished his coffee and stares straight ahead, one leg draped over another, both forearms on the table in front of him. He watches the shoppers of the shopping center, a steady stream of recently parked folks getting out of their cars and locking up and marching forth, and the shoppers walking back, back from the mega drug store, back from the supermarket, back from the family restaurant, back from the humongous retail outlet, walking slowly, at angles to each other, in all directions, crossing paths, pausing, looking, swinging, stopping, starting again, watching, whispering, sighing, wondering, and not, across the lines of the parking lot, the majestic parking lot, and the dance of the walkers to and from, the stores, inevitably all assembled and dis-, in the parking lot… In front of a wall awkwardly located in front of a blue sky, with no buildings around, two young women stand, one crouched with a cell phone, the other waiting, impatient, looking in the direction of the coming bus… On the sidewalk, in front of a row of shops, a tall man holding the hand of a girl who is skipping, walks. His gait is steady and his gaze fixed in front and even though the little girl skips and breaks off the rhythm and even though individuals walk into or come out of the stores he passes, he does not let go of the hand or look askance. He stares straight ahead and even now that the girl is not skipping anymore and now that he's past the shops and walking in front of a wall with old posters a dozen of the same and then another dozen, he does not turn or modify his gait or his gaze, and when he walks past the girls waiting for the bus, he does not turn to look or acknowledge or even say hi, even though the little girl not only looks but is fixated, on the waiting ones and the passing cars, her head facing the street, her stance awkward, un-free, while the man holding her hand continues to walk, on the sidewalk in front of the wall… And, as always, from above, at night, from her balcony, Mrs. Delectable wonders whatever became of her daughter, so sweet and nice in high school, showing such promise, French club member and president of the student council, and then she vanished, joined an unseemly band of bandits, never to be heard from again, although she'll be back, Mrs. Delectable thinks, Dolores will be back, she always comes back, her motherly refrain (O the motherly refrains how they shall follow us to the graves), Dolores will be back, Dolores will be back, she always comes through, my Dolores will be back…

Cars passing by, cars passing by, counting cars, more and more, counting more cars, passing cars, a gray Saab 6000 passes, a green Mercedes, minivan, passes, a Chevrolet pickup, passes, a Ford Expedition minivan, a black Honda Civic, a red Jeep Wrangler, a light blue Oldsmobile, a black Honda Civic (another), a white Ford minivan, an old Volvo, a blue Barwood cab, a green Jag (personal license plates), a dark blue Mercedes, they all pass and pass and pass, a big Jeep truck, they pass and they pass and they pass, hypnotic this traffic flow, a thing of wonder this traffic flow, so orderly, so mesmerizing this traffic flow, so meditation-inducing this traffic flow, poetry in motion truly, if only one were to focus on and de-objectify the poor vehicles, think of them as living beings in motion, as stars or celestial bodies in motion, as instances of light sprung onto an unsuspecting sky, as a paean to free-flow imagery freed from the mind implanted upon the canvas of reality...

It is before this mechanical and O so this-worldly ballet, that A., after his defining act, looks heavenwards, smiles, and once again, thinks about: the next steps.

O malevolent forces once again tempting me to show my cards before it's time, is it here that the secrets shall be spilled? Here that the gory details of the rumblings will be unmasked? Here, that the movement's every detail shall be described? Heresy of sorts, or shall I go on? (O mythological figures watching over the shoulders of woebegone souls, administer please, a dose, if not of righteousness, of clarity at least!)

Yes, there is, basically, a revolution brewing, and yes, this is an account, based on a true story at that—hard as it is to believe. (A note of caution though: you should highly distrust that odious dichotomy, fiction and non-, and disregard even your honest tale-teller's declarations: fable, fantasy, farce: terms such as these do not even begin to do justice to the fabrications wrought onto that fabric dubbed 'reality'.) But: is this an affair of true, genuine revolutionaries: who've thought it out, analyzed the ideologies, the foundations of the system, the gross inequalities, the corruption and the injustices—and have determined that a takeover of cozy suburban Whooton (in which no less than one hundred percent of the five original leaders were born and raised) is in order? Or is it another load of crock fed to whomever wants to go for it, made up by a bunch of call 'em what you will assholes rationalizing the daylights out of a whole bunch of individual neuroses and unhealthy motivations? Did they really think and say No more asinine movies at multiplexes No more swarms of fat folks through the up-

per-level food courts of humongous malls No more immaculately kept streets and avenues and boulevards devoid of a
single walker even No more orderly lines of cars dutifully stopping at signs and lining up docilely in one file at the stop light
even though there are two lanes and the left one is totally empty and no car dares go in it just because thirty other cars have
lined up in the right and that it's better to follow and be safe—
or is that just me, I, moi, Mr. Narrator-man (a party, marginal,
at best, to all these shenanigans?!), projecting my own fantasies
on the poor characterly inventions, living vicariously through
them? Uncertain, uncertain at best, are the answers to these
queries, I must confess. But surely, it is precisely the point of
this sacred account to touch on the subtleties associated with
the intentions and the actions of the players during the entire
campaign. And I promise to invest energies and powers galore
in unveiling and demasking the quite preposterous details of
the entire episode, I do. But as we go on, as we follow this
potentially lost and pathetic bunch on their journey and see
their program through even though we could just have ignored
their stories and gone on with our happy lives (which I wasn't
entirely opposed to, except that a funny thing happened on
the way to the market to get some late-night snacks), as you
wonder what the hey else is going on, what with all the cars
and the parking lots and the traffic flow, wonder do, wonder (a
different acceptation of the term), with me, benevolent reader,
and watch, and wait, stand amazed and in awe, almost, with
me, and wonder, and just ask, ask again, and the answers will
come I promise, in due time they will, keep asking, why it
might be that all around you the cars roll and the cars stand,
look around and you'll know, generous reader, patient reader,
look around and you'll know, what it's all about, where all the
mysteries lie, parking lots and traffic flow, all the cars that roll

and all the cars that stand, all these cars, all these parking lots, all this traffic flow, parking lots and traffic flow, parking lots and traffic flow, the delirious rhythm of our lives, parking lots and traffic flow, is this what it's all about, a portrait, after all, behind this grand mask, through this grand charade, of parking lots and traffic flow, in all their majestic, pure, undaunted, unadulterated form.

So. There is a revolution and there is not, there's a story to be told, and there is not... What concerns us at the present time is that a question arises: Why the 'burbs? Actually, questions arise (double shift of the 's'—physically, grammatically): a) Why the 'burbs? b) Why this 'burb? c) Why?

That a *General Theory of Suburban Angst*, along with a *Critique of the Lifestyles in These Here Parts* (and the subsequent values and relationships spawned by the policies in place and the frameworks in vogue) would offer us another angle into the motivations for the revolution, of this there is no doubt. There is even less doubt however, that a new order of things—a new way of being—was envisaged. The old system had to go, the leaders thought, the new one had to be implemented. Out with the old, in with the new, they would mutter under breath in the early stages of the planning. We will take the suburbs back, and make a new suburbia. Change the culture. Change the ways. Take it back from the greedy developers concerned only with their profits. Why shouldn't it be our profits! Heck, aren't we paying taxes?! (They were not, at that point.) A slogan was then adopted, a new chant formulated, for a New Suburban Order was to be generated. Except that the debate over the nature of this chant did not come about easily: between Hail Suburbia, Hail the Suburbs, and Hail the 'Burbs, a passionate séance was held between the Original Five (so dubbed by themselves early on). Forceful exchanges, angry retorts, even the breaking of a beer glass. The first, by a vote of three to two, was defeated for its impracticality. The debate raged between the second and third, the second winning over by a thin three to two margin, based on notions that Hail the 'Burbs simply could not be taken seriously enough in the upcoming recruiting effort. And so it was: Hail the Suburbs went the chant, Hail the Suburbs, Hail the Motherland Suburbs.

Why this suburb? It was the one they knew, it was the one they held dear. It was the one they needed to take back. It was their Home. Hail the Suburbs. Why? Because they're revolutionaries, that's why. Hail the Suburbs.

So. On the morning of the first operation, A. is preparing himself on the exit ramp, putting the finishing touches on his dishevelment, practicing in a whisper his line, his O so important Ostrich in a Cadillac Ostrich in a Cadillac line, and the necessary gestures that were to accompany. A nervous moment of course, a great moment, others would say, a turning point, if all goes according to plan. A., the current leader, putting himself out there, preparing, for the ultimate sacrifice. Now: we know how A. did, we know what he had to go through, we know it wasn't as easy as it looked. But wouldn't a general portrait of the goings-on before and after A.'s encounter with Steve, which depictions would have the merit of situating in a wider context the struggle, provide us with an even better, more detailed grasp of that gory episode's birthing, if I may? Wouldn't all that, pray tell Mr. Narrator-man, allow a singular glimpse into the psyches associated with and the goings-on surrounding that great momentous event? Lo, a voyeuristic peek, into the whole shebang? Will you please Mr. Narrator-man, will you take us around, on a little tour, of the goings-on, please!

Shouted Sememe I

O please, please, Mr. Narrator-man,
O Mr. Narrator-man
Tell us your plans, your sure-fire plans
What you got cookin' there with your clan!

The voices in your head that is, and
Your wrists—since you still write long-hand! (You dinosaur
you!)
What you got going on over there even though it might be
Banned—
And
Not only in this or that land
Not only by the oppressive, dictatorial, tyrannical,
ignominiously cataclysmically self-legitimized gov-
ernments telling this or that person what to think,
believe, do, not do, where to go and not go and
when and how and why
—but also by all the other gangs!

Yes, Mr. Narrator-man, do tell us, your plans
Where you'll take 'em
How you'll make 'em
O Mr. Narrator-man, tell us your plans
Won't you?

Will do, reader-folk, will do. Situating the abduction/se-
duction and murder of Steve at 10:57 a.m. Eastern Standard
Time (9:57 Central, 7:57 Pacific),

at 10:33, on the same exact ramp,

a Honda Civic, driven by a gray-haired elderly woman, breaks slightly as A. appears on the emergency ramp and is pulling his shirt over his pants and fixing his hair (disheveling it, in fact). She wonders (in that moment where she gets a glimpse of A. as she drives by) what the young man might be up to, but just as quickly speeds away, not entirely uncomfortable with the notion of not intervening when she is not certain of the merits of the circumstance, especially since

twenty minutes before that,
coming down the stairs of
her son's garden apartment,

she had twisted an ankle and almost fallen to the ground, rescued only by her still considerable reactive senses which allowed her to grab the railing, prevent the potentially nightmarish and debilitating hip/back injury, sit on the stairs and get her bearings back (no need to go back up and bother the son), before limping to the car and getting in and along. She needed to get home, and fast, to lie down, to nurse the injury. All this running through her mind while

Mappolo Rei, one of the Original Five,

is nervously downing brews—yes, that early! He knows what's going down, and he knows it all has to do with the Cadillac that he and A. pressured Saminski (surname) Gabor (first name), a Hungarian expatriate owner of a car dealership (and youth soccer coach Rei had once met at a clinic given at the middle school soccer fields for eight-year-olds fully geared in shin guards, cleats, and splashy uniforms, and that Rei had stumbled upon because he had nothing better to do—serious!), to sell for close to nothing. The nerve-racking moments propel him to experience all kinds of anxieties and launch many a petty reconsideration. Feeling the pressure surely. Succumbing to it almost. He even questions his participation. What's so wrong with how things are right now anyway, he wonders but does not voice. Who the hell am I to lead anyone?! And what can we really do to make it all so much better?! What do 'wrong' and 'better' really mean anyway—and this is not a petty recourse to relativism at the eleventh hour either. Just some lucid analyses, clairvoyant queries, one could say, unbecoming a true revolutionary. Besides, he's always been keenly suspicious of A. and his true motives anyway. Something else was always at work. Something that he can't quite define. Rumblings of upcoming coups, all this indecision? Conspiracy to undermine? Rei shakes his head, almost as if to banish the uncouth thoughts from his system. He slams the empty glass on the bar, but the two old patrons sitting at the edge don't budge (they've been peering at him anyway and they're always there, all day, every day, always). Almost immediately, he orders

a kamikaze shot—

symbolic, the order, but pragmatic too. He wants to be shot (no pun intended) when the hour has come. 'You all right?' the bartender, napkin in right hand drying small glass situated in left, asks, calmly, rhetorically. 'Fine,' Mappolo answers dryly. 'One ka-mikaze, please.' (The fake politeness will not save you from suspicion Mappolo, you know it. You don't repeat an order, you don't rush a bartender, you don't play the cool dude, certainly not in a dive along the route with unsavory characters. Count your blessings, boy, that they're not on top of you already—and sit still.) The bartender looks at him for a moment after putting the napkin and the glass down, contemplating his next move. Luckily, he remains composed and, his eyes still on Mappolo who is not returning the favor (eyes cast downward), walks to the shelves and picks out the appropriate bottles. No other sound, no music, no movement.

10:40, gas station, attendant is

a young man by the name of Eddie (with an 'i' and an 'e') 'Ayee' Perez. Present scribe believes the genesis (and development) of Eddie's nickname can be attributed to the confluence of two factors: one, that he always had to emphasize the 'i, e' whenever he spelled his name, and also because, philosophically speaking, at a human, buddy level, it was well-known that he would always 'be there' for you, always watch your back, he-the-man sorta kinda deal, he be, There, Here, Ahi (in Spanish), Ahi, A—yee. You combine the two and there, the perfect symbiotic union, the perfect nickname: Ayee! (Not to mention that the moniker stuck even more as Eddie would scream, rolling down on the highway in his dad's old Pontiac, windows down, head stuck out and hair flowing around, a chant akin to the great war cries, as if to emphasize his feelings of liberty, his passion for life, his sense of wonder, scream: Ayeeeeeee...)

He is sporting a goatee and a gold cross around his neck with a visible tattoo at the top of his right arm. Steve's Corvette has pulled into the full-serve station and he's asked the friendly young attendant to 'fill'er up.' His good nature and friendly demeanor spark a conversation within the confines of which he discovers that Eddie is himself an avid rollerblader ('Rollerblade acrobatics, my major,' the surprisingly quirky and quick-witted Eddie says!) and skateboarder, which prompts Steve to open up the back trunk and invite Eddie over to check out the electric scooters while the nozzle in the car automatically pumps in the gas (its drone a part of the soundscape). 'Wow,' exclaims Eddie when Steve takes out one of his favorite specimens. 'Here,' Steve says, 'try it.' Eddie says, 'How much do these babies go for?' And Steve says, 'Got this one online, two hundred, think I gotta good deal.' Eddie says, 'I'ma check it out at Sal's, they got some bad ones in there.' Steve says, 'You do competitions?' Eddie says, 'Thought about 'em but don't got the time.' Steve says, 'School?' Eddie says, 'Yeah, wanna get a scholarship, you know, blade acrobatics.' Then he laughs and says, 'Just playin' man, I wanna get my physics scholarship—get a full to State.' Steve says, 'Physics ey... Mister P.' Funny of course, since Steve didn't know that Eddie's last name was Perez (he did know his first name was Eddie, thanks to the name tag). 'That's right,' Eddie says, cognizant, he, of the double-ontondrah, and of his counterpart's coincidental pun-tification.

Before Steve's 'Mister P.' comment, the gas pump had ticked back to its neutral status, the programmed-in amount reached. Eddie walks back, takes the nozzle and puts it back on the appropriate pump. He says to Steve, 'That's ten dollars,' even though he knows Steve knows, since that's exactly how much Steve had asked to be put in, and further, since that's what the meter on the pump said, or did it, actually.

'Says ten o one,' Steve says smiling. 'Is that all right?'

Eddie signals that it is and Steve takes out a twenty and hands it to Eddie who swings a hand in a pocket and takes out a wad of cash, folded bills which he straightens expertly with one hand in order to take a ten-dollar bill out with his other, which he hands to Steve.

'Thanks,' says the latter. 'And good luck.'

'Thanks,' Eddie says. 'You too.'

Hmmm... Good luck? thinks Steve as he waves and pulls out, since when do gas station attendants say good luck to clients leaving their islands? Granted he didn't say, Good luck, he said, You too—but that's what it meant. Does Eddie know something Steve doesn't and that at the precise moment we wouldn't either if a certain episode that chronologically occurred later had not been told first in this narrative? Is he somehow connected? Part of the dark underground? A special agent of sorts? He does come across as a perfect candidate, a young, intelligent, seemingly harmless worker... Did A. and his underlings provoke one or another of their anonymous associates to somehow recruit him, bring him into the fold, seduce him with their rhetoric? Perhaps, perhaps... And we shall find out soon enough...

Steve, in his car, presses on the gas pedal and, oblivious to the circumstances of his departure, speeds away.

Hypnotic Freeway Reverie, With Air Guitar
(In I Minor)

Dreams of nightrides among the weary with the wind through the driver's side window, headlights in the opposite direction zooming by, with what solitude I come to conquer you, O world, Steve whispers within, I, a mere vagabond, stranger to these pages, exiled from the physical world, planted among the wayfarers in their flights of fancy...

From the fangs of bridges to the looping cables and steel structures and banners holding aloft the arcs of light floating in dark blue skies, along these roads, I summon thee to appear, Youth, once in a while at least, to remind us of the glory of the species, and of creation, and of imagination, and of knowing the madness within, not to mention the toll plaza that oft appears before and after such joyrides on the bridge.

And Steve again peering into the horizon and at the treetops and at the flight of birds and the heavy lumbering of a truck in the adjacent lane, and recalling the tortuous roads along the coastal highways, at dawn, at dusk, with the blue of the sea and the blue of the sky that merged, and the hills and the mountains, how he swerved around them, how he accelerated, his sunglasses giving him the feel of otherworldly invincibility, how alone on a hilltop he would swerve off and peer down below at the winding road, all the winding roads along green pastures and sunny oceansides he'd ever driven along, the endless highways along the deserts and the busy highways along the east coast with their factory-like structures popping up, and the stench of marshes covered now by super asphalt lanes, how he sees the lines, the lines on the pavements, the fragmented lines on the pavements, on freeways or in two-lanes, doesn't matter, his grand obsession, how the lines go by, a rhythmic passing by, the lines and the memories, the lines and the dreams, the lines and the screams in secret locales, the lines and freedom, yes that's right, the lines and freedom, the lines and the passage of time, the lines and how they draw the ephemeral on the canvas, the lines on the pavements of highways or small boulevards or even alleys at night in the deserted suburban hamlets, how they enchant, how they make us know who we are, Steve peering thus and remembering so, allows the song to invade his being again, and the song invades again as he speeds down the highway, speeds down peering through the glass at the unfolding of the highway, the breaking lines that coalesce into one another, fragments merging into the whole, the road that is all his now, in this darkness, in this night, there is only one song, O Teenager in the Basement, despair not, drown not in the ignominy of the circumstances in which you find yourself, brave the times and adhere not to the lust for self-destruction, in the side room, alone, you don't necessarily have to put away the guitar, but strum it with a happier melody will ya, not necessarily gingerly no, but at least, at least, at least—

O teenager in the basement
Don't bang your head on the pavement
Stand up and rock yes
And make your statement
Sing along
Drive along the highway at night
And shout out
Never again
I'm never again
Never again
Gonna seek no treatment
I'm my own joy and drug
I'm the addict
Of contentment
O teenager in the basement
Rockin' your guitar
In your undergarment!

The evening before, at Eddie Perez's girlfriend's,

in front of the tube. Eddie, you goin' to work tomorrow, says the girl. Gotta go baby, you know I gotta go—Eddie. But you said you'd take the day off, remember, my birthday?—the girlfriend. I know baby, I know, we're gonna go out tomorrow night, what you need me during the day for—Eddie. They've huddled up and are cuddling hugging on the couch, limbs intertwined. She's being cute, she knows it, but she does really mean it—that she'd wanna go with him all day—but she understands. All right baby? Eddie says, conclusively, stroking her hair, the remote in his other hand, I'm all yours tomorrow night, but I gotta go to work. Tomorrow day, I gotta go, he repeats, switching at least eight channels in the space of five seconds (*Guys and Remotes: A Sociological Study of Responses to the Deficiency of Male Hormonal Impulse Control*, by...), emphasizing the drama and setting up for the cliffhanging event to come—

while, simultaneously, in the gym,

converted gym that is (bleachers empty, cheerleaderlessly imposing the sadness of empty houses of fanless quietude), on the parquet floor where usually the Wild Boars beat up on opponents on their way to three straight state titles (you cannot bring yourself to picture the scene without the members of the basketball team running up and down the court waving arms, stirring the crowd, the crowd now stands, chanting in one voice, excited voice no doubt, dee-fense, dee-fense (in his mind's eye, A. switches from one image to another (whatever happened to those glorious days, A. now thinking inside, when he was a star on the soccer team and he would come and catch the basketball team whack the other schools and they'd all go to one party after another), he sees and hears the varieties of bodies—lean and leaner, tall and taller, with the occasional chubby kid riding the bench thrown in in the spirit of participation—the varieties of shots, lay-ups and three-pointers and reverse and straight dunks and even fancier reverse double tomahawk three-sixty monster slams, the gestures, the scowls, the chest-thumping, high-fiving shimmies and other assortments of innovative individual I'm-the-man celebrations, the hugs after some hard-fought down-to-the-wire thriller, the player intros before the games, the team chant all gathered in that little (annoying) circle, arms extended, sweaty palms and tips of hands touching and so on, the happy parents jumping up and down in the stands, the nervous parents yelling one or another obscenity at the hapless refs, light and sound and cheers all around, characters in a drama, actors in a ritual dance, bodies and movement, the coach (pacing), the refs (whistling), the clocks (red, bright, ticking), the scoreboard (shining), the fans on the other side of the floor (in one group appearing as if one body, swaying), the past failures (flashing by), the memories (…), the hopes (sinking), the dreams (unfulfilled), the American version (being lived, to its fullest, green yard and garage too, along with mortgage payments and car payments and credit card debts and—), the neighbors' annoying kid (mowing the lawn on the family's new lawn mower), and the game again, the game and all the digressions it precipitates, the actual changing of the score, the fouls, the shouts, the howls, the shots, all coalesce into one free-flowing hallucinogenic haze, coming in and out of being, changing hues and metamorphosing shapes, one tapestry enchanting, fashioned out of the involuntary merging of the cacophonies on display, A. himself now caught in a whirling daze, as if his presence had been somehow manufactured, as if he'd been driven to the locale only to be transported by vengeful powers into some other realm, as if he simply could not distinguish, control, keep pace, the excess of information invading his body, his mind, his space, with the brutality and the vehemence of an invading army, as if, as he watched the young players running up and down the court trying to put the gosh darn ball through the hoops, there was nothing that truly mattered, as if winning was the last thing on his mind, last thing he could care about, last thing he should be present for, the slants, the parents, the hands, the chants), dee-fense, dee-fense, dee-fense…), A., after an address to the assembled (no more than a dozen), and a continuous round of cheers and nervous anticipation and anxious excitement from the small group, says: 'Folks, it's on!'

The morning of, 7 a.m. sharp, A. is awakened by the big man/big woman superstore Doss's catchy tune:

In a place like Doss's
In a place like Doss's
There ain't no fusses
Just lots o' plusses!

The rapid-fire voice of a pitchman then rattles off a slew of items on sale, from sweaters for the fall to his or her bathing suits for these last precious weekends to the practical give-away of the sandals and the t-shirts. Weird, A. thinks to himself, how the fake excitement and nervous urgency of the seemingly happy-go-lucky pitchman, and Doss's mission in general, and the ads themselves, and the image of row upon row of clothes at clearance prices in the interminable aisles under the terrible lights and the crappy elevator music, not only do not induce physical sickness, or physiological reaction, but how they soothe him, how they bring a weird lightness to his senses, how they comfort his being. He's never bothered to analyze why, consciously, in fact, he does not really want to know why, conceptually. The effect is valid enough, no matter the degree of absurdity: why Doss's tune after all, and not a thousand and one other tunes… But he will not think about it, he will not, there are times when one must not think, too much that is, allow the legitimacy of the effect, allow the supremacy of the sensation, allow the body to lead the way—and yes, this, this, reasoned and reasons A., this is one of those times, when he must just accept his reverence for Doss's catchy ditty, and move on, shameless, guiltless, lo, fully enthralled by his feelings when the juicy jingle suddenly awakens his senses...

Groggy, both hands on head scratching scalp, sitting on top of his futon, legs swung to the side feet slightly above the ground. In his head, images of the day ahead (a strategy, to calm his nerves, and to fulfill successfully the tasks), images of fragments of his life (a walk with his mother, when he was eight, next to the shore; a goal he scored during a street soccer game, when he was ten; his first kiss, at a party, dancing a slow dance), and yet another melody, his own, which comes to him, it happens every time after the Doss anthem, a robaï, a limerick, a nice little genre-mixer, genre-breaker of sorts, a new genrahh (how could it be O how could it be):

> *There was a guy always liked to see*
> *The glorious day the great elm tree*
> *Yet he chose to play*
> *In a dangerous way*
> *That game: How Can I (Really) Be Free!*

It is followed by a metaphysical haiku, as he walks to the window and looks outside, a weird feeling in the air, a solid feeling in the air, ohh ohh, what is this feeling I feel, O yes, I got to pee:

> *Tree in the distance*
> > *Through the window with leaves*

Under
Calling—you gotta pee

to me. Tree knows, can see it, in my panicked visage.

But that was just a haiku and the presence of the officers of the law (increased presence), along with the fact that it would be much easier to just stumble to the cozy bathroom inside, won't allow the tree's exhortation to come to fruition. So A. takes the easy way out and walks to the john and opens the door and stops in front of the mirror. Checks out cheek and lifts toothbrush, neatly deposited in one of the holes of the holder on the left. Brushes teeth, puts toothbrush back, quietly approaches face to mirror, pulls skin of cheek to check out another irregularity, and then, softly, as is his morning ritual, recites a verse from one of his all-time favorite poems: *Et toi songeur solitaire des quais, quels furent les secrets de ton royaume?* which loosely translates into:

And you solitary wanderer of wharfs,
What were the secrets of your kingdom?

(Ahh! He just loves—loves!—that one!)

And yes, he does subsequently lift the toilet seat (habit, good one), and he does pee.

He shaves, shits, showers (triple-'sh' morning ritual) and dresses and walks down and takes a bus to a small coffee shop located in the shopping center four miles down. He enters and orders a medium coffee with milk and sugar and smiles at the friendly teenage cashier who recognizes him since he's there most mornings and asks him, How you doin' this morning, as she takes the order and says, as she punches the order in, Will that be all? She almost expects it to be all, A. never gets anything else, not even a muffin, a bagel, a doughnut. Someone else hands her the coffee which she in one motion brings to A. Twenty-one cents is your change, she says, then hands him the two dimes and the penny and adds, Thanks again and have a nice day! A. thanks her quietly and as he's turned around walking toward the bar-type area in front of the window where he'll be spending some time, he thinks, Thank god we're acting (confirming it all, no doubt), that's just it, I cannot *stand* how they do that, in the same exchange pretending to be your buddy and recognizing you and all, and throwing the same generic *crap*, like a bunch of *robots*! Automatons, he's thinking! This, *this*, is what we gotta change! *This*, A. thinks, still torturing himself, this is what's *wrong*! This is a true symbol of the ailments that affect us! This and the bland, cliché-spewing, scripted-gestured, controlled-from-afar-like-a-device-ness of local-news anchors! The nerve of her and her cohorts, to ask questions the answers to which they care not at all to hear! Thank god we're here! (Did he mean it, you're asking, did that really upset A. that much? Was that what the revolution was all about? That!? The faux friendliness of TV-speechified young automaton teens?!)

Yes, this, more than anything else, including the fact that most minimum wage employees were working for five and a quarter an hour (wage at time of initial publication) and still going the extra mile to benefit the company's shareholders at the expense of the lowly customer, this was worse, to A. anyway! Soon, after he'd spent a little while looking out the window at the parked cars, at the

Ford Taurus, blue, the Mazda
Protégé
    taupe, the

    blue Volvo 760
        turbo,
        the:
            Toyota Previa
                minivan,

the ToyotaCamryAccuraMDXFordTundra
    (blue),
    the burgundy

To

    yo

        ta

            RA V4,
            and the
Saturn

holding his cup and drinking with slow lifts and sips, he
goes across to the public library. He'll spend some time there,
reading the newspapers, checking out some magazines, checking his email. At around 9:30, he will walk to a nearby taxi
stand, where: he will take a taxi to the destined exit.

(Next up: III, with still no attempt at chapter headings, the
entire exercise undermined by the anguish of conventional opera-
tions imposing their laws on the narrative; or, in guise of a chapter
heading, how we shall proceed, in a third volay ('volet', with-
out the accentuated twang), of our extended prose sonnay (same

twangy element applied to 'sonnet'), shall we say—correct pronun-ciation, by the way.)

3

The hero A. ('hero' in the sense of protagonist of a fable, a fairy tale, a farce of sorts, and in no way a personal hero of narrator's, or imaginary narrator's, or imagined narrator's, or literary I's, in the sense of one to be emulated or honored, obviously, censors and civil servants, please note) is walking up the road, carrying Steve's remains (the meaty parts) inside a sack. He'd taken care to clean out the remains in such manner that no animals would be attracted, then placed them in a hole close to the tree closest to the big tree under which the Cadillac was parked. He had then taken a back route, a few minutes through the woods to end up on a small street (treelined, lampposts, 2 cars per driveway) which he walked on until he made a left on a wider street (treelined, lampposts, 2 cars per driveway) which led him a few minutes later onto a wider avenue (treelined, lampposts, 2 cars per driveway, shops in shopping center) that connected these small communities to the scattered convenience stores and shops constituting the *soi-disant* sprawl.

He is at the bottom of a hilly street, and he knows that the sack on his back may begin to weigh quite a bit by the time he's reached a desired place. He thinks about the mall, not that far away after all, there is a huge one a few blocks up he knows, and even though nobody else walks in these here parts, and even though the strangest of occurrences is to have

a walker actually walking on the sidewalk, he's not opposed
to the idea, even with the heavy bag on his back. There is a
small mini-mall too, even closer than that one, with only two
levels and a manageable number of stores. He's frequented that
one as well, and he could go again now, buy a smoothie perhaps and sit on one of the comfortable chairs in the middle,
and just watch the shoppers with their plastic bags filled with
junk. Or he could get his smoothie and stand by the railings
and lean over the railings on the second floor and watch the
shoppers on the first floor in the main walkway, with the kids
in the strollers and the older kids pushing the strollers and the
oldest kids getting on their parents' nerves and inviting them
to lose their patience and shout. A. now sees himself standing
above the railing watching the crowds, watching the boys and
the girls, watching the migrants, watching the teens, watching
the O so excited consumers rushing from one great bargain to
another, watching the consumers consume, watching the consumers consume some more, and more, and in-between get
hefty so that they can consume even more. A. is now smiling
at the thought of such rituals, he's had enough really, those
days are gone, although he takes pleasure in watching, even if
just to confirm the importance of the mission, and how he'd
like to if not outlaw malls outright, then definitely outlaw the
personages in the form of families that dot their interiors. He
even remembers the mall's Santa Claus, and how a picture with
Santa would cost something like nine ninety-nine, and if you
wanted one sitting on Santa's lap it would be even more, a
few bucks more, fourteen ninety-nine! A.'s sense of dread is
mixed in with his smile at the depravity of it all, no way he
thinks, no mall, except that there was always the food court,
the Food Court (I should write) at the Mall, and such a choice,
he thinks, was precious, so that even if he outlawed the crowd

at the mall, he'd let the food court stand, what with its precious offerings, its wide selection, how you can grab pretty much anything and sit at one of the tables in the middle. And now again his focus back to his immediate concerns, back from the revolutionary zeal to this: he's thinking if he goes to the food court at the mall, he could sit at one of those ugly and cheap orangish reddish tables, Steve's remains on his side, some appetizing Chinese food or Thai food or whatever he'd choose to order in front of him, surveying the scene, fatsos and freaks walking the premises, poor old migrants again wiping tables and emptying trays in trash bags and changing trash bags and mopping the spills of wild children, or careless adults, or a combination thereof. Food Court at the Mall, O beloved Food Court at the Mall, A. begins to whisper another favorite ditty,

Food Court at the Mall
Come and see and eat y'all
It's a wonderful space a wonderful place
Eat all you want and never feel too small

O Food Court at the Mall, O Food Court at the Mall, A. goes on whispering, whistling the tune, in his head,

O Food Court at the Mall
O Food Court at the Mall
Save me from boredom save me from the fall
Into irrelevance and mediocrity
Summon the deities and help me heed the call!
O Food Court at the Mall
How can I get it all
All I mean!
The chicken fingers and the Thai noodles

A little taste o' spicy ribs
Kebabs and hearty yogurt sips
Fancy soups from the lady with the poodles!

He ponders where to go, maybe catch a movie, at the multiplex, he loved always to watch movies at the multiplex, inside
the theatre in the middle of the day, when only the scattered
poets and painters and bums and retirees attended, when it
wasn't really time to go and watch, maybe he'll do that, go up
to ticket booth, the bored cashier behind the glass waiting to
print a ticket, and walk around to the ticket attendant who
doubles also as the old-time usher, completely out of it, who
snatches his ticket and shows him in, where he'll join lots of
teens and more of the restless, the jobless, the lifeless, in the
middle of a hot afternoon, and then, suddenly, No—in his
head the definitive exclamation, with a capital N—almost out
of nowhere, but with total conviction, no go: no mall for now,
no multiplex, and not even the food court, for now anyway.
He chooses to stand and watch and ponder in the street, and
in his stillness, in the beatitude of stillness, in the quietude
and serenity of post-amazing-feat accomplished, he wonders,
where to next. He keeps walking and looking, and constant
switches of the bag from right to left shoulder are in order. He's
walked quite a bit when:

a 7-Eleven appears yonder, atop the hill

where the road curves, right next to the pizza place with the
bright red sign and the worn-out letters that you know just
haven't been maintained for a while, like the 'p' and the 'z' (the
second one), each of which is missing a piece of its contours, a
bit like chipped teeth, or chiseled cement blocks, or the corner

of a secondhand coffee table that you go get at a thrift shop (not the chic-looking ones but the admittedly worn-down versions you find, well, around the neighborhoods of this humble bloke's). The second 'z' even offers what amounts to an elegant artistic contrast with the first 'z', almost as if a percentage sign, the vagaries of chance (and natural elements) decidedly conspiring to wear out the mighty last letter of the alphabet in perfectly symmetrical fashion and right at the very points that would entice the unknowing spectator to assume that the owners might have gone beyond the call of duty (especially in the usual domain of the preoccupation of pizza joint owners who, more often than not, demonstrate a conspicuously uncanny absence of aesthetic concern (or taste) in the overall décor and management of their establishments (save for their nifty red-and-white square tablecloths found in some, my favorites), not to mention attention to graphic design) to make sure that their joint stands out among its competitors and its neighbors, an absolute necessity if you want to survive in business in this day and age. What with this pizza place itself situated next to a small car-wash operation (at present sporting only a few idle young men in an orchestrated (in and out, solitary, waiting…) movement), the entire lot situated across a bus depot, which translates into: waiting passengers (some loitering outside, others with weary and tired faces either slumbering or staring absent-mindedly into space on their extremely uncomfortable seats), the bus usually driving up this very road (A. saw only two, during his long walk up the hill) and turning into the relatively small parking lot, the passengers snapping to and automatically (as it happens in these parts) forming a line (bags on shoulders, bags on ground, bags on both shoulders at times with baby in arms, baby cries, the occasional complaint of a particularly worn-out passenger), the stoic driver standing at the door and giving instructions and taking and ripping tickets and managing the crowd with utmost professionalism, the passersby looking disturbed at the scene, the line of cars at the intersection obediently responding to the traffic lights and carrying on what feels after a protracted following of the scene without thought or judgment or critical inquiry, like an orchestration, an otherworldly choreography of machines in their elegant automatism, beauteous motion with its quiet, almost unnerving majesty, in a landscape without idle chatter, without cacophonous rattling, without noise...

And in this landscape, this somehow solitary landscape, A. is looking for a drink, because, he is, thirsty.

He enters. He knows he does not look suspicious, and he knows also that thanks to his relatively careful treatment of the meat, Steve is not in an unfathomable fantastical turn, going to come alive or storm out of the bag in this venerable convenient store. At least not yet. 'Stevie,' he whispers even, the disgusting lout, the heartless monster, 'you behave now you hear. Don't you mess with me in here.' (The (almost) homonymous hear/here delighted his amateurish prosaisms to no end.) A wicked smile is flashed, to no one in particular, in the classic fashion of the monstrous (yes, keep repeating until it sinks in), despicable, revolutionaries without mercy.

He does not see anyone he knows, and that is perhaps for the better. A quick glance around to ascertain and he notices in the back Golayab Dol, a diet guru who'd started his own business a few years back and was having, incredibly, a great amount of success—attributed in the press to both his extravagant marketing strategies and the fact that he'd hit the market at the right time—and whose products all the soccer moms and their friends were drawn to and perceived as the next most important fad. Gol Dol, as he'd come to be known, had attended A.'s high school for a year, sophomore year to be exact, subsequent to which his aunt—his parents had remained in his native country, where that was A. could not recall—had transferred him to a private school. He'd flown under the radar that one year, magically managing to avoid each of the clans, and inconspicuously disappearing just as he had appeared. It was only after his business success, and the TV commercials espousing Master Gol Dol's dietary revolutions that A. and his cohorts had gotten a whiff that the fellow had attended their school. And only after Dol was the honorary recipient of an alumnus award, for both Achievement in Business and Giving Back to the Community—in addition to the prize received from the municipality—all given to him at a lavish high school alumni reunion (followed by a sedate and measured lecture that, according to attendees, drew only a polite applause), was it cemented that Dol did indeed attend the school, and he had in fact succeeded in business. A., one night seeing the commercial, suddenly recalled an episode where, that very sophomore year, in what was the first or second week of school, he'd been involved in a minor episode with Dol, helping him, as it turned out, coming to his rescue at just the right moment, as he was about to be picked on (the process—the slight shove, the gathering in a semicircle of the clan, the bullish tone—had already started) by one of the cliques. Dol had walked away unscathed, untouched, unaffected really, and had politely thanked A. on the spot without ever really mentioning, or making a deal of it during the year, or in subsequent years. But regarding Dol's identity, there was no doubt—and now that he was seeing him here, tucked away in the back of the 7-Eleven... Gol Dol turns around and also catches a glimpse of A.—but no, no grand acknowledgment, no sudden recourse to friendly small talk: just a nod (A.'s initiative) and the nod's echo (Dol), appropriate for a 7-Eleven chance run-in.

Now, the annals of all of the world's literatures, dear reader, all of the world's mythologies, all of the world's tales, are, I would hope we can agree, strewn with marvelous accounts of amorous passions and loving encounters in the most unexpected of locales, and, often, between if not polar opposites, then the farther reaches of various poles. One could cite any number of extravagant flings among heretical folk-heroes of a particular era overcoming the conservative obstacles laid out before them, folks finally able to flaunt their victories arm in arm. The tragic consequences of an innumerable array of blasphemous bondings—one tribe with another, one neighborhood with another, one so-called race with another so-called race—are familiar to audiences world-wide, and often the subject of massive commentary, not to mention adaptations of all sorts, for they do indeed enlighten us do they not, on the prickly essence of our beings, lest we forget all the illegitimate liaisons, the penalized rendezvous, the state-sponsored imprisonment of many a humble folk engaged in those modes of relations not only not sanctioned during a particular era, but that deeply quote unquote offend some organism or body or institution, whether they be represented by one or many human entities. In all of these disparate cultures and geographically diverse lands, a wholesome conglomeration of sayings has come into being firmly implanting into the various consciousnesses the notion of a sudden burst of desire surfacing to the fore. In our day, in our most sacred and sacrosanct of languages, 'love at first sight' is an expression that I, and I'm willing to bet, you also (finger of a figure on a poster coming straight at you), hold particularly dear, even though it has come to be used with perhaps excessive freedom. Well, this is what's surreptitiously happening within the confines of our fable, our novella, our, say it loud say it clear, new genre, our fabella. We have, fortunately or un—and even though our 'characters' and the very fabric of their beings are far removed from the usual concoctions, namely the healthy mixture of DNA, social and environmental factors and chemical predispositions, along with an array of cultural forces and of course, natural causes, that fashion our live human brethren—stumbled upon such an occurrence indeed.

A., upon a first glance left at the magazine rack after his sighting of Dol, raises his eyes and… spots, across the store, a solidly hot-looking babe in a cut-off shirt and jeans. His eyes instantly meet hers. It's… Except that he's not sure whether this constitutes the proverbial 'across the room' since, well, it's not a room he's inside. (The interlocking of the eyes is no illusion though, and, it seems to me, that's all that really matters.) And so he wonders: approach, or not? Wouldn't it serve me better to ignore her, at least temporarily, infuse a bit of uncertainty in her mind, inject a bit of intrigue in her soul? Plus, what about Mappolo? And, what about my promise to myself, to limit, in more ways than one, the, shall I say, flings… What about… Hesitation, however, is not called for here. Not under what are swiftly turning into sacrosanct circumstances. One day forth, A. does see the future mausoleum's welcoming plaques, they shall designate this most sacred of locales a shrine, or at least a museum, the store in Aville, or Aburg, or Acity, where King A. first set his eyes upon his future queen! ('Cause he will need to have a queen, unless times change so radically, but he doubts that, really he does…)

He's thinking to approach, the lone uncertainty being whether he'd even slightly turned her off by rapidly glancing—after the meeting of the eyes—at the shiny belly-button ring on her amazingly flat, tan and curvy stomach. Wouldn't legend have wanted that his eyes remain (the key is the absence of that swift to and fro), remain, I repeat, on hers? (Perhaps, but truth-telling is my forte, my mission, my, ehem, calling, and deviation from the chosen path, however practical for the legend, I cannot permit.) Wouldn't mythology have preferred a prolonged and uninterrupted silent exchange? Even as the hot chick's considerably chubbier, shorter and green-and-purple-haired friend in loose pants and horrible-looking shirt continued her banter; even as baseball-capped teenager with a box of cookies under one arm and a huge cereal in the other momentarily stood in their line of vision and blocked the uninterrupted exchange, what with his indecision in selecting his bag of chips (the layout of the store, decidedly, was not designed with cross-the-room flirtations, or loves, in mind); even as a small group of Spanish-speaking migrants (Mexican, A. could tell) raised a mini-brouhaha; even as the cashier from 'one of them countries *pa'llá*' (as A. fondly recalled his Puerto-Rican friend J. Rivera's moitié-condescending, moitié-endearing reference to folks from those far-away countries) kept repeating prices? Shouldn't his eyes have, again I repeat, stayed affixed to hers? Perhaps— but the sad reality is that they hadn't, he hadn't allowed this most undaunted and unperturbed of miracles to come into being. Yes, he'd peeked. At her midriff. At her boobs. Better to admit it than deny it. The question was, had she noticed, and would she really mind if she had? ('Why would she,' A.'s inward consciousness generates the linguistic phrase, unheard obviously but in his own mind, 'isn't the first glimpse what counts—and besides, she must love it if she flaunts it, no?')

He turns momentarily, unable to bear the weight of his colossally important questions. He feigns being interested in the items stacked out at the very edge of the aisle he is closest to (sugars—brown, granulated, white, different size packs; salts—iodized and not etc.), but very quickly looks up again. She's turned, is facing the refrigerated section, now even slides open the sliding door and is in the process of selecting juices, soda, milk, who knows, when her friend quickly glances back, in the way of those who've been told a thing or two about the subject of their gaze! Encouraging, A. thinks.

A., of course, can not fail to notice her well-proportioned, fabulously round and undoubtedly firm buttocks, with the skin of the back portion atop getting his juices flowing even more. The tight jeans, her long, shapely legs... Why do girls do this to us, the thought races through his mind, why do they do this! This new examination of her fabulous proportions, he's happy to convince himself, was certainly not provoked by his wandering eyes (even though it was making the encounter less and less of a candidate for inclusion in the hall of fame of grandiose, mythical, universal, romantic love stories). She had, he thought, knowingly and purposefully, launched the whole mini-show. She had given him that unmistakable come-hither look. She had enticed him, some might even say hypnotized him. She was: seducing him.

He walks up now with a determined pace and by the time he's reached the refrigerated section, she's turned around. He's going to pick a bottled soda, a juice, he's pretending, and so stops, right in front. Uncomfortable moment, or perhaps awkward I should say, yes awkward is a more judicious word. She doesn't quite know how to act: get out of the way, actually carry on and do her best, say something? 'Oh!' she lets out, staccato. 'Sorry!' She nudges to the left as A. swings the Steve sack to his right shoulder and moves closer to the sliding door. 'No, no! No problem,' he says—and this, *this*, is when it was all confirmed: he (this time for real) fixes his eyes on hers, she returning the favor, neither budging, neither even pretending to be engaged in any other activity, neither following through with the logical continuation of the itinerary (he not sliding door, not even looking at item let alone picking it out, she not carrying on, not talking to friend), and, in fact, retaining physical positions (she facing sliding door, neck turned right, he, at an angle, facing the sliding door also, neck turned left, and slightly hunched) which, without a doubt, confirms their betaken-ness with one another. The friend even walks away, getting the clue—and further cementing the what may now legitimately be called flirtatious (if not yet amorous) encounter.

The hero A. smiles and she returns the smile. Her greenish/grayish eyes are even more beautiful up close, he thinks—and that soft, smooth skin... Not to mention breasts thrust forward, natural too, thank god (he's thinking), he's sure of it, no enhancement, besides, she's too young, although you never know, not nowadays anyways...

A. puts the sack down. He, at his five feet sevenish-ness is about two inches taller than she (a perfect queen, he's thinking) and so slightly bends down as he leans forward and whispers into her ear (start the violins): 'I'd love to lick ice-cream off your belly button one day—that is, if you'd allow me, madam!'

He comes back up, smiling, didn't know him to be such the smooth operator, not A., not the A. I'd made up and known up to now, especially not with the females. She's giggling, blushing, turning slightly away.

'Listen,' he says, in a much more gentlemanly manner, and with a smooth, soothing, relaxed tone, 'my friends and I, we're going to have a party later tonight—if you wanna...'

For a moment, she pretends, or wants to pretend, that she needs to play the game, the denial, the uncertainty at least (the trailing 'I don't know...' even races through her mind), but she realizes, recognizes rather, that she was party, was she not, to this entire affair, she gave the eye, the look, she stood there, she turned around, he knew all of this, no more reason for...

'Maybe,' she answers—'call me.' (Wow, A. confirms, what a soft, sensitive, seductive, voice!)

Swiftly, even as she had passed between the first word and her next two-worded utterance (that had nevertheless been uttered as though one sememe: 'callme'), she had dug into the tiny handbag, taken out a torn piece of paper and with her lip liner (dug in same bag), scribbled—something: she's folded it into an even more minuscule square and now handed it to him. She turns around and catches up to her friend as A., standing helpless, follows her with his, yes, eyes. Dares not open the paper, and so carefully deposits it into the little mini-pocket situated above the regular pocket of his jeans. Wow, he's still thinking, wow wow wow wow, wow! How mysterious. How... She, at this tender age, knowing how to... She, at the cashier, their items rung up and placed in bag (the friend had already started the process), now, before taking off, does she, does she, please do, he's thinking, please... Yes: turneth around and depositeth a last furtive glance upon her knight's awaiting, expecting visage. Her friend says, Let's go, and so she swiftly turns and they're both out the door. The cashier looks at A. and smiles—the generous smile of recognition on the part of strangers in sympathy with a minor victory, with those they want to show, silently, their 'way to go' to. A. cannot resist: he quickly takes the little squarely folded page out and opens up, one fold after another. 'Shit!' he exclaims quickly. 'Goddamnit,' he then says louder! The matter? This: all there is on the piece of paper is a phone number, no area code, with some of the numbers barely distinguishable—and no name.

And no name, he's thinking, goddamnit, how am I going to... He folds the paper back, deposits it in the little pocket, weary of losing it if placed in bigger locales and gets, in a manner of saying, a hold of himself. He's got bigger fish to fry, after all, metaphorically and literally, and he knows it. 'Get a hold of yourself asshole,' he mutters inwardly. And so straightens up again, bends down to lift his sack and swings it on his shoulder, looks about, and then, what did I come here to get, thinking, ah yes... There, before even having realized, a clue that ignites memory. There, he sees:

a very large cup, atop the counter,

seemingly used: a big gulp, getting bigger, and bigger, and bigger, and huger and huger and huger (as his thirst in some weird way transports him into a hallucinatory dreamland). He walks toward the actual resource center, where the various sizes are stacked, pulls out the largest cup and brings it to the soda fountain, lifts it, presses it against the ice lever, situated in the middle of the fountain, pulls it away as ice still is cascading down (he does not want too much, does not want to be ripped off), swings cup under soda lever, presses until liquid fills cup to brim and even overflows, stops, pushes lever again in swift thrusts, each time instigating a sudden slush of soda that comes with that silly swoosh noise when a lever is pushed, allows the soda to overflow again, then shakes the whole cup, backhand flips the ice at top out, now it's looking good, now he's satisfied, now he's getting his money's worth. Picks cap to put over but it's the wrong size so picks up next size and places on top of cup and then grabs a few straws—you never know, you might lose some.

A sudden call is heard (as A. is contemplating how many straws and napkins he will steal): 'A., is that you A.?!' A. turns. 'Well whaddaya know!' slaps him on the back with a big grin on his face, the tall and gangly and awkwardly unbalanced and unkempt fellow. 'It *is* you! I knew I'd recognized you!'

It was indeed one of those occasions when a fellow walks into a convenience store, for, precisely, convenience, and gets what can safely be said to constitute its opposite: running into old acquaintances one cares nothing for, leading to awkward and certainly unnecessary exchanges that seem to last a lot longer than they actually do. And as in A.'s current case, at precisely the wrong time, under the worst of circumstances.

'Heeeeey,' A. responds, attempting to strike a delicate balance between polite, distant friendliness and the deliberate communication of a lack of desire to chat. 'Sonder, what's up?!'

'You tell me buddy!' the fellow now recognized as Sonder responds. 'What have you been up to?!!'

Unfortunately, A.'s worst nightmares have come true and he stands there and chats with old Sonder Saktchek, a former colleague at the car shop where for a while, between gigs, A. had moonlighted as a receptionist slash administrative guy. Big car shop too, involved in all aspects of automotive repair, from collision damage to glass work to refurbishing and the like. It turns out that Saktchek was still gainfully employed there, was still married, 'Happily I might add,' to Mrs. Saktchek, still took Sonder Jr. to his little league baseball games ('I managed the team for a while, while ol' Johnny Paltruks recovered from a triple bypass, now that was a trip!'), and still religiously got a few old pals to come over on Sundays to watch the football games. He also had four daughters (two from a previous marriage), a house full of pets (dog, two cats, fish, two hamsters, one for each of the girl's rooms and another forthcoming for little Sonder) and a set of matching bikes. Sonder Saktchek was a family man now, a loud and loving father and husband fully enjoying the spoils of father/husbandhood. And although reader has been spared the impromptu meeting's more excessive details, poor old A. was not—until Saktchek himself, looking at his watch, exclaims, 'Oh my gosh, I gotta run my man, good seeing you again, you be good now,' his little basket full of items for the family filled to the brim.

Is that it, A. is thinking as Saktchek runs to the register and pays and twists and waves as he exits quickly, his entire mindset perturbed, one, by the actual meeting, and subsequently, by the inconclusive exchange. His attention turns again to his own needs, after what can be called a relatively eventful or eventless 7-Eleven experience, depending on one's expectations and precedent. For A., a regular despite how he fancies himself to be on the path, this was, let's call it, not so atypical. He's gotten most of his needed items too, although a snack could be enticing. He considers: chips, a candy bar, an unappetizing hot dog or a slice he sees in the machine keeping them warm, or maybe… an item from:

The Encyclopedic Dictionary
of shitty junk food calling on the ruined palate,
all temptations on full throttle and angel on
little shoulder saying now now don't go

Candies; cakes (slices of pound, cheese, carrot and others); cereals (small boxes); Cheetos; chips (greasy); chocolate bars (a variety to choose from, as we all know); cookies; crappy fake fruit juice; corn in a can; doughnuts (mini version); doughnuts (maxi version); fruit (fruit?!! actual fruit? as a snack? right!); gums; gummy bears; Hershey's kisses; ice-cream; juice-bars (various flavors); lollipops (various flavors); M&Ms (have to have own category); muffins (in a plastic bag); nachos; (really, really old, grubby, grandma-skinned) pizza slices; plantains (fried); popcorn in a bag; power bars (healthy I guess); puddings; raisins (dried); Reese's peanut butter cups; slices of ham; Twinkies; wafers. (Please fill in neglected items—and check your favorite.)

Or… No, rather a fruit yogurt, strawberry, his favorite. These little yogurt cups make for good snacks always, and the consumption is quite convenient. Yes, why not—he'll do a yogurt.

We catch A. next standing in line, one big gulp in the left hand, three straws sticking out of his pants' left pocket, the yogurt cup held uncomfortably by the same hand holding the sack over his shoulder.

A peculiar thing happens as he is waiting. He was certain that there were only three customers in front of him, and the two who'd come behind him. But when he turns his head straight again after a momentary meditation, his eyes transfixed on the far wall filled with non-perishables such as detergents and soaps and lotions of all kinds, he notices, standing at a slight angle but definitely in front of him in the line, a fourth fellow, a very tall, lanky, unshaven man with a troubled look. He is not absolutely sure that this fellow was not in front of him, but he's pretty certain. He detects these tricky situations, has an eye for 'em you could say, especially in relation to queuing up. His presumption takes a drastic turn for the worst when he decides, uncharacteristically (he customarily lets these things go), to take action:

'Sir,' he says, tapping the large fellow on the shoulder, 'the line is over here.'

At first, big man on campus thinking himself big man in store just because he's a big man, completely ignores A.'s overture. Does not even bother to turn around. In fact, one might offer the conjecture that he really and truly did not feel the tap, what with the puny timidity of the one finger tapped thrice totally unfelt on his massive shoulders... Thought of a fly surely, our big brute...

'Sir,' A. repeats (he will not let it go, emboldened by the earlier heroics), this time louder, more forceful and utilizing the entire palm of his right hand on the big man's shoulder.

With all intention to intimidate, the fellow slowly, methodically, revealing a super mean stare, turns around.

A., big man in fabella, is not the least bit intimidated. He's been through worse, much worse. These pesky Americans always think they're all that and real bad, little do they know what kinds of street smarts the rest of us acquire through life!

The man does not say anything. Has crossed his arms at his chest hulkingly, standing before A., as if to say, How can I help you?

Our hero A. is cognizant that the exchange is being noticed. The ones behind him obviously are looking, dreading in one way the outcome (most definitely for A.'s sake) but surely applauding his courage to take on the big fella. But also, around the store, the already belligerent interaction has drawn the attention and interest of a potpourri of two-minute shoppers, namely: Franklyn Furmbutts, at the fridge, a contractor, on a break (curtsy please, Franklyn... thank you—); Monti Mellonsire, a regular guy who wants to be a real estate broker who wants to be a TV host in order to one day be on a sitcom and be a star; Hank Hulbooth, an expert in historical enactments whose next project involves some enactments in the parking lots of several shopping centers, which he believed had been unjustly erected on old historical sites; Yoluzbeth Licktchups, a nurse's aide, in the aisle adjacent (Yoluzbeth, if you will please, thanks...); ten-year old Jojo Bitarbiat and mom (guys...). So, A. thinks, there's an audience, great...

Not budging, making sure to look at the baaaaaaaaad aaaaaaaaasssss duuuuuuuuuuude in the eyes, A. says: 'You cut in line man. And I was telling you that the line starts there.'

Woh!—As in: a) exclamation; b) synonym of misery. No mincing of words here! The onlookers are impressed, and afraid. The cashier, worried. The little boy, staring, mute. The big bad man is slightly taken aback by A.'s seriously badass attitude. He tries to regain his composure and says, meekly, but trying to be mean: 'Is thaaaaaaaaaaaaat soooooooooo?'

'That's so,' A. says without missing a beat.

He even brings his arm up and extends it backwards, index finger pointing, as if to emphasize: there!

(Emboldened, did I say? By the greatness he sees in himself and that he can no longer deny? Is he crazy?! And what would I do if the guy beats him up! What happens to MY story! And what about his cowardly shaking in his boots when he thought Steve had a gun? Is this whole courageous turn compatible, consistent with his personality? But, what O what personality, I would ask! Is this not the very fabric of all our beings, this schizophrenic unpredictability?!)

The big fellow now is beside himself. This little shrimp of a creature posing as a man, pointing to the back, for me?!! Did he just do that to me?!! Even worse, now pretty much all the occupants of the store (Monteskiew Audams, a truck driver, John-Paul Sartra, a spoken-word artist, dancer and actor, Andray Brittany, a gun dealer with white hair, Pierre Roller, a French jazz pianist, John Jobonline, a headhunter at a downtown firm who lives in these parts, Henry Deeate, a motivational speaker who mostly tackles issues related to diets and weight-loss among a host of multicultural clients) are honed in on the confrontation. He grimaces, emits even a small growl, pulls up his sleeves, and makes as if he will in one swoop grab A. and lift A. and slam A. to the ground and, if he feels like it, stomp on A. But A., anticipating the move, quickly takes a step back (stepping on toes of fellow behind him who goes 'Ouch!' and A., 'Sorry!') and... Round 1? One fall? No limit? Cage match? Bets?

Not even, O voyeuristic, O sadistic mongrel of a reader, not even! For, our hero A., cleverly and with all the street smarts he could muster, as he had taken the step back, had also taken care to simultaneously reposition his body so as to be able to take precise aim and swing the sack with Steve's remains all the way over, windmill style, and crash it mercilessly right on top of the head of the big man, who, like a huge lug of a tree, like a big-ass building or mountain, crashes to the ground, where he remains motionless, out cold.

The audience bursts into uncontrolled and ecstatic applause. Cheers follow and folks even come up to A. and shake his hand and slap his back and say 'Way to go man' and 'You tell him mister' and 'Good for you dude!' And also give him high fives and tens. The cashier, with the help of a couple of others, drags the man's body out, pulling his arms and holding the legs, him still on the ground, on his back. A., back in line, whispers to the Steve sack: 'Thanks buddy, I owe you one.'

When his turn comes up, the cashier tells him how much it'll all cost, and A. pays, and the cashier gives him his change back, and A. says thanks and turns and walks out, waving his arm to all, the sack on his right shoulder, a generous, and enthusiastic applause accompanying his exit.

With his slurpy in one hand (right) and the pieces of Steve's cadaver in the sack thrown over his shoulder: like a troubadour how he traverses the desolate landscape of suburbia on his way home…

And despite the sudden jerks precipitated upon the sack by Steve's unusually healthy heart (still beating, still beating, a bit like that Persian poem from Iraj Mirza where the mom's heart ripped apart by her own progeny on command of his lover, speaks to him still, asking 'Are you all right my son?'), A. walks: purposefully, pensively, proudly, holding his huge drink—slurping on his straw stuck in the hole of his cup.

4

O Ostrich in a Cadillac, Ostrich in a Cadillac chant! O unfortunate exclamation birthed by a deprived and delusional jokester madman, a young turk who once upon a forsaken night lost all manner of inhibitions and came up with You! O First Line but never last from which surely a spew of cheap imitations and subversive reactions will flow probably within the confines of this very book! Pardon, I say, pardon the freelancing floater's uncaring 'Why don't we just shout out something totally whacko' attitude. He's a bit on the eccentric side if I may, this young fellow, but I swear, I'd say he had multiple personalities if I didn't know better. Although… Come to think of it… I can't really even proclaim for certain that he doesn't! All I know, and I say this with some degree of trepidation and guilt, since I am, after all, the one under whose auspices he has morphed into a genuine creature of the page, the guy does swing between totally wild bouts of depression and anxiety and a happy-go-lucky attitude that contravenes his fanatical devotion to sports and a weird swinging lifestyle of sorts. Quite the *cas* in fact, a pendulum swinger of the worst kind, totally unpredictable, an almost impossible character (key word is: almost), who, without really meaning it, gave birth to you when everyone else was stuck. Oh they knew the method all right, just couldn't come up with a drawing factor: until, that is, this most imaginative of blokes, in drunken stupor and exhibiting the indifference of an alien invader, came up with you, O Ostrich in a Cadillac, Ostrich in a Cadillac chant, sullying, perhaps forever, the noble image of that wondrous bird, not to mention the otherworldly reputation of the classic automobile. He did make it happen in a way, he did give you to the world. He, yes, but he who? We've met him in fact, at his most anxious and vulnerable, when he was sitting downing shots at a small dive, not just anxious and on the verge of regretful commiseration with his self, but even semi-guilty, although not really. None other than the future hero of this gory tale, none other than, O once upon a time there was, once upon a time there was not, a fellow by the name of...

> *Oyo, Oyo*
> *He was a gentle soul, a child at heart*
> *A cherubic face in the cold dark night*
> *Ohummm, Ohummmm...*

> *His name was Mappolo, Mappolo Rei*
> *Never knew his daddy but that's okay*
> *He's a saint and a savior anyway*
> *His name is Mappolo, Mappolo Rei*

—yes: Mappolo, Mappolo Rei...

Alas, I shall not as of yet disclose the source of the poetic fragment I have just here introduced (should not have, probably). Nor will I share the story of its genesis, which soon you shall all be privy to—so sad, so sad it is... But he's alive and well as we read, alive and well, and now more than ever a central figure and not just in our tale. 'He'? 'Is'? I write again nonchalantly... But who, who pray tell, who is this Mappolo Rei?

A hero for the ages?
Delivering all from cages?
An actor on stages?
Ex-reader burning pages?
A wise man among sages?

All of that, all of that, and more...

He is someone who:
in his bedroom, has: a futon on the ground, a writing desk with two drawers and a lamp on top, a bike against the wall, which he rarely rides, an extra closet full of both workman-like and splashy clothes, several plants (details unnecessary), and a small alarm clock.

He is someone who:
on the rack drilled on the back of the door of his bedroom, has: an always semi-wet towel, two pairs of pants hanging, one with a belt and one without, a shoulder bag, a sweater he rarely wears, and a cap.

He is someone who:
in the pockets of the pants with the belt on the rack, has: around seventy-five cents in change (always makes sure to replenish), his keys, several old receipts, a phone number or two (always makes sure to replenish), no wallet (keeps it somewhere else).

No to-do lists anywhere (not on boards, tables or calendars).
No medicine in the medicine cabinet (does not believe in pills, tablets or pain-killers).

Toothbrush? Yes, obviously.

Shaving cream? Absolutely.

Electric razor? Sheeeeeeeee! No way! Regular razor with blades, or else skin is very messy.

He is also, like all residing here on this celestial sphere of ours, the proud owner of some quirks, and some history too, don't you know...

One: he had a peculiar habit that truly distinguished, and not necessarily in positive ways, his initial interactions. Indeed, Mappolo Rei would purposely refrain from engaging in any salutary handshake, independent of the circumstances, the social (or financial) status of the other person, or the parameters of the meeting. Worse, he would purposely retain his right hand in his pocket while allowing the left to float freely, knowing very well that the contrast would irritate, if not frankly unnerve, his counterpart. Upon the awkward refusal to extend (upon the other's), he would merely either go forward (if the encounter were occurring at a point of passage, at the door, say), or simply stand, in both cases without explanation (particular allergies, skin disease), humorous asides, or even strategic introduction of conversation topic. The responses of his counterparts, as you might well imagine, would run the gamut: from vehement reprisals to quiet acceptance to addressing of topic at later date. No form or degree of the reaction, however, ever managed to precipitate a reconsideration on his part. Nor did anyone ever understand why, just why, he had ever gotten to this point.

Two: he fondly recalled an episode from his brief college tenure (he dropped out after the first year), which he believed (and I acquiesce to his request for inclusion) gave a particularly illuminating angle into his life path. Indeed, he was most proud of a comment made by a gray-haired, gray-bearded professor his freshman year during a private meeting the old prof had arranged. Backdrop is that a total of four students had signed up for the course (just like Mappolo wanted it: go to the least popular classes, to the wild and unrecognized professor's) on Pragmatism in America (obviously not to learn pragmatic lessons from it, but to engage with what he thought were the 'ideas'), two seniors (one a philosophy major), one sophomore, and he, a not-so-wide-eyed freshman. A few weeks into the course and two papers and a midterm later, the prof had summoned our young hero to his spacious and book-lined office (what for, he feared, he did not know) and despite an initial pose of glacial austerity and severity, had commended his work and congratulated him on his 'gifts' (he remembered that word distinctly), while expressing some rather unflattering reservations about his superfluous arguments in his paper (would be treated much more severely had he been a major in the department, he was told), and literally told that great things could be expected of him, that he was potentially 'a great one' if—but the prof never really said if *what*, or a great *what*! And Mappolo, despite his genius, perhaps because of it, would have loved a slight direction. All of which had touched him deeply and was even more appreciated later on, after his academic career had come to an abrupt end, since the very great things never did materialize, and the awaited greatness had long ago been forgotten. Perhaps, though, he reasoned in quiet moments away from all the hullabaloo, his current endeavors constituted a new mixture: after all, had he 'succeeded' and been a professor of some sort, another writer, another poet, a philosopher, a radically original combination thereof even, *even there*, there was a dash of mediocrity, a conventionalist death wish that he simply had to reject. Perhaps then, just perhaps, he indeed was onto those great things: it was *up-to-somethingness* that really counted, and that the professor had deciphered, yet not been able to name. *Up-to-somethingness*: Mappolo was proving his adeptness at that particular and subtle characteristic, had succeeded in giving credence to it in manifest reality. He had become, indeed, a *revolutionary*—without doubts, or reservations. None of which explained the terrible and obscure moments of sudden anxiety that invaded his entire being (body, soul, what-have-you) and led to unbearable tremors and panic attacks and questioning of his involvements. The invisible scars of up-to-somethingness, or simply the consequences of unconscious mechanisms he simply could not control? Why, after all, was he so adept at undermining his talents and his capacities, why and how did he manage to ef up anything even semi-decent or positive that had a potential of happening to him, why did he treat those who could help him so nastily and hang out with folks he could barely stand and who for sure were going nowhere? Why did he not just allow himself to flow within the regular streams of the social fabric, another thread in the quilt, a decidedly happy element, a troubled yet content element, radical or not, deluded or not, why was he stocking and shelving items in a small market in a small shopping center in a suburban outpost?! O questions eternally unanswered, O impervious actions forever destroying every potential of anything good happening, O gray-haired and gray-bearded prof of my ambitious days, where art thou when you are needed!

Three: in his drawers, Mappolo Rei had assembled a plethora of writings that would fulfill any archeologist's dream of unearthing abandoned projects, or the clever and scholarly archivist's thirst for being treated to a treasure-trove of manifestoes. Among the potentially forgotten yet just-as-possibly nation-building tracts, one could find: The Selfless Manifesto, which propounded a philosophy of service and generosity through an actual, physical undoing of the layers forming what one might call one's self (along with all sorts of fancy drivel on 'subjectivity'); The Exile from Exiledom's Manifesto—for all those who are not even at home in exile or in some expatriate-fashioned delusionary garden; The Sycamore Manifesto—named after his favorite tree under which to meditate; The River Manifesto, which he considered among his best writings—and within the confines of which his tone and style adhered to levels of literariness he coveted—and which did not stoop to polemical ranting and raving (in fact, subsequent to the writing of The River Manifesto, he thought seriously of burning all the others, getting so close as to hold them over a fire after a ritualistic dance even, but not having the courage after all); The Tyrannical Manifesto; The Dreamscape Manifesto; The Weary Teenager's Manifesto, not to mention The Manifesto to End All Manifestoes—a bold and guttural cry for freedom from all shackles. There was also an array of scattered poems, observations, arguments, irreverent shouts and screams and various booklets, ranging from a collection of bad Sufi-loving, mystical-leaning, love poetry with much use of syllepses rendering the efforts totally resistant to translation ('You drink the Wine of my Spirit and I circulate in your veins, the Blood of Life') to a volume of philosophical aphorisms ('The Burden of Man is only a function of his understanding and his lucidity'), to a compilation combining funky phonetic phosphorescent frolics ('Forget fame and forever feign indifference') and meta-aphoristic elaborations ('An aphorism a day makes the gloomy doom go away'), not to mention a work containing fragments of a literally illuminated manuscript (it had a built-in light inside). In a separate drawer, false and imagined past and future interviews with himself as both revolutionary leader and post-revolutionary victorious prophet gave some great insight into Mappolo's psyche while providing prime material for the future Historian of the Revolution's research concerning the movement's poetics and politics. A cursory sampling… Question: 'When you started out Mr. Rei, would you ever have imagined such a glorious homecoming?' Answer: 'I always wanted to work for the people, I wanted to liberate our people, I dreamt of our independence and our freedom, that's all I ever thought about.' Q: 'When you were forced into exile, did you ever, ever, doubt?' A: 'Never doubted—that is: I never doubted, not myself, not the will of the people, not the ultimate victory of the revolution.' Q: 'There's a funny anecdote, when you were eight, a child at school, you know that one, I think it was quite illustrative, can you expound on that a bit?' A: 'At school, yes, I was eight, and a group of ten-year-olds started picking on a friend of mine, I wasn't around mind you, and it wasn't with me that they had any beef, but somehow we heard about it in the hallway, and I was the only one who came to the rescue I guess you could say, and I made sure to tell Sedi, my friend, to go away, and I confronted the bullies, all by myself, got beat up pretty good I must admit, but I'd rather that than… I couldn't bear to see Sedi scared like that… I could handle it better I thought, psychologically, emotionally, no—better me than him!' Q: 'You really truly are a hero Mappolo Rei!' A: 'There are no heroes in the world, my sweet, only workers.'

And finally: lest we forget that our future hero could also be part of a huge family—with all sorts of drama and secrets—or tribe—with many an example of rebellion, and not too few instances of struggle between continuity and rupture, tradition and modernity, duty to collective body and individualism—or history, he concoted not just one but two family 'trees', albeit not really the familiar versions but nevertheless versions that attest to Mappolo solidly being able to be part of an inter-generational saga of vast, epic proportions (if only the author hadn't scoffed at the notion), culled, both the 'past' and 'future' illustrations, from Mappolo's own files (originally done in his own handwriting and with all the smudges, but which we ultimately decided not to include here). Branches bearing the names of Mappolo's family members, his lineage, his offspring, even distant ones, in both directions. And yes, their offspring, the next generation and on and on. Two family trees, but extended ones. Real extended. He wasn't kidding. No kidding with Mappolo. None.

All nice and good. A dose of present (continuous), some (recent) past, and a tree-like summary/illustration of the Great Past and even Greater Future. But what had preoccupied our schizophrenic friend-prophet, especially in the period preceding his more intense involvement in the revolution, was none other than The Ghastliest of Preoccupations, the Mother of All Anxiety-producing Mind-bending, Life-revising Searches, the most Unforgiving Prompt of all your Missteps and Stupidities throughout Life: a Job Search. He, like you, like me, like pretty much most everybody who ever walked the face of this god-damn blue ball (save for the aristocrats of yore (and progeny)), was involved in a: Job Search! Say it loud, say it clear, with me now, one, two (and louder, and louder), the man was—had been— looking for, looking for

A JOB!

A JOB!

A JOB!

And so was looking for, in all sorts of ways, all sorts of (simultaneous spelling-out with arms and other body parts)

J – O – B – S

JOBS! JOBS!

JOBS!

(Worthwhile to go into detail about Mappolo's employment predicament? Yes, we do believe so, for, as it will amply be demonstrated, the process and the product (here, the job) will allow us a deeper understanding of his psyche and his emotional disposition, not to mention that the job itself would make significant contributions to Mr. Rei's involvement in the revolution. So… Here we go.)

Q. How did he intend to limit his search? What was he looking for?

Several factors went into his calculations. First and foremost:

a job with as little human and machine interaction as possible. One that would limit all need for switching of linguistic universes, not to mention the mental occupation of colliding ideological tracts. Unhindered, uninterrupted moronic work, with no need for thought, reflection, or creativity. That's what he wanted.

Q. What kind of parameters did he take into account?

This one's good. For indeed, Mappolo Rei could boast of being the actual inventor of the CFB Quotient—The Conceptual Framework Bearability Quotient, a measure he had insisted should be at the very top of job-seekers' considerations. (Which prompted him to think of the potential bestseller, *What Matters When You Go Looking For Work That Employers Won't Tell You Even If You Ask, Repeatedly.*) To make it simple, the closer to zero the CFBQ number, the more job-seeker friendly the job. In case of a perpetual indecision, the job with the lower CFBQ would be chosen. Also, would come into play such factors as: 1) pay, 2) schedule, 3) benefits, and other niceties that he acknowledged were often the first (and only) important considerations for a majority of folks.

Q. What did his résumé look like?

Not like much actually. Didn't believe in putting down an objective, and further thought that a skills-based format best suited him, since he didn't have much experience to begin with—nothing of note, anyhow. So he did the 'qualifications' paragraph, then went ahead and did the 'work experience' (he had to put something), and finally, further 'applicable skills' and a quickie on education. Good enough, he thought, good enough for now.

Q. Did he intend to attend seminars and job-placement workshops?

Not! Rather, we find him (this episode now takes place before the beginning of this chronicle) on a stool, at the Say 'n' Sigh diner, open all night, with Marla the waitress repeatedly filling up his white mug without so much as asking, where an early brainstorming session delivered the following results:

1. Data entry dude at a warehousish building;
2. Phone survey operator at a company with a building on the edge of the sprawl;
3. Movie projectionist at the local movie theater at the mall;
4. Dishwasher at the Mexican restaurant inside the mall.

He then proceeded, as had been his wont all throughout his life, to determine the French *pour* (elements they had going 'for' them) and the *contre* ('against' them). He would also take into account miscellaneous considerations (MC) and potential regret factors (RF)—a measure he'd designed that actually took into account those elements within each engagement that would lead to regret one's involvement. This measure had the merit of considering 'fears-down-the-line' when the regret factor would kick in (one year, three, five, ten, indicated by a first number, as in RF 1, RF 2...) and the 'depth factor' of regret (from 1-5, one being the lowest). The numbers would thus appear as RF (1, 5) or RF (3, 4) etc...

This is what a cursory evaluation produced (still on the stool, sideways, occasionally turns and picks up cup and sips).

Data entry: moronic degree of engagement, comes nevertheless with potentially excessive interaction with frustrated middle-aged administrators. Might take themselves seriously—and, certainly, the data too. MC: can't think of any. Overall RF factor: given the uncertainty as to the possibility of having to take on way too much data with your 'boss' breathing down your neck, RF would run something like 1 and 4, thus RF (1, 4). Overall CFBQ: 1.5.

Phone survey operator: little contact with higher-ups. Harmless, but potentially unfruitful. RF (2, 3). CFBQ: 1.1. Actual work: asking questions, getting answers. MC: being on phone all day might damage ears.

Movie projectionist: theory is that while film is running, one is totally free—but a break, or any other sudden misfortune, might induce extended panic. Little interaction, although high machine interaction. RF (3, 2): quite minimal, since, at worst, a skill is learned. CFBQ: 0.2. No conceptual framework, other than there's a theatre, folks come in, pay, see a movie. (The critical engagement with the foundations of the movie industry and the type of film-making and film-seeing it generates is another question.)

Dishwasher: pretty much left alone. No interaction. Work can get overwhelming at times though. RF (1, 3), in case of fights with coworkers. CFBQ: 2—if only for the ethnic and nationalistic fervor given to the joint. MC: the irony would be delicious: a former sports-camp counselor, with dishwashing experience during his one year at his venerable higher education institution's student center, promising himself to do anything but, desiring absolute independence, ending up washing dishes in adult life at the establishment of a barely English-speaking trio of Mexicans who'd started as busboys only two years earlier (illegal, was their entry), and who'd conceived the fabulous idea of bringing mom to work, and marketing *Mi Mami* as the only genuine, authentic Mexican-serving restaurant within a fifty-mile radius. No, there would be no sense of failure or a sudden what-am-I-doing awakening. He did not fear the irony—cherished it, in fact, embraced it. That would be the ultimate logical extension of the American Dream: going back to busing tables, washing dishes and floors, a reverse pioneerism. Why not him, after all? He would be the one to put it in motion. The ultimate pioneer-negative. Why not?!

Mappolo puts his pen on the counter as he swivels the chair back facing the mirror opposite. A fatigue (mental) visible on his face. A sort of exasperation—congratulating himself nevertheless for at least putting it down on paper. Back curved head tilted upwards, hand goes to coffee mug, handle grasped, mug brought to lips, pause, and sip.

'Dja figure it out?'

Marla was standing a few steps away, at the edge of the counter, one elbow on top.

'I don't even know yet,' Mappolo answers, an appreciative smile on his face.

'What are you… lookin' for a job?'

'Yeah, actually,' Mappolo says. 'Kinda.'

'What kinda job?' Marla asks after a pause and a quick refilling of another fellow's cup, sitting there, close to the edge, a couple of seats away from Mappolo.

'That's the whole thing. Actually, I'm lookin' for, sorta, a dumb job.'

'Well, welcome to America!' Marla says with that awkward humor of hairup waitresses. She pauses and adds: 'We sure got plenty of those!'

And then, it was there, at the Say 'n' Sigh, April 15th, that the suggestion was made. The ensuing discussion between Mappolo and Marla had elucidated for the latter the former's goals, and the elements and the components he was looking for in his next employment. It hadn't taken her long to come up with an idea. Not that she had truly grasped all the 'factors' and 'quotients' Mappolo had concocted to give legitimacy and meaning to the aspects that were relevant to him, but she had, indeed, listened closely, and had been, while he kept on with his explanations, mulling over in her brain the recommendations she would give him.

So when she'd suggested ('Why don't you give a call to my friend Joe Betashnik, he owns a small market, you could stock the shelves and run errands?') that he take on a sort of all-around gopher gig at her friend's small market, with the emphasis on stocking the shelves, a weird, some would say creepy and eerie, excitement had come over Mappolo. Almost like an illumination, certainly a most satisfying feeling of fullness. He had never been able to admit to himself that the idea of living creatures being slaughtered and then served, in whatever format, excited him in a peculiar way that went beyond the actual sumptuousness of a juicy meal. Something beyond, that he'd never dared challenge within himself, let alone question, or analyze. In addition, he'd always fantasized, when strolling nonchalantly in the relatively quiet aisles of the mega-super-markets in the shopping centers (the gourmet as well as the regular ones) about one day holding down one of the stockboy positions: there they were (would be), CD players in pockets and headphones on (their long hair tight under the arch of the headphones, but flowing in the back, tattoos showing, on the arms, on the forearms, and on the backs of necks), sometimes you could hear their music halfway up the aisle so loud they had it (a perfect place to work and lose yourself in other worlds with the pummeling of the hard rock drums), oblivious to their surroundings, mechanically opening the cardboard boxes (with an enviable degree of precision and skill, a sequence of snappings and cuts right where it counts), moving the objects on the shelves to their destined places of repose (O what maneuvering of limbs, O what coordination between head and arms and eyes, breaking down and pushing down to the side and placing in right spot at perfect angle), ripping open again the boxes that didn't cooperate (and shouting to another shelf-stocker down the aisle, or passing by, sharing a laugh or teasing or telling a joke, loudly, as if there are no shoppers roaming these same aisles, as if they can allow themselves all liberties, as if acknowledging their total irrelevance and replaceability, they could be as annoying and loud as they wanted, who cared really if they got fired, what would they be getting fired from, Mappolo heard himself thinking, what would I be getting fired from!), filing the new items on the replenished shelves and in turn pointing the yellow price guns and in exhilarating fashion sticking the little price tags, going from one to another specimen with such expertise as to unnerve and render anyone at the top of their profession envious, of the speed, the agility, the coordination, the deft maneuvering, the flexibility (of the body, given the necessary contortions), the accuracy (could stick the tags just about anywhere), the consistency, of the yellow price gun handlers. Sight to behold indeed. (He did wonder, in parentheses, if his second fantasy had been a concoction, or an extension of the first troubling desire!)

What better now than to combine his present preoccupation, his present search, with the private longings of so many years?! What better than to just, as the saying goes, go for it—and let the chips fall where they may? What better—and he found no harm in the fact of so many other clichés racing through his mind, each time reinforcing the previous one's general indication that his pursuit of market stockboy might be the best option available—than to take Marla's proposition seriously? So he'd turned to Marla again (he'd been looking straight ahead now for quite a few moments contemplating) and asked: 'You think he'll need me to put the prices up on the items too—you know, with those guns?'

'The price guns?'

'Yeah!'

'Couldn't tell ya,' Marla had responded. 'You'd have to ask him.'

And so it was, once upon a fortnight of a revolution, before any of the methods were discussed with his peers...

A few days later, after placing a relatively harmless call to Betashnik (the question of the price gun had come and the answer had been... affirmative: 'If it excites you!'—Betashnik humor), he'd found himself aproned (Betashnik insisted on the apron) and emptying the contents of a big box on the shelf. The parameters were met, and without question or worries. Betashnik was a generally agreeable sort of fellow, with a unique (perhaps worrisome) sense of humor, his bald head (two puffs of hair on either side) and his considerable gut giving his five-five frame the appearance of a relatively sincere fellow running his own small market with a good dose of cynicism, two kids, a cat, and a home with a garage, further out in the boondocks. The regret factor was essentially nil, there was no one he had to interact with, and Betashnik himself only occasionally called him up on issues. (And yes, in the back of his mind but not so distant reaches, he always did wonder, what in the hey would I be getting fired from—and that lack of anxiety, that total absence of devotion to his occupation, that acknowledged recognition of his profound carelessness, allowed him a free-floating attitude.) In fact, after only a week, they developed such a thorough understanding of each other that their system in itself functioned marvelously with little to no dialogue. The CFBQ was, in turn, as low as it could go, and the only 'miscellaneous consideration' he could think of was that excitement, that quite provocative surge of adrenaline he felt when he was putting the stacks of ribs and especially, *especially*, chicken legs, in the refrigerated section. A positive, in other words, although he'd had difficulty acknowledging it. The pay was what it was and the schedule flexible. (Remarkably, Mappolo had never factored salary into his considerations. Not really anyway, even though officially he'd considered it. Could it be that he truly did not care, about: money???!!!) Betashnik had kept the business open until 2 a.m. usually, but was somehow persuaded by Mappolo to keep it open all night, that he'd make up the cost of being open—what with the late-nighters, the teenagers for sure. 'They got no place to go I'm telling ya,' he told Joe, elaborating on all the kids hanging out in the parking lots, in the parking lot at 7-Eleven, in the parking lot at the beer and wine deli type place, the kids hanging out in the parking lot at the Mall, after their multiplex viewing, and their Food Court visit, and how they'd go on all night if they could, except that they couldn't, and so they'd go to another joint, to the parking lots of their schools, where it was dark, where no cops looked for them, where no security dispersed them or told them to go home, why not open all night, unofficially but sort of in a tempting way, as the teens hang out, in the parking lot, 'I'll tell them to pretend they're drinking soda, I'll come up with something Joe, you were a teen once remember Joe, Teenager in the basement/Hanging on to your life/Banging your head against the pavement/Never one to let go of strife... You've been there Joe, leave it open, let them come, let the teens in their basements open their suburban homes and flee, and hang on the hoods, of their cars, among the other cars, with their peers, in the parking lots of their lives, in your, Joe, your parking lot!'

Soon, Mappolo persuaded Joe to let him work through the night, a total graveyard shift, his favorite, when the teens whose lives were all close to being shattered would swing by, how he'd put it to convince Joe... Except that mostly they didn't, they stayed in their basements, they smoked their joints, they drifted out of their homes and the planet in general in their basements, and so he, Mappolo, had the best of all worlds: he was alone, contemplating, meditating, no one there, blast the music, stock them shelves, think, and, occasionally, run to the register and do a transaction. Quite brilliant on his part. Most of his preferences were met, and he'd succeeded in retaining his most productive hours for himself. Best of all, he had what each and every one of us, deep within, craves more than anything. He had, albeit not a glorious one, albeit one without much status, or income, or cachet, he had, that thing, that thing called, a job.

When he hears the knock, Mappolo hesitates and then sits up on the bed. The knocker knocks again. Twice, pause, twice, pause. Another? Yes—another!

It's A. To announce? Could it be? Is there... Yes, one more: the knock that usually does not accompany! The message! The news! The first day? As planned? Could it be?!

Mappolo hurries to the door. Unlocks. (Heaves a required deep sigh for dramatic effect before opening.) Turns knob—and opens.

Good old A. has entered and walks all the way to the couch, where he lets flop the sack on the ground. Stands and looks at his friend, his comrade, his guerrier-in-arms. Askingly, Mappolo looks at A: Is it—he's saying with his bewildered gaze—

could it be?! A. answers, with words: 'It is!' he says. 'It is!'

Mappolo slowly walks to A. Then, with a passion and abandon belying his previous calm, he thrusts his arms around A.'s neck and lowers his head into A.'s shoulder, weeping. A. taps him on the back (slightly), and raises his eyes: he understands, of course he does, he knows what they've gone through—but he does manage to keep his composure.

A weeping Mappolo raises his head and grabs A., hard, one hand each on the side of the comrade's face: 'We did it!' he shouts, startled and relieved and anxious and exhilarated, all at once in a heap of unidentifiable, nameless emotions. 'We did it!' he continues to weep. 'We did it!!'

5

'We haven't done a thing yet,' A., cautious, demanding, austere. 'The revolution has just begun!'

Ultimately though, unimaginably, uncompromisingly, unconsciously, they'd done it. Pulled it off. Gone all the way. Hit one outta the ballpark. Unfathomably. Almost, one is tempted to say, almost impossibly.

The first of Mappolo's deeds is to go to the phone and call Betashnik: 'Joe, listen, can't make it tonight, emergency... Wha?... No... Well... I'm tellin' you!'

Joe always understands, Mappolo thinks. Besides, if he doesn't, too bad! What choice does he have. What can he really do. (Ahh, if all the powerless (including students) realized how easily they could rebel. Give themselves permission. Allow themselves. Not fear freedom, the true kind! But...) Joe does argue though. Appealing to Mappolo's sense of duty. His obligations. His unwritten contract. Mappolo reminds him that they in fact have a written contract, albeit an informal one (four lines thought out in drunken stupor and as a joke, a sort of parody of corporate contracts, when both with Sonny Williams the custodian of the elementary school close to the shopping center went on a drinking binge inside the market), and that its provisions do not (I repeat, Mappolo insists), do *not* include exceptional devotion!

Joe, the question goes, will you stand this kid's irritating

sense of his self, meaning, his need to prove intellectual superiority, to have the last word in every argument? Isn't it time to
boot him out, show him the door, as the saying goes, a goodbye
and a good riddance for the (long!) road? Don't have a choice,
really, Joe responds to the beleaguered narrator. Besides, the
kid works well. Take the good with the bad. So what if he sets
his own hours and closes some nights. I'd be closed anyway. So:
after 1) some prodding, 2) vehement yet empty threats, high-
pitched at that ('You're not going to fire me, Joe!'), 3) gentle,
needy appeal to the financial needs of the institution, 4) exple-
tive-filled rant targeted at no one in particular, this all coming
from Mappolo, Joe acquiesces. Has no choice, really, so…

Mappolo hangs up the phone. Embraces A. again. 'Let me
see,' he says. But A. is unmoved: 'Relax man,' he says. 'What
are you all worked up about?'

The excessively cool, nonchalant disposition of the commandant is wearing thin on the lieutenant. He (the latter)
knows full well that he (the former) is as ecstatic as he with
their first coup. And he (the latter) acknowledges that there is
more to be done, much more, that the struggle has just begun,
that there will be many a desperate times and grand sacrifices,
but heck, isn't this one worth celebrating? A little outing? A
little cruisin'? More so since it was planned on this special day
for a reason?!

Mappolo suggests as much to A. who in turn acknowledges
that he was thinking about it himself. Mappolo says that his
machine (a juiced-up red Jaguar with tinted glass) has been
ready for just such an occasion. A. says he was thinking more
like a stint at Leggs (a strip joint off route 121, more than a
hundred girls a night). Mappolo says, 'That too, how the hell
we gonna get there anyway?' A. says, 'True, true,' his voice
falling off (decrescendo). Mappolo says they could just ride

around, get a couple bottles or maybe go to Antonio's and then cruise the streets and hit on some chicks and then go to Leggs. A. says, 'Ho ho easy there cowboy... I'm kind of pooped.'

'Pooped?! Are you kidding me!'

'I know I know, but hey....'

'Man, I gotta spruce you up don't I?'

'Listen, let me just hang here a little ey... Then...'

'Then we're off. I'm not even listenin' to your tired crap.'

Then, Mappolo, doing like some of his friends, says, 'I'ma dump a bucket of ice on you maself!'

Mr. A., Commandant A., General A., the future Supreme and Untouchable Leader of the Great Venerated Land, A., laughs (a fatigued laugh, granted), the last, conclusive laughter of a man on a mission who's accomplished the mission, lying exhausted on a desolate street after a long trek, or saved after a shipwreck, or, as in our case, sprawled on the couch, one leg on top of the arm of the couch, body contorted. A., greatest revolutionary leader of all times, closes his eyes. Has lived quite a few (mis) adventures since the early morn, to be sure. Opens his eyes again. 'Lieutenant,' he calls on Mappolo. 'Commandant,' answers Mappolo. 'We've got to start cooking!' A. says. 'We do, we do,' Mappolo answers. Then he pauses. 'Where though?' he adds.

Dilemma? Roadblock? Unexpected detour? Not even. These fellows have thought it all out. Nothing will stand in the way of the uprising, certainly not minor details. Hail the Suburbs.

'Turn on the oven,' A. says. 'We'll put it on low heat. We gotta take the skin off though, and clean some more. Can raise no suspicions.'

Simple enough, Mappolo thinks. 'Now?' he asks.

'Yeah, why not?' A. answers.

A. has stood up and is going to enter the restroom. Takes the bag on his way and brings it into the small kitchen space at the far end of the hallway.

'You gotta start,' A. says. 'I'm gonna jump in the shower.'

'Go,' says Mappolo. 'I got your back.'

Not a question of having my back, you idiot, thinks A., just—which reminds him (A. again) that somehow, in some weird way, he's still weary of Mappolo's ways, his inclinations, his excessive enthusiasm. Almost too intelligent, A. thinks, almost as if to make up for all his failures, his total unfulfillment of his potential.

'I don't need you to have my back,' he says after the preceding thoughts had indeed raced around in his mind, and curtly, unaware that the process in his brain had not been visible or accessible, and so that the comment came across as unnecessarily aggressive to Mappolo, who, after the playful and warm exchanges, was taken aback: 'Ho!' says he. 'Didn't mean to offend the commandant! Relax dude! Get in the shower and take your time yo!'

Twenty minutes have passed. An eternity? Not really, feels just like that: twenty minutes.

A., refreshed, renewed, with a better perspective on today's accomplishment, is much enthused. He walks into the kitchen (towel around neck, one of Mappolo's bathrobes adorning his frame) and sees Mappolo hard at work on Steve's remains, in the sink and on top of the counter. He walks behind him, presses his body against his and puts his right arm around Mappolo's waist.

Mappolo, upon feeling A.'s touch, stops the work, raises his hands. A. gently turns Mappolo around, keeping his right arm around Mappolo, then raises his left hand and strokes Mappolo's hair on the left side.

Their faces approach, necks tilting (both to the right), and lip to lip they launch into a quietly passionate, certainly heartfelt (after the day's drama), and wet, kiss. They separate momentarily, Mappolo hangs his arms on A.'s shoulders, his hands dirty and smelly (Steve-smell), from all the peeling and cutting.

A. looks at him, deep gaze into his lieutenant's eyes, almost as if to apologize for his pre-shower antics.

'You're a bad boy, you know that,' Mappolo tells him, gently, smiling. 'Way too bad!'

They smile again and A. kisses Mappolo on the cheek (O sinister travesties engulfing the passionate, untamed souls of young pansexual lovers in heat...) and then, one last time, on the lips.

One hour later. Scene is the living room in Mappolo's basement apartment. Commandant and lieutenant are both showered and dressed, nothing fancy: nice jeans, nice collared shirts, Mappolo with a black t-shirt under, A. without. The various parts of the body are in the oven, on low heat. It will take a few hours, the time they do their rounds. Unwise, perhaps, unsafe, as well, some would say, but they are confident that no unforeseen accidents will befall them.

They figure, in the car, driving around, in the same streets they'd seen widened and asphalted and beautified, along the roads with the shopping centers that had popped up and gradually turned into upper-level gourmet versions of themselves, along the roads where new libraries and doctors' offices and corporate headquarters had been erected, and highways expanded and exits widened, where the latest and best automobiles were taken straight out of showrooms to be driven, they figure, driving around a landscape that is barren despite wealth, a landscape that is barren because there is no one walking on the sidewalks and no kids running in the streets and no impromptu soccer games or basketball games in the side streets, barren because it is quiet and dead and because you see no one, no one, you hear only the rumbling of the cars, barren, always, because with all the work and productivity, there is no life, no life of the type that counts, they figure, driving on this barren landscape which is their point precisely to jolt out of, this dreariness that soon they'll rule (the right deity willing), that they're still all right, that the disappearance of Steve will for a few hours at least not be reported, and that, subsequent to any potential discovery, it will be a few days before it's news. They were counting, in effect, on the quite hands-off approach of the local authorities as far as out-of-the-ordinary sightings were concerned. They surmised Steve's car could sit for days on the ramp before anyone might bother to approach, peek, wonder. All the drivers in the cars would keep looking straight ahead, straight at the road, the long road before them, their music blasting, or their radio talk show hosts ranting and raving with callers espousing one firmly held opinion or another. They would look through the front windshield at the road, lost in their own reveries, drowned in their own worlds, ignoring completely the goings-on, someone could get lost, someone could get raped, someone could certainly get murdered, a parked car on the side of the road, no one would bother with that, and even if they did, even if they slowed down at the roadside irregularity, nothing would come of it, nothing would stop them. It helped that Steve's car's windows were tinted black too—that would keep away a good portion of curious passersby or troublemakers of all sorts, teens especially. A. had made sure, before their ride down the hill on the electric scooters, that all the doors had been closed, and the trunk too.

When A. was telling Mappolo the details of the day and of his encounter with Steve, the young Mappolo Rei had been admittedly fascinated by: a) the good looks of the abductee, b) the electric scooters. How did they ride, he wondered and then asked his companion/commandant, whom he knew to be weary of putting on his feet anything other than flat-soled shoes. Pretty good, A. answers, and you know me! Maybe we can get a couple, Mappolo says, but A. reminds him that he'd hidden them in the trunk of the Cadillac, next time they're down there they can pick 'em up, why get new ones, those looked pretty new.

Mappolo pulls into the parking lot of the strip joint, open all day and night. It is, strangely, not isolated. In the same shopping center, in fact, there is a food mart (a couple recently arrived from Honduras managed the place, they're always there, with their little girl running around, always there, always making all the money they can, working hard for a better life), a golf store (Mappolo forever had wondered who actually buys golf equipment, or how stores dedicated to golf could survive, but they did, and in fact, this store had gotten bigger with the acquisition of a soccer store next door and was thriving), a Chinese food store (will I ever be able to abandon this greasy food, A. now ponders, will I ever be able to go on without some General Tso's, or a little Lo Mein for takeout), a home appliances store, a sandwich-making shop (with the picture of a hearty sandwich on the logo), a hair-cutting place, a beer and wine store (the owner was a long-haired, Texas-twanged, heavily-tattooed, cowboy-hat-donning rancher dude but very sweet man who'd abandoned the prairie for the comfort of the 'burbs, without necessarily giving up his tequila), a little coffee shop attended on weekend mornings in particular by families of at least four in the ownership of particularly large-sized SUVs, a pharmacy (not a chain), an eye care place, and a jewelry joint at the end of the row of stores. Across the street, another shopping center, with even bigger signs, taller signs, cleaner signs—and with a little Sun Trust Bank erected in an isolated yet charming way in the front of the parking lot, surrounded by a host of shops, ready to meet your every need, and your every non-need.

In-between the two shopping centers of course, and in front of these terribly inviting stores, the object of A.'s and Mappolo's deepest affections, the subject of their dreams and, admittedly, nightmares, the central figures in this here little fable (a lot more on this matter later on, trust me), the subject, even more degenerate to admit but I must, of their sexual gratifications, the source of such niceties as the establishment of status and feelings of superiority over your fellow beings and endless opportunities to show off whether on the road or in the garage, or out in front, and the bestest of tools for picking up, chicks or dicks, whichever you're into, the first and last hero, the ones with whom the buck stops, none other than the venerated, worshipped, counted and exchanged and bought at auction or at the dealership, with the used versions' immortalized salesmen occupying an incomparable niche within our fragile psyches and our national consciousness: automobiles—cars to you and me. Cars and more cars and still more cars, passing through, creating the gorgeous, just gorgeous, traffic flow, holding the attention of a meditative A. and a rapt Mappolo, passing cars and their even more gratifying parked versions, in the two huge, humongous, parking lots.

A. begins to doze off into a meditational trance of sorts while he watches, peers, rather, a panoramic sweep, at the parking lot, where he sees pure poetry, motionless, this time, but poetry it is nonetheless, zero doubt, poetry immobile, the purest of forms, the very scene that had prompted him to briefly consider becoming a poet in the first place, the apple of his not only eye but being, a gallery of priceless pieces adjoining, he sees…

> *The black Honda Accord, and a white Porsche Carrera*
> *The gray Toyota Camry, and a blue/gray Land Cruiser*
> *Blue Dodge pickup (surely driven by an old loser!)*
> *The good Oldsmobile 88 4-door, and a gray VW Jetta*
>
> *The red Dodge Evergreen, a pearl Taurus, as in Ford*
> *A Nissan Quest SE, dark green, and a dark blue SAAB*
> *Girl holding daddy's hand walking to car about to sob*
> *A great Jeep, and a red station wagon, an… Escort!*
>
> *A black Honda Civic, another black Honda Civic*
> *And I could go on and on and say hondacivic hondacivic*
> *hondacivic*
> *Not to mention the blue Chevrolet pickup*
>
> *A white Toyota Tercel and a black Honda… Acohhhhrd!*
> *Aco-ho-hord! Aco-ho-hord! Aco-ho-hord!*
> *And the Caddy invisible rolling down for the stick-up.*

(Yes, a sonnet: for the scene is a work of art, and it needs the vehicle that most formally announces the archetype of the literary arts, a sonnet.)

The great revolutionary leader A. continues to gaze at the cars, almost as if penetrating the steely frames and the cushions inside, as if becoming one with the many features, the power windows, the power locks, the generic colors, almost as if staring into the eyes of savage animals, in the middle of a forest, or a desert, thinking, contemplating, waxing nostalgic, in a weird and obviously peculiar type of way. A. had frequented these locales before. And every pause in the parking lot inevitably reminded him of his experiences as a child, a teenager, a young man on the verge of adulthood. The big sports store, he nostalgically recalled, eyes fixed on the steel front doors out of which walked young boys carrying huge bags with their daddies and their mommies, was where he projected movies, the one movie theatre in town that was open past midnight, how he loved those shifts, the showings of The Rocky Horror Picture Show, the flying popcorn, the whizzing soda cups and wrappers, the ice thrown at the screen, all in perfect harmony, the hooting and howling and the loud singalongs, the whole annoying accompaniment of the followers of the cult classic, how he loved it all indeed. They annoyed him then, but he later learned to appreciate their rage, their frustrations, their childish neuroses. In a way, the sources were quite similar to the ones that were at the very roots of this revolution. Now it had come full circle: he knew you don't replace a movie theatre, even one showing the latest garbage of Hollywood with a massive sports store without paying a price! Nor was it a personal obsession or the constant churning of everything into revolutionary rhetoric once you're on the path that drove him to associate every desire, every longing, every annoying tidbit with his current enterprise. They were genuine, the concerns, sincere, real. He was a child of these parts, after all, he'd grown up on the playgrounds only a few miles from here, he'd taken groceries through these same parking lots, he'd participated (half-heartedly granted, but he had) in the youth soccer leagues and he could not bear to see the transformations: large multinationals he held so dear taken over by even larger even more multi multinationals, conglomerates of his youth replaced by even more powerful conglomerates! He did not cast himself as the particular bearer of any ideological flag no, he only knew that this order could not last—should not last—and he'd give until his last breath (the very last, he always joked, he might keep—to redress and subvert and change things 'from within!') to the revolution. Hail the Suburbs, he murmured, his only true love now, this cause, his one and only companion. (Mappolo had not failed to point this out in several fits of anger even though he himself had designs on the revolution grander than even those of A.'s.) And as he stood there now the passenger door still open, his forearm resting on top of the frame, Mappolo out and turned and peering in the direction in which A.'s gaze had been fixed, he could not help but think of those simpler days, O when he was a teenager, and in the basement, granted, when a smaller parking lot stood there, in all its heroic splendor, its incomparable majesty, its sufficient succinctness, and which by the way, could easily have held all the cars parked here, now, in this oversized goliath of a lot, the

white Chevy Glazer station waaaaaagon,
the black Mercedeeeeezzz
190E, the pearl Nissan Maaaaaaxima,
the dark blue Hyundai
Elaaaaaantra, O teenager in the basement
cry not for a Honda
Accoooo-ho-hoord,
a Dodge Grand Ca-ra-vaaaan, an Isuzu
Rodeoooo, a dark blue Chevy
Cavaleeeeahhh, a Pontiac
Gooooodcitay, a red Accura Integraaaaahhh

and a whole lot more too, whole lot more cars it could have
held, A.'s parking lot of his childhood, A.'s beloved and cozy
and warm and not immaculately kept but definitely worth a
thousand of these football fields posing as parking lots, lot!

'You all right baby?' Mappolo asks him, softly.

Our hero A. peers ahead, his resolve, his spirit, the grotesque
unwaveringness that makes of great revolutionary leaders the
actual myths and monsters that they inevitably and invariably
become, intact. He does not answer.

'Hey—' Mappolo barks back—whereupon—

'Let's go—' A. slamming the door and snapping out of his
parking lot meditation, and, dare I say, blues.

It's real early still, as far as the strip joint is concerned, a
sparse crowd is attending, a mix of construction and other
blue-collar workers from a site nearby and some professionals
in their coats and ties (loosened, invariably) sitting mostly morose, quiet, in dreamlands it seems holding their drinks, except
for a scattered group of younger college kids laughing loudly,
calling on the girls, buying their drinks, carousing.

Leggs was a relatively large strip joint, designed quite differ-
ently from the classic downtown spots frequented by a much
wealthier clientele. A great wide rectangle formed the counter
of the bar, with a long runway in the middle with three sliding
poles, occupied perpetually by a minimum of three dancers.
A VIP room was available, but other than this private hiding
place, there were no comfortable chairs, no velvet curtains, no
fancy couches. The patrons would scatter and plunk down on
the stools around the rectangle or around small tables, and,
mostly alone, look straight ahead, transfixed by the movements
and the lights, drowned in their proverbial sorrows and regrets.

A. knew the owner well, one Richard Kossowski, they went back years, before the latter had made it big in the entertainment business, and so Λ. had quite the free pass, at the door, at the bar, and mostly with any of the girls he wanted. The managers, the ever-changing cast of doormen and bartenders were all in turn made aware of his identity and his importance. They also knew of his all-encompassing sexual appetites, and were told to make all attempts to facilitate his urges. No one seemed to mind, certainly not after D. Koss (as he got to be known) often instructed his staff to make this particular guest feel like royalty (not knowing, A. laughed to himself, that he soon would be just that).

When A. walked hand in hand with Mappolo (he was not one to hide his habits, or his desires), the only wayward glances would come by way of stooped clients—most of whom would simply turn back and ignore the oddity (unusual for Leggs, anyway). After his quick fix in the parking lot, A. is determined to forego thoughts of the coming complications and to simply let loose and enjoy. He and Mappolo join the other patrons in cheering every doffing of vestment, every sway of the hips, every seductive glance and every sudden ripping off of even the smallest lingerie. Mappolo calls his favorite girl over, a statuesque bronze Amazon goddess with plentiful breasts and ample nipples that seem ready to burst our of her bikini top, starts to flirt with her and even gets a bit too close for comfort, which prompts the princess to pull back, tap Mappolo's forehead with a finger and tell him to behave. 'Watch your little boy,' she turns away and carries on the bill-collecting seduction tour. A., floating in that uncertain, ambiguous zone between enraged jealousy and shared excitement, himself turned on to significant degrees by the tigress's antics, smiles, turns to Mappolo and envelops his mouth in an all-out French kiss.

Girls saunter in, girls grabbing clothes and bills file out, a perpetual wave of lace, leather, exciting thongs and panties, along with butts and breasts in, literally, all shapes and sizes. Even Monti Mellonsire, the fellow who wanted to be a real estate broker who was trying to make it as a TV host so he can somehow get a gig on a sitcom and soon become a star, is there. He is sitting alone, leaning back with a drink in his hand, with, amazingly, comically, tragically, a two-boobed hat on his head. A. had not known him to be of such ilk, all sorts of weirdos came to strip joints after all, he just didn't seem the type, especially when Mappolo sees him masturbating under the table, with such glee, his boobed hat going back and forth, O that Monti, Mappolo thinking, that pathetic, pathetic Monti.

Mappolo in a mild drunken stupor now approaches a superhot gal in a thong, topless, doing a closeup for one of the patrons and nudges him aside: 'What giveth thou for a paltry one hundred dollar tip, my good lady?' The words trickle out, fast, but the nudged one is getting pissed. Before the girl has a chance to answer, said fellow pushes Mappolo back, hand swinging and says: 'Watch it fella!' Mappolo feels it: it was hard, it was considerable, it was real. A. follows the action from a few feet away and soon lunges forward. No time for Mappolo to get in trouble, he thinks, rightly. He jumps into the fray as Mappolo is straightening himself out, the girl a few steps back now. 'It's all right,' A. says, surprising the bartenders by his cool and his reserve (as a patron that is) unaware that unique circumstances are prompting 'Big A.' to refrain from insults, provocations and punches. 'It's all right, he didn't mean to,' he tells the bulky man, as he helps Mappolo to straighten. 'I'm gonna get that sonnova...' Mappolo blabbers, to which, his protective pal: 'Easy boy, easy...' He takes him away from the scene, back to the back and through a maze of bodies, towards the door. Taps, before exiting, the doorman on the shoulder, and shakes his hand. 'Good seeing you again' he says, diplomatically, even though this was the doorman's first night on the job and so no way that A. had ever seen him, but he thinking, you never know, when you might need someone.

The conduct of revolutionaries post establishment of their regime after victory, or even post first coup, has not heretofore been the subject of a wise man's how-to-book. No best-sellers exist with titles such as: *What To Do Before, During and After Takeover of Your Community*—or the more radical, *Etiquette for the Real Revolutionary*. No. The volumes gracing the shelves of our libraries and our bookstores do indeed cover such topics as how to get somewhere and how to behave when you get there, but only when the 'somewhere' constitutes a recognized locale or position—within a system, an established paradigm. Nary a word, sadly, on how to behave when your 'somewhere' rests on the assumption of the total undermining, voire destruction, of that system.

No way to criticize, therefore, our carousing couple as they ride their Jag down the lonely boulevards of the sprawling landscape. They watch the shoppers walking out of the supermarkets carrying their bags walking to their cars and opening the trunks and putting the bags inside and walking slowly to the driver's side, they watch the young boys riding their bikes and laughing and riding faster and leaving a smaller boy, a brother, behind, they watch the drivers back from work lost in their dazes at traffic lights staring ahead, so numb, so listless, so pointless it all seems the faces say, the gazes tell, they watch the bankers and the accountants and the real estate brokers and the mortgage brokers and the school teachers and the travel agents and the hotel workers going through the drive-through of the bank putting checks inside containers, and then the long line snaking around at the drive-through fast food, heads popping up almost as if in a cartoon, from the SUVs and the old station wagons and the latest sedans that all look alike, families of four, of two, of five, all obediently packed behind one another moving up, ever so slightly, tires rolling slow, signs above and all around, they watch the poles that shoot up in the skies with advertisements, inviting in, happy deals and happy meals, landscape dotted in the green and the yellow and the red and the blue of the sky and the trees and the large billboards, they watch the cars slowly file into the grand parking lot of the mall, the cars that move in and out of the slots, the bodies that move in and out of the cars, the constant shifting of motion and stillness, of human shapes and automobiles, the steps they take and the tires rolling, an organism alive in the body of Suburbiana, in the parking lots how the organism is molded, how the organism molds and makes itself, a beauteous organism, its cells the human shapes, the heads of humans turning, going down, going up, the automobiles, rolling, slowly, rolling, fast, O Organism in Suburbiana, O Organism in Suburbiana, what kinds of creatures will you be fashioning, what kinds of future nincompoops will you be molding, O Organism O, O soccer moms and hockey dads and your collection of shirts and shin guards, crazy parents shouting deserving of your Silent Saturdays imposed by administrators sick of your uncivilized behavior along the sidelines living vicariously through your children, you pathetic pimps, O Organism what kinds of viruses will you make grow, will you place, O Organism with the screeching of the lost, the poor workers voiceless penniless working midnight shifts, gas station attendants on the verge, of what exactly, not nervous breakdowns, perhaps another murderous rampage in our O so tranquil treelined streets, although most are polite and greet you with that twang, if they're not migrants, which many are, O Organism, save yourself, save us all, from this fall, a fall it is I assure you, where into I'm not sure, which abyss, which inferno, which dark vault or black hole, but a fall it is, and not just an allegorical or metaphorical one, a fall, a real one, a long one, a nasty one, a naaaaaaaaaaaast-eh one, O Organism in Suburbiana, let me put in my riff please O please, O Organism in Suburbiana with all your teenagers, O Suburbiana and your teens, O Suburbiana and your teenagers, O teenager in the basement, O teenager in the basement, into this world you've come,

Now forget all your woes
Go and pay yourself some hoes
Teenager in the basement
Let go of you anger let go
Let go of your inhibitions let go
Let go of all the gloom and doom
That rests still within your soul—let go
It's nobody's fault it's all just the way
All the empty streets surrounding you
The empty lots and soulless folks
They're just a bunch of fucks
O teenager in the basement
Breathe deep now
Breathe hard now
Stay in
The game and just, just…
Make sure you win
That's all
Make sure you win

O teenager in the basement
Heed my call—
And make sure you win!

Mappolo and A. roll down the windows elbows out, both sides. An occasional automobile passes, they shout out, depends who's inside, of course, a duo of horny (and hornier) schizos on the prowl.

To an elderly couple, a smart aleck comment that makes the man (driving) shake his head but not respond (for fear), while wife (surely) in passenger seat (pulled way up) stares ahead and pretends she's heard nothing (to which apparent indifference—that Mappolo knows to be an attempt at ignoring him—he says, 'Smile old witch!'). To a young man driving in a Porsche, Mappolo sends kisses, bunched up fingers released to air bouquet-like, and says: 'Where to cutie?' With a pair of young and extremely pretty ladies in a red Honda, the boys begin with some clever flirtatious quips. Both of the girls smile—then feign indifference. 'Don't play that game now!' Mappolo says. 'You know you love it!' The girls smile again (grin, hands on wheel for driver, grin, twist of the head for rider). 'Why don't you follow us?' Mappolo unrelentingly suggests. 'We're going to the market get some booze.' The girls giggle, look at each other. 'Yeah?'—Mappolo says, asking, suggesting. 'Go!' the driver-girl says. 'You comin' or what?' Mappolo throws out. (Driving all the while, these exchanges? Fearless and without conscience? Should they not, at least, park?) 'Go!' the girl answers giggling still, both hands on the steering wheel. (Why the tease, thinks Mappolo, betaken, bewitched, beholden—why not just make life simple!) He turns, smiling, then speeds away. The girls switch lanes, go right behind. Soon, Mappolo makes a turn, drives down a mere four hundred yards, turns left, slowly drives another two hundred, left again and into a parking lot. The girls are not… O yes, they are, behind. The lot is full, as usual. Lots of customers in these parts, what with wholesale prices on most items, and giant sizes. Mappolo finds the first parking spot: 'You guys go,' he mumbles to the girls since they're behind. The driver thanks him and rolls right in-between the two white lines while Mappolo slowly goes on to, oh, a Jeep pulling out, puts the blinkers on, waits, good, Jeep driver waives to Mappolo, 'What, not leaving?' mumbles our hero, 'Yes, yes!' seems to gesture the bloke, going out. So go! Mappolo thinking, and then the jeep pulls out and Mappolo turns and directs the Jag into the spot. A. has been, as the narrative has made clear, quite silent. Tired, for sure, but preoccupied also—although he'd promised to let loose… Just that he knows, Mappolo cannot be a worthy heir, no way, there are going to be big problems, he keeps demonstrating it, how are we ever going to… No, A. is the skeptical type, he does not trust, he does not trust… He's usually known what to attribute it to, but he's not much of a psychoanalyst, especially when it comes to himself—and that explains the nature of his relationships: with himself, with others, with the world. He's not necessarily only suspicious either, just cautious he likes to think, and sometimes even he wonders if he is too good of a guy, despite appearances, perhaps he gives the aura of an unfriendly distant bloke, but he is, after all, too loving, too trusting, or so he ponders in the uncertainty of his own gloom. But as far as the revolution and Mappolo go, despite the good signs, he cannot be overly trusting and so better be safe before sorry, and so, decidedly, he just cannot let loose, not tonight, vibes in the air, premonitions, call them, just that peculiar, ba-a-ad, feeling in the air…

'Let's go,' Mappolo tells A. as he swiftly and as if in one motion, takes keys out, exits, and slams door. A. walks out in a more orderly manner and sees Mappolo walking towards the girls. The four get together finally, right there in the parking lot. Introductions. Mappolo: Mappolonius Rei, folks call me Mappolo, Map if you prefer. Elaine Johnson: Elaine Johnson. Jennifer Hotkoss: Jenny, you're funny (to Mappolo). A. dry, curt: A., just like that. Elaine: Just like that? A.: Yep, just like that. Pleased to meet you A. (Elaine), Pleased to meet you (Jenny), Ditto (A.), Let's go (Mappolo). What are we gonna do in there anyway: Jenny, seriously, but with a good attitude, and a sexy voice. We're gonna shop, Mappolo smiling, joking, s-h-o-p—shop.

Inside though, they do that (s-h-o-p, shop shop shop!) and a whole lot more. In fact, as soon as they've entered, Mappolo already playfully has his arm around Jenny, and he takes a shopping cart and tells her, Hop in, she blushing, does hop in and adjust her body inside, A. shaking his head, Mappolo's inconsistencies baffling, even to him, but he's tagged along and is politely speaking with Jenny's friend, they were obviously not much into each other and besides, A. was still smitten with the girl from the 7-Eleven, could not get her face (or body) out of his mind. Mappolo pushing the cart with Jenny inside, her legs like a frog's hanging out over the front, increases the speed and zigzags through the aisles. He yahoos and ballyhoos and screams as they ride through the pet food section and the refrigerated section and through the front section with all the fruits and the little salad bar, and doth doff his imaginary cowboy hat and even giddy up kick steps while he picks up salt (they needed more for Steve) and two types of sugar, lofts them high into the air shouting, Catch, and Jenny, playing along bringing her hands up in an uncoordinated kind of way, half-turning head and half-closing eyes, letting object come to her and only then gripping, does catch. Through the breads section they go and Mappolo twists around and juggles loafs and a couple of smaller rolls and lobs behind his back a pita bag that he himself catches, then approaches Jenny and smiles and deposits the variety in the cart and says, Gotcha. He wants to kiss her, the proximity ignites a weird fire within, this improvisational clowning around, and plus, she seems to like it. They're hitting it off somehow, no doubt, and she does too, it seems, want him to kiss her, but he refrains, respect factor, and plus, after all, Mappolo is sort of taken, even though he has a deal with A., the open relationship and all, especially since... In front of the lobster tank they stop and Mappolo approaches face to tank and goes, Kootchykoo, with his fingers tapping piano-like on the glass and Jenny laughing and then Mappolo turning around and doing an approximation of a lobster face and lobster claws in movement and Jenny laughing some more and Mappolo saying, You like lobster my dear, and Jenny still laughing not answering and Mappolo adding, Because I'll be your lobster all you want and you can munch on me all day and night I promise. Mappolo wheels around and Jenny laughing he stops at the front of an another aisle and picks up a disposable camera and says, Smile, to poor Jenny slung in the cart and she plays along and does a grimace and an ugly face and Mappolo pretends to take a picture and says, Beautiful, but then he does, indeed, take the camera, and places it, in the cart. Then, right there in the middle of the aisle, to the imagined hip-hop beat and the imagined audience gathered swaying arms and limbs in front of the stage, what the world will hear soon, recites his

Shouted Sememe II

performance poetry in the form of a rap
(finger twisted meekly in a mini-version
of what would truly be, on stage,
one of the greatest shows on earth,
a much more pronounced bend,
along with an angry and anxious face,
with microphone almost touching the mouth,
almost swallowed,
switch of hands, gestures contortions and—)

They say it can't be
All a mystery
Who are you to see where you'll be
But I'm just free, don't join no gangs
Hate the greed, will show my fangs
And they will see, can't mess with my plans.
I'm all I need 'cause I just kill yo! Dang –
No more beep 'cause I am
I am
I am
A revolutionary a king to be
A thing to see
A prophet with glee
That will be my destiny
For the revolution
Is coming and I am
I am
And will be
One with the people!
No more: oppre-shun!

No more: depre-shun!

No more: devasta-shun!

Don't shun

Me

                For I'm the lord.

That will be

I repeat

        My Destiny.

Mappolo after getting a quickie applause from a scattered few who'd gathered or were going through items in the aisles themselves, bows and bows again and thanks the folks and then wheels the cart around and now Jenny saying, Mappolo get me out please I'm getting tired, and Mappolo jokes, Are you sure, and wheels her around doing a tchoo-tchoo train sound and she laughs but she insists, I'm serious Mappolo my back, and Mappolo says, Ah but my dear you are my prisoner, bringing one arm up and lowering his pitch and doing like a monster-creator from somewhere like Transylvania and then comes back up (in pitch) and says, Just kidding, and then, gentleman that he can be, stops, extends arm in gentlemanly way and pulls her out and bends and curtsies and kisses her hand and then says, Your wish is my command. Then he says, Wanna get some free snacks, they give out lots of freebies here. Jenny laughs and before she's even answered she's whisked away to Mappolo's favorite stretch, where the employees dutifully make and distribute miniature freebies, and folks make lines to snag the items, chicken salad on a cracker here, a taco there, the latest in salsa sauce served on tortillas, everywhere. Jenny, stuffing herself and once even fed by Mappolo who then wipes off the saucy onion that fell on her shirt, laughing says to Mappolo, again, You're funny! Then, looking about, says, Where's your friend… and Elaine? Mappolo says, I think they stayed up front. And so the two move slowly, stuffed and with cart, walk up and sure enough see A. by the cash registers, looking bored, leaning against the front end of one of the lanes reading a magazine—well, 'reading'! Mappolo reiterates, Yeah they're there, and so they continue that way and, as they approach, Jenny says to her friend: 'You guys! Why didn't you come with us?!!'

Her question is ignored as A., now surveying the content of the cart, sternly, to Mappolo, says: 'Where's the booze?'

Mappolo says, 'Woops,' and is turning already and heading to the back and walking away says, 'Be right back.' Indeed: quickly, he's back, with two six-packs. Which he places directly on the belt, already occupied with the items Jenny and Elaine, in their kindness, are helping A. take out from the cart.

Lots of shopping going on in this surreptitious tale, I know! All I'm trying to be is a realist—really.

6

This epic tale of revolutionary upheaval and romantic tragedy, this panoramic depiction of lives lost and suppers
gained which also incidentally happens to be an expert rendition (with the precise hues, I dare say) of an entire epoch in the
great tradition of those painters of centuries-ago somewhere
telling of an entire historical era in one masterly scene, this ode
to the daring of a few brave souls willing to bear the brunt of
their contemporaries' ignorance, ridicule and, worse, hysterical
lynching, this panegyric to the vicissitudes of chance, the cruel
consequences of planned programs, the tyranny of ideas and
the tyranny of counter-ideas and the tyranny of the lack thereof, this sonnet of majestic fervor and phantasmagoric leanings, this superbly crafted novelistic gem destined to prompt
the crazed adoration of eager teenagers (plus mommies and
daddies) freezing their butts off at the local mall's lone chain
bookstore waiting in line fearful that said store might run out
of copies: is about to take a turn to what the French would call
situation absurdo-comique (a phrase that is easily 'translated' by
the non-French-speaking public, given that only pronunciation, spelling and word-order adjustments are necessary) and
which we shall adapt simply by: doggone mess.

For it is as the current *personnage principal* (main character)
of the *récit* (tale, account) is about to place *les clés* (the keys) of
the *appartement* (apartment) inside the keyhole (keyhole), that

he remembers Steve (shit!), and whispers to Mappolo, 'In the car, can you go see and take the ladies with you, wanna make believe I forgot the right keys and we need 'em to open up this door—don't say anything just pretend, but we're not gonna just let the girls walk in with old Steve in the oven!'

Got it, Mappolo gestures for the sake of the ruse. And, obviously, the ladies are confused.

'Mappolo's gonna get the right keys, can't get in without 'em,' A. lies. 'I'll go check what's up in the back. You can go with him.'

A. moves away while the ladies walk back to the car with Mappolo. A. quickly enters and makes sure conditions are such that the ladies don't even get close to detecting anything or get too curious about what must probably by now have a weird smell.

Jenny says to Mappolo: 'Like, what's going on! That was weird!'

'Yeah?' (Mappolo)

'Yeah! *I* think!' (Jenny)

'Well, yeah... Maybe... But it's all good...' (Mappolo)

There are more important matters at hand, however, than these silly niceties. Both for the characters to address, and for the setting to embrace.

Mappolo comes back and opens the door with his keys he pretended to take from the car, and the three enter with the shopping bags. After all have entered and wiped their shoes off, Mappolo invites the girls to go into the living room. A. greets them and says, 'Ah, found my spares'—as in keys—'welcome!' But he was troubled. Visibly troubled, and more. In the meantime, he had rushed through to remove any visible signs of Steve or activities related to his body parts, but more needed to be done. He excuses himself again. 'Be right back,' he says, aloof and alarmed.

Forever the worrywart, A. has gone to the kitchen again to make sure they had discarded all items, leftovers, extra skin. He also wanted to trash anything visible that might alert the unsuspecting guests as to the pending feast. As far as signs and alerts are concerned, everything is fine, A. concludes. Mappolo had even taken out the garbage, and put a clean bag in. But then (and here is where things go awry, where the plot thickens, the focus shifts, the... O fearful deities), he pulls open the oven door and notices that a thigh, a big piece he himself had taken great care to clean, cut and sort apart, is missing. How could the thigh be missing? That's what A. would like to know. Mappolo, A. can see from the kitchen, is leaning against a chair. Mappolo senses an irregularity (must have), for he turns around and catches a glimpse of A. Better not be jealous, he's thinking, unaware that A.'s current concerns far outweigh such trivial emotions. Mappolo has a peculiar smile that to A. appears to be a pretense of concern. A. looks at Mappolo with renewed, reinvigorated suspicions. Never did trust him that much, despite appearances.

'Mappolo,' he calls out.

'Yo—' says Mappolo.

'Come here a minute, please.'

Mappolo turns back to the ladies and says: 'Excuse me one sec girls—be right back.'

He saunters into the kitchen. 'What's up?' he says nonchalantly.

'Listen, Map,' A. begins (Mappolo knows trouble is brewing, A. calls him Map only when he's anxious, angry, or both), 'the leg is missing. I'm gonna ask you straight up. Did you take it, did you hide it, did you eat it already?!' (His 'already' has that intriguing double-function: a) semantic, temporal precision, and b) filler, within sentences utilized for a wide range of purposes and sometimes without any good reason at all.)

'What are you talkin' about A., what leg, what...'

'Don't mess with me Mappolonius!' A. heightening the tone (there he goes, thinks Mappolo, with his big-ass father figure condescension). 'Did you take the leg or didn't you?'

'What freagin' leg are you talkin' about? What—'

'How many legs are there in this house that are not in use, genius, think!'

'I have no freagin' clue what you're talking about!' (The reader will have noticed that the good-citizen spirit of self-censorship has led me (I, the actual authorial voice) to substitute, repeatedly, for most characters' actual uses of the f-word, the more bearable and less objectionable f-word, with similar connotations. Which strategy has not precluded my use of the actual f-word when it was well-nigh impossible to substitute anything else for it. You are at liberty to decide which of the two has been used by particular character at particular juncture when the less objectionable f-word has been transcribed.)

Mappolo is adamant, seems to be sincere.

'You have no idea what I'm talking about ey,' A. says, irritated. Grabs Mappolo by the forearm, drags him two feet and still holding him pulls open the door of the oven.

'That leg!'—arm extended, index finger too—'I'm talkin' about that leg! There was a piece of leg in the other—'

'Shit!' Mappolo says. 'You're right!'

He pauses before his next attempt at a murmured, hesitant, explanation.

'So?' A. says, noticing that Mappolo had not followed through. (Also, he'd let go of the forearm.)

'So what man!' Mappolo lets out suddenly switching tones and with a pretense of having been offended. 'Of course I don't know what happened!'

'Then what the…' A. is beside himself, cannot control himself. He needs to chat with Mappolo. A long chat. A private chat. A chat that will perhaps turn into something else. He suddenly turns around, walks through the kitchen and into the living room. Too bad the girls are in a good mood—given that A.'s going to ask them to leave.

'Girls,' he says as he gently leads them to stand, 'I'm sorry I'm gonna have to ask you to leave. Emergency. 'Til soon, ey.'

'Is everything all right?' Jenny asks innocently as she's being escorted to the door. 'Is Mappo all right?'

'Mappo?! Yes, Mappo's fine!' A. says. 'Believe me, he's fine. Just that there's an urgent matter.'

Mappolo comes out as well. He's angry, but understands. There's a matter that needs to be addressed. The girls aren't sitting anymore, obviously, so, better not fight. He's come to the door, standing now with A. 'Sorry ladies. Serious—if you wanna leave a number, maybe we can…' It's too late for that Mappolo Rei. Girls who've been escorted out without explanation by folks they've barely gotten to know don't leave numbers with said folks who come across as freaky, no matter how much of a good time they may have had in the supermarket with the shopping cart and the lobsters and all. Besides, you shoulda asked for the number then, you should know that by now, mister playboy gigolo man, you get the number when things are going well, no matter what, because, as is well demonstrated in this case, you never know!

'Well…' Jenny thinks about it, half-turns towards Mappolo, seems like she's really taken a liking to him, but…

She's dissuaded by her obviously more cautious, more lucid, friend, who's shaking her hand vigorously, while dragging Jenny out. 'No thanks,' Elaine says curtly as they exit—and as the door slams, heavily, behind them.

The plight of at least a one followed by several zeros living in suburban hamlet now depends on the goings-on in an anonymous-looking yet crucial (in its historical importance) basement apartment of a simple family home. Could it be? It could. Revolutionary fervor has brewed in even less exotic locales, and certainly in more sinister, run-down neighborhoods. But does the relative tranquility in these parts point to the inevitable present and/or future failure of the work of renegade young men drowned in visions of grandeur and fanatic zeal?

Once again, the reader must generously be reminded that all throughout the big H word (I have quite the ambivalent position as regards enunciating syllables of sememes ('History') I know to be without merit, their place in the canon of disciplines a mere acquiescence to the simplicity of their formal/ linguistic/structural models, and their appeal to the masses), upheavals have occurred in the most unexpected of places and most unexpected of times.

But what of that pesky progenitor of downfalls, great and small, talking about 'division within the ranks' of course, especially betwixt elements thinking selves incomparable leaders? Could it be that despite what after all amounts to slight progress in their grandiose enterprise, there is already a rift that will undermine the entire unfolding of the change of regimes? Again, a distinct possibility. Movements have been halted in earlier stages still, rendering their leaders, their plotters and surely a handful of self-styled martyrs utterly irrelevant and completely unknown in the great annals of similar events. But I digress. There is a man, and another, in a dwelling in the suburbs, post celebration but with celebratory mood completely vanished. There is a crucial question (the answer to which could prove devastating to the fates of a whole array of institutions), and there is a dilemma. How shall the situation be addressed? How will the plot go forward? How will the characters develop? How will this hand o' mine decide the fate of so many? Will a silly misunderstanding spell the end of the battle? And the war? Such a grandly conceived plan, carried out pretty nicely too I might add, abandoned subsequent to a petty lovers' quarrel? Is this it? (The branches of the tree, outside, swaying, a dog (Sanjab, the neighbor's, a weak, one-legged, one-eyed disease-prone specimen) barks, weakly, the clouds pass, gently...) Premonitions? Natural energies in harmony with the moods of human occupants of the planet responding to the bitterness ensuing? Nonsense? Superstitions all? Delusions? Shall we await a new chapter to divulge the secrets? Or even in a spirit of newness and radical narrative gestures, abandon the topic in order to return down the line to it? No, I say and decide, the matter shall be resolved, without further delay: a swift and clean resolution.

What in fact will occur is this: A., having gotten a hold of his self (and his excessively volcanic revolutionary leader's temper) will sit his ass down on Mappolo's couch, telling him what it is that he thinks he saw, then ask, politely, for an explanation (if Mappolo has one to offer), calmly listen to his beleaguered lieutenant's version, then... hit him over the head with a hammer he's hidden under the couch? (No, no! Easy, imagination gone wild, hard-to-reign-in-senses of beleaguered narrator— easy!) Rather: calmly propose, if Mappolo is unable to provide the necessary conjectures, that they seek the appropriate remedies? Done? Not quite: up to that point (at 'then', five lines up), calmly, A. follows the script to the tune of perfection. There, however, endowed excessively by his creator with unmatched fervor, he rebels, indeed, against the path marked by the pen: against, yes, the progenitor of his entire selfhood! Oedipus conquering! Hero of all Characters everywhere! Death of Authorial Father! Go to hell, so to say, to none other than yours truly—despite generosity, goodness, favor of even making him leader, granting him first hero status, and *personnage principal* at that too! (Listen to them all how they sing and dance! Parade in the streets all the characters of so many tales! Characters of folk tales and historical tales, and a whole bunch of novels and novellas too! Horns blaring and cars shaking and monstrous balloons in the likes of their brethren abandoned to the skies! Such the party, the fiesta! Great!) That's what you get, I guess. Tears I shall not shed however, A., you will get your just desserts, I only feel a bit wounded, your turning your back, but heck, I know how it works: endowed you with the sight, and foresight, and hindsight, taught you well... Pat on my own back now ey? I'm not upset though, I can take it. How it goes. Telling you though, you screwed up big time A-man, you'll get yours! One doesn't so easily turn one's back on one's creator! You'll get your comeuppance—and a lot sooner that you could even imagine!

Then... he erupts, in one motion stands and slaps with the back of his right hand the lamp (old, grandmotherly) off the side table. (And this, *this*, is what I'm referring to: this was not planned—and he, A., just did it! Took it upon himself to get up and create the drama and the raucus! Unbeknownst to his maker!)

'You son of a freagin' gun! You freagin' liar! You are one dumb s.o.b. Mappolo! You know that?!' And he surprises all, including me, by sitting back down, swinging his left arm down, and pulling, à la magician a rabbit out of the hat, a human leg from under the couch. Cut off right at the ankle, low at the hip.

'And what's this?!' he barks, holding up the accusatory item trophy-like. 'Huh, how do you explains this, Mappo-man?!'

Mappolo cannot believe it. The situation, that is, and himself. Out of hand, decidedly. He truly could not remember doing it. A side of his personality he did not want to acknowledge maybe. Certainly, maybe. But this time, he really didn't even recall physically dragging the prized item. What had come over him? What kind of evil entity had taken over his soul? Maybe A. himself had planted the item—these are, after all, times of potential real conspiracies, and not just imagined, given what's at stake. Did he, could he... (Bonus points: can you figure out when it was that Mappolo hid the leg under the couch? The answer can indeed be found in the book, what with a bit of persistence and close reading.)

Mappolo Rei, feeling depleted, somehow vanquished, could not summon enough brainpower—or energy—to fashion a conspiracy theory. It could have been no one else, after all, not even the neighbor's dog, not the girls, obviously, it was him or A. The unfortunate *suite des événements* (course of events) had even sapped him of all argumentative energy. In a way, he didn't even care anymore. Rather admit what may not be true than prolong an exhausting search. And besides, it was probably true, it was probably him, although he could not confirm...

'I don't know what to say,' he says, puppy dog eyes in full effect for maximum sympathy, beaten in a way, but standing tall (standing strong).

'Of course you don't!' A. responds, haughty and condescending as usual. 'Go, take it back!'

He hands Mappolo the leg and Mappolo, obediently, takes

it back into the kitchen. When he comes back, he finds A. putting on his coat, at the door.

'I'm going for a ride,' he says.

Mappolo, hesitating, softly, asks: 'Alone?'

But A. is out already. Did not hear Mappolo's last question, or pretended not to have. Surprisingly though, A. had not slammed the door upon his exit.

Mappolo slithers on the couch. Gazes quietly ahead, in a quasi-daze. Then, weirdly, something comes over him. Something strange, a pure sensation, an anger, a deep-felt sense of seizing the moment and scripting his own destiny. What is it though, exactly? What is this thing that comes over him? Does it have a name? It is mysterious. It is troubling. It is nauseating (literally: he wants to throw up). It has no name, he concludes. What it does is that it provokes a sudden outburst of tears. And a melodramatic follow-through in the form of both hands coming to cover face—plus convulsions and wailing. Slight tremors too, can't be hidden. How sad. How terribly ironic too: fellow who swings between his macho outer self and his soft, sensitive, call it wimpy even, inner self. Confused fellow, unpredictable, all over the place, in an uncanny, extreme, kind of way. Can't control his urges. Can't shake off the years of meat deprecation. Can't come to terms with the tyrant within. The demon within. The, yes, cannibal—cannibal!—within!

Mappolo Rei, do you hear me? You cannibal, you never could control your urges, you misogynistic pansexual freakozoid! You never did manage to get the most of your talents because, because what, because something inside you, a beast you never did recognize, and you knew it was there since you've been six, admit it, always prevented you from committing your entire personhood to the tasks and ambitions at hand. Just that the other you was a truer you, a purer version, devoid of degrees and decorations and demands, a self that was much more you—than you, O cannibal!

All I ever wanted to be was a lanky American writer-dude working in a used-CD store, behind the counter, with my glasses on and my shirt hanging outside of my worn-out jeans, old t-shirt untucked, you say? That's what they all say, but that's not what happened is it?! Remember in his basement hideaway, Danilson Doyka dozing off into dreamlands when you were a senior? He'd gone off to college and come back and dropped out. It all frightened you didn't it? You promised you wouldn't be like him, no not you... And yet, at the same time, he was all you wanted to be: a college dropout, and thus, to you, by definition, a genius. A god who could not swallow the crap they tried to feed him in school, shoulda coulda woulda dropped out of high school even, if he'd had the guts. You wanted to avoid being like him, at all cost, and yet, at the same time, you were gonna do your darndest to emulate him. Worse: do him three times better. Remember all his hallucinations? His trepidations? His illuminations? Your goosebumps, at the ungodly sights, sitting by his bed while he did all he shouldn't have? Like a little twerp going to see his master you acted, admit it Mappolo! Were hallucinogenic drugs being used as a catalyst? Or just to pass the time? Depression? Addiction? Insanity? All of the above? You took it all in, Mappolo Rei, you ungrateful bastard, your mom worked her butt off and left her native land to come here and drown in debilitating work and sacrifice her entire life and get you to be somebody and what did you do? She had you, here, went back, came back again, gave up her life there! She cleaned toilets and mopped floors and cleared tables and then got a night job cashiering! Do you even know who your daddy is, Mappolo-man? Huh, do you? Who is your father, Mapman, or should I say, Who's your daddy, Mappolo Rei?! Did you ever get to meet him?! Did he ever contribute? One penny even?! And this was your gratitude to your mother, you worthless pimp! Do you remember how at homecoming you stayed at that dufus Reza Irani's, the Iranian-American? Yes, homecoming, do you remember it? They say the homecoming queen had the hots for you Mappolo Rei, remember her, Zee (for Zita) Ecks, that was before you ever even thought of 'x', 'y', and 'z' as anything other than the last letters of this alphabet, and before you knew what s-e-x in 'sex' stood for! She died, Mappolo, car accident, drunk driver, she and three pals! And here you are, living your life to the fullest! Emad Kolkoon. Name ring a bell? No? Doesn't ring a bell or you're just not answering because you don't want to remember? Typical, ey? The need to forget/banish from thoughts? Surprise, surprise! He was the running back slash cornerback on the last great varsity team recuerda?! Best team ever in the history of the school, dude! Pretty much all went downhill after that if you'd indulge us and recall! Although you won't, we know that, but that's all right. Sort of beside the point. Know where he ended up? Emad the Emerald Man? Emerald Emad heading up to State to play for Coach Urfila! Gonna get a full scholarship and sock it to you! Even became a chant for rivals! Got some real chances of playing in none other than the, say it loud, say it clear, En, Ef, El! Well well well! Not quite how it turned out! Your Emerald, Mappolo, your cruisin' buddy, Everybody's Emerald, daddy Mr. Ambassador of Egypt Emerald, gonna be the first great Arab-American in The League Emerald? Minor success at first at State under coach U., soon in his doghouse, goes to bench, junior year is not even playing, quits, badmouths coach and then drops out. Serving five years now, assault and battery. Three prior convictions. That was his fate. Quite the fall ey, Mapman? No rags to riches story to tell of, I'm sorry, and I'm not even going to go into the riches to rags ones, like Babak Barami. Like Felix Giordano. Like John Fixmanter. Like Joey Lasko. And I could go on and on and tell you about the rags to more rags to more rags! Sons of custodians and welders and deliverymen and mechanics doing guess what: welding, collecting, delivering, fixing, with the shiny stars among them none other than a few proudly donning the uniforms of the armed services—local (Police Officer Nospl), national (Sergeant Daniel Padduck), or global even (Nam Dan Kuong of Interpol, thank you)! Otherwise, it's rags and heaps of more rags, and still more, bathed in the comfort and the convenience of this world! Ahh but of course Monti, remember how he wanted to be someone who wanted to be a real estate broker who wanted to then be famous! Still at it, sacré Monti! At least he was, is and remains, consistent! What about Rick Rubble? Remember him, voted Most Likely to Transcend? He got a scholarship, reserved for Persons of Greenish Hue who can prove some link to the Ancient Grasshopper Peoples of the Plains. He even started his own Society to Provide Safe Haven to City Grasshoppers, Mappolo, did you know that? You used to dig that guy, but, hey, he went on his merry way, and actually accomplished things! The one and only! Couldn't have hung out with him, no sireee Bob! Remember Dave, that voracious reader and early student of the classics? Mister Dave Tomas! Sitting in the back of the room! Acting like mister cool! Being cool! Looking good! Who used to joke around like that Mappolo Rei, do you recall? Perhaps a fellow who went by the name of Mariano Reyes, sweet-faced and chubby-cheeked, a bit on the insecure side, but really nice, remember him, Map, that was you, you son of a gun, you!

Well Dave Tomas too committed suicide two years out, after his own binges, after he too dropped out, did you know, Mr. Rei? Boy, your bunch really made out good in this world, didn't they! Him sitting next to you in class thinking you his buddy, his friend, mister supporter-man, mister good-friends-look-out-for-each-other man, dudemeister, in person! A whole lot of looking out for him you did, you traitor! In his basement too, they had to fetch him, he'd burned himself to death, Mappolo, a plan—grotesque, gory, gruesome—hatched up in a vision come to him after an impromptu late-night tryst at a popular bowling alley on route 121, the sergeant concluded, a drug-induced state into nirvanic nurturance. He'd seen it all, the terrible tragedies, could not bear it apparently, could bear no more, and could see no hope, no way out, it's said he was screaming as he burned, no way out, no way out, no way out!

Go now Mappolo Rei—go and get in your ride and drive downtown, drive all around town with your shades on, it don't matter if it's dark out, get behind the wheel and throw your headgear on and put your hands on the wheel and steer, steer clear of memories, Mappolo Rei, steer clear of all your dimwitted moves in life, all your regrettable actions, all your fuck-ups and your boneheaded decisions, steer through the boulevards and the streets of your childhood and bemoan your fate, steer away and go along the lanes on the highway at super speeds without regard to the cops who might get on your case, steer and cry Mappolo, steer and cry your heart out, no one will see those tears behind the shades, coming down, at light speeds as you fly down the lanes of regret and despair! Go and park in the parking lot of the shopping center of the mall but just make sure you don't park in the disabled spot or even in the newly created spots reserved for 'expectant or recent mothers' (true, that), the fines are hefty nowadays, or better yet, go in

the parking lot of your old school and peer ahead dazed, con-
template, in your haze, and the haze of all your delirious rushes to judgment and impulsive moves and... But no, not that,
that's just too nostalgic, too depraved, better go back to the
mall, there the sanctuary, there the only sanctuary, park and
enter from the upper level, straight to the food court, and sit
your ass down, Mappolo Rei, where you also sat in your late
teens and your early teens and every year in-between, and cry
and shout and scream inside, no one will hear you Mappolo,
shout and scream your head off, they'll walk around with their
trays, with their huge orange trays and cups, the fat hanging
from their waists and their necks and their cheeks, go and sit
and scream and sing, Mappolo, cry, Mappolo, weep and cry
and sing, Mappolo:

O Food Court at the Mall
O Food Court at the Mall
I'm just walking around in a daze
With a cloud hangin' over me in this maze
I just don't know what to choose in my uncertaintyyyyy
Is this meant to be as hard as tri-go-no-metryyyyyyyy!
O Food Court at the Mall
O Food Court at the Mall
I love to wash hands in your bathroom's stalls
So clean and shiny I feel like a doll
Hangin' out and checkin' out the crowds
Wanna give all my friends a call!
O Food Court at the Mall
O Food Court at the Mall
I love the walkers and the workers roaming your halls
How happy they seem and content and light
One with the universe accepting their plight

Even though they seem totally out of it within these walls
Hunched over their trays munching on the steaks of their
dreams
On their lunch breaks too what else could you ask for
They're happy happy happy lickin' on
Their American cream!

Sing your head off Mappolo, no one hears you at the mall, no one cares for you at the mall, unless you're there to cruise and pick up chicks, no one cares Mappolo, not at the mall and definitely not at the food court at the mall, under whose maddening lights the world of suburbia precipitates the banishment of the solitary soul.

O *voix intérieure* (interior voice) of imaginary characters exposing beleaguered souls and giving backdrop of entirely unexpected and seemingly nonsensical behavior, is it fair that you bare, so cruelly, a man's inner struggles? Wouldn't it be fair to let us in on the mindset of the antagonist also in this situation, behind the wheels of a vehicle tormented, driving on the road with the music blasting, angry beyond words, a peek at least, in light of the current crisis, only fair to smoothly switch into another voice, another mind, how funny it seems now that you never could commit at the beginning, the indecisive hesitations, the flippant remarks, the 'ahronknows' you would send C.'s way upon his overtures. What if he's pushing it, exaggerating, you used to think. Then they got that poor Johnny's kid. Trumped-up charges and all. What a bunch of crock! Made you mad, A., didn't it, made you have all sorts of visions, all kinds of flashes akin to those of folks who have near-death experiences. Made you rethink your whole involvement in this all-too-real movement. The trajectory of it. The hows and whys. The random events and the sudden decisions that had made you go in one direction even though you would have been perfectly capable of going in the opposite... No, you had to be part of it now. No more doubting no, no more hesitation, even if you did have to resort to a preposterously sinister plan hatched up by what most would label a firebrand group of coldblooded killers, domestic terrorists with no regard for human life. You had a feeling, truth be told, not just tagging along, just not seeing any other options. The labels aren't your problem though, you don't make 'em, you can't break 'em. It's the undesirables that like that game. Historians in particular. Public policy wonks. Pundits. These are the folks that come to mind, all blended together in a massive talking head of sorts, Historianspublicpolicywonksandpundits. God you hate them, A., and you know what, some day, if you got anything to do with it, they and all their cohorts and their patsies will pay, hey hey...

We find A.'s car (which he'd left at Mappolo's the day before) parked at an angle (across a white parking line), occupying, illegally, two spots, in front of the McDoogal's, a lone relic of old time supermarkets, without the glitzy neon or the flash of the current crop sprouting all over, with a weathered edifice, peeling walls even and a row of bubblegum machines dispensing not just bubble-gum but miniature football team helmets too like in the old days. Good thing he'd decided to go back home and take his car to Mappolo's after the morning adventure. Mappolo's dramatics can be counted on, he thinks, good to be able to get away when you need to!

The parking lot is rather empty, scattered cars here and there, a red Ford Escort, a blue Lincoln Towncar, a Toyota Camry, a white Honda Civic, a Honda Odyssey, a VW Cabriolet, a black

Nissan Maxima, a burgundy Buick Regal, a Chevrolet Corsica, a blue Volvo V70 station wagon. McDoogal's is closed now, it only makes sense, not the twenty-four hour super competitive joints of today, just a rusty building with some shopping carts in front, and a weathered name on the top.

We find A.: melancholy, sitting still in the car, elbow out, peering solemnly at the vast expanse of black asphalt unimaginatively painted with white thick lines. As a poet peers into the ocean from a lonely boulder or the ruins of an ancient city, as the exile peers into the imagined home he has so longed for, as the general in defeat peers into the flames of his beloved land, A., here, peers into: his beloved parking lot. And sees there: the big, white Lincoln Navigator, the blue Saab 900, the classic blue Oldsmobile, the white Nissan XE, the BMW 325 ci, the black Subaru Legacy, the white Ford Taurus, the black VW Jetta, the red Ford Escort. Then he decides to get out, walks to the rear end of the car, leans against the trunk, hands folded at chest, looking one way (at the desolate scene in front of McDoogal's), then the other (at the cars passing by with the number of passengers inside, passing, a blue sedan with 1 passenger, a gray Honda sedan with 1 passenger, a black Mercedes with 1, green Toyota with 2, green sedan 1, red Dodge van 1, black sedan 2, beige sedan 2, beige sedan 2, black sedan 1, black Subaru minivan 2, gray Honda civic 2). What he must be thinking. The regrets. The doubts. What to do. Solemnly he turneth again his visage and peereth into the front of McDoogal's. Noticeth there a bent-over worker unloading boxes from a delivery truck. Surely a new batch of grocery items, since the store is closed, and is, was, remains, famous for its fresh vegetables, farm-picked fruits, organically produced produce, before organic became a whole category and industry of its own. Averteth then his eyes for he can no more bear this sight. The slow withering of an old world he knows. The unfettered withering of the sights, the sounds, the smells, of his childhood haven. Alas, if only he could go back in time, or forward in time, where all the complexes and the multiplexes and the supermarkets and the megastores adhere to his likes, to his desires, his—

> *O Cineplex*
> *O beloved Cineplex of my youth*
> *I'm just on a journey to recuperate my lost years*
> *I want to drive around and park and get to you*
> *Walk to the entrance and order a ticket and get some*
>   *popcorn*
> *And plump my butt down I do*
> *And rid my soul of anxieties and fears*
> *O Cineplex of endless youth*
> *I remember the shoot 'em-ups we used to catch with the boys*
> *I remember the quirky flick I watched with Stacy Dellimoys*
> *And the Rocky Horror Picture Show*
> *O what a thrill O what a blow*
> *Except that I used to project it and then clean up after*
>   *the communal*
> *Joy!*

But they will, he promises, they will conform to his whims. I am not leaving this life without making sure, O Cineplex, O Cineplex,

> *O Cineplex of endless youth*
> *All the parties ended up at your doors*
> *Now where are the friends all scattered*
> *And working at Mickey D's and Walmarts and other*
> *Big-ass generic stores!*

Shall he elect the coveted hall and title of Exile, A. wonders as he glances at a paper coke cup at his feet with the straw inside still intact shooting through the lid? Surely that will add to his legend, to the myth that shall become the ultimate triumph! Yes, exile, is good for fame, we all know that. But if he just packs bags and catches plane or train out, how is he an exile if he can just come back? He must somehow be arrested, tortured, or something. Provoke a persecution even, if exile, the condition—and the title—is what he craves. No, he concludes, exile ain't for him. Besides, he concludes again (last, promise), the genius of this joint is that it renders exile impossible (with all the status and following the term ignites): you can always come back—you just won't matter, and you'll be eliminated, in less controversial, less dramatic, more pertinent ways (and which shall lead to no one caring what the hey you're up to). No—no exile, no gain, but then again, no exile, no pain, and so, no gracias, to exile.

There are few solutions, A. thinks at this great moment he envisions will one day be remembered as are all great momentous occasions, like the one with Moses on the rock, or... Well, you get the point. The moment when A. had his Vision, and his ultimate Conversation (granted, here it's with himself, but no less important), and launched the new era, in the Parking Lot. As for more immediate concerns, he must basically continue his doomed relationship with Mappolo and the others, at least until the victory of the revolution is assured, whereupon he can turn around and have Mappolo, the clear danger, along with a few other associates, arrested and killed for their despicable crimes, whatever they turn out to be. Besides, there is no other way. He must simply pardon Mappolo's current indiscretion. It is not a surprise, after all, he should have expected it, seen it coming from such a fragile, troubled and unreliable soul. Sitting again now in his parked car with the door ajar and one of his legs out, looking out still at the Banner Glass store across the way, and the Chinese food restaurant and the Superior Transmission, and Jimmy's Auto Body, he marvels at all he sees. He always had marveled at all things, at all of humanity's inventions and rituals, somehow someone made this, somehow folks ended up where they ended up, somehow someone works here, in the morning, has a shift, then is off, and quietly goes to the back and punches out and then if there's a uniform, like a hat or a shirt, takes it off and hangs head and walks out and... Somehow, at all the little things in life, he always marvels: at jobs, at rituals, at how folks go to work, and sit at their desks, and call people, and begin their days, and accomplish things, and have around them all their mementos, the pictures of kids, in the cubicles, those sanctuaries, the folders in the cubicles, the books and memos in the cubicles, and happiness of course, happiness and contentment in the cubicles, comfort and convenience in the cubicles, health insurance for sure, in the cubicles, benefits with the cubicles, happiness, cubicles, contentment, cubicles, health insurance, cubicles, happiness, the cubicles, the cubicles, the cubicles...

I'm happy in my cubicle
Happy in my cubicle
I won't let you be cynical
O cynicaaaal!
It's all a joke anyway and I'm quite happyyyy
Might as well make some moneyyyyyy
That's what my dearest uncle saaaaays
Be happy in your cubicaaaaaaaal!
You're not picking trash off the streets
You're not cleaning or sweeping dirty streets

You're a professional with your nice attire
A most respected fella in your communityyyyy!

Yes, at all things in life he marvels, and perhaps nothing more, these days anyways, than the cubicle, the very cubicle he had spurned—for greater glories, he was sure.

He puts his hand in his pocket and pulls out the small piece of paper with the 7-eleven girl's number on it. He'd made sure to take it after showering and changing! He should give her a call, he's thinking, give her a call and start a whole new life, a new chapter for himself and in general, the A. Era... He could start now, why not now, now is as good a time as any... Mend his ways, settle down perhaps, but definitely, at least, give up the whole Mappolo affair, never was meant to be, they were too different, and plus, Mappolo liked girls way too much, and me too, he thinks, always have preferred girls, perhaps this was the sign, a whole new era, Mappolo would understand, he was mature enough, comrades-in-arms... Yes, A. thought, yes, I will call, and find out... And then, in a whisper (actually uttered and not just in his mind, although there is no one around), he says: 'I, A., after the takeover is complete, shall mend my ways, and save myself, and my soul.' And then, after a pause, he says: 'And I'm gonna give that hot chick a call, for sure!'

7

Mr. A. strokes his imaginary beard. Mr. A. pulls on the handles of his imaginary moustache. Left eye blinks quickly in succession, a tick set in motion when he's agitated. Heaves a deep sigh. Peers into the distance. A motor vehicle administration sign, with an arrow, informs him where the office is. A Jeeper's World of Fun with colorful neon lights in the distance. A trinity church with a god pronouncement of sorts on the info board. A Hooters is down the pike, along with the movie theater, the big book store and the super sports store and all the rest of the super stores that make this hamlet pretty much like all the other hamlets with all the same great super stores in pretty much the same exact configuration, with all possible consumption right there at your fingertips. Right there. How fabulous. How amazingly fabulous…

A. hangs his head. Thought? Meditation? Resignation? Whatever. He suddenly gets up and walks to the trunk. He opens it, thinks, closes again, comes back and slides in, with gusto, as if with a definite destination and purpose. Everything resolved? Maybe. Keys? Woops. He'd left them on the trunk. Back out (door on driver's side had remained open), walks to the trunk, picks up keys, walks to door, hops in, closes door, the sudden panic of keylessness replaced by a sense of the irony of it all. Irony of ironies, actually, since he'd gone through so many in the past not even twenty-four hours. It seems like he's resolved matters, like he's got things to do, places to go, stuff to figure out. That's what his determination and scowl say.

Scowl with a smile too, sign of a certainty, a dangerous wisdom of sorts. Further irony of ironies though, for A. has barely thrown the keys in the ignition that a Chevy Impala, circa 1976, suddenly swerves in front of him: 'What the...' he's thinking. He's got room behind to maneuver, but he is taken by the suddenness of the event—and so does what comes naturally, and might actually come back to haunt him. That is, he opens the door, violently steps out and forges forward toward the driver's side window of the oversized sedan. No need to be so aggressive and in such a rush to settle matters though, he discovers, for before he's reached the Impala, said vehicle's driver himself has slipped out. Tall fellow, sporting sunglasses (Ray-Bans, authentic ones, A. judges in that split second, a connoisseur of such luxury items), menacing, to say the least.

'You A.?' the driver asks curtly, coldly, meanly—and in a deep, deep baritone.

Our hero A. doesn't know how to respond. If he tells the truth, he could be in trouble. If he tells a lie, he could be in trouble. If he plays around with the meanings of words, however legitimate his challenge (such as, 'What do you mean by *you*'), he could still be in trouble. Opt for truth over lies, then, daring over hesitation. 'Y—' he begins (phonetic rendition of the letter), but then reconsiders. Slight panic. What's wrong with being afraid, he ponders. Of death (physical), or the destruction of your career or life by one or another lobby, organization, ideology. Better safe than sorry. Better cautious than calamitous. So, he mumbles again, 'W...' (phonetic, again). Quickly though, a further reconsideration. Who the hell is this dude anyway?! And why should I tell him what he wants to know? Clearly, calmly, a last reconsideration, and:

'Who wants to know?' he asks, with a strong smart-alecky overtone.

'You A.?' the unimpressed and burly brute asks again, not even bothering, as a switch to insistence would impose, to properly place the 'are' in the first part of the question.

'Listen pal,' A. responds, 'I'd be all for bringin' over the blankets and the bottles and the baskets and a-hangin' out or picnickin' and all, it would please me to no end, really it would, but right now, I ain't in the mood, and am actually in a hurry, so if you'll please excuse me...'

He has taken a mere step away that the back doors of the Impala suddenly thrust open, two men in pink suits (like the driver's) and dark shades jump out and grab a hold of him and drag him into the backseat—all in one swift, smooth, swoop. The driver straightens the collar of his jacket, takes the obligatory glance left and right, and goes back in the car. A.'s car's driver's side's door remains open, the whole vehicle itself still parked at an awkward angle. (A future wanderer, a curious thrill-seeker or a mere passerby, using a bit of judgment, would surely be able to conclude that something had gone wrong in these here parts, something had gone awry, something tragic even, perhaps terrible, certainly just gosh darn awful. Ahhh, if only we could see the faces of those future, unknown discoverers.)

Strangely, A., in the back between the unidentified kidnappers, is quiet, resigned. His eyes fixed to the ground, he does not shout, rant, rave or even ask: who they are, where they are taking him. His mind is blank, terribly blank, almost as if he recognizes the end of an era, the futility of existence, of wonderings, of queries, of the whole shebang really. (O how swift are the swings of bipolar fiends...)

The two men in the back blindfold A. midway through their trek. They hold him firmly, on the arm, on each side, then proceed to handcuff him. Exercises? Playful torture of some sort, A. wonders, the haughty, naughty thought? Even if there were other factions, what would they want with him now?! Worse, how did they know where to find him? No, this scenario of a runaway rebel group snatching him either for kicks or as a full-blown attempt to try to eliminate him did not jive, was unlikely, highly unlikely. Steve's kin? Warned before you know it? A high-placed executive our happy-go-lucky cowboy, despite his appearance, his demeanor, or even information he'd divulged? Now his associates snatching his murderer? Time of revenge? Brutal, tribal, mano-a-mano vengeance?

Highly unlikely too, if for nothing other than a detail Steve himself had revealed on the way down the hill to the Cadillac, and that your polite narrator consciously omitted, thinking it a minor aside and a minor detail—but which now I must readily communicate (illusions of god-like omniscience be damned) if only in the service of informed judgment. Namely, the following info: that Steve had admitted he had 'dabbled in some hanky-panky type business, if you know what I mean' (this after the initial salutations and upon expounding on endeavors he was involved with other than his singing/songwriting career), upon which after a slight shake of the head and simultaneous raising of the eyebrows and further maneuvering of the neck, A. had communicated to Steve that not really, he didn't really know what he meant, upon which the now long dead and chopped-up but then embarrassed Steve had had to slowly move his head back and forth, forward and back, struggling for a decent way to say what he needed to say, the words just not coming, or was it that there was no way of sanitizing his dubious involvements, 'skin flicks, you know,' he'd

suddenly blurted out, surprising even himself as to the timing
of the utterance, to which he gave in, after further considerations, 'tits and ass, chicks and dicks'—and he would rhythmically run each expression off, tip of his tongue type thing,
with the heightening of the pitch, as if a question, each—upon
which, finally A. getting it, Steve had revealed that he'd gotten
into some hot water with some dudes who'd found him in a
far-off porn store (yellow neon lights, cheap flashing bulbs,
contour of naked girl long hair flowing on her back and hips
lying down on her side, mermaid-like, with a darkened door
through which figures looking down would walk out, half-way
covering their faces but not really, not guilty of anything after
all, except perhaps slightly ashamed, although without reason),
him dropping off some of his 'work' ('my own distribution system'), and reminded him to not get too ambitious, not get too
greedy, or else the consequences might be severe, prompting
him (Steve) to think they might have been with not necessarily
the mob, but a mob, a gang of sorts, that could do him harm,
that's all he was concerned about—point being, Steve was operating on his own, independently, with colleagues obviously,
but not within some sort of grand scheme, probably why it
didn't 'pan out the way I thought it coulda,' Steve emphasizing
at the end of his explanation to A.—point being, Steve most
probably was not being avenged by members of a 'criminal'
unit (not the organized kind, anyway) and so, it made no sense
to think that for A., since he knew already, what I'm just now
admitting (recognizing that reader is privy to info as much as
character A.) was not a minor aside.

What else then? An unrelated incident? But I've paid all my
bills, A. thinks—or have I? Besides, this is not the usual method authorities resort to—not for trivial non-payments, is it?
Have things changed so dramatically? And if so, where have I

been? No, he surmises (sad, sad, panicked and afraid), the only probable culprit is one he knows all too well... The only possible scenario, one he could never have dared imagine, although it does not completely surprise him. Is this how things are to unfold after all? Certainly not written so, certainly not what he expected. But he should have. Truth is, he should have. The difficulties lie where you don't expect. And where you await the laborious times and struggles, at times, all flows, smooth...

The car stops at a nondescript hovel, a few exits after where A. had accosted the fellow depicted as Steve, that very morning(!!), although it seems now like so long ago, so so long ago! (It has been quite the day, A. thinks in a flash as the car is coming to a stop!)

A. is dragged by his captors out of the car and up a row of stairs. He is shoved through a door that the driver has opened and held open. He is pushed again, stumbles, stops, is pushed again and finally dragged in the middle of what feels to him like a barely decorated large anti-chamber. They shove him down on a small, fragile chair. Pull his arms back, tighten (little scream by A.) and attach them by rope to the chair. They do the same with his feet: attached to the feet of the chair. Feet to feet he sits, unmoving... and thus recalls singing to Fiora (his friend's daughter) the 'feet to feet' lullaby, which now he whispers inside, to bring himself to a modicum of calm:

Feet to feet they carry on
Soldiers under a burning sun
Sisters holding hands
Brothers marching on
Fathers mothers daughters and sons
To the tunes of a thousand and one flutes
A thousand and one giant balloons

Favorite voices of cartoons
A thousand and one marvelous tunes
They march on march on
Soldiers on the fabulous trek
Called life
Wonderful they say so wonderful and bright
So full of happiness joy and light
A thousand and one beautiful sights
And more and more and more candle lights
(No matter A. that you're an orphan
You're an orphan with might—)
O yes they carry on
Fathers mothers daughters and sons
On this merry way they call
Life.

Two close calls today, A. murmurs inwardly after finishing his soothing song, now what…

Book I: The Room

The blindfold suddenly comes off. His eyelids flutter, the light bothers him. He shakes his head. Pretty right about the surroundings, he congratulates himself, quite accurate indeed. On both sides of him, one of the big guards is putting on his shoulder a hand. Hard too. Unnecessary he thinks. Says as much: 'You need to press so hard, fellas?'

'Shut up!' the ex-driver now lead guard, by deportment and comportment, shouts.

'As you say,' the proud warrior sarcastically swings back.

The chauffeur-cum-torturer slowly walks toward him. Stops

and frowns. 'Don't fuckin' joke with me you cock-suckin' son of a bitch,' he utters, articulately, and shall we say, forcefully. He's also let fly a monstrous slap-cum-punch to A.'s head, who, helpless, almost flips back on his chair, held back by his two personal guardian angels.

This ain't no joke, A. thinks, in pain and already bruised and bleeding from the nose. But something, call it perverse pride of a revolutionary, a spirit of resistance, *kerm*, in my O so long ago abandoned mother tongue, rises in him—and:

'This ain't no joke now, is it?!' A. says loudly, enunciating fully each word, separating one from another.

Torturer-cum-major-pain stands and looks. What shall I do, he's mulling in his head, the filthy pig. But he simmers down and does nothing. Ready for the next opportunity when he'll pounce on him and destroy his sorry ass. There is a proverb and there is not, a tale of the folks, a song of the people, that says, continually beware of the monster who thinks everybody else is a monster. He'll get his due, and his just desserts. Not entirely accurate perhaps, but a wisdom lies therein nevertheless, in the baroque (for a whole bunch of reasons) tradition of the folktale.

Book II: The Entrance

The room, then: a bare, depressing hall with a few trivial objects and a photo of a morose general, crooked, on the wall. On the seat, hands and feet tied, right side of the face bruised, the great man of the ages, the grand leader of the revolution, A. On his sides, two huge guards. In front of him, an even huger brute. In the air: a nauseating premonition that something pretty nasty is going down, and that it's not, repeat, not, going to be pretty. (Then, there is a silence—almost as if all

the players, A. and the guards and the narrator even, the chair
and the rope, the wall, the emptiness of the hall, all of the
sounds, and the unheard sighs and the air even, floating about,
were suspended, as if the supermarkets and the cineplexes and
the megaplexes and their songs, and the teenagers in the basements, all the depressed and despaired teenagers in all the dreary basements of single family homes or attached townhouses or
fancy mansions, and the food courts at the malls, and the large
signs shooting into the skies, the warehouses and the gourmet
coffee shops, the family restaurants and the health clubs, had
all been stripped of their facades, had all been exposed, had
been unmade, as if all that remained, as if all that had ever happened, along with memories and desires, and ambitions and
cravings, and lusts and battles and wars, had suddenly been
eradicated, and the monuments of their triumphs razed to the
ground, as if all the rhythmic comings and goings of passersby,
the entrances and exits, through the doors of shoppers in the
shopping malls, the choreography of cars and folks, the balletic
motions of the automobiles in the cities' streets, the crisscrossing of walkers, the silhouettes, the shadows, the outlines, had
all been untangled and unmade and exposed, almost as if unreality with vengeance had entered the confines of the hollow
chambers, and unleashed its ruthless, venomous forces, fangs
and teeth and snarls of all kinds, onto the unsuspecting, as if
nothing matters, as if all the senses have failed or will soon, as
if reality all along had been a most devilish ruse, and so the
world, and so its woes, and so within it circulating, wondering,
the men, as if nothing within or without mattered, all without
consequence, or legitimacy, there are no men in suits standing
guard inside, there is no dark and dreary chamber occupied,
no empty walls and echo-filled halls, there is no torturer, there
is not on a chair a man sitting his hands and feet bound with

a rope awaiting what, his comeuppance, his execution, there is no wall without color and the crooked portrait of a general and peeling paint, there is no quiet rumbling of invisible machines, no one, there is no one, about, no sound, no words, no breaths, no air, there is no one, there is no one, there is only a silence, only a silence, unforgiving.)

Soon, a noise is heard beyond the door, a crackling of sorts. More distinct now: someone moving objects, now stopping. Sounds of steps. Several steps and again, the rhythm. Can tell. Something going down. Can tell. Everything stops. Doorknob, right before A.'s eyes, turns. Door, slowly, opening. Open now. One man, wearing a cape-like robe, walks in, pompous and with pretense, flanked by similarly attired associates, they with shades on, and arms crossed, à la bodyguard.

All together, in perfect synchrony, they take one step, then another, closer to the chair. The two associates stop, the cape-wearing man moves forward, four paces more. He is standing two yards away from A. and now looks down at him.

'Ohhh shit!'—A.'s reaction (with both the 'o' and the 'sh' elongated) perhaps says it all. But not enough. Certainly not enough.

Book III: The Shit Hits the Fan

'Shit is right, mister!' Mappolo says. 'No one, I repeat, NO ONE, leaves Mappolo Rei to cry his eyes out on his birthday, you dig!'

He pauses, takes a deep breath. 'After all the times you made me feel guilty—you bastard!'

(Necessary Switch to Theatrical Mode)
Dramatis Personae
Mappolo Rei, associate and lover of A., revolutionary;
A., associate and lover of Mappolo Rei, revolutionary;
Eddie Perez, ex-associate of A., now swearing allegiance to Mappolo Rei; Laverneus Doggerel, relatively new recruit swearing allegiance to Mappolo Rei; Monti the real-estate-wanna-be guy; the guards

Scene
Suburbs; room in a ramshackle warehouse; outside: parking lot with cars parked nicely inside white lanes

Shocked A. (*Sarcastic and angry*): You are one fucked-up dude, Mappolo, you know that, you're a freak!

Mappolo, (*Genuinely beside himself*): I'm a freak!? I'm a freak!? Did you hear that boys, I'm the freak! (*The guards all shake their heads and smile nervously*) I'm the one who came up with the little ritual to frighten the citizens ey, mister! One by one, one and all, I'm the one who came up with that ey?

Wounded A.: You don't know what you're talking about Mappolo! Take off that robe and that silly crap and get these things off of me!

Mappolo (*Laughing the requisite laugh*): I don't think you get it, big A. I actually have the distinct impression that you do not, repeat, do NOT get it! Don't you boys, don't you think he's not getting it! (*The guards, again, acquiesce, gesturing as if to say sure, whatever…*) Listen, faggot-ass faggot, this is it! End of the line *pour toi*! Bye-bye big A. No more…

Anxious A. (*Agitated*): Mappolo, you're not stealing this revolution from me, you freak! You hear me, this is my revolution!

Mappolo (*Prancing about*): Oh no, I'm not going to steal it from you, mister, because it was not yours to begin with, asshole! You came up with the method shall we call it, but that's because you are pure evil, the devil incarnate, a disgrace to your race! I just gave you the chant! The *idea* of the chant, asshole! Do you know anyone who eats a finger or two a week? (*Mappolo looks sarcastically around*) Boys, you know anyone, two and a half human fingers? What does that come to, I wonder (*Finger, no pun intended, to the chin, in the manner of a contemplator*). Hmmm...

Humiliated A. (*Snapping*): Fuck you faggot!

Mappolo: No, no, let's get this straight. The faggot, is you. That is: you're the faggot. And soon, you are a dead faggot. Bye-bye faggot song will be sung for you! All right, mister, let's roll.

Exeunt one guard. Enter another guard—and Monti.

Strategizing A. (*This time with a distinctly more panicked urgency*): Mappolo! Take these ropes off of me and let's go home! (*Then surprised at seeing Monti walk in*) Monti! Monti, what the hell!

Mappolo (*Looking at Monti and then at A.*): Monti thought he'd drop by and pay you a visit. Ain't that right Monti? (*Monti nods*) He knew you'd appreciate it. Say, 'Hello Monti,' A., come now, say it, 'Hello Monti!'

Despairing A., simply lets out a loud grunt and rolls his eyes.

Mappolo (*Crueler than he ever imagined himself to be*): Not only are you a dead punk, but you will have the great indignity, my good man, of joining your many victims in the freezer, for I, for one, shall take great pleasure in devouring your cooked limbs, not to mention your crooked nose, and your curly cock, and your cut-up tongue, and your cooked-up parts, and a caramel cake too, for dessert, especially a certain one which I know you to be quite proud and fond of.

Mister A. (*Almost giving up*): You son of a bitch! You piece of garbage!

Mappolo (*Laughing*): Go on, go on, darling! Shower me with love do! You've been at it for quite some time now…

(Mappolo then begins to hum and brings his face closer and closer to A.'s, and subsequently raises his voice and sings louder and louder as he carries on, O teenager in the basement, O teenager in the basement, Save me now from my predicament, Save me now from my prediiiiiicament. The last 'predicament' Mappolo shouts roughly and insistently, switching keys, and as if letting out a howl into the night sky. Then he suddenly stands and raises his two arms and peers demoniacally at A., upon which all the guards and Monti and Eddie mimic Mappolo's grandstanding and stand as well, soldier-like, heads straight staring ahead, like their Leader, upon which Mappolo brings one arm back down violently as if a signal, upon which the whole gang launches into the anthem.)

> *O teenager in the basement*
> *You really think you're gonna be a rock star*
> *Or a famous actor driving around in a fancy car*
> *O teenager in the basement*
> *Don't hold your head so low*
> *Don't hate your 'rents don't blow*
> *They're not to blame just wanted the best for you all along*
> *Why—they got you the basement for you to grow!*
> *O teenager in the basement*
> *Think about your predicament!*
> *Get your chin off the pavement*
> *Get your soul out the gutter*
> *Get your mind off the stripper*
> *Get up and make a statement!*
> *I am, I am, I am—*
> *A teenager in the basement*

Sick—and tired!—of strumming my lonely guitar!
Sick—and tired!—of dad's old beat-up car!
Sick—and tired!—of staring at blank walls!
Sick and tired, sick and tired, sick and tired
Of fakin' all my higgggggghhhhhhssss…
And passin' out on the
Cheap-ass
Devil-red
Old-style
Lazy-chairish
Motha-fuckin'
Beeeeeeeaaaaaaaaan baaaaaaaaaaaaaaaaaaag!

(Pause and everyone catching their breaths)

Mappolo: You know what, little A., and I mean, little, A., I don't wanna hear this anymore. *(He turns to Eddie)* Eddie, get rid of him please, will you? *(Repeat in a form of query/command with that straight rise of the voice)* Please?

(BACK TO PROSE)

Eddie takes a few steps toward A., stops, pulls out a machete from the belt of his robe-like garment, and in one swoop, beheads him. The head rolls a few feet away. The headless body shakes and goes through convulsions. The head's mouth utters incomprehensible syllables. Shut up, Mappolo turns and shouts at the head, enraged and slightly incoherent. Mappolo is quickly out of the room. Eddie too, turns and walks out. The guards behind A., their hands on his shoulders, eerily, have not taken them off. Until now. They look at each other, then askance. Someone has to clean this mess up, they know. A moment of repose, before the next task. Anyone would need a reprieve from this—even they. After all… Well… Well… No need to…

Book IV: The Number, the Teller, the Portrait, the Departure

Mappolo has ordered the pockets of all clothes to be emptied and the contents turned over to him. They are, subsequently, to be turned over to a charity of his choice. The head and body are cleaned, both washed and cut, the former to be preserved, the latter for future consumption at the grand banquet—perhaps the greatest of banquets. Also, the guards got the phone number of the 7-Eleven lady out of A.'s pockets and smartly, did not turn it over to anyone but to Mappolo himself. 'Hmmmm,' he muttered, 'interesting…'

O agents of fortune, O agents of vengeance, protect my feeble fingers from excessive engagement in the details of this gory tale. This adventure gone awry. This ill-advised, ill-begotten fable and farce. I cannot insist enough on my own premonitions that the sour would turn even more so by, say, midway through the grand portraiture. Will the reader believe (I urge him, her, and all transgendered avatars) that I take no pleasure in exposing the lurid, untold, unwritten realities of the revolution. I proffer no perverse pleasure in remaking the account, in recounting the more outlandish aspects of the events. I admit, in fact, the great trepidation I forced myself to overcome in order to recount accurately the goings-on and confess, further, to a troubling sense of dread I have perpetually had to lull to inactive inefficacy in order to continue to tell not only this story, but, indeed, this history. Such descriptions, such awakening of dormant images give me no more satisfaction than an unparalleled sense of thirst in the middle of a desert. Really. But at the same time, I acknowledge, I cannot keep from elaborating, from progressing, from digressing and transgressing and a whole lot of other words ending in '–essing'! A profuse disease of the hand—mechanical, I concede. A weakness of the spirit, in acquiescence to the powerful pull of Eros, undoubtedly. Perhaps even a whiff of chicanery, of street-thuggish thirst for redemption and clever acquisitions—a small dose of playfulness, surely. But gore for gore's sake? Please!

Yes, tolerant leader, benevolent reader, the events herein portrayed are not of the lot to provoke cheesy sentimentality, I realize that. Nor are they much good at providing misty-eyed developments for even the most sensitive of personalities. A narrative with a poetic bent—not quite: no reveries solitary on a nameless wharf, no quiet recitation book in hand along an anonymous and glorious shore, no private readings among the sophisticated and philistine to enliven a dreary night, or ignite passion, poetic, I mean, epic passion, passion of the epic, in the accursed heart. None of them, I admit, not even a bit of gratuitous porno, to make one band! But fret not. Accuse not. Do not turn away in anger or disgust. I had no choice but to be true to truth. That shall follow me to my grave, I'm sure of it, perhaps even cause my early departure to it, but, well, is there an alternative? Seriously. I too would rather have seen A. and Mappolo reconcile, hug, kiss, make up, and in their case, even fuck. I too would rather have appreciated a turn back to eliminate the confrontation in the kitchen that launched the whole messy shebang to begin with, and the tense situation, and the accusation, but, truth be told, that was just the tip of the iceberg. We can all imagine how the root causes and the build-up to Mappolo's bloody coup preceded not only that episode and the flare-up, but, I dare say, the very fabrication of the tale within which the two were birthed, and their story, fashioned:

in other words, a long time ago. Granted. Of course. I would rather have no one killing no one, for no purpose, not even as a free meal. Not even for the Ultimate Triumph of the Cause. And yet, the revolution, did I, did I not, raise my left hand and salute, bend index finger and little finger (without any other finger) and profess devotion... Hail the Suburbs, Hail the Suburbs, did I not, also, dream of—all irrelevant, irrelevant I say, immaterial: what's told is told, what's made (up) gets old. What's told, in addition, is truth: within the confines of tales, anyway, which means, probably, always. And what's 'truth' will allow indiscriminate embellishments, decorations, exaggerations... Let us move on.

For even the personages in the midst of our fairy tale have engaged in just such a trek: have set on going homewards that is, on cleaning up, on reviewing the day, taking stock. The guards, annoyed, but recognizing that duty was calling upon them to fulfill their mission, had cleaned the floor (mop in the back, ready) and cleared it completely of any trace of the impure A. They did with his parts what Mappolo had demanded, one sack for the head, two sacks for the rest. One of the fellows had even taken the portrait of the general down, revealing behind it a huge hole in the wall that the old and obviously meaningless (some old Soviet crap) painting had helped cover. It was placed on top of the chair, this itself brought back to its original spot, in the corner of the room. Each of the guards had then doffed the pink jacket, thrown on a jean jacket for one, leather for the other, and left the premises. Eddie, in turn, had gone back to his girl's (Oooh, Eddie, you smell so... so fresh—the girl) and engaged in some deliciously devious and splendidly sumptuous sexual shenanigans. As for Mappolo, what can one say, really. A long, long, looooong day, for sure, and he was feeling, not quite remorse, no, but something akin to it. He was feeling more than a little blue, and no amount of contemplation, meditation, or reflection, would do. What he needed, and he prided himself on knowing himself, was occupation: physical at least, and mental, perhaps. To get his mind off of things, rather than continue what would, after all, constitute senseless deliberation.

Reprieve from the Terrible Events Going Down to Mention Folks Around Town

All around Whooton, even as tragedy had struck so deep within, even as the world was about to crumble, even as evil was showing its many faces, the citizens carried on, as if naught was a-happening. Totally oblivious, totally without care, pretty much as happens everyday everywhere. We won't go through everyone of course, it's impossible, but to give a taste of the diverse population populating this hamlet, in a testament to all those around the world yearning for and struggling to ac-quire the American Dream, let us not, not, be so pithy as to not include at least some names, our favorite ones too, a who's who of whosedom, when it comes to names that sound like other names and mean all sorts of different things if one thinks about them, especially in a cross-pollination of modern spoken languages.

Let us, then, without further ado, list the many characters that will have gone without mention even though they inhabit the same locales as the revolutionary wannabes, and work hard and earn their hard-earned dollars. Here we go: Earl 'Huss' Kant, ex-philosopher-king turned attorney-queen, John Ali, ex-boxer turned preacher turned preacher-doctor, Salmon Fleisch III, Jack (the Gripper) Grund, Dick Seaman, Geron-imo Alamo, Jesus Mohamed, psychotherapist specializing in varieties of schizophrenic behavior and multiple personality disorders, James N. Cricket, Ariba Downs, MD, who used to live uptown on the west side and had her office downtown, on the east side, but now just lives in one of the houses in the cul de sac, Phil 'Rhino' Girafski, Kei Kodja, MFA, Koo 'Kiki' Howser, an ex-general thought to have disappeared who was in fact just enjoying a few years of anonymous living in a remote island but had now decided to join and contribute to civilian life, Richard 'Cat' Kiriakos, a showbiz impresario and a leader in the transgender community, Jimmy N. Crocket, a Broadway dancer known for his extravagant pieces, Al 'Hoop' Lah, a basketball playground legend from Harlem, New York (shout out to the homies in the 'hood II) whose high school career (junior high, even) had agents and teams frothing at the mouth, but who somehow never lived up to all the expectations, and moved to the quieter side, Solange Padres, born in the Ivory Coast of a Mexican father and Senegalese mother, who later on rejected all ties to country, family and folk and, paradoxically, joined (yes, joined) an anarchist movement, Sondra T. Omeydo, a leader in the organic foods movement, Angelica Sinn (hmm... now let's see, what kind of profession could she be in), Sue Meenut (please), L. Icky Midoo (oh yeah), Koon Tchon Tank (not to be confused with), Koon Khon Hunk (I will I will, promise I will), Don Deal Jr., LouLou Khorkhoray, Ahmed Ahmadi, Sid Sidovsky, Sam Samuelson, Jacob Washington, Joseph Madison, Jehovah Franklin, Abraham Lincoln, Dinayro Cashman, Shush Jishman, Tchador Weil, Dast Footman, German Frank, Suk Mahdool, Duane Shat, Anne Reed, Annie Reedy, D.D. Reedy (no relation), DDS, Tikk Tock, Luna Teek, Sal Omay, Yool Assies, Salaam Siya, and, of course, Elias Nombres, a clown, impersonator, singer, and all-around nice guy. What of them? Well, it would have sufficed to pretend that we wanted to list the whole lot in order to right the injustice whereby only loudmouths and shouters and screamers get any attention, what with these folks just going about their business (perhaps with many among them dedicated to the deciphering of the mysteries of the world, who knows), but that, unfortunately, is not the sole reason. In fact, the preceding personalities also had this in common: they were all standing in line waiting for the doors to open at Bobby's SuperStore for the Early Bird Special (6-9 a.m.), where, what, a sale of course, would greet them on all items within the hallowed halls. Not just any sale either, *the* Sale of the Year, the Post-Holiday Sale to end all such events, of course! And we took advantage and picked out some folks at random and interviewed them, just to get a feel for the average citizen's pulse. Among a host of interactions all pointing to the fact that no one knew or cared about anything other than what the store was offering, a minimal sampling... Question: How is this sale turning out for you? Answer: Oh god great, I love these bargains (Ms. Padres). Question: Did you ever think you would get a deal like this Mr. Washington? Answer: Not in a hundred years (he laughs), but of course, next year will be better we hope (we all laugh)! Question: Mr. Jimmy N. Crocket, you've just won the great bonanza, how do you feel? Answer: Well gee, Mr. interviewer, I feel like Jimmy N. Crocket, ha ha! (Back to you, Narrator, at Book V, Narrator's interviewer's persona's voice interfacing with fake characters reporting from the field.)

Book V: Exterior Voice and Interior Voice, in an Awkward Embrace

'Joe,' Mappolo says, on the phone, 'changed my mind. Think I can come.'

Mappolo is lying on his couch, undressed, but showered. Betashnik is pissed off but all right. Had made plans to close, but what the hell. 'What happened?' his voice can be heard on Mappolo's receiver. 'Nothing,' Mappolo says, in a bit of a weird mood. 'You all right?' Joe's voice asks. 'What about your emergency?' 'Fine,' Mappolo says. 'Taken care of.' He sounds down, Joe can feel it, has gotten a good feel for the kid by now, but prefers to drop it. Let the kid be, Joe's inward thoughts can be detected on Mappolo's receiver, probably another boy drama. (Yes, Joe knew about the pansexuality, quite the open-minded bloke, although a stereotypical ascription of personality to his physique and his manners would not have allowed the just evaluation of Joe's openness. Mappolo had dared anyway, made a remark, one night, close to the soda machine, when a cute young man had walked by...)

Mappolo in his living room walking about taking stock of the day. The celebration has not gone as planned, obviously. If only that loser freak hadn't chased away the girls. What the fuck did he want with the leg anyway! Couldn't it have waited! Checking up on the leg goddamnit! Can't he just keep his nose in his business! You hear me A., you fuck, in heaven or hell or wherever the freak you are, what the hell did you want with a piece of leg to begin with! Missed your friend Stevie boy's sexy calves? Goddamn you!

He slumps on an old, velvety (faux velvet of course), red, modern-style chair he has in the corner. Not traumatized, far from it, but, frankly, lonely. He'd really thought they'd turned a corner with A. Really thought they were onto something special. Sure they'd had their differences and their tiffs but who didn't? They'd always found a way to make amends, kiss and make up, so to say. Find that common ground. But now... Thought he had to go looking for the leg! Bastard! He wants to think there is possibly a way to fix what he'd done, but, not really. Perhaps undo it all, or believe in some otherworldly powers, but, again, not really. There are no ghosts in Mappolo's world, no reincarnations, no energies that travel back and forth. There is only life, to be lived, and then: whatever. And he was determined to live the first and perhaps only one to its fullest. How dare he, he thinks, his facial expression changing in tune with his emotions. Calling it his revolution! What nerve! He got what he deserved! Bastard! Mappolo picks up the phone and contemplates. He has no one to call. Puts the phone back down. Ponders. Picks up again and dials. 'Eddie?' the utterance. 'Everything good?... Yeah... All right... Bring it over tomorrow... Yeah...' Puts the receiver back down. Stares ahead. He's gonna have to chase and hit on a whole bunch of boys and girls. Start the whole damn process over again. Give a few more years of life, laugh and cry, break up, make up, put that whole damn wheel in motion, again! 'Way to go!' he screams, at no one in particular, but at A., it seems. Granted that he chased even during his fling with A., but it was different, a sort of conquest mentality he just couldn't outgrow, the cheap thrill, maybe even to provoke A., who knows. But he did, sometimes he thinks, maybe really love him. Although, it's doubtful. Just wait until this damn thing is over, then they'll be crawling over each other to get to me. Beggin' me to fuck 'em. Beggin' for blow jobs! At no one in particular, he shouts: 'Just you wait and see!'

Mappolo Rei then stands up and goes to the washroom. His shift is coming up, and he needs to prepare. He long ago had abandoned all other plans and ambitions, the revolution essentially dominating his every thought and move.

And now, it needed his strong leadership even more. (Thank god he'd attended some leadership workshops in his youth at a local non-profit, or else…) His sure guidance. He was now the undisputed leader, the lone member of the Original Five still alive. Poor A., thinking he'd get away with things! Hah! Well-deserved, he mumbles again inwardly. Look who's standing now, the one they all laughed at and scorned. The kid! Wherefore art thou, O dead leaders of the revolution ey, what hath you sewn amongst your flock? He laughs. The lord sayeth that whoever messeth with Mappolo Rei hath it coming to their asses! The lord insisteth that you don't, repeat, do not, fuck with Mappolo Rei! Especially not on his birthday! Ain't that right A.! The lord, that mean mofo, insisteth some more and laugheth, Now look where you are, now look what you begot, all ye who deigned, who dared disrespect the great leader of the greatest revolution, Mappolo Rei, look at you now! Mocking him and ordering him and telling him what to do! Burn now in hell, you unrepentant douchebags! And salivate over Mappolo Rei's triumphs while you rot, slowly, O so, O so, O so, slooooowly. Mappolo snickereth again to himself. But quietly composeth his self. Must not get a big head. Not now. That could be foolish. And too sad. No. Must concentrate. Get a hold of thyself, and thy faculties. And thy judgment. Must lay the groundwork for the next phase, the next phases, truth be told. His work is cut out for him, he's well aware. But he's up for it—up for the fight. And up to it—up to the challenge. He'll be calm, the whole way through. Calm and never cocky. Calm, confident and collected—and always cool.

8

Dawn of the revolution, period of incubation of thoughts and the laying of the groundwork for actions: preceded the narrative. Gatherings, buoyant conversations, passionate debates in undisclosed locales as well as Poppy's down the pike and several coffee shops around town: ditto. Rituals of belonging, invention of signs and signals, elaboration of lingo and manners of proceeding, establishment of secret meeting places, of codes of conduct and behavior: all followed the first rumblings pre-narrative and were excluded from the work, mainly for two reasons, a) fear of repetitiveness (been there done that, in terms of the narrating of the upheaval), and b) drive to keep our account relatively short in terms of space, consideration of audience's time, genuine will to have this artifact fit into back pocket for solitary enjoyment on park bench, on bar stool, at dinner table, at rest stop, on the sofa… Interminable disagreements and subsequent elimination of ex-comrades-in-arms in purges of all sorts by the cruelest, cleverest, most cunning: way too violent for inclusion. Consolidation of power and preparation of the splashy first attack: left out, eleventh-hour revision. Thus and so, ladies and gents, an ensemble of meetings, plannings and proceedings led to A.'s heroic first hit, that much we know, and that's where we chose to start: in medias res… But sooner than thought, the as-yet undetermined, unarticulated laws of human nature created the

rifts we have seen at work, what with the upheaval and elimination of A. And now? Treetop in a hypnotic sway, whistling
of birds, garden in full bloom, extension of branches and leaves
towards direction of light... And now: if you allow, the rest of
the *récit*...

The news of the disappearance of Steve was broadcast several days later. Culprit? It seems that his wife had called the authorities, and when the latter were notified that a vehicle was
left on the exit ramp bearing the registration number that they
matched to Steve's, bingo: they put two and three together and
presumably got five, which proceedings got the witch hunt
underway. The talk of the suburbs turned to the mysteries surrounding the grizzly abduction of the poor traveling salesman.
In department stores and huge multiplexes and convenient
stores, the theme dominated all discussions. Opinions ranged
far and wide, and conspiracy theories of all kinds made the
rounds, from revenge motives to payback scenarios to gang-af-
filiated hits. At least momentarily, however, Steve's story, dead
man that he was, was the talk of town.

The Epic History of Mr. Deadmun Jr.

Rumor had it that despite his overall cheery demeanor and
simple ways—neighbors saying he was such a nice fellow, students saying he was always willing to listen and help out, if not
particularly a great musician himself, colleague L. Bob Adams
insisting he was a good pal who always had your back—Steve,
aka Beng Dychman, was involved in a prostitution ring of
sorts, acting in, directing and producing home videos selling
for no more than nineteen ninety-nine, available on a web site

by the name of Sux and Lays Videos (S & L Videos). And that, as fate would have it, something somehow somewhere must have gone terribly wrong. Without respite—and the privileged and informed reader's knowledge notwithstanding—the rumors and theories circulated, at each turn a layer of fabrications and phantasmagoric, unfathomable details heaped upon the previous inventions, spinning the entire sequence and nature of events out of control. (At one point, I heard a dialogue in an outdoor café between a young businessman and the teenage waiter who evoked the 'sick way they'd shot the poor guy' after the violent break-in to 'get back' their stuff, upon which the slightly more mature businessman asked the fellow how he knew and was he sure, because he'd heard otherwise, to which our young and industrious worker had answered, 'Yeah, totally, they even say the guy was wearing a wig and make-up he was so scared they were coming for him!')

No one, funnily, thought a revolution was brewing. In fact, the entire affair had spun so out of control that more attention was being paid to Steve's past, real and imaginary, along with events and people in his life, bogus involvements—preposterous and monstrous involvements—than to the circumstances that had brought about his disappearance. To the point where an editorial was dispatched by his utterly disgusted current wife to a local magazine, the Be (with one 'e'), in which she basically elaborated on the 'sickness' of contemporary society's preoccupation with unearthing heaps of fabricated dirt on a most loving and honorable husband, father and son (no one up to then had known about the 'father' part, a slip of sorts on the part of 'wife' (quotation marks now because, frankly, who the hell knew what was going on, who knew the wife actually was the wife, and not just a wife, or a fake wife, or maybe even a decoy, or a transvestite sex-worker masquerading as wife, paid off handsomely by whomever (she did, I must confess, exhibit manly features and a gravelly voice in her interviews)), that not only did not put out but managed to further fan the flames of rumors, and prompted extended investigations by adults and teens alike who get off this sort of dirt-digging stuff, revealing that yes sir, not only was Stevie a proud father of one, not even two or three, or four, no, but five children, all born out of wedlock, with four different women, all now still residing in the south (one, a waitress at a lonesome diner, in Alabama, residing in a trailer on the outskirts of a little town by the name of Jimani, where she was raising their only daughter (she loved him still, rumors went, high school sweethearts, somehow separated by fate, and, granted, Steve's wild imagination and other-worldly ambitions); another in Tennessee, now apparently working as a real estate agent, what with her having gotten her associates degree and passing the exam, she was on to better things and making a life for herself why not (was steadily dating a local politician too and they were contemplating tying the knot, Steve's daughter Kim not necessarily disapproving but also missing her daddy who did stay in touch although sporadically, and he did love his kids, really he did, and they knew it, and they loved him back); a third working as a cashier in South Carolina, staying now with her parents, still bitter at Steve for his broken promises and what she found out, only now, he was involved with, now definitely she was going to protect their two daughters from him, better, she thought for a moment, that he's disappeared out of their lives, hopefully forever (only to quickly repent and make the sign of the cross for having allowed even the thought to cross her mind); and a last gal, the latest of Steve's flings, with whom, she admitted herself, 'It was never meant to be anything serious, just that we kind of liked each other and couldn't get enough of each other and one thing led to another'—she was twenty now, three years after her first tryst with Steve was currently caring for their one-year old baby, and dancing at night, in a local strip joint, and occasionally doing tours, during the holiday seasons, she enjoyed it, she admitted, was hot too, great body, even after the pregnancy and delivery, wearing costumes, Santa's hat and reindeer bells, with thigh-high boots and reindeer antlers, she loved it, she had to confess, and so did Steve, and yes, she did still have a soft spot in her heart for him, something about him, how he carried himself, a sweetheart, no matter what anyone else would try to tell you)), instead of 'bringing together the resources to find the real culprits and halt the evil design they have on our precious community.'

She went on to blast the media, the police, the dirt-diggers of various persuasions and in her own words, 'Quidam: that nameless ethereal entity, within and without each one of us, fascinated more by the reign of the unknown and by elaboration upon and perpetuation of silly and baseless gossip, rather than the rational collection and analysis of solid evidence.' (All were impressed by her eloquence.) She did not address ('I shall not legitimize the preposterous accusation by any form of defense') the most troubling rumor that somehow she herself had been in on the coup, had planned the murder with associates in order to reap the inheritance of the Sux and Lays Videos future empire. It was also confirmed, by solid investigation and the turning out of many a roomful and vaultful of such tapes, that Steve, our own nice-guy Stevie boy, aka Luke, had indeed, confirmed and sworn upon this day of the month of the year, acted in, directed and produced, as Beng Dychman, many a video, although, based on the nonchalant interviews I conducted with witnesses, there was really nothing too shabby about any of them, nothing really illegal and certainly nothing too graphic or gross, just a whole bunch of fetishistic frolics.

No one, funnily, expected a revolution to break out. (I shudder, I hesitate, I repeat, I sling my arrow even, as I attempt to forget the other Revolution no one expected to break out (or did they?), but to no avail!) Nor did the news, potentially of great import, and certainly getting good ratings locally, gain prominent national attention. Not even a furtive glance. After several weeks in fact, it was totally off the radar screen, even of the local channels. So Steve's saga was quickly forgotten, by citizens and authorities alike. Only remnants remained, of an imaginary life, pieced together by rumors, hearsay, half-truths, gossip, and opinions. As further indication that the topic was completely passé and irrelevant, pretty much everyone also forgot that they'd even forgotten, that there'd been anything to forget, having moved smoothly, indeed, to the next hot topic, the scandal, that is, involving one Ernest Aloysius Dollaway (irrelevant to our tale, as a person, and a story).

'Good!' Mappolo Rei couldn't be happier. What all of this, and the moronic attitude pervading the community, was going to do, was to allow the implementation of the programs without too much scrutiny. The meticulous planning that was required for the various stages, the use of his imagination to conjure up creative ways not only to bring about the changes but to consolidate power and make sure it never ever, ever, slips through his fingers: all of this he could now undertake almost invisibly. On the necessary purge of elements deemed hostile to the well-being of the new regime, post-takeover, he had meditated long and hard, and even taken notes on random pieces of paper. 'On the Elaboration of New Methods for Creation' became the actual working title of another article, the original piece of paper on which it had been noted first finding its resting abode in his back pocket. (He took it out after a long night, before hitting the showers.) 'On the Threat of Anarchy and Hostile Attacks' was yet another title he had scribbled on another random napkin, attempting to make sure he was well-prepared for everything. He had even fashioned charts and diagrams determining not only the sequence of events but the various outposts, each person's duties and obligations, precise timelines for the new resistance and even a bibliography, with many a famous title and many a not, from obscure theorists of revolutionary angst to actual architects of revolutionary upheaval and ultimate victory, including works of revolutionary dreamers who failed to drive the point home, and to show that failure was a real possibility, if not an option. A song even, Mappolo-man wrote, aptly titled 'Revolution Come Carry On'—which the band Bogoloo took a liking to, performed, and ultimately recorded.

And so, no, with all that was at stake, and the details that demanded his attention, he did not mind one bit that the citizens were distracted, encouraged it in fact, would himself have devised a way to manufacture the distraction had he been savvy enough. But it had not been needed: the fiasco had taken a life of its own. 'Good!' he shouted again in his solitude.

In fact, those first nights after his putsch, at work, in the quietude afforded by the utterly mindless task-oriented job—which also afforded him conditions for meditation and creation through ritualistic mechanical repetition (stock stock price, stock stock price...)—he was able to clearly set the new agenda, chart the new path, and design the next phases of:

yes,

a, the,

theee

revolution.

The Inspiring Gathering at the Dawn of the New Era

And thus and so, on an evening soon after all the brouhaha about Steve had died down, Mappolo calls Eddie Perez, Laverneus Doggerel, Sanjip Ray (with a 'y' and no relation), Kriistaa Applbottum, Elvyra Apeltchiks, Askar 'Agha' Goli, Sonya Gullardovski, Tonya Aldamarin, Dolores Delectable and several others to his quarters. Present as well is Gol Dol, who hovers about with his newfound success. (He's been recruited to provide financial backing. Mappolo has even promised to make him Treasurer of Revolution the non-profit organization if, in Mappolo's own words, 'The revolution in the real world thingy doesn't work and we have to take it in a different direction.') Mappolo feels confident, serene, untroubled. He knows he needs to rally the troupes. Unify. Ascertain the loyalties. Reconfirm. Talk and smoke a little. No more putsches, no more betrayals. He must avoid them at all cost. He must persuade the group that there was no need. Or scare them into wanting no part of it. He was no fool, not he, not Mappolo Rei, he would not be another in a long line of vanished ex-tyrants no, he would see it through, not another in the long line of trailblazers and theorists defeated at the end and forgotten while the meek and unimaginative followers got well-off off the fruits of their labor. (He would even recall some of the works from his bibliography. He would not flounder. He was the last standing of the Original Five. And he was going to show it, and make everyone know it.)

Everyone is sitting in the living room of Mappolo Rei's apartment, some lounging on the sofa, some on the ground, one (Sanjip) leaning against the wall. Mappolo, subsequent to all sorts of salutations, walks to the middle of the room, raises arms and brings them down as if asking for the audience to calm down and let him speak, even though no one was really saying much, all decidedly quiet on the front. Mappolo takes a deep breath and welcomes everyone and does an icebreaker and tells a couple of jokes. Then he gets serious and details the plans. They will not drag the process on too long, he says. He calls on them to be courageous, to be brave, to basically suck it up and hit one for the gipper, the gipper being, in this case, not only he himself, but the very principles for which they were fighting. Then, in what surely must go down in the annals of history as one of the most awe-inspiring sports-cliché driven incitements to revolutionary zeal one will probably ever hear, encounter, read about, or invoke, Mappolo Rei, an admittedly zealous sports fan and quite the addict when it came to watching his favorite sports on TV, and who would, by necessity, fall asleep to the lullaby of sports talk radio in the wee hours of the morning, launches into a session unmatched by the most vociferous of preachers, or the most bloodthirsty winning-is-all-that-matters-minded of coaches.

He waves his arms again as if asking for quiet, pauses, clears the throat, and launches:

'We are not going to drop the ball, my people, we are not going to ride the bench all our lives, we are going to get in there and kick some butt!'

All those present cheer. Hip hip hooray, they shout. They feel an unmatched pride. An adrenaline rush. Shivers down their spines. And they even pick up the thread:

'We're gonna step up to the plate! And slash some heads!' Eddie Perez says.

'We're gonna get in the starting lineup! And cut open some hearts!' Sonya G. says.

'We're gonna look those linemen in the eyes,' Laverneus Doggerel says, 'and we're gonna change the play at the line of scrimmage!'

'We're gonna throw a fastball, a whole bunch of fastballs actually, right down the middle,' Dolores Delectable shouts, 'and eat some fresh body parts!'

Mappolo Rei allows the excitement. He is getting to them, he thinks, good, we're all on the same page. He points up, looks downwards, looks heavenwards again and down again and closes his eyes and in a deep sweat, opens his eyes again:

'Sanjip Ray—are you going to rock 'em and sock 'em and eat 'em alive?'

'Hey hey!' Sanjip Ray sings and sways.

'Laverneus Doggerel, are you going to call audibles and let the chips fall where they may?'

'Hey hey, hey hey!' Laverneus Doggerel chants and sways in rhythm.

'Elvyra Apeltchiks, are you going to be a role player all your life or are you going to get in that starting lineup and be a star?'

'Hey hey, hey hey, hey hey!' Apeltchiks says. 'Hey hey and a hallelujah!'

They all sing and sway and do more of the same, an assembly in a trance, a gathering in the deep throes of communal sharing, understanding, upheaval. The rush is necessary—but not enough, Mappolo thinks, ever the worrywart. Time to get to some nitty gritty. Draw some plays. Execute. Xs-and-Os man after all, this Mappolo Rei, even if unexpectedly so. Gonna pull himself up by the bootstraps Mr. Rei. And play some knock-down drag-out ball games. All participants are standing, ready for instructions.

'Already boys and girls, it's time now for us to buckle our chinstraps and go after 'em and butt some heads! We're gonna take it to the hole! Can't have more turnovers or takeovers right? We've shot ourselves in the foot and the head long enough! Gotta take hold of the situation, take some good shots and play some defense, cause you know they're gonna be coming after us with their tanks and their sniffing dogs. Make sure we don't get any of our shots blocked either. Any questions?'

Apeltchiks raises her hand: 'We gonna go for it on fourth?' she asks.

'It'll depend,' Mappolo says. 'Obviously, it'll depend on the circumstances.'

'But what if we run outta steam?' Dolores Delectable asks.

'Then we're just gonna have to catch our second winds and give it a hundred and ten percent!'

Mappolo even points to his Head Case with Steve's head shining in the middle, reminding all that trophies were symbols of victory, the spoils of triumphs!

'We want the heads!' Mappolo Rei says. 'We are a glorious tribe! And we shall collect the heads! And display the heads! And count the heads! After we munch on the flesh of course. This is one that we can be proud of. That is what we are. So let's doggone fill that Head Case until there is no tomorrow!'

'Anything else,' Mappolo asks. The assembled shake their heads and look at one another. Shake their heads some more. Mappolo, despite the frenzy they've gotten themselves into and the obvious determination on their faces and in their hearts, feels restless, a bit fearful given the uncertain future. Like a soldier going into battle, like a child on the first day of school...

'Listen, men and women, we're basically on our one-yard line, driving ninety-nine yards with under a minute left and no time-outs. That's how you gotta look at it. But we're gonna throw some spirals, you hear me, we're gonna open some holes, run through them and all the way in. We're not gonna settle for no field goals, repeat, not gonna settle for no field goals. No ties. We are going to win, and rule, cops and cop-killers alike be damned. We're gonna throw our best pitch on a three two count, and you know why, because none of us—and I look around this room and I see one brave soldier after another, one angelic soul after another—because none of us were afraid to go up in the batting order and hit that homer! Am I right?! Would you be sitting here if you had been? No, of course not. No one here settles for playing DH. We're all a bunch of star quarterbacks who throw vicious blocks on opposing teams' linebackers downfield after a reverse to the wide receiver. Ain't that right?!'

And he punctuates each of his long-drawn exclamations with emphatic chants of: 'Hail the 'Burbs!' and 'Hack those Heads!' and 'Flash that Flesh!'

The frenzy is getting more out of hand than ever. 'Hallelujah hallelujah,' the assembly begins again, truly taken by Mappolo's inspiring words.

'We, I say,' he says, 'we are a bunch of undrafted free agents who played on special teams and gunned their way down that field and worked our way to the practice squad during preseason and subsequently played, played on those special teams on losing teams, and then moved on up to our destined positions on winning teams, and cannibalistic clans—ain't that right?'

And Mappolo Rei again shouts, 'Hail the 'Burbs!' His arm extended, his neck flung back, he finishes: 'Hack those Heads, Flash that Flesh!'

And the congregation once more was up in arms and, hallelujah lordin' in a trance, repeated in deep ecstasy, 'Hack those Heads, Flash that Flesh!'

'We, I say,' Mappolo shouts, 'we give one thousand and one percent, always, we are able to run and stop the run, we say yes coach yes coach yes coach, we don't rock the boat but we don't take crap, we play 'em one game at a time damnit, it's worth repeating, one game at a time, we are, in fact, a bunch who were told to hang up the spikes and instead went out there and swung the bats and swung the bats some more and got into that lineup and weren't afraid to get up and hit the home run in the bottom of the ninth, two on two out, seven five the score, seventh game, ain't that right, my good people?!'

They all sway, they all even pray and stand up almost as if controlled by an otherworldly presence, one line, arms all interlocked, chanting:

The Great Anthem of the Great and Noble Future

Don't get us wrong, we ain't goin' down
We're not benchwarmers waiting around
Happy to risk it all and go for it on fourth
Plowing on and forging forth
Land that triple axel (wooh!)
Crash those boards (crack!)
Smack that pretty boxer (pow!)
Drive that car (vroom!)
O don't get us wrong, we'll head-first slide
We're not sissies sitting on the sides
Happy to plan and ready to execute
Taking aim and ready to shoot
Kick that ball (damn!)
Swing that bat (bam!)
Give it your all (yeah!)
Get that sack (oomph!)
Don't get us wrong, we ain't going down
We're no showboats looking for a wow

Happy to report, lunch pails and hard hats
Going to work, hitting hard the mats
Take that hook (whoosh!)
Sink that putt (ping!)
Curl that kick (yowza!)
Make that shot (swish!)
Hail the 'Burbs! Hail the 'Burbs!
Hack those Heads! Hack those Heads!
Flash that Flesh! Flash that Flesh!

Then they run to the corners of Mappolo's room and pick up pillows and then scatter and pose like cheerleaders and use the pillows and some other garments like pompoms, legs open and arms raised, bodies swiveling down and up, hips to the left, hips to the right, arms up, arms back down,

Em, ay, pee, pee, oh, el, oh
Mappolo, Mappolo
He's our man, our one hero
His name is Rei, ahr, eeee, i
But he's our king
Our one Rey, ahr, eeee, y
Why why why?

Then they all approach, boys and girls, all as if a mob converging towards a fleeing rock star, sliding to him teasingly, making as if to grab his shirt and pants and wanting more, and more, as in private parts,

'Cause Mappolo, Mappolo, Mappolo Rei
He's just that, a great lay.

(Switch to query tone)

Mappolo Rei, hey, Mappolo Rei
Will you—ah-say
Will you please, make our day?
Pleeeeeeeeeeeeeeeease...

(This one was a real come-hitherish, tease-me-not-you-bad-bad-boys-and-girls-you tone of voice, with eyelashes a-flutter and necks sliding back and torsos twisting slowly, and a screechy whispery voice...)

Whaddaya SAY!!!!!

And then: assembly in a trance with pompoms hopping up and down,

Hey-hey, ho-ho
We're all here so let it go—
Hey-hey, ho-ho
Nasty A. had got to go!

They all collapse then, sweaty and out of breath, onto the couch, the chairs, the floor.

The (kind of) Great History of the Great Revolution (October-August)

When all came to, Mappolo, in a much more sedate and calm way, begins to end the session, this most awe-inspiring sports-cliché driven summoning of forces and spirits, by more inspired, inspired, words: pointing to the historical record and reminding folks of the hard path they'd taken to get to this point, prefacing his new speech with the salute and some 'Hack the Heads!' and 'Flash the Flesh!' exclamations and an exhortation to fill the Head Case.

'Boys and girls, men and women,' he says, even though there are only a few men, a few women, and no boys and no girls, 'last winter, when B. led our first attempt at the takeover but gave it all away for a house, great benefits and lifetime security not to mention free wireless service, that devil incarnate traitor-fuck'—the 'other' Mappolo is about to burst out, but he, happily, controls it—'sold his soul and left us all out to dry. For what, you may ask? What else but more convenience, more comfort, more luxury. And more convenience. Surprise surprise. B. always had been a coward, if you ask me, but unfortunately, no one did, not when it mattered anyway... I could tell, every time I looked in his eyes, every time I heard him talk on his phone, every time I saw him in his pathetic attempts to excite and inspire us all, I knew he was bogus, a fraud all the way, I knew it all along, I knew it all just flowed from his pathetic used-car salesman's training, not that he freely volunteered the info either, not that he was proud either, but that's all he was basically, a crook—and he knew it! He got what he deserved, I say, and thanks to C. But recall those dark days, at the beginning, we said then, those of you who were with us then, recall'—only Apeltchiks, in fact, had been there, and soon, Sanjip Ray—'we said we're gonna hold our heads high, walk outta here with our heads held high, and we're gonna come back, and we're gonna stick it to them. We said, I, in fact, said, then, to all those who felt betrayed by B.'s rationalizations, that we were a bunch of point guards, that we were gonna take it to the hole next time, no more standing around and clearing out and letting whoever go one on one, we're gonna take their best shots and put the ball through the uprights. No, we were not going to go O for the world series—no siree, not us, no way. Then, as expected, as we know, inevitable as it is, along to leadership positions moved up C. and D. No rags to riches story in either of their cases, not even a riches to rags one. In fact, no story at all, unbelievable as that may seem, which makes us have to invent one! Well here we go: C. promised to get everyone involved, no superstars, he proclaimed, not on this team, his refrain. That he was gonna play everyone, one through twelve (basketball), all fifty-three (football, pro), all eighteen (soccer), all sixty (football, college), all one hundred (football, college: what it looks like, when they're all coming out of the tunnel and the band is playing that god-awful college fight-song), all twenty-five (baseball), but what happened, he really wanted to be not only the QB, but also to call his own plays and if we let him, run and catch his own passes! Pitch and catch, then hit, get on base and come back and hit again and be a pinch runner! Boxer, ring-master and ring-girl parading between rounds, all at once! He, in other words, not only wanted to call all the shots but he also wanted to take them. All of them. And if he were to miss, he wanted to rebound and have everyone clear out again and he calls the next play, takes the next shot and so on and so forth! What a way to go! C-man leaving his ice-cream truck and his part-time mechanic's duties to run a revolution! C-man hitting the happy-tune button driving around in the summertime in all your neighborhoods, now he's had enough, no longer a lonely ice-cream dude, he would fight or die, he wasn't sitting in no truck sliding no cream in no 'hood no more. Ain't that a trip! No worse than other such grand momentous events in the history of our species, you could argue, and you'd be right, but that an argument does not make!

Well! Was it a surprise when D. thought enough is enough is enough and carried on with *his* putsch! Sure, some said he was just frustrated because his daughter was dating a dreadlocked Rastafarian, and that he might even have impregnated her, but so what. Whatever the pressures he was feeling, he thought the putsch was pretty justified. And in retrospect, it all becomes clear. That's why nothing ever got off the ground: infighting, undermining, power-grabbing and wresting away authority. An infernal cycle. And what did anyone accomplish? Where did we get? C. is now lying who knows where, in some unmarked grave, what with D.'s cruelty prompting him to forgo the casket and in the great tradition of the great revolutionaries of the places we won't name (they know who they are), sent a couple of goons to C.'s family's house and demanded that they reimburse the Committee for the bullets wasted on the tyrannical C.'s execution! Off to another promising start ey! Now along comes D., and what does he do? Sure he gathered the troops and shouted some slogans and made some promises, but what, does, he, do? As in, accomplish? Just managed to alienate his mates some more, go solo, hog the ball, dribble in circles, scramble and get rid of it, always guarding, jealously, the glory he did not, as yet, possess, deluded Hall-of-Famer that he fancied himself. Should I mention, I should not, but I will, that D., that damned D., rode the bench everywhere he went! Junior high basketball team, high school basketball, even the summer league, they just let him on the team! Delusional nincompoop! We've seen plenty of those, and in power too, but D. was really rewriting the whole book on them even! So along comes... The A-train, A-man, A-meister... A... monster is what he was... All the way around, back to the beginning, literally, aleph it is, beginning of all things... Is it any wonder that I, alone, stand before you now, I alone, the only fully, legitimately named bloke on the block? Was it not meant to be? Is it coincidence, chance, fate? I doubt it...'

Mappolo trails off. Everyone mulls the proposition. Never had thought of that one, it was true, he was the only one of the Five with a full, syllabically conventional name. Now, as to what that meant... Most of those present just decided to go along, did not doubt, did not question, objectively that is, Mappolo's lack of, what was it, *nom de guerre*, *nom de plume*, or just a *nom de... nom*? Whatever, they all think right now, whatever.

Mappolo is not finished. 'Well, brothers and sisters,' he launches on his final soliloquy, 'the time has come: I, like you, all these years, have bled big blue. The time has come to get the ball across that goal line, sprint and catch 'em and win at the finish line, pull back with a big shark the fishing pole, jump high and smash the ball over the net (volleyball), end the match on an ace (tennis), double-eagle the last hole and win by one (golf), curl a free kick into the upper corner during injury time (soccer), do an Alley-oop McTwist on the last chance (snowboarding), and a triple-lux-triple-axle at the last turn (ice-skating). We,' he finishes, 'shall write our way, our own way, bar none, to the Hall of Fame, the Mother, I say, of all Halls of Fame!!'

The audience rises, a hearty ovation is given, a passionate applause thunders throughout. Mappolo jumps down from the coffee table from which he's delivered his last words and shakes the hands (yes he does, he finally does, he does indeed!) of all his admirers with genuine sincerity (both hands around the one hand), walking from one to another, as if a general in a parade, in a grand showing of force. 'To our great success!' he cries. 'To the success of the great revolution, Hail the 'Burbs!'

The modification in the chant has not been lost on the

group all along this session. Most are okay with it, and besides... What can they really do...

'Hail the 'Burbs!' the chant goes up.

Everyone then begins to munch on each other's flesh, some biting on calves, some on arms, some attacking legs, others breasts, some even kneeling and eating out some butts.

Amazingly, as naked as they'd gotten, as tempting as they'd made themselves, as seductive as some of the girls were with their thongs on and their see-through bras, and the boys even with their thongs, as much as the relative poses and positions taken by different members would have called for it (O that raising of the butt on her knees on Mappolo's futon Elvyra Apeltchiks, O that macho pose arms flexed facing the vertical mirror hanging on the wall Eddie Perez, O the come hither look fashioned by newcomer Daunte Delabad), orgy-driven as it all seemed, somehow, amazingly (and this perhaps could be traced to the previous promise to keep all such erotic adventures out of the account), there was not only no penetration of bodily orifices by other members' members, but there was not even any finger action or use of toys. In short, no sex at all, and Mappolo would be first to admit that he was not one to discourage such shenanigans. No: incredibly, impossibly, the devoted members of the corps controlled all sexual urges, and engaged only in their most delectable of pleasures, in what to most constituted perhaps not only a pleasure beyond the pure and raw sexual but perhaps the very foundational rationalization on which they had propounded their active participation in the revolution, or this para-commandantist play-acting: none other than their primal cannibalistic urges.

And thus and so: small and big bites, the occasional ripping apart of a small piece of flesh greeted with glee by both parties, amorous munching, sensual swallowing, murmurs as they crawled to one another, and kisses even to the injured parts. And the perpetual reminder that they would not totally rip each other apart here, that in fact they would always be there, for one another, a show of solidarity, the eternal show of solidarity. And the whispers as they crawled and munched were heard:

> *Teenager in the basement*
> *Wallow not despair not*
> *Get off your rocker and dance*
> *Through fate and the 'rents and chance*
> *Get up and make a statement*
> *O teenager in the basement*
> *Put on your tunes and tune out your gloom*
> *And wallow not in this predicament!*

It is time now to go and execute, and leave the great leader to rest. They all pay their respects, tell Mappolo how much they admire him and how fortunate they feel, happy, truly, to be thus engaged, in this movement of liberation. One by one, without doubts and smiling (aaargh, that pathetic serene smile and look of the convinced!), they walk up, kiss his hand, curtsy and file out of the room.

One by one, one and all? Not quite: although he too, had walked up and lined up and kissed the hand, there was, ever-present in his heart, a most definite hesitation. And when he had finally exited the apartment, he thought, but did not articulate, distinctly, in these very terms: 'Mappolo is a complete narcissistic madman, not to mention a total douchebag.' Then, he thought, unbowed, that could mean trouble, big trouble, for all of us...

The name of the doubter, the name of the foe? Reza 'Rey' Irani, a bad-ass fellow with a whole bunch of issues himself, who, on the way out, did not fail to mention the idea to Eddie Perez, who, kind of, agreed.

'You should tell him about it,' the loserish yet wily Irani told Eddie. 'He likes you.'

The next night, at work, while restocking anchovies in the canned goods section, in his apron, at 3 a.m. the store empty, Mappolo has a Vision, an Elham, an Illumination. He slithers to the floor, in convulsions and with terrible shakes, a seizure of sorts that renders him unconscious until, about a half hour later, when a client, looking for some toilet paper, starts shaking him: 'Hey... Hey buddy, wake up,' the man shakes, gently at first, at the shoulder, and a bit more violently afterwards. 'Wake up.'

Mappolo, coming to, groggy, shaking his head, weary, just then realizes that his being chosen has been confirmed, that a message, no doubt, from the guy up above, confirmed that very night, was sent: that he was to lead the flock to the promised land.

'Hey mister!' the client says again. 'You work here, right? Hey—wake up...'

'Yeah yeah, wha...' Mappolo mumbles his answer at first. 'What's up, when... yeah...' And he's lifted himself half-way up, half-sitting position, his legs extended still.

The man (burly, bald) asks: 'You know where the toilet paper's at?'

'Huh?' Mappolo responds, still not totally with it.

'Toilet paper? You guys got any toilet paper?'

'Yeah...yeah...' Mappolo answers. 'Over there, all the way back.' He is pointing to the last aisle, his other hand running through his hair.

'Thanks,' the man says, and he stumbles on over, while Mappolo, as if still in a daze, mechanically follows the short chubby dude's steps (in his decades-old Hush Puppies) to the last aisle.

Mappolo gets up, shakes his head, tells the customer he'll be right back ('No problem,' the reply), goes to the tiny dirty bathroom in the rear (reserved for employees) with the broom and the buckets taking most of the space, splashes a few doses of water on his face and, groggy still, splashes some more until he feels slightly rejuvenated. What has happened to him is a miracle, he thinks, a sign, from up above, or down below, but he's hoping from up above, but definitely from some direction. In front of the mirror, in the bathroom, he already can see the future history textbook's entry,

How Mappolo Rei rose from the ground and began the great march that brought about the total liberation of everyone

He smiles. Victory is close at hand. He smiles again. They have no more time to lose. He frowns. The path is fraught with danger. He grins. No other option but to go forward. He heaves a very very very, *very* deep sigh. Gotta watch out for the traitors.

He walks out. The customer is quietly, patiently standing at the register, nonchalantly going through a tabloid newspaper.

'Oh great,' he says in a nice-guyish kind of way when he sees Mappolo.

He pushes forward his eight rolls of toilet paper in a pack, and puts down the Gatorade bottle and the cereal boxes he's somehow holding under his arm.

Mappolo rings up the items and slides them down and grabs a bag and puts them in.

'Fourteen forty,' he says dryly.

'Here you go,' the bloke says, handing over a twenty-dollar bill.

Mappolo takes the bill, puts it in the register, counts the change and gives the customer all with the receipt that he expertly snatches from the machine.

'Thanks again,' the balding bloke says. 'You have a good night.'

'You too,' Mappolo Rei responds, even though it's, well, the morning.

And as the man's silhouette disappears into the darkness, Mappolo thinks, Get ready for me O world: for I have gotten up now from this goddamn floor!

9

*How Mappolo Rei, upon his Awakening,
summons the lieutenants to his abode to spell out the directives for the next phase*

How they all come with the best of intentions

How the next phase is planned

'Eddie, you got Wednesday, Sanjip, Thursday, Tonya, Friday. Remember: once the car has actually pulled into the ramp,
he, she, is all yours. No way you're losing them guests now
you hear. Don't come across as too panicked either. Fine line
between real panicked and too panicked. If they see you're too
panicked, they might just think to heck with it and drive off.
They gotta think there's a child in danger down there. Life and
death thing. Got it? Heroes and rara stuff. All right?'

'Right on!'—the enthusiastic response.

'Now let's get up and go through it one more time.'

Everyone up. Arms extended. Fake contortions of the face.
Small hops. Like a chorus of cheerleaders, men in the platoon,
football players doing drills on the field, one and all, all for
one:

'Ostrich in a Cadillac! Ostrich in a Cadillac!'

At different rhythms though, with different voices, it all
seems out of sync.

'Sonya, please, don't just hop and shout, right?! It's more
than that! Feel it in your gut! Think of all you're fighting for!
There's hopping and there's hopping with passion! Not shouting! A call! Liberation! Freedom! Feel it! Please! Come on now,

again! And let's not just go through the motions, all right! Let's go let's go! Everyone set. And… Car is driving by, slowing down and…'

'Ostrich in a Cadillac! Ostrich in a Cadillac!'

'Good, good!' chants authoritatively Mappolo. 'Very good! Much better! All right now, this is it folks. This is really it. I'm thinking by Friday, maybe set up another site, off Route 4, you know that exit right after the one with the gas station…'

Eddie Perez is shaking his head. Close to his heart. Not a bad idea, he's thinking. Says as much, after inward deliberation.

'That's a good idea!' he says. 'I think it'll work.'

His opinion of Mappolo still is unchanged. But you have to give the man his due. It is, after all, a good idea.

'We set then?' Mappolo in a cheerful manner asks.

Everyone nods. All happy. All ready.

'Great!' Mappolo says. 'Great!'

How Eddie Perez with unusual gusto and efficiency leads the circle in the number of kills (literal, in this case)

Saturday evening, 7 p.m. Mappolo doesn't work on Saturdays, when the feast was planned. All abductions had been cut and chopped and cleaned and frozen. That morning, Mappolo had arranged a few barbecue grills in the garden and allowed all the body parts, seasoned and soaked, to get ready to perfection. The day before, Applbottum had also purchased the booze and they'd put the legs to marinate overnight. Mappolo had set up the dining room table real nice also—as nice as he could. Bottles of wine on ice, his best china out.

Once the folks have all arrived, one by one, ready at eight, the first thing Mappolo does is toast: 'To our great success, to the success of the great revolution, Hail the 'Burbs!'

'Hail the 'Burbs!' the chant goes up.

Mappolo then walks to the glorious Head Case where he has meticulously assembled a select number of heads of abducted motorists, a reminder of their great triumphs and symbol of their persistent commitment to the ultimate victory. He stands in front of the Head Case and silently stares, looks it up and down, counts even, and recalls some episodes. Proudly gushes, almost cries. But holds his tears through great effort too, and simply smiles and makes a sign to all who acknowledge the great path, the great headway they have made on this journey to power and freedom. Mappolo then turns around and raises his glass. Everyone follows and, arms extend, glasses cling, arms retreat, lips bunch up, open up slightly, forearms bend, glasses at an angle, contents sipped, and swallowed.

'I have the great privilege,' Mappolo begins after all sit down, 'to present this Fleshy Leg Award to our young revolutionary, Eddie Perez.'

Everyone claps. There's jealousy, of course, and envy. Everyone wanted the award, it goes without saying, but only one could actually have it. (Except for Josh: there really was not an envious bone in his body—and it showed. He applauded heartily, smiled, cheered, hollered a lonely 'Yeah!' and some dog-barks even.) Plus, Eddie had done a truly amaaaaaay-zing job. Eddie stands up and grabs the award from Mappolo.

'Eddie assassinated sixteen undesirables and counter-revolutionaries on Friday, and gave us the great opportunity to be able to engorge on a variety of delicious, flavored, slices of human flesh. How many was it again Eddie, eight and eight?'

'Eight and seven,' Eddie says, 'plus the little boy. And a little dog too.' (Addeth he gleefully.)

'There you have it! Well, in any case, kudos and bravo and mashallah! Fabulous work my man!'

Eddie is about to sit when colleagues, prompted by Sanjip Ray, shout, 'Speech! Speech! Speech!'

Eddie stands up again and timidly thanks his mom, his dad, the spirit of the revolution, his mentors and Mappolo, 'and all those bullies in middle school who launched me on this path!'

Everyone laughs. Everyone sits.

'Enjoy!' Mappolo enthusiastically shouts. And, in perfectly choreographed synchrony, a group of four nastily dressed super-leggy super-sexy long-haired big-breasted mavens in French-maid outfits and eight-inch high heels bring humongous trays of exquisitely fragranced human body parts to the table.

'Enjoy, my friends!' Mappolo shouts again. 'To your heart's delight!'

(Genuinely happy for Eddie and fearful that his enthusiastic encouragement had been lost in the excitement, Josh walks up to Eddie's chair, smiling, and from a few feet away already, begins his call that ends with Eddie standing up, twisting a quarter-way and getting a hug and a few quickie taps on the back: 'Duuuuuuuuuuuuuuuuuuuuude,' clamors he, 'congrats!')

How the operation off Exit 4
was launched with great success,
thanks especially to the new leggy recruit

One of the above-mentioned cocktail waitresses, actually. She'd inquired about the reasons for the festivities and been seriously turned on (both literally and tropologically) by Mappolo's explanations. She'd volunteer, she had proposed, 'So you can learn to trust me.'

'Doesn't work that way, hon!' Mappolo had clarified. 'Once you're in, you're in—no two ways about it.'

'I'm in then!' the blond bombshell had bellowed. 'I'm in!'

After a night of devious and deprived sexual scenarios worked out to creepy, bizarre extremes, Mappolo had entrusted her with the new operation at the newest exit. Unable to secure from Gaborski a similarly worthless Cadillac, his bodacious babe would have to adjust the chant to the new circumstances. With those boobies and that booty, he reasoned, sure to haul 'em in! The morning before, he took her through the motions again, just to eliminate any final jitters. Surprisingly though, she was quite comfortable, very at ease, extremely confident.

'One more time!' insisted nevertheless the increasingly paranoid Mappolo. 'Let's do it one more time.'

And he'd go through the motions and the scenario, You're on the curb, a gray Honda's making its way to the exit from the road, you can see it, you're prepared, aaaaaaaaaaannnd—action:

'Parakeet in a Pinto,' babelicious bobbled up and down. 'Parakeet in a Pinto!'

'Great, great!' Mappolo shouted. 'Fantastic! I think you're gonna do great. Marvelous!'

That night, Bernadette (her name) was instructed to go back to Mappolo's pad and to wait (under the sheets, in sexy lingerie). She reported, once upon her lover's retreat, that she'd gotten rid of a record twenty-eight counter-revolutionaries. The bodies were in the freezer, she said—had to hitch a ride though, couldn't carry it all, obviously.

'Obviously,' Mappolo thought, 'but didn't they ask you what...'

'Didn't ask,' she said. 'I made sure of it.'

Atta girl, Mappolo thought, smiling slightly, jealous though, he had to admit…

'There's another thing though,' she said.

'Tell me,' Mappolo said.

And Bernadette told of how her cravings had gotten the best of her and that well…

'Well?'—Mappolo inquires.

'I kinda helped myself—a neck—and balls—two pairs. I left the limp penises though, couldn't handle it.'

Mappolo, in the pose of a ponderer, says:

'Twenty-eight… A neck and some balls… I guess it's all right…'

Then they both burst into a silly laughter… And that night, for the first time ever, they made love—true love that is, the untainted, unperturbed, romantic kind: no toe-licking or high-heel-sucking sessions, no dildo-brandishings of any kind, no fetish masks or harnesses or ropes or leashes, just totally legit, and not sinful: him on top, she beneath, missionary style and official version and all, the truest, truest and most honest of loves.

How in the spirit of the new romantic turn
their relationship was taking
Bernadette Bunns tells Mappolo
she'd rather be a stay-at-home wife
('And, maybe mom?' she lets slip)
of a revolutionary rather than up there on the front lines

'But honeeeeeey,' Mappolo exclaims upon first hearing the news, 'you're our best out there! You know how to close the deals! You know how to finalize those sales! Bernie 'Done Deals' Bunns—remember?!'

This was a few weeks (vagueness in the spirit of imagination filling in) after Bernadette's first triumphant entry into the Drive-By Cannibalism movement.

'I'm tired of standing there and jumping up and down, Mappy honey.'

'So we'll get you a Chevette down there, or an Audi, or a Mercedes, a Lexus, Countach, you name it, we'll change the chant every day. I think I can get Gaborski to give us some deals. Huh? Whaddaya say?'

'I don't know Mappy, I mean…'

'Come on baby, Bluebird in a Benz, Owl in an Audi—can't you feel it?!'

'Well, what about you? How come you're never down there doing the dirty work?!'

Woooooooooooooooooooooooooooooooooooooopppp—siiiiiiiie!

Tension coming! Not a good get! Faux pas! (Elongate please if you will, dear reader, the last syllable of each exclamation, raising simultaneously the pitch of your voice; yes, go back please and indulge me, with the three expressions.) How dare she, after all, question the leader of the revolution!

'First of all,' a genuinely pissed-off Mappolo says, 'I'm the leader, I don't do dirty work. Second of all, missy, I was doin' the dirty work of this goddamn revolution when you were still parading in your silly little maid's outfit at bachelor parties all night, all right?'

'Thirdly—' Mappolo pauses, retreats (anger-wise) and lowers slightly the voice, 'I have a weakness.'

'A weakness? What kind of weakness?'

'Like, you've never noticed?!'

'Well…'

'O come on Bernadette! What do I do when we get together

and munch on the flesh, huh? Don't tell me you don't know!'

Bernadette, taken aback, opening wide the eyes, raising of eyebrows, twitch of the face...

'What's this?'—Mappolo, aggressive, pointing to one, two, several big teeth-marks on Bernadette's legs.

'The hickeys?'

'The hickeys Bernadette, yes, the hickeys! Why are they where they are?!'

'Because... that's where you left 'em?' (Interrogatory affirmative tone.)

'And I left 'em there and not somewhere else be-caaaaaaaaaaaaause...' (Condescending male lover talking down to partner tone.)

'Because?' Mappoloman repeats.

'Because... you like it there I suppose. You like my thighs! I don't know!'

'That's right, Bernadette, that's right! Bravo! Kudos to you Bernie baby! Because I like thighs! I—like—thighs! I like thighs Bernadette! I like thighs too much you see! These boys and girls I'd be leading down to their doom, their carcasses wouldn't last a minute! One thigh, another thigh, and if I'm doin' the thigh thing I'm doin' the legs and so on and so forth! Don't you get it!'

Bernadette got it. She wanted no part of being pushed around by some demented deluded whacko fanatic! If she was not going to be a housewife, she was going to get rid of him and be the queen, or she was, as the proverbial saying goes, outta there. The first thought, although quite tempting, would be too much hassle. She opted for the second—and the morning after the dispute herein reported, she was gone. When Mappolo woke up, he found a note: 'I love you Mappolo Rei—but my love is too strong. It will bring us down.' Corny and cheesy, awkward even, poorly written and with poor spelling too (she had 'wil' instead of 'will'—which I took upon myself in the transcription to correct), but nevertheless touching, heartfelt, sincere—gotta give her that!

Mappolo Rei, alone again, loved her even more.

How Mappolo Rei, flanked by his royal troops, in the parking lot of the Doowat Shopping Center, addresses the crowd

Mappolo Rei standing on his dishwasher liquid box: 'In other words,' he cries preacher-like, 'you're with us already, or you'll be forced to be with us. Ain't no in-between, no gray areas, no complexities or ambiguities or subtleties thank you. Us or not-us, you pick. And I know you've heard this kind of crap before, but hey, too bad. We are an unstoppable force. A force to be reckoned with. With the revolutionary spirit. Spirit of Revolution. Revolution, spirit. Two words that go together well.'

He leans toward Eddie Perez to his right and instructs him to start the next sentence with whichever word finished the last one—and to tell the others to do the same, and so on and so forth. Perez shakes his head in a sign of acknowledgment. Mappolo finishes, '… and great search for justice!' A few isolated claps are heard.

'Justice for the downtrodden,' Perez says and looks at the colleague's suddenly panicked expression.

'Justice for the downtrodden,' Perez repeats with emphasis, gritting his teeth in a definite sign of annoyance. Still, no response from the clueless comrade.

'Downtrodden of the land,' Perez continues—upon which

the next one's enlightened face reveals that she finally got it: 'Oh... Oh, all right, got it!'

'Land of the freaks, home of the crazed,' a certain Persylla Sillipurr says.

'Crazed new world,' Dolores Delectable says.

'World without hunger, a world without debt,' Rey Irani says.

Most of the folks in the parking lot had dispersed, some laughing, literally thinking the troupe to be members of a performance group from the city doing a weekend gig of some sort in these here parts, others thinking them a bunch of bored unemployed zealots. But no one, amazingly enough, took them too seriously. And no one recognized the individual members (they all were wearing face-covering scarves), and no one, at all, suspected that this bunch of scrawny-looking jerks was behind the rash of abductions, disappearances and murders of countless drivers over the past few weeks.

'An invitation has been extended for all to join!' Mappolo screams at the top of his lungs. 'All those who ignore us will suffer at their own peril!'

How the weatherman was kidnapped,
thought potentially to be made a pawn in negotiations,
and his fate decided at a local arcade,
it being real loud and noisy and all,
and so Mappolo and cohorts can discuss in peace
with no fear of eavesdropping or retribution of any sort

The deal on the local weatherman is this: that they'd kidnap him first, think about the rest later. (On his knees, the latter had gotten at the moment of abduction, sudden spasmodic fits, eyes popping out and howls ringing out, prayers and pleadings spewing uncontrollably, mercy for family, friends, and family once more, 'if not I.')

A quick verdict by The Committee to Protect the Righteousness of the Revolution, Be That as it May, led to a meeting at the arcade, in the mall. (Pause here, another long parenthesis opening: who would suspect a gathering of revolutionaries at the arcade, a meeting of future leaders of the globe's leading thinkers, cornered by the noise and chatter of teenagers at the neighboring games? No one, that's who: the perfect disguise, the perfect 'hiding-place' to plan some horrible things, what with the endless array of teens gathered around with girls teasing the boys pulling at them wanting them obviously, even little kids running around, in and out, shouting, crying, screaming, the bigger ones shouting back at them, to leave them alone, to go sit there, to just be quiet, and even to shut up. A concert of noises and beeps and crashes and fake gunfire and folks killing each other on the make-believe screens, screams, from the players and from every corner, yeahs and hoorays, shouts, hugs, tricks, kisses too, slaps, all around and from all parts, the little girl from under her sister's watch rebelling letting go of her hand as big sis is not paying attention, paying no mind to the little one and so she runs away, just a dash, directionless and big sis smiles at the boy she's clinging to and sighs and tells him to wait up and turns and shouts Washana and takes several giant steps (towards Washana), except that resourceful Washana skips and glides some more through the tree-legs of this forest, her forest, until big sis grabs her, by the coat, pulls her back, and they walk back to the boy, him getting ready now, his turn at the pinball, he was patiently waiting, now fixes his cap and straightens his torso and readies the arms, and a quiet man ready for battle steps up and suddenly like a ticked-off madman pushes and hops and yells and pushes some more, more buttons, hops, yells, damns, yos, whooshes, more yos, and again and again and, damn, one lost, two to go, did pretty well though on the first ball, turns and quick kiss on the lips of the girl holding Washana, quieter now she, in her own little dreamworld gazing all around soaking it up, so it seems. Next door a group of four hark and bark in turn and yack and look left right and shout out an obscenity here, another there, group of pals, slaps and silly punches in the air and poses of thugness all a pose though, they'd be first to admit, they know... Next to them, three other boys engaged in similar chicanery except that at least they got a couple of girls with them, maybe not with, but there, next to, hitting on, hitting with, whatever, all around and all about rising the grunts and voices and the hollers, the teens trying to get away from overbearing parents, munching on their chips and their burgers and their fries and their nachos, all the idle ones, hanging, all around, about, playing, laughing, cajoling, all, except, except for our four, our bunch, our creepy creepy wannabe revolutionaries, who do they think they are, you must wonder when you get down to it, just play the goddamn games but no, gotta go, for it all, and assemble here...)

The Council, huddled around a Pacman game (still around, that sucker, I was just there), was to determine how, if at all, the captive could be put to good use.

'They trust him,' Dolores Delectable says, wisely. 'He's a soothing presence, you know, comforting, trusted. He's the one they turn to, cozy under the comforter after a hard day's work, remote in hand, here he comes mister friendly weatherman man, with his soothing voice and his graphics behind him making us feel like the world is all right, all is in its right place, a magician of sorts this fellow, a seer, a friend, looking out for you even (who else on TV looks out for you, directly, oh so genuinely), looking out for us (actual quote, 'Bundle up when you head on out that door!'), the kids even (actual quote number 2, 'Kids on the bus stop tomorrow make sure to have that hot breakfast!'), the house even (actual quote number 3, 'It's sunny but cold so don't let the sun fool ya!'). He's their friendly neighbor, their trusted companion, the one who tells them what to wear, what to take. I tell you, we can use him good: if he tells them to switch, they switch, if he gets hurt for any reason, then watch out, the mobs in the streets. They swear by him, I tell you, they swear by the weatherman; and so, he's the best bargaining tool we've got.'

'He'll betray us!' thunders suddenly the dissenting Elliott Nagooski, stern unblinking gaze and all. He adds: 'He'll tell them to switch and once we let him go, he'll turn around and stab us in the back. I tell you, I know his kind. Plus,' Elliott pauses, his facial expression changes, 'plus... I actually, literally, know this guy. We went to Walter Johnson together. Played a little ball too. He's the kind, you know, sit in the front of the class, junior year he even brought an apple to the chemistry teacher, made it look like he was kiddin' and all, like a joke, parodying the whole idea but that was a guise itself, the parody, his whole act, the guy meant it I tell you, ass-kisser that he is, it was just like him, and everyone knew it...'

'What does junior year have to do with our goddamn plan?' Mappolo barks back at Nagooski.

'Everything,' Nagooski says forcefully and defiantly. 'Don't you get it... All's he wants to be... All things to all people, at all times... Why do you think he's the weatherman?!'

Mappolo turns around in frustration. Did Elliott have some sort of beef with this guy or what? Some unresolved complex of sorts? What kind of grade did he get in that class anyway? Elliott was, after all, a dropout, a wicked and tortured soul who did go ahead and take classes at the local community college after getting his GED, although he was a smart fellow, no doubt about that. No one could figure out his agenda though, and that was the big issue: what he was up to, what he really wanted, whether he was just a slave to his cannibalism, in ways that, lo and behold, not even the other cannibals in the gang could relate to… His father's suicide? The conjecture had once been brought up, between Mappolo and A., of all people, and it could not be discounted that the event precipitated his unapologetic forays into extreme cruelty. Maybe his mom abandoning him when he was a baby: that alone can scar you for life! And then when the first wife left him… Poor Elliott, Mappolo thinks, who knew he'd turn out to be such a screw-up. But then again, Mappolo thought, I was a dropout too, although I at least got into a good school! So… To Sanjip and Dolores, his other trusted advisors, he says, askingly: 'Well?'

'I say we keep him, not hurt him, see what happens…'—Dolores.

'I say we let him go… Mistake from the beginning, just let him walk… Don't need him anyway…'—Sanjip.

Mappolo turns to Nagooski.

'Elli, and you?'

'I say we get rid of him. Cut him up, chop him up, miam miam miam. Isn't that our motto? I mean, you guys are giving this populace way too much credit. Besides, it's too late. We get rid of him like everyone else. Ain't gonna be no riots, trust me, they'll just go along with the next guy they're fed, next guy they put in front of that camera. You know it too. All just cardboard frames. Don't matter who fills them. Make you believe anything… Want anything… All just frames…'

Then, getting more and more agitated as the weatherman's fate was obviously prompting digressing thoughts, he says, softly (strange, the softness of his voice at that juncture): 'I'll cut him up myself… You guys don't worry…'

The decision is now Mappolo's. He excuses himself as he always does at times of such great stress and tension, walks a few paces to the Galaga game, bends over, drops in a couple of quarters in the slot and begins to play.

Quite expert at it and always trying to beat his own record, Mappolo considers this his domain, his chamber, the room where the toughest decisions are made, his rock and boulder, for meditation and contemplation. Half hour later, him back, the three associates by the side of the legendary leader, waiting, eagerly.

Mappolo takes a deep breath, raises his arm, puts a hand on Sanjip's shoulder (to his left), another on that of Dolores (to his right), and stares straight ahead:

'Elliott,' he says, turning to him, 'he's all yours.'

No one panics, no one shouts or is upset or overjoyed. In fact, no one shows any emotion. Not as if they'd won a date or some other privilege on a game show, no. Nothing. Except that, Nagooski does smile, that is true, and it must be pointed out.

'But,' Mappolo adds, 'save me the thighs, will you?'

Elliott smiles again: 'Will do, boss, will do.'

(Oooh, Mappolo thought upon hearing the word 'boss' in context, I like the sound of that!)

***How revolutionary Drive-by Cannibalism
was accelerated and the populace
warned again of the impending takeover***

Macau in a Mercedes! Finch in a Festiva! Loon in a Lu-minary! Eagle in an… Eagle (Jeep)! The Vision was now un-

daunted! The Ambition was now immeasurable! The Con-
clusion was now inevitable! Capital letters all around for this
Revolution! This Populace! This Leader!

On command of Mappolo, the number of posts were increased. In addition to the two stations manned by different
folks on a rotating basis, several more were set up, including
one at the exit to The Great Price Company, the most ambitious project yet, given the higher number of cars passing. And
yet another before the last exit to the freeway. A Cadillac had
been procured for the previous, but none for the second, where
a Dodge was the only vehicle available.

A great many motorists had thus succumbed to the particularly grotesque form of devastation perpetrated by these
unknown thugs. The authorities were helpless. They admitted as much ('We're helpless!') and admitted to the population that they'd done all they could ('We've done all we can!')
and couldn't do more ('Can't do more!'). Amazingly though,
not too many people cared or asked questions. Or even wondered. Whatever the authorities said, they kind of went along
with. And the authorities soon said that despite their being
helpless and having done all they could and not being able
to do more, there was really nothing to worry about and the
whole issue would soon subside. Further, no national troops,
guards or military personnel were called to duty in this suburban hamlet, no one quite knows why. For a very slim minority
though, things, to borrow the words of young seven-year old
Nathan excluded from participation in a youth soccer game
(that his team had apparently won) because his mother had
been ordered off the grounds for excessive heckling of the poor
teenage referee in a previous game, sucked.

What's for certain is that the physical landscape of an idyl-
lic place was a-changin', what with no one, not even petty

thieves, engaging in any way in clearing the emergency lanes of the great variety of motor vehicles (that one usually sees either in balletic motion on freeways, or in halted stop-and-go thrusts at traffic lights, or serenely parked in parking lots right next to one another next to one another, unoccupied yet somehow, somehow, tranquil, unperturbed, awaiting only the next arrival of their masters), all now queued up in an awkward, troublesome, eerie way, without drivers or passengers, and with that uncanny suggestion that none were forthcoming, that a perfectly fine and fabulous car, with money due on it for sure, was just sitting there, abandoned like an unwanted puppy, left to fend for itself in a cruel world, like the horse of a fallen soldier in wars of long-ago, like a child who has lost mommy in a vast chain store (drug, grocery, toy), like a lone antelope somehow gone astray and now alone in the wild, the herd having moved on. Amazing. One would have thought that at least the dealerships would send agents to pick some cars up, or that the emergency route services would post a warning of some sorts. But, noooooooooooooooo! Nothing! Nada! The lone voice rising was that of Mappolo Rei, who, on this the last Saturday of the month again gathered the troops in the parking lot and with the weary citizens dutifully doing their shopping before going to the mall for more shopping, once more from High Atop His Dishwasher Liquid Box, told them to beware, for the takeover, was close at hand.

How the attempts by citizens to come to grips with the various disappearances fell short

How the preparations for the takeover intensified

But where O where had all the motorists gone?! And why were their cars abandoned? No one knew for sure. The mystery was grand. Real grand mystery. 'Maybe it has something to do with those folks we see at the exits jumping up and down,' a brilliant nuclear physicist living in the area had voiced in a scarcely attended town hall meeting. But his loony suggestion was quickly dismissed and other potential causes explored. No explanation, however, was agreed upon and so no explanations were given, and everyone just agreed that you know what, the events were incomprehensible and that was that. Let's just pray and move on.

Meanwhile, Mappolo Rei and the Drive-by Cannibals had successfully recruited a whole bunch of eager new members ready for the final takeover. The plan was a multi-step process.

First, block all entries into the hamlet by closing off the exits from the freeway: delegated, this most crucial of tasks, to Dolores Delectable. (Delectable Dolores Delectable! What a name! In the annals of the great real names parents give us! And your nickname an echo of your surname! Never did mind it though Dolores. She'd always been popular in school. Well-liked among the jocks as well as the nerds and the regular guys too. Most likely to succeed even, she was voted in the year-book... Still, something bigger, perhaps that same idealism that had prompted her classmates to bestow such early honors on her, had precipitated her abandoning all conventional paths for the future. She never did regret it though (she either truly believed or tried to convince herself), even now she was well-liked by everyone, without even trying. And it was conceivable, and not impossible, that she leave the ranks and join again the civilians, get her full-time job in conglomerate office, dedicating herself to one good cause or another. Her mom would have gone for that, it was never too late, never too late, pondered Delirious Dolores Delectable, pondered Delicious Dolores Delectable, O Dolores how I long still for your touch, how I'd give anything to feel again your silky hair, your long legs wrapped around me, Delirious Dolores, my Dolores, my Dolores, how we should have eloped then, when we had the chance, before this whole mess started, I warned you, I told you, but always your idealism got in the way, always you needed to, wanted to, ahhhh, I cannot even finish the sentence, cannot even go on, perhaps an ode to you this whole account, an angry ode though I say, in your memory, for you, dedicated to you, O Dolores of my pains, Dolores of my dreams, wherefore art thou Dolores, O my Dolores Delectable…)

Second, have people in the parking lots of major shopping centers ready to announce that a takeover was taking place and that the new leadership was about to seize power: small suburb, twelve major shopping centers, eighteen million minor ones, hmmm… Mappolo reasoned that maybe Apeltchiks could drive around from one shopping center to another and just deliver the news, yes, that was a better idea, rather than have someone stationed at each, for cryin' out loud, the goddamn shopping centers outnumber the entire revolutionary corps! Delegated, thus, to: Elvyra Apeltchiks. ('All you have to do,' Mappolo had excitedly explained to Elvyra, 'tell them that the takeover is taking place. That's it. Everyone will roll with it.')

Third, contact local radio and TV channels and announce over the airways that the takeover had taken place. No seizure was necessary, no forceful entry called for, no violence. All that was needed were calls to the various stations, for them to make the announcement. On a.m. talk shows, the task was easy enough. On f.m. and TV, a little more delicate, but surely the urgency of the matter could be explained to the operators and a quick bringing-up-to-date suggested. Most would go for it, the bet was, and then one news agency, one channel, one program would pick up the startling developments and the bug would spread by itself. Finally, local police and the forces of the law would be contacted and ordered to join the new government or lay down their arms, surrender completely, and no blood would be shed. The theory was that with the momentum, most would volunteer to join the new government, and that a smooth transition would take place. If all went according to plan, Mappolo would soon be calling Delectable and ordering her to unblock the exits and let the flow begin, and saying, out loud, the revolution has been victorious. At the very thought of the utterance, Mappolo felt an energy flow through him: the revolution has been victorious, he mumbled within, the revolution has been victorious... Wow, he thought, wow, he imagined, wow—he whispered, wow.

O people of the Suburban Motherland
O diners in the Food Court at the Mall
Now will you heed the call
O people getting fat at the Food Court at the Mall!

Arise all you dining fools!
Arise from your plastic stools!
Arise and salute this greatest of falls
O patrons of the Food Court at the Mall!

The revolution has been victorious
Extend your arms and put on a happy face
And grow your beards even—not!
O patrons of the Food Court at the Mall!

The revolution has been victorious!

That phrase, Mappolo in wonderment in ecstasy gazing silently ahead, that phrase almost made him come, it's true, but it was more than that, honest, a grand dream is what it was... Wow, he whispered again within, wow, it truly was all worth it, it truly was all worth it, even if just to utter that one, brief, phrase. The completion of the task was close at hand, unbelievable as it seemed, it was close at hand. The revolution... has been victorious.

How Mappolo's interior voice once again (again!) gives itself permission to intrude

You see there Mappolo Rei, you almost didn't believe it yourself, didn't believe, thought for a while there that nothing other than a loser I was, working away, plowing away, thinking I know, that one day... They said no child with Dehir's Syndrome could ever make it, alive that is, let alone past the sixth or eighth or twelfth grade, or college, for that matter. So what if your phobia presented unforeseen problems where others know no such thing and take their conceptual beliefs for granted: it's not your fault that you have a perpetual fear of the conceptual framework presented to you, lo, imposed upon you. A perpetual state of paranoia it is not. You did try to do something about it, Mappolo Rei, give yourself that, in good old American tradition, did give more than a 100% and try to change things, enlighten, educate, but no one would have it, what for, they live their permanent state of comatose belief quite nicely thank you. You made your own discoveries, Mappolo Rei, remember, the last half of the descriptive analysis of the disease, which you contested was crucial, for it was that which distinguished it from the immensely more prevalent form known as anxiety. Or depression. Depression anxiety paranoia, in whichever order: of course they want you to believe that, but you overcame, you knew better, you knew it was just a matter of not accepting things as they are, because you, Mr. Rei, are a revolutionary, and the ways of the world as they have been drawn, they ain't for you. Say it loud, Mappolo Rei, say it clear: your day is coming, fearful of conceptual frameworks that you proudly proclaim you are, your day is coming! And you can now call that half-assed bitch Mariann Sussvoll, that old girlfriend of yours on the cheerleading squad, who through her excessive trysts and self-love and an abundance of confidence made your self-esteem plummet, and you can tell that bitch and her full scholarship and her nauseous career as a corporate executive to shove it all down her newest boy-toy's ass, then promptly go to hell, better, to then come back and suck yours dry, you, Mappolo Rei, and better no armchair therapists now smiling discovering that this whole revolutionary gig is just a response to the scars and the traumas of adolescence left by that cunt, they'd know their fates too if they try (please, go ahead, say it, try, say it!), because you, you, Mappolo Rei, el rey indeed, de los suburbos, the king of all kings of all, all, all, suburbs, shall now, ruuuuuuuuuuuuuuuuuuuule!

How the delegated tasks go according to plan and the revolution, victorious, takes over

The entrances to Whooton were blocked. Passing motorists didn't much care, and the few who wanted to exit were told there was an emergency in town, and all exits were closed until further notice. No one really seemed to mind. In fact, they were understanding and helpful. In the shopping center and at the mall parking lots, the news of the takeover failed to provoke much of a stir. Most folks seemed to be pretty much a-okay with the news. Few revolted, fewer still bothered to ask questions. And even fewer than that seemed to care. Didn't matter. Nothing mattered. It all just rolled along. They would go, day after day, just go along with the regular routine. Get up and shower and clean up. Get dressed and drive. Get in the car and turn it on and pause and turn, arm resting on passenger seat's back. Lean and pull out of the driveway, slowly go along their treelined streets and up to the traffic light and right or left, then on to the ramp and the highway, maybe some have stopped and grabbed their coffees and now, music or talk radio hosts accompanying them, they bring the coffee to their lips and smile and frown in accord with what's on their car's radio, merrily driving down, then all of a sudden, road rage, some nasty words hollered into the windshield will do, quickly compose self, bumper to bumper stop and go traffic, the sun in their eyes, stop and go, stop and go, more curses and then drifting away, one with the machine they drive and drift away, somehow they get on the highway and it all goes according to plan, they drive along and not get in any accidents and in fact get off the correct exit and go into the parking lot and park and say hello to attendant and get into the office soon and say hello to the receptionist. Slow march to paper work on desk. Sit ass down, sigh (inward for most), check messages and email, get back to folks, meeting soon, hey how are you good and you thanks and you good, reports, discuss, back to office and return more calls, hey what's up what's doing, not much and you, check some email, respond, water-cooler time, water-cooler gossip follows, water-cooler small-talk next, the game or the elimination of the candidate on reality show, lunchtime soon which means lunch break, already thinking of what to eat, planning that is, wander out to the court at the mall and eat, O food court at the mall, we welcome you with open arms that's for sure, or come back and eat at the cubicle, the grand cubicle, O the cubicle O, it's true I do have a boss, don't necessarily like taking orders, have this on my desk at, I'd like my coffee with, it's all a matter of, being there for someone else, but still, but still!

I'm the cubicle maestro
Like my uncle says I let it show
I'm happy with my cubicle
So haaaaapppy with my cubicle!

I'm not telling tales in the subway caaaaars
Singing songs in the dirty paaaaarks
Taking handouts from a rich-ass sugar daddddyyyyy
I only wish I were a trust-fund babbyyyyyy!

'Tis true I like my cubicle
'Tis a place so magical
I like all the folders I work on all day
I like the memos and thumbtacks and emails
And I love! Just love! All the letters sent my waaaaay!
Not to mention: pictures of my famillllllllayyyyy...

Food court or cubicle for lunch: verdict will have to await result of emergency meeting in boss's office. And that's just that.

Again, I repeat: no one knew what was going on. And perhaps worse: no one seemed to care!

The exception to the rule proving the rule, a young man with long dark hair, shouting an impassioned, 'Never, never, Whooton belongs to the people!' was simply ignored, in accord with Mappolo's directives of limiting all violence and senseless shedding of blood. (Contradiction? Not really! Why make a fuss after all, the idea was, let them scream and not matter, let them contest and dissent in the void, rather than kill or censure or imprison them and make martyrs of them all.)

'Great!' Mappolo said when his lieutenants came back with one after another good news about the completion of the takeover. 'Let the festivities begin!'

He ordered Dolores to open the exits, and the traffic flow went back to normal. The calls to the stations also went according to plan, although the responses were not of the desired ilk. Incredibly, and to the bewilderment of Mappolo and all his cohorts, all national and international news agencies and all all-news channels and other propagandist formats totally failed to pick up the story and failed to report the incredible developments. There were no news choppers hovering above and no blimps floating about. No cameras and no crews and no annoying reporters to notice that... that... there was no movement on the ground? That, in fact, absolutely nothing was different and absolutely nothing was happening? Is that why no one requested to speak to the leader of the movement, and so Mappolo could not clearly and proudly rebuff their request, and could not let his people know to tell their people that there will be an announcement that evening, at 8 p.m., a press conference of sorts, because none was forthcoming?

In other words, told that The Takeover (capital letters now!) had been completed, and that the revolutionary government was now in place, none of the representatives of the news media decided exactly to skip Mappolo's speech, since they never had intended to cover it, which really means, by extension, that there would be no press conference! 'Who the hell are these jokers anyway,' one news media mogul was heard telling his associates on his private plane when asked if they should go ahead and cover the happenings in the far-flung hamlet: 'To hell with 'em!'

'Fuck 'em!' Mappolo in turn enraged had exclaimed when told of the media's attitude and decisions. 'They can all come suck my balls!'

Finally, when the police and other forces of the law were contacted to join the 'new government' by the young recruit Sindull Doolpop, she reported that 'Yes! They're in!'—for indeed, a desk-clerk on the other side after telling her to hold on and after talking to his superiors about what he should say, giggling, had answered her, 'Sure, count us in, count us in,' and had hung up, still deliriously laughing it up with his colleagues in the background.

But no, Mappolo Rei and his cohorts would let nothing stand in the way of these celebrations. The road had been long and tough (although not that long or that tough, if you really thought about it), the suffering great (not that great). No one, repeat, no one, would stand in the way of these celebrations!

For good measure, Mappolo took the Jag to the parking lot and swerved noisily and parked the car (illegally, again) across two lanes, right past a terrified woman who dropped her shopping bags staring incredulously at this, no doubt about it, madman, mouth agape, hands in front, while several others, including a lady in front of the bank, close to the drive-through, quickly turn around, as sudden unusual screeches tend to incite one to do, only to watch this out-of-control freak jump out without even turning off the car, leave the door open, open wide the arms, throw head back and twist: around helicopter-like and scream, 'Fuck 'em aaaaaaaaaaaaaaaaaaaaaaa aaaaaaaaaaaaaaaaaaaaaaaaaaaaaaaalllllllllllllllllll!'

10

The freezers had been emptied again and once more the French-maid attired beauties had paraded around in Mappolo's dwelling. Party again! Donkeys had been brought in for some no-way-I'm-not-censoring-scenes-here types of depraved fun. Dancers of all kinds had giggled and wiggled and pranced around like there was no tomorrow and paused before the ever-growing and quite impressive Head Case, wondering aloud where those had come from, and on occasion looking and asking about the provenance, the price, the proprietor, and the prospects of their one day resting in a great museum. In what amounted to a scary moment that did mercifully pass without incident, one of the invited strippers seems to have actually recognized one of the heads in the case, turned in fact and told her pal, 'You know, that's incredible, that looks like this guy I've seen a bunch of times, that's his head, hadn't seen him for a while, I thought maybe he didn't like my,' and then she'd stopped cold and banished the possibility from her thoughts (perhaps having recourse to the common human automatism that banishes the unthinkable—the uncouth unthinkable— from one's system), and even followed her comments with a sudden skip and scream and joining of the carousing crowd, which did bring a sigh of relief to Mappolo, who'd been warned by a scrupulous associate to pay attention to the unfolding potential drama.

The party had gotten so loud in fact, so crowded (crashers had crashed and helped themselves, unaware they were feasting on human flesh), and so out of hand, that a whole bunch spontaneously transferred the good times to the big party room down in the basement of the condo where Sanjip Ray lived.

The revelry lasted through the night, with Dionysian overtones manifesting themselves to quite preposterous extremes, followed by pure orgiastic activity unbecoming a light-hearted narrative such as this. Question was: now what? It is true that in their original formulations for the necessity of the revolution, and through the many debates and discussions, hurling of insults and objects, back-stabbings and back-slappings, ass-kissings and toe-lickings, and even the *rédaction* of a mini anti-manifesto, *What Shall We Do: The New People's Revolution of this Great Suburban Hamlet Known as Whooton*, certain policies had been formulated. But over the months, through the struggles and the internecine warfare and the daily grinds, these lines of thought had been, excuse my French, flushed down the john. To the point where, absent all irony even, Mappolo, an otherwise intelligent and industrious fellow as we've come to know him, could not even remember what the whole thing was about, and what, if anything, they were to do now. Sure, he recalled some vague notions about helping the poor, utterances on concepts such as equality and justice and more parking space and a better management of the traffic flow, some drivel on the reform of tax laws and minor quality of life issues like potholes and traffic lights that don't switch quickly enough—but truth be told, he couldn't remember much else. Neither excessive preoccupation with wresting power away from A. (sure it was planned, of course, just looking for an excuse is all…), nor his subsequently increasing paranoia had been of much service in the creative conceptualization and implementation of new paths. His zeal for sports and for following them on TV, and his excessive taste for long celebrations and orgiastic festivities were also wearing thin on some of his lieutenants, those frontline soldiers who had gone through, *pardonnez mon français*, hell and back, jumping up and down and leading strangers astray and murdering and chopping them and then eating them along with pals. More than anyone else, Eddie Perez, the valiant (yet eclipsed) youngster, still wide-eyed about the possibilities the revolution represented, and even more convinced of Mappolo's increasing irrationality and delusional sense of grandeur, decided he was going to confront the leader—now is the time, yes it is.

Eddie Perez, gas station attendant by day, rock 'n' roll dreamer by night, was indeed a peculiar type. An idealist of sorts who most agreed could easily have studied some productive trade or even gone on to major in the humanities at a prestigious East Coast liberal arts college in pursuit of a lucrative career in politics or a plush one in academia, he had somehow slid down that inescapable path of gloom and wretchedness that seized the soul of the young and unsuspecting in this outpost, perhaps all such outposts. A talented guitarist who'd actually had a whiff of *enfant prodige* status (he'd even performed with a blues legend on stage at the tender age of twelve), a genius pointed out early in childhood on which of course he did not capitalize, he became, as his slide mercilessly continued and intensified, more and more disenchanted and disillusioned about rescuing his own future, not to mention soul. Whence the slight inconsistency in his behavior, since he did, besides the need to satisfy his cannibalistic urges, actually care about the direction of the society that had done its best and in part succeeded, to ruin him. Legend has it that he even dated, albeit for a few inconsequential months, none other that Dolores Delectable, Dandy Dolores, *my* Delicious Dolores. His rock band was a well-known entity around town, playing the small circuit of clubs, even coming close to inking a modest but nevertheless significant deal with a not-so-major recording label. Fell through though, and Eddie was not surprised, these types of things rarely happen the way they should. And so he, liberal leader of the band, along with its mostly changing cohorts, survived with meaningless and menial jobs in the day, getting high and drunk and angry at the world at night, treacherously close to the abyss with suicidal thoughts swirling deep within. The only possible salvation? Through the one and only possible recourse, of course, the revolution as always, the revolution—or else, art.

> *O teenager in the basement*
> *O teenager in the basement*
> *Never fear your debasement*
> *O teenager in the basement*
> *Don't give up the runs along riverbanks*
> *Don't just knock your head against the tanks*
> *Stop the rockin'*
> *Blow off the hiphoppin'*
> *Halt all the rappin'*
> *And the bad-ass school pranks!*

When he'd written that song, when he'd jotted down the whole anthem of this lost and lonely bunch, Eddie Perez, the immortal bard of the 'burbs, forever to be known as the singer/songwriter who gave the world Teenager in the Basement, never would have guessed how prophetic his words would one day sound:

O teenager in the basement
O teenager in the basement
Don't be silly
It ain't all that bad not all so gloomy
New kids will come and you'll grow old
With a job and a car and pets and a family
And your own teenager
Your own teenager
Your own teenager
Do you hear me
Your own teenager
In the basement
O your own teenager in the basement
Wallowing in his or her predicament!

And here's where he lets rip into his world-famous chorus:

O teenager in the basement
O teenager in the basement
Wake up from your slumber
O teenager in the basement
Think about your predicament!

Get your chin off the pavement
Get your soul out the gutter
Get your mind off the stripper
Get up and make a statement!

I am, I am, I am—
A teenager in the basement
Sick—and tired!—of strumming my lonely guitar!
Sick—and tired!—of dad's old beat-up car!

Sick—and tired!—of staring at blank walls!

Sick and tired, sick and tired, sick and tired
Of fakin' all my higggggghhhhhhssss…

And passin' out on the
Cheap-ass
Devil-red
Old-style
Lazy-chairish
Motha-fuckin'
Beeeeeeaaaaaaaaan baaaaaaaaaaaaaaaaaag!

It is the morning after these greatest of festivities, Mappolo is just recovering and has decided for the time being to continue to reside in his humble quarters (as the press release conveyed, for he would continue to be 'a humble leader, without pretense or pompous ways'), that Eddie goes to see the leader.

Eddie knocks and enters (the door has been left open) and sees quite the mess in the living room. He goes toward the bedroom, knocks and again, purposely, strategically, not waiting for a reply, immediately opens and barges in.

'What the f…!' Mappolo from under the sheets, startled, jumping. A young man also suddenly jumps up panicked and wraps some sheets around his obviously naked body and scurries into the bathroom.

'Eddie! What the fuck are you doing?!'—Mappolo.

'Hello Mappolo, do you have a minute?'—Eddie.

(Eddie never said hello, not only not in that tone, but basically never even the word. Always a hey, a hi, a variation thereon—but hello? Uh-huh, don't think so! So, something is up:

all of this racing through Mappolo's mind in a nano-second.)

'A minute?! What the fuck! No I don't have a minute Eddie. What the—!'

'It's important,' Eddie insists, calm and collected.

'Goddamnit!' Mappolo mumbles as he drags his tired body out of bed.

He walks to the bathroom and knocks and says: 'We'll be in the living room Eddy hon.' (Another Eddy, thinks Eddie, but is it with a 'y' or an 'i e'?—I confess I merely used the more common/logical option, uncertain of Mappolo's new plaything's spelling preference.) 'Don't sweat it, all right, take your time…'

Throws pants on and walks Eddie out to the living room. 'Want something to drink Eddie?' he says, with obvious irritation but also with obvious big-brotherish sentiments for the young man, even though he's not even older than him! Mappolo is, after all, a gentle soul—and knows how to appreciate a job well done. Eddie answers curtly in the negative, that he's fine, that he just wants to talk. Mappolo, sliding on the couch with his robe over his jeans and throwing his feet on the still cluttered coffee table (knocking a glass and a shoe out of the way, actually, to let rest comfyly his feet), asks the young man what's on his mind.

Eddie says, It goes something like this, I don't know that I like what's going on, and Mappolo says, What do you mean Eddie, what do you—what's going on, and Eddie says that with all the parties and the celebrations and festivities, Is this why we killed and cut up all those people, is that what the revolution was all about after all now, nothing changing, was it necessary? And Mappolo, now getting a good sense of the threat that Eddie might currently or one day pose, but not wanting to let on to his recognition, and loathing with every second that passes the young traitor more and more, says, I don't understand what you're trying to say Eddie, what do you mean what's going on, what IS going on? And Eddie says, I don't even know, really, I mean, all this stuff, all this booze and this, this fucking and these banquets and all this coup crap; and Mappolo says curtly, Actually I don't Eddie but I'll think about it, you know I respect you so I'll think about it. And he's already gotten up and has forced Eddie into escorting him out and Eddie's up and half-heartedly walking out sort of nudged out to tell the truth while Mappolo tells him that he promises him, he'll be thinking about it.

On his way home, Eddie Perez is reviewing his mission. It's not how he wanted it to go frankly. Somehow in the presence of the mythological figure that Mappolo was fast becoming, he'd become timid, uncertain, hesitant. Which is really weird, because he never felt that, as anti-authoritarian as he was, he'd get intimidated or cheated in such circumstances. Lost track of his plan even, let alone the forceful confrontation he'd dreamed up. Too bad, he thought, but he should not be so hard on himself. There was a long road ahead. A great future. A bright and wondrous future!

That same day, shortly after six, soon after Eddie had been back from work and lounging in front of an afternoon talk show exploring the topic 'My Lover Wants to Kill Me and I Just Found Out', there was a knock on his door.

'Who's there?' Eddie shouts, tired.

Knock knock.

'Who's there?' Eddie shouts again, louder, tired still, and slightly annoyed.

Finito, a voice says.

Finito who, Eddie says.

Finito Parati, the voice says.

The gang then barges through the door. Eddie Perez up in panic, the television's sound drowned out by the commotion and the hullabaloo but the figures still prancing about with participants fuming and angry faces and punches thrown and subtitles under evoking studio audience's feelings, three masked men grab Eddie, one putting him in a chokehold and holding him down as the others hit him and bring his arms back and put handcuffs on him and keep beating him as the young lad lets out primal screams muted though quickly by the hood placed on his head while the television's sequence of actions, that no one has watched (except for I), eerily, supernaturally, I'm tempted to say Impossibly (with a capital I, even though it's an adverb), mimics the live actions in the room with, I'm guessing, the 'potential killer' being subdued by the host's army of security detail. Eddie, meanwhile, is dragged to his feet—he struggles—and is further dragged through the door and, I presume, taken away to some as-yet undisclosed location, the door to his place violently slammed, and definitely shut.

Which does, if I may, beg the question: when a television is on and its watcher has been kidnapped by turncoat ex-comrades, does it still have images prancing and cutting rapidly on the screen? And, more importantly, do the commercial breaks, still, come, on? The answer, I claim, matters less in this as in other such cleverly designed philosophical conundrums than the fact that the question gets asked. That, by itself, 'confirms' the 'legitimate' 'existence' of the 'phenomena' inciting the 'question' in the 'first' 'place' '.'

What follows is…

A gory episode
in which Eddie Perez becomes the first
post-revolutionary casualty
of the Rei regime (reader discretion is advised)

The car in which Perez finds himself stops. He is dragged
out and led into a place that smells, yes, no mistaking it, of
pancakes. His straitjacket is opened only for his arms to be
pulled further back and his entire body tied to a column. Pain-
ful, the ordeal, goes without saying. Once his arms are tied, his
feet bound, and another set of ropes around his frame tied, the
hood is lifted up. Alas, he thinks, I knew I smelled pancakes.
Sure enough, Eddie Perez's sense of smell is correct. The Old
Pancake House in the Flynt Shopping Center has been trans-
formed into a prison execution chamber of sorts. The chairs
all out, the tables too, although the booths, attached to the
ground and the sides, have been left as they are. His abduc-
tors leave their masks on but Eddie recognizes, at the front,
Applbottum. He cannot speak, for they have stuffed a sock,
literally, in his mouth, with tape over it. Lucky enough that
he can still breathe. His eyes, in the manner of those about to
be cruelly executed, pathetically roll left and right—as if a disabled child, wondering what's up and coming in the world all
around. Eddie should have known this, Eddie thinks using the
rhetorical strategy of superstar athletes referring to themselves
in the third person singular. (Why? Possibly to distance 'himself' from the fate 'he' inevitably is awaiting!) You should have
known Eddie, what made you (slips) think you(slips again)'d
be immune, why the hey didn't Eddie realize, think, before
acting, who the hell told you (slips once more) to listen to
that godforsaken bozo loser Reza Irani (the constant mix and
shuffling of first and third person pronouns and proper nouns

sadly commenting on Eddie's confused, traumatized, chaotic and panicked state), why Eddie, why (O teenager in the basement)...

A contingent of four more masked people walk in, rhythmic gaits, with guns at an angle on right shoulders with left arms still in harmony with their steps going back and forth. They stop about ten yards away from Eddie Perez, guns across chests, both hands atop. Another walks in and stands half-way between Eddie and the firing squad, his line of sight perpendicular to the shooters' (and Eddie's, in the opposite direction). He yells a barely decipherable yell, then he raises a baton and yells something else, whereupon the shooters are prompted into lifting their guns and aiming at Eddie. One other yell, the baton comes down, the guns discharge. Eddie Perez wriggles and slithers and goes through several convulsions. His eyes are wide open, his head sunk back against the pole. The yeller approaches and pokes him with his baton. The yeller signals that that's it. The yeller motions that the firing squad can relax. The firing squad at ease. The yeller leaves. The firing squad follows, exiting as it had entered. Two others dressed in white walk in, untie Eddie Perez and place his lifeless body on a stretcher and take him away.

Another gathering
(in which news of the execution of Eddie Perez
reaches those who most closely had associated
(in a manner of saying) with him on the front lines)

Present, among others (with AEB and NC ratings indicating 'Already Encountered in Book' and 'New Character' in parentheses): Sanjip Ray (AEB), Sindull Doolpop (AEB), Pfaula Ponderghast (NC), Deltha Thunderbunke (NC), Dick Koonkasif (NC), Rey Irani (AEB), Dolores Delectable (AEB). All somber, deep in thought, surely thinking about, torn between, reflecting upon, meditating on their allegiances. They already know. Everybody knows. Part of Mappolo's plan: make some examples. No dissention will be allowed. No doubts allowed.

Poor Mappolo, thinks privately Sanjip Ray. Despite his hyperbolic claims and the sports-cliché-spewing exhortation to push forth the revolution, and despite his further assurances during the festivities that there would be no more hierarchies and no more oppression, that this would be a government for the people by the people, in the truest sense of the word, Mappolo was now caught in the throes of self-aggrandizement. In the logic of humanhood. In its despicable, no-way-out logic. Survival and enrichment. Zero-sum games. Games, yes, all intertwined. Impossible web. Inescapable, unchangeable phenomena. One clog in the gosh darn system. Just another part. Element. In the vast laws governing our existence. The very fabric of our circulation. Fuck!

'So?' Pfaula Ponderghast asks, matter-of-factly.

But none among the morose bunch could summon the strength, or the energy, to respond in any shape or form. Eerie silence. What to do. The idea of forming a whole new block to counter Mappolo's faction seems reasonable, desirable even, some suggest. But the prospects of victory in such a case would be, at best, uncertain, what with Mappolo's recent consolidation of power. 'Perhaps Eddie deserved it after all,' Mimi Miramay (NC) says. 'We don't know what happened between them!' (Trying quickly to fit in despite her recent joining of the group (wearing a business dress for the occasion too), show some balls and prove she's not intimidated, establish herself and prove she could take on a leadership position if necessary, prove she would not just fade into the background, and that in fact, one day, she was gonna take the whole damn thing over.) Yeah but Eddie, a protest is heard (dashing me-first Mimi's ambitions at least for now), I mean Eddie! How in the world would Eddie have deserved that!

'Perhaps a conversation with Mappolo,' Pfaula Ponderghast suggests, 'might shed some light, reveal some misunderstanding. We should really try. At least to get a sense of where he's at. And what's up. What they should all expect.' Pfaula Ponderghast was impressive. Intelligence and eloquence. Reserved yet cool analysis. Plus, she had a knockout bod. Mr. Sanjip Ray, her beau, was part of this admiring group. And he feared not to let it be known.

'Bravo, Pfaula,' he says. 'You're very right!'

That was probably best, Sanjip Ray went on to suggest: 'Not to act hastily, talk to him, get a sense of what he's thinking, what he's feeling.' It was too early to panic. Too crucial a friend to abandon, without at least probing. Too soon.

Meanwhile, a directive is circulated by Mappolo Rei

Plastered on the bulletin boards inside the supermarkets, next to the ads for home vacuum cleaners, next to the ads for babysitters, next to personal ads with the numbers at the bottom semi-cut so they can be ripped off, plastered on the bus stops even though it's probably still illegal, plastered on another bulletin board inside the ice-cream parlor in the gourmet shopping center, plastered on the bulletin boards of elementary schools and high schools and junior highs, distributed by uniformed members of The Revolutionary Corps to all cars at intersection (ordering the drivers to roll down windows and handing out the flyers), to teenagers walking in the mall (force-fed, even though most would try to brush aside the flyers shoved in their faces), to residents of homes for the elderly and for young delinquents, to residents of condos under their doors (à la restaurants soliciting without permission), to residents residing in townhouses or single-family homes, to shop owners and managers, in most all stores in the shopping centers and the malls: a long set of directives outlining changes in policy and… Attempt definitely at covering all bases. Exhaustively.

People of the Suburban Motherland

The Takeover is complete.
The Revolution is victorious.
The people have all joined with the revolutionary forces.
You need only relax. Not much is asked of you. The following
changes will be brought about in the following weeks.
Fret not, just accept and go on, and you'll be fine.
You know how it works.

Then, a list of changes and information was provided in small type.

1. The following street, square and neighborhood changes are in effect immediately: Democracy Boulevard is now Revolution's Way. Heroes' Square is now Revolutionary Square. Revolution Avenue is now Democracy Street. People's Shopping Center is Heroes' Plaza. World Plaza is People's Square.

2. The Old Pancake House, Poppy's, Daddy's Fried Chicken, are all temporarily closed.

3. At least for now, any showing of skin past the elbows and knees, men and women, is disallowed, except for when I (by the way, hi, my name is Mappolo Rei and I'll be serving as your new revolutionary leader) ask for them to be shown.

(He had scribbled something illegible in the margin of the original, to which I did gain access but which, I also, unfortunately, could not decipher.)

4. Say 'please' when you ask for something (this includes the thug wannabes harassing the overwhelmed, hardworking and underpaid cashiers at any number of our fast food joints), and 'thank you' when you are given something. Reclaim politeness! Let's bring back some morals around these parts!

5. Hey by the way, Sammy (NC—editors) and everyone else, did you hear that one about the girl in the ice-cream parlor? You're supposed to tell it like some dude from Juysee! Something like: guy goes up to her, says to her he says, lady, what would you like, it's on me, and the girl blushes and does the timid retreat and even pulls a half-sighed oohh, and the guy says he says, what flavor do you like, and the girl says she likes vanilla and the guy says that's just what I got. And he pops out his weenie real quick like a cowboy his gun and shoots his load on her, had gotten it hard already, and laughs and darts out of the parlor and runs away with two dudes waiting outside for him. Pretty nasty I think too, but something genuine, really gross about it that I like.

6. Folks, don't start all right. Chill out. It was a joke. Crude and rude and gross and sexist even maybe but whatever. I'm the leader of this goddamn joint now so I can allow myself a few pleasantries. That's right. Besides, I'm now

7. nostalgically contemplating a quiet retirement somewhere sunny—not! (Here, Mappolo seems to have perhaps just jotted down a false note to get his friends to relax and not worry.) *I have plans, and they seem a'ight if I may say so myself, but they don't, like, necessitate my presence. I can delegate. Besides, the more invisible, the more absent, the more my legend will grow. The more deified I shall become. Who'd give that up just to stick around for the day to day grind and this whole freagin' rat race?!*

(Mappolo after the revolution and Mappolo before: two distinct creatures, and it did not escape the notice of his brethren. Not just in action, but the tone, the mannerism, the approach, the style...)

8. From the Journal of Mappolo Rei I: I have seriously considered, well, I guess two things, although I was, before actually beginning to write this, gonna tell y'all who'll one day get to read it, only about one. But I'll do both, why not. First is, I've thought about moving, some community somewhere, matters little to be frank, just to where there's openness enough for the pansexual community. And enough deer to hunt what with the dearth of human flesh. I think Bernadette is quite capable of running the day to day. Besides, who we foolin'! This goddamn place don't need anyone to run it! It runs on its own, despite what anyone might tell you! Well-oiled machine that it is. Plus, I have no patience at all for the inevitable bitterness that's going to surface. So, why not. Second thing is: suicide. I've thought about it. Now that we've won (even though no one knows, and no one cares, and nothing's changed), there's nothing left to accomplish. We'll see.

9. An aphorism a day, that's the way, wouldn't you say. To save thy self last, save them others first.

10. Dear Elliott (AEB): although I did invite you to do what you will with you know whom and do with you know what, what, to give to you know whom, I'm feeling now a bit squeamish about the whole thing. My own aphorism (see previous item) hath revealed to me my blindness to the suffering of others. Hath awakened in my previously childish, histrionic, self-absorbed self, an awareness of the human condition's worse traits. I'm having second thoughts. I don't know what you think about all this but, if there is another way, won't you think about it. And let me know. Through Bernadette. If not, our previous deal stands. Let me know where to pick it up. Again through Bernadette. She'll do me the honors. (P.S.: Excuse my quasi-permanent withdrawal from the midst, just the duty of the revolutionary leader. Don't hold it against me and say hi to all the folks. Still love all o' youz. Hugs and kisses.)

11. And the band played on and the band played on...

12. I don't know about this whole main character thing. Ever since 'my' 'murder' of A., my pre-emptive strike so to say, I'm feeling the heat. Feeling like I'm losing myself. A sense of myself. As if I'm not the same person anymore. Fear of success, perhaps, but I would not be surprised if I somehow were to write the script to my own doom.

13. From the journal of Mappolo Rei II: Did nothing today. Hard to get up. Feeling a little blue. Eddy with a y came over, stayed all night. Wish he hadn't. (Next day's entry: Did nothing again today. Rolled around in bed is all...)

14. What if the plot rebelled. Just got up and walked away?
What would become of me (Mappolo, that is)? What about A.'s
remains in the freezer, and 'I', that little pest of a pronoun float-
ing around never telling you (the reader!) who he is and what
he's up to? What then, who do I talk to about that?...

15. Front-in parking only in shopping center parking lots!
Please! Cooperate with the new forces of the law and all will
be a-okay. (Call 1-888-555-6661 for up-to-the-minute info
on all street name changes + changes to the names of schools,
buildings, and public landmarks.)

What the...

That's what most of the cast thought when they saw the
driveling directive. All these inner workings of the Drive-by
Cannibals for public consumption?! All the personal information?! Tasteless jokes?! Journal entries?! What the fuck!! He's
totally lost his mind, said Sanjip Ray. He's going mad, opined
Delectable. Kookoo, concluded Thunderbunke. No doubt
now. A conversation was definitely on the agenda. Oh, and
there was, indeed, something else.

Something else

When Sanjip Ray and a contingent of the revolution's ultimate warriors go to see Mappolo, they find a small gate erected
a few feet from the front door, with a simple sign that reads:

Off-limits

Residence of the Ultimate Leader of the Ultimate Revolution

(In case of emergency, call 301-555-0506)

Rey Irani recognizes the number as Mappolo's. Hasn't even bothered to change numbers, the idiot. They cross the street with the contingent and walk to a pay phone, the four gathering around the old booth while Rey takes it upon himself to do the honors. A few moments pass before Rey hangs up and updates the folks.

'Machine,' he says.

'Did you leave a message,' Sanjip asks.

And Rey answers that he hadn't that should he.

'Yeah—I mean, what else is there,' opines Sanjip. Rey Irani steps back to the phone, picks up and calls back. Waits—and: 'Yeah... Mappolo?... This is Rey, just calling to see how you holdin' up, it's Wednesday... And, well... Me and a few of the folks here, we just wanted to see if we could talk to you a little—just about what's comin' up and stuff, all right? Not urgent but it would be cool if we could do it soonish, sorta... So, give me a call back if you can, 301-555-8631, or you can call Dolores or Sanjip... Again, hope you're well and we'll talk... All right... See ya...'

Hangs up and turns to waiting folks.

'Well?'

'Yeah.'—Rey, matter-of-factly.

They all disperse afterwards, anxious and worried about the future: theirs, their quote unquote city. They even hug and kiss and hug again, almost as if feeling the coming of the apocalypse, or, at any rate, a certain type of apocalyptic moment.

Strange, thinks Rey Irani (by the way, I know that I needed to perhaps mention this earlier, but feel free on Irani's pronunciation: could go Eerani, or Eyerani, or Eyerahhni, or whatever...) as he walks to catch his bus, echoing one of Mappolo's quick comments on his list of 'directives', now that it's won, over, there's almost nothing to do. That fucker's right, he thinks of Mappolo, no thrills, no risks, no doubters, no naysayers. Ahhh, he sighs, for the good old days when unsuspecting motorists would drive slowly onto the emergency lane and back up and come out of the cars and ask us what the matter was. Ahhhh for our lies, our seduction, our leading them down to their doom and that fateful Cadillac (skipped the Pinto and the Audi he did, mister Irani). Ahhhh for that moment of truth: the plunge of the dagger into their unsuspecting hearts (the old woman from the drugstore, the suit-wearing L. N. Jahandi, whom he'd recognized from print ads), their exposed necks (Sylvam Sontaigi, a high school friend turned successful developer, who'd even recognized his pal and patted him on the back and said, 'Gee, I'm glad I could help you out buddy' before...), their backs (the school teacher, the magician, the manager of the humongous sports shop). Some were even cut down with several shots to the leg before the final coup to the heart as they lay a-screamin' (Jackie Chang, sister of Donny, ex-cheerleader in S. Ray's sister's boyfriend's high school, plus that guy he'd always seen sending her coffee at the coffee shop). All of the images, all of the hackings and the sadistic inner urges and the slashes and the spewings of blood and the screams and the worm-like wrigglings and the last pleadings and the last breaths and the panicked faces and the contorted limbs and the out-of-joint hollers and the final daggers and the executions and the chopping and the bagging and the bragging, all the images race through Irani's mind, as if a collection of triumphant reels, a database of fabulous accomplishments, a string of highlights put together by his own nostalgia as a tribute to the struggle, the war, the movement, that he'd so glamorously, fantastically, luckily, after all, maybe just luckily, been part of, good old Reza Irani!

He walks now dejectedly to the bus stop, where no one else is waiting. He waits for a while, and waits some more, and waits some more, and, still reeling from the images in his mind, still somehow nostalgic and lost, he becomes engulfed with the traffic flow, the same that had so mesmerized others within this tale, myself included, somehow sees the cars passing, the wondrous traffic flow, and begins to check out the makes and models if he can, but definitely the number of passengers, just to get a sense of the ratio of cars to population, a matter of importance after all for one supposedly caring about life in the 'burbs, a sedan he sees passing with one passenger (1), a minivan passes with three passengers (3), another minivan with two (2), a red van (1), a white SUV (2), a beige Cherokee (3), a gray sedan (1), a black Benz (1), another black Benz (3) that leaves two and drives away (1), a dark blue sedan (1), a green sedan (1), a van (1), a Toyota Camry (2), Mercury (1), minivan (1), Maxima (1), black Benz (1), minivan (1), 3 passengers, 1 passenger, too much now, all he sees are silhouettes, vanishing silhouettes and the numbers and soon not even shapes, he sees these dark thingies and counts, two, two, two, two, one, two, two, one, one, one, two, two, one, two, two, can't take the passing cars anymore, sorry traffic flow, and bored, turns attention to the parking lot (O O beloved parking lot), and to forget the mortgage payment, to forget the car payment, to recall the protest march he became part of what seems like so many lost years ago, he counts, moronically, mechanically, he just makes out the shapes and whether car is parked front in or back in, looks and waits, looks and waits, watches and counts, without protest or sound, counts the cars parked in the parking lot, a blue sedan front, a gray sedan back, wait and watch, a gray sedan back, a red minivan back, watch and wait, a green Jeep back, a blue sedan back, a beige sedan back, a gray sedan back, wait and wait and watch and watch and a gray sedan back a gray minivan back a blue sedan back, white minivan back, beige minivan back red sedan front red van back beige pickup truck front blue sedan back white minivan and can't, just can't, just can't take it anymore now just wait, and wait, and... and then as if by a sudden injection of poetic inspiration, the beginning of a sonnet is revealed to him, another in the long line, another sonnet, a real one this time, ode to the great suburbia, not some Food Court at the Mall ditty, not some bogus Ode to the Cubicle, and certainly not a depressing and depressed suicide rock riff dubbed Teenager in the Basement, no sir: a real sonnet, a real sonnet ode to the sonnet as a form, the grand poetic form, the Ur-form, a sonnet indeed that he begins to formulate:

> *The cars on the freeway pass by these lost dreamlands*
> *No one gets out or stands to watch or feel the show*
> *The drivers just sit and make sure they don't go slow*
> *Watchers watch and open the doors in the white sand*

A sonnet that he nevertheless abandons as he sees his bus approaching (the rest is left to your imagination, O gentle reader)... Whereupon, his head hung, Irani takes one tired step after another and slides his card in the slot, turns and walks to the mid-section of the bus and sits down.

The something else: when he gets home, he notices that he had been faxed (for those who had it) or delivered (those with faxes got both the fax and the delivered letter), an *Avis* from the Great Leader of the Revolution, Mappolonius Rei, in so many words informing them all of his future inaccessibility. 'For purposes of security and in order to keep a watchful eye on all counter-revolutionary activity,' he would not avail himself to the public unless the event were previously announced. All members of The Revolutionary Corps were instructed to continue the struggle and to work towards the implementation of the policies they fought so hard to bring to fruition. A note at the bottom informed them that a meeting would take place every Thursday at Chez Dovra, with Great Rei's personal assistant, one (don't blush) Bernadette Bunns. Progress reports were due to her at such times, subject to Mr. Rei's review, who would get back to the various committees in due time for the actual implementing of said policies. The exclamation at the bottom read: 'Hail the 'Burbs!'

Rey Irani, beside himself but holding it all in, could not help but mutter deep within, Screw them aaaaaaaaaaaaaaaaaaaa aaaaaaaaaaaaaaaaaaaaaallllllllll!

11

W hen Rey Irani walked into the one-bedroom
apartment he shared with his younger sister on the ninth floor
of generic suburban condo building with lots of older residents
and an exercise room downstairs and an outdoor swimming
pool, he was too tired and too fed up to complain again about
her lack of ambition and resolve, not to mention her overall lack of togetherness, a trait he blamed on one of her best
friends from school she'd run around with junior and senior
years. She was always moving in and out of their parents' (big
house, lots of stuff in it, even further out in the next suburb
over), in and out of dead-end jobs (Hallmark Card shop at the
Mall, coffee shop at a different mall, waitress at a hip night
spot downtown…), in and out of school (junior colleges at
that). Somehow, she'd never gotten the educational bug, the
bug that would have propelled her to the proper station in life
and allowed her to reap the financial rewards and a standard
that was the norm in those parts. Unbeknownst to her folks,
she would regularly skip school, hang out with what is universally known as the wrong crowd, smoke, drink, get high, and
party 'til dawn and then all the way through to the next day,
take long road trips, fuck, experiment with designer drugs, go
into trances, have sex with multiple partners. During one of
her stints at the junior college, she'd even had the inkling to
start up a start-up, a hybrid diet center/health spa/beauty sa-

lon/lounge/internet joint that miraculously had a whiff of success, before one of the friends she had concocted the business with overdosed and someone's good lord be with her, passed away, taking with her not only her expertise in management, but her daddy's ninety-eight percent funding of the venture. Irani-*père* had busted his butt, giving up a cushy position in the civil service to try to provide for his family. He had arrived full of hope and ambition, only to be shut down over and over. He'd started a small business selling vacuum cleaners that soon failed. He'd gotten a job at a local shop in the mall in the men's shoe section. He'd soon abandoned that and set up with business partners a limousine service that went under. Finally, he'd settled in as a real estate broker making enough to feed the family. Mom had followed a similarly unsettling if perhaps less turbulent path, soon realizing that she too needed to now take up a new profession, despite her reluctance. The parents had indeed always been there and insisted on the importance of a good education. They'd provided, cared, perhaps too much even, created all the right circumstances, financially at least, and certainly modeled the hard work ethic and behavior in the great, great tradition of immigrants working their asses off to make it, have the first-generation kids grow up to be somebodies and brag back home, *voilà*, my son daughter doctor so and so, engineer so and so (and, starting in the '90's, computer geeks and people with MBAs even were made a big deal of), waltz around and parade their specimens in the enterprising yet annoying immigrant community. (Annoying, did you say? Yeah well, I guess I did...)

And there they were, two versions of total failures, one full of promise and talent who'd been led astray never to find her way again (sis), the other a mediocrity by all official and un- measures, legitimate and il- criteria, who'd jumped early

enough on an absurd revolutionary bandwagon to fancy himself a second-tier leader of sorts, yet all too cognizant of his
minor and quite irrelevant contributions, his totally dispens-
able services, perhaps even well aware—more than most—of
others' impressions of his just tagging along.

That he'd urged his personhood (his brain and limbs) into
action just to satisfy the cannibalistic urges he'd always known
he possessed, of this there was no doubt—and he did not deny
it. A weird adrenaline rush, a sudden excitement, a definite
burst of energy always came upon him at the sight of barbecue
grills and exposed human flesh (so often together, in the garden, in the park, dad flipping the burgers and he, little boy of
nine, wondering what the devil was inside him, why did he,
why did he, not want *this* beef version dad was so rapturously
singing the praises of, 'The best, grade A import,' but... but...
spit it out Rey, they've all come out at some point, Mappolo
too, his was revealed even in the book, spill it out Rey Irani, spill it out, what you want is human beef, human, beef!),
so much so that later on during his teenage years, thinking
himself the lone creature on the planet with such urges, he
was almost driven to suicide, especially since he was soon acknowledging the admittedly horrendous, monstrous, erotic
sensations that were awakened within him at the thought of
the barbecue of arms, forearms and necks (his particular fetish). Later on though, actually acknowledging the feelings
by accepting inwardly the phraseology and the nomenclature
('Yes, I'm a cannibal,' he would stand and say in the mirror,
'and that's an all right thing to be'), he learned to postpone the
self-destructive urges, and to just be, to just let it be... And it
was only fortuitous circumstances that finally led to his meeting A. in a run-down porno shop on E Street downtown (he
could not recall how they'd gotten on the topic), and learning

of the revolution, especially of its methods and preferred modus operandi. Hallelujah he'd sing to himself. Finally, finally he'd found a way out: a rationalized, wonderfully self-serving mechanism to satisfy his deep-rooted desires, to channel his energies, to direct his obsessions, all the while claiming he was engaged in a higher struggle and a whole array of unrelated, and bogus, causes.

It was only later, after a meeting with A. and the rest of the gang, that he found out Mappolo also was involved, and that he was a leader, albeit a minor one, who'd come up with the idea independently of A. and D. Impossible to leave at the time though, irrespective of his antagonistic feelings (mutual, he was sure) towards Mappolo, ever since middle school when the fucker had... Well, never mind... Fate has tricks up its sleeve, Irani mumbled to himself in guise of a wise aphorism, better learn to trust it than fight it, yes, the time will come...

Tired, fed up, but angry also, Irani closes the door behind him and walks in: 'Hey,' he says, subdued, to sis.

'Heyyyy,' sis responds, affectionate, concerned and hearing in bro's salutation not just a slight measure of sadness, but also of consternation. And it should be made clear, as soon as possible, that, despite their occasional fisticuffs, the two loved each other like no brother and sister ever could, literally.

She gets up, comes over, gives big bro a big hug. Even takes remote and turns TV off.

'No, no, leave it on,' Irani says.

'Leave the TV on? But you were...'

'Ah—leave it on, what the hell!'

She turns the TV back on. He wants to sit and stare. Wants to feel like a zombie. A moronic zombiesque couch potato.

What he wants to do and feel like just now. His right as an American citizen. An upholding one at that. Inalienable right. Goddamn right it's his right, he thinks inwardly. Shoulda taken that path long ago. Nine to five it and then come back and plunk down. Day job it and forego the night. Get up and shit shave shower and make a cup of coffee and wear the suit and take the elevator down to the Japanese-made car, drive to work listening to the morning entertainment on the radio, get to the office with the briefcase and say hi to the receptionist and go to the cubicle and sing the praises of the cubicle, put the rest of the coffee on the table and check the messages and stand up momentarily and look around from above the fray at the tops of cubicles and the colleagues hunched over on their phones inside the cubicles, and then smile and happily wallow in professional functions, in the merriment that is working in the cubicle at the company, and shout the praises of the cubicle, and leave the cubicle to go to a big meeting in the conference room and then leave again the cubicle to go out to lunch and return to the cubicle to work and then leave again the cubicle in the early evening to go to happy hour, where, happy as he may be, he'll miss the cubicle. What did I ever have against the cubicle, he begins to sing, should have gone the cubicle route and sung, should have gone that route yeah, and sung:

I'm happy in my cubicle, happy in my cubicle
I won't let you be cynical oh cynical
It's all a joke anyway honeyyyyy
Might as well make some moneyyyyy!

That's what my dearest uncle says
Be happy in your cubicle!

You're not picking trash off the streets
You're not cleaning or sweeping the dirty streets
You're a professional with your nice attire
A most respected fella in your communityyyyy!

You're not escorting unruly kids after school
(Or during lunch or recess in school)
You're not telling tales in the subway caaaaars
You're not—singing songs in dirty paaaaarks
Taking handouts from a rich-ass sugar daddddyyyyy
You only wish you were a trust-fund babbyyyyyy!

I loooooooove—My Cubicle!

Stupid adventures! Revolution! (Interior voice again? Yessiree Bob, right on, it does not—not!—discriminate!) He does indeed stare ahead. Unmoving. Eyes too. Arms. Legs.

'So what happened?'

She's kind. Generous. Understanding. Still, Rey does not answer. Not at first. Still sitting zombie-like staring ahead. Seems like a regular guy, probably is a regular guy, but somehow... Then he awakens. Something monstrous in him rising. No physical movement gives away this metamorphosis no, just the air about, the sensation, the energy—and finally: the words...

'What happened,' Rey Irani says, 'is that I'm gonna get that son of a bitch motherfucker. I'm gonna cut his throat, then eat it, right in front of them all!'

Amazingly, neither his nor his sister's expression changed much. No panic or fear or O-my's. Sure, the mere articulation puts into motion muscles in his face and throat, but other than this causal determinism, only a slight anger is sensed, and that in his eyes, widening and then back to normal. She does not budge. She was the only one in the family (in the whole wide world, actually, other than the revolutionary wackos he'd been spending so much time with) who knew about his frightening desires (needs), and she came not only to accept, but to encourage him to 'realize more' his 'full' self. She also knew how proud he could be, how passionate. Still with one leg raised and the other bent on the couch next to him, she says:

'Who? Him who?'

'That son of a bitch motherfucker fuck!'

'Mappolo?'

'Mappollah! Ayatollah Mappollah!'

'What happened?'

'Nothing happened. I'm just gonna cut him up, that's all.'

'Rey, come now…'

'Come now nothing. That's just that. I'ma cut him up and eat him straight.'

'What happened? What did he do? Come, now Reyo, hellooh! Who you talkin' toooo?'

Reyo, called thus only by sis and appreciating actually the intimacy of the name, for the first time since his sitting down, moves: turns to her, that is, then brings arms around and thrusts them on her shoulder and squeezes hard.

'Goddamnit!' Irani says. 'I knew this was going to end this way! I knew it wouldn't work. I fuckin' knew it! Fuck!'

'But you guys have it all won,' she says, sincerely—and not just to make him feel good. (If only she'd known of the rifts in the leadership. But no, she mustn't! At least not yet.)

'Nahhh,' he says after having looked at her an awkward moment more. 'Better not get into it.'

'Reza Irani! I order you to tell your sister what it is that you're so upset about. Hell-oh-ohhh…'

'He just…' Rey is in thought, refraining now, staring ahead

at nothing. 'He's an egomaniac tyrant, basically, what can I tell you,' he says, relatively calm. Somehow, sis is not surprised.

'Are you surprised?' she says. 'I mean, what did you expect?'

'Not really I guess,' Rey answers hesitant. 'But then again...' He trails off.

'You know they killed Eddie? Butchered the guy! Poor Eddie!'

'Wow!' she says, honestly surprised but not overly dramatic or overly in shock.

'Stuffed a sock in his mouth and everything. Rumor is Mappolo's gonna eat him all by himself. Set an example.'

'Goddamn!'* she says. (*This time, yes, there is shock.)

'I don't know that one though, it's a rumor,' says he. 'I'm sure he's gonna eat the whole thing. All he wanted was an excuse to get rid of Eddie. He always wanted him the whole way, you know it too...'

'What are you guys gonna do?' she asks.

'Don't know yet,' Irani says, purposely neglecting to tell her of their failed attempt at contacting the leader. 'He's sending these dumb-ass letters that he's now off-limits, the fuck. Off-limits!'

'Off-limits?'

'Won't be seeing anyone. Will be operating invisibly. In the background. You know—the legend, el commandante. Afraid goddamn fuck!'

'You want me to talk to him?'

'You? How you gonna talk to him! He's...'

Rey doesn't finish. Last thing he wants, for her to get hurt. Plus, he knows she knows. Mappolo's weaknesses, that is. Plus, they even had a fling long ago, Mappolo and sis. Lasted only a few weeks. It's true that she was hot, Rey could recognize that in his sister, outside of... Tall, long legs, great ass. Great proportions. Tanned. The smoking had aged her slightly but also gave her a mysterious look. Irani considered the offer, but—

'I think we're beyond it, tell you the truth… Thanks for the offer though…'

He pauses and picks up: 'We need a real response. Something big. Something…'

'Don't tell me,' sis says. 'Do *not* tell me.'

'I think so,' Reza Irani says quietly. 'I think so…'

Of love and counter-revolutionary
sentiments and meetings
in secret places with all sorts of rabid
and angry extremists
plus smoke rising

Locale: Sonya Gullardovski's garden apartment, third floor, number twenty. Off exit 18 A. (Precision added, 18 B going South and A being North and several of those now present having gotten lost until they made their way back, even though directions were properly given.) Topic: The overthrow of the current revolutionary regime. Conditions: super secret, high security. Scene: Danny Moore at the door, holding a rifle, hidden, Bobby Lott on the balcony surveying the parking lot (names changed to protect the identities). All seems calm, serene even: the neighbor from the first floor, walking in the parking lot carrying her groshuries (in deference to her, the pronunciation: she always, always, accentuated the non-existent 'sh' in groceries) from the car, smiles and cuts a quick Hi! upward, to which Lott responds by a similarly staccato Hey.

Vonya Injakoosh, the unofficial Secretary of Communications, asks for the attention of her comrades, for she is going to present some 'news' and reports from the fronts. Herewith the items on the agenda, which you can guess would have been expanded upon and discussed: four counter-revolutionary insurgents had been shot at the Old Pancake House, arrested while plotting in the ice-cream shop; a group of ten other dissidents had been left with maximum security at Daddy's Fried, temporarily being used as a prison for political extremists and enemies; Poppy's was also being turned into a holding area of sorts, this for even graver acts thought to potentially be conceived to potentially be committed, potentially against the new leader of the potential Revolution, to potentially overthrow him. So far, only one fellow had been arrested, and that, the field spies had ventured, only in order to not have the damn place sit empty.

There was also talk of a counter-movement (and to be frank, talk of a counter-counter-movement) that was rapidly being extinguished since only a handful (half a dozen, say) of participants were said to be heavily involved. Their commitment was not in doubt, but their qualifications were: it was reported that the group was constituted of several bored teenagers thinking it a summer diversion with no particular political theory at the foundation of their beliefs or actions, no history of political involvement, no leanings or ideological attachments of any sort. Their forces were being squashed, conveniently enough, by Mappolo's, quite rapidly and efficiently.

Vonya I. then puts down the paper she is holding up in front of her face as her brethren look and listen on. 'That's it,' she quips. (None of this information was enough to stop Dolores Delectable, my Dolores Delectable, from finally admitting her attraction to Sanjip, what with the atmosphere of openness and the apparent malaise prompting her to recognize that there's only one life (probably) and that you must live it to its fullest... So she corners him at the most unexpected time (Sanjip with his raised glass flattened backwards against a wall). 'I think you're beautiful,' she says, rapturously (and drunk), adding, 'Inside I mean, and out!' Sanjip, politely, and in a seemingly fake attempt at being discreet (head tilted sideways, eyes rolling, fake smile momentarily appearing), whispers, 'Doloressss! This is not the placccccce!')

That was, indeed, in the words of sexy madame Injakoosh, it. Mappolo in his silly world, those loyal to him also in their silly worlds, them in the counter-coup clan in their silly big world, and a whole lot of plotting going on. But what needed to be said was that it was all too real—all too real indeed! That despite all appearances, despite the tranquility and the serenity and the comfort of suburban existence assuming no revolution would ever be instigated from within its borders, it was possible, and it was happening, and better beware, O comfortably and conveniently naive citizens!

Other than that, few visible transformations were in store. The facades of the houses were still made with cheap material, with folks buying into breathtakingly boring complexes and thinking themselves successful in the midst of the mind-numbing monotony. All the townhouse complexes still looked alike, save for the colors of the tiles on the roofs. A plethora of obese specimens still walked around with an array of 'diet' and 'health' food products. That lonely, whacked-out, deranged dude (Al Rahboro, I think his name is) still walks (the nerve!) on the sidewalk (oblivious to the zooming automobiles and the fact that he's the only one). Bob, the friendly gas station attendant, still waves when drivers pass by. The mall, as tyrannical as ever, cedes no ground whatsoever to those pesky little mom and pop operations (au contraire: gets bigger, better, brighter, busier, with scheduled Santa and lines forming too at X-mas time). And traffic, O beloved traffic...

Traffic flows smoothly and flows some more, and flows and flows, with its parts (the automobiles) following obediently the laws, flows from shopping mall to shopping center to home, and back, to summer camp at school to soccer practice at the grounds in the junior high, to the food store, from one parking lot to another to another,

Amir Parsa

SUDDEN BREAK IN
THE NARRATIVE
to allow for a
STUNNING
ADMISSION

On the part of humble scribe, Mr.
Narrator-man posing as I,

*and in lieu of any other type of explanation
or elaboration and to make sure future
generations are not led astray by
fabrications of institutions or
senseless pontifications*

*I know that for a variety of reasons that shall go unnamed, I've
kinda sorta had to make up all sorts of quote unquote characters,
from major to minor, from dead to alive, with proper names and
all, with scenes and images, even a plot or two, occasionally shifted
to ensure interest and attention, and to keep boredom at bay (just
like I used to do when I was teaching sports to little kids, ages four
to fourteen). Now the truth: rubbish all! Phantasmagoria! Fabrications propounded in bad faith! Concoctions all, I must confess,
just to get people's attention! Plot-twisting and setting and descrip-
tion and character-building? Baloney! Ba, lo, ney! Obviously all
just a whole bunch of posturing! I couldn't care less about all that
drivel! And it's probably quite obvious! Truth be told, they're just*

convenient asides propounded for the liberation of my one and only obsession, a fixation I could describe to nary a close colleague, a loved one or a lover, let alone anyone with any degree of influence or power in giving to the world this priceless gem of a satirical masterpiece: that unforgiving component of our daily lives, that crucial ingredient, that permanent fixture in the fabric of our movements, that element that I tossed, why in the past, rather, toss, and turn about one sleepless night after another, object of my affections and obsessions, vilest perturber of my tranquility, inconsiderate invader of my peace not to mention dreams, that space where souls wander deep in thought and where they take out their cell phones before they go into their favorite shops and chat: where slowly, cautiously, carefully, automobiles pull in and out, in and out, between the wondrously drawn and immaculately kept white lines: where abandoned wrappers of sandwiches and napkins from the coffee shops on the ground point to Absence itself, to the barrenness of life, I say, of all of existence: where we used to hang out on Friday and Saturday and actually even on some weekday nights freshman sophomore and junior years high school, doors of cars open and some of the guys hanging on the hood ('on' and not 'in' then), engaged, some (not me!) in all sorts of 'illegal' activities: where I made out (and that was it) with Tori Parsieti, and later on got to second base, with boner and all, with Joony Szanz, and to third with Dolly Djivali: where once, Manny after the club unable any longer to hold his pee swerves crazily and opens his driver's side door before the car had come to a full stop even and dashes to the fence under the lamp and brings down pants (not just zipper) and lets flow and sighs, oh Manny's last great sigh, how wondrous it seemed then, his joy so profoundly could be felt (it shall not be revealed what other types of activities Manny would engage in at same locale with equal urgency): where, once, a sad man holding a briefcase walked and saw me looking at him from behind the window of a shop and nodded as if to say that I also one day would be there, and switched the briefcase to his other hand and looked down after fixing the collar of his coat and walked to his car and before entering stood, I saw him stand, before going in, and peer, into the distance, just standing, and peering, and taking a deep breath, so unusual it seemed: always and again yes, again and always, that sacred space, that temple of clarity and transcendence, that heavenly sanctuary, that serene valley of repose, talking about... the parking lot, of course, and better still, in its plural form, parking lots! Parking lots, parking lots, parking lots! That's what this whole damn book portrays: parking lots and also, to almost equal degree, traffic flow. Parking lots and traffic flow! And if folks ask what the book is about (a question I abhor and whose premise I really do not even allow let alone answer), that's what I would say. Parking lots and traffic flow! And if it increases my anxiety, and brings me to an uncontrollable boiling point to admit it, so be it. I mean, is there any way, any single possible manner in which I could have just come out and said it, told anyone (bared my soul and then gone ahead and promoted and advertised and then immersed myself into bringing about the book), that it's all about parking lots and traffic flow? No, I couldn't have. And that's just the facts. Whence the delay, whence the impassioned, liberating tone of this admission. Not about a dead man and his remains, you ask? Not really, I answer. Not sex, sex, sex, in all its varieties and lists, lists, lists, of all sorts? Not s-h-o-p, shop, shop, shop? Not gratuitous violence, proper names and the suburban landscape? Not revolution? Not character-creation or fiction-making? Not the very process of turning reality into artistic artifact? Not parentheses and thus pauses, hesitations, digressions, desires, memory, forgetting, images of elsewheres and othertimes? Not another punctuation mark, as in, the apostrophe, or the period? No! I say. No no no no no! The resounding answer is: NO. No it is not, and I'm not being funny or cute or humble. Just the truth. Those are all just props! It's all about parking lots and traffic flow. Parking lots, and traffic flow.

See for yourself reader: where do the most important 'events' of the book take place? Where does A. go for his meditation? Where is he kidnapped? Where does Mappolo go to exalt in his triumph (clue: woman walking out of bank, mouth agape at the screeching of Mappolo's Jag)? Why does the narrator moronically list cars and how they're parked, and even has the balls to describe passing cars in the traffic flow?! Where do the Drive-by Cannibals gather to tell the populace of their duty towards the coming revolution (image: Mappolo on his dishwasher liquid box)? For Christ's sake, isn't the whole launch of the book formatted around a clever subversion of the entire idea of parking and parking lots, a deconstructed post-post-post-modernist derivation, what with a Cadillac PARKED UNDER A TREE, and the parked Cadillac's back side only visible and the unsuspecting motorist being seduced and led to a PARKED CAR, all the while PARKING HIS OWN CAR on a lane exceptionally created by the good managers of this great society specifically for EMERGENCY PARKING on the roadside? Is it becoming obvious now? Am I getting my point across? In the torture sessions, and the subsequent murders, why are the details of the PARKED CARS still narrated? And the poetic peerings into the PARKING LOTS? Please! Would that ever occur if author did not intend to make the lots and the flow, thee, I mean, theeee, main characters? For heaven's sake, to attempt to make poetry, of all sorts and genres at that, with PARKING LOTS and TRAFFIC FLOW? What kind of demented desire is that?! Made my point? Believe me now? Will you? And since we're at it, onwards to the more important queries, and exhortations. I ask now: how could the American literary canon, especially the classics, go on without a book that's all about parking lots and the traffic flow??? Not a bit hypocritical? Or short-sighted? Or exclusionary? I mean, don't we need this? Doesn't the Canon need this?! A book that just like our own human selves, is devoted to them, worships them, plans life around them, is basically a slave to them, seriously could not function without them, can't get enough of them, brings them up whenever!? Please, seriously, you guys, you gotta put this book in there, we gotta have something with the main characters being parking lots and traffic flow! I mean, don't we? Don't we?! Don't we?????!!!!

(Police reports withheld, let it still be confessed that the author was even cited for suspicious behavior snooping around in parking lots and jotting down, like a mental patient, the makes and models of parked cars, including whether they were parked front in or back in, and on other occasions counting the number of passengers passing cars contained, plus their colors and who knows what else. When confronted by the undercover shopping center manager (query: 'Sir, what are you doing!?') the profligate subject seems to have been oblivious to his demoniacally weird behavior, for he is said to have actually answered by saying exactly what he was doing, as in, I'm jotting down the make and model of parked cars, their colors, and whether they are parked front in or back in.)

RETURN TO NARRATIVE

flows smoothly, in this serene and tranquil hamlet, without a noise, without a honk even, without a walker or anyone heard shouting, in perfect peace, tranquility, serenity, and more peace and more tranquility and more serenity. Mappolo Rei? The Revolutionary Corps? The new government? Whatever.

Nevertheless, threats of a possible invasion (metaphorical, literal) from the adjoining suburb are considered. Apparently betting on the potential chaos and disorder reigning in Whooton, along with the fragility of the leadership, the leader of suburban neighbor Pebbleville has been contemplating an offensive for several reasons: more parking space (bigger, if not better, parking lots) and more square-inch space between white lines; more land for constructing parking spaces (being further out from the city, more land was available); more useless buildings to raze down to create more parking space.

'I doubt they're reliable though,' Deltha Thunderbunke (AEB) unexpectedly intervenes on the matter of the threats, 'and two, I don't think they'd actually go for it, when all is said and done.' (O Deltha Thunderbunke, O Deltha Thunderbunke, you've always had that giddy kind of spunk, where would we be without you, love!?) Deltha Thunderbunke, another very impressively intellectually gifted gal with a devotion to the cause that was unequalled, always put her analytical acumen to work wonderfully with her insights and her instincts. She is quite approachable too, and does not at all come across as rabid or intolerant of other views, despite an intensity in her face and gaze that might suggest the opposite. O Deltha Thunderbunke, what would we do without your spunk?...

The assembly nevertheless agrees that a much more serious threat is growing ever more powerful by the minute, and that it is presented by none other than the current, albeit short-lived government, and its tyrannical dictator, Mappolo Rei. And that all those present better take stock of the danger for surely, they are on some list, somewhere, 'as we speak.' This from Rey Irani, who's managed to act like the head of the whole proceedings, even though none have been officially designated. That is what really needs to be addressed. If not, each one, and not so long from now, they'd be getting theirs at the Old Pancake House, at Poppy's, or some other newly designed abode of torture and suffering.

Hear ye, hear ye, they chant again, hear ye hear ye…

A declaration of independence, prepared by Fol Lokoway (NC), a gifted and active member of the new group, is signed. A vote of confidence is taken. A pledge of commitment is concocted and recited by all members. A ritual of greetings is created. Form of communion. Form of salutation. Belonging. Oneness. Like so: right hand on hip, left on the forehead, pledge is said, the hip sways right, stops, then left, pauses, then right again, upon which the hand on head makes a circular motion and then several full revolutions on the forehead, after which the two hands are brought briefly together in front, fingers interlocking, and placed on the heart. An exclamation follows, shouted, as loud as you can. The exclamation is: Hail Suburbia!

The ritual is repeated several times, after which, Rey Irani, growing impatient and now somehow ensconced as leader of sorts, shouts: 'Enough already!'

Now, the thing left to do is this: decide what they actually are going to do. Opinions vary, as opinions are bound to. The attempts at negotiations with Mappolo are futile, they generally agree. They have failed in the past and will fail again in the future. So, no negotiations.

Rey Irani, in a surprising (to his colleagues, not to yours truly) demonstration of bloodthirsty savagery and a true craving for some good old-fashioned warmongering, continues on the trail. Despite the appearance of force too, he suggests, with his goons and his fast food joints turned into fortresses, the guess here is that Mappolo is a lot weaker than he lets on. In addition, he only has Applbottum, and a relatively new recruit who manned the Parakeet in a Pinto station on his side, from the actual force that brought about the revolution. A lot less formidable a force, the assembly reckons, than he lets on. In other words, no need to go underground. 'But staying over, or on top, on the ground,' Rey Irani warns, pausing strategically to let the effect sink in, 'can only mean one thing.' And that thing, that thing...

They never thought they'd end up here. Not in their wildest dreams. Or nightmares. How everything had kind of gotten out of hand, frankly, some thought privately. All this, just for some human flesh! Jesus... How had they gotten to this point?... Shall they just acquiesce?... But how would they?... They would never be able to lead quiet lives, if they let go, that is... How does life ever get away from one so quickly?... How do the years go by and you end up where you end up?... Did I really intend to be here, standing among these creatures?... Did I really ask for this?... Did I precipitate this?... How many silly and stupid decisions one makes in a lifetime!... And is forced to make as one goes on!... How to go on, is the big question... How to go on... How...

Contemplative moods... Inward queries... Whispers and wayward glances... Are there no more options? Is this really it? Seems like it... Well... One more round of votes. The question is asked, and the command made for all those for, to say 'aye'—and all those not, to say 'nay.' The ayes outnumber the nays. Unanimously. And so...

'That's that,' says an obviously delighted Rey Irani. In an underhanded and totally unexpected and sleazy way, he had risen to, not just a leadership position of sorts, but, possibly, The Leadership position. To the surprise, yes, but also the chagrin of his brethren, who could not reverse things at this point. The weasel had gotten his way, his absolute dislike for Mappolo finally, finally finding an outlet... More importantly, the dreaded thing, that 'thing' that was worrying them and igniting all sorts of hesitations inside, that thing was...

The Civil War

How the savage within all would be unleashed and madness unabated reign. How evil in its many incarnations and manifestations, its guises and its dis-guises, would wander the bleak and bombed-out boulevards. How previously friendly and even bowling-alley sharing neighbors would turn on each other, victims all of their delusional feelings of the necessity of belonging to one group or another. How neighborhood watches would crumble in the face of rampant, mordant destruction, suspicious activity being the only kind of activity around. How company softball teams would disintegrate and disappear and the whole league disband, what with all the negativity and division and dislike of teammates and foes alike.

O Saturday afternoon barbecues postponed who knows how long hopefully not through the fall we'd like to tailgate and catch some college football. O popcorn unpopped (closure of movie cineplexes), O sales unshopped (consumer spending down and higher taxes), O cafés ironically teaming with people (no confidence in phones or faxes)! Deliriously how the crying children from the arms of their mothers are pulled away by farcically evil occupiers. Monstrously how the soldiers of doom knock down walls, break down doors and slowly, gratuitously, abduct, rape, slash, kill, and kill some more, and kill some more. Flames atop towers in the distance, fire rising, rising, ashes falling from the skies and the ruins, fireworks in the nights lit with the blood of the weary, the wounded and the lost, bombs, falling, falling, smashed, the dreams and the pictures of long-ago lusts, falling, the worlds, falling, still, falling, slowly, as if the last cry of dawn, falling... Bombs from up above and bullets from all around: the mall is a fortress and from the rooftops the snipers pick out shoppers still shopping, in the midst of this rapturous hullabaloo, unbelievably, disbelievingly, they're still shopping in the middle of a civil war! Even though the mall's parking lot is now a no man's land! *Their* parking lot? A no-man's land?! *Their* mall? O how is it possible for this to happen here?! *Here*! To *us*!!

O malevolent forces of evil unleashed by evildoers from overseas probably! Certainly! All those barbarians always start these things and not us! Can't go shopping at the mall?! Are you kidding?! Wherefore art thou Trojan Toyota? A giant one too is needed to place inconspicuously in the middle of the parking lot and wait, on the other side, in the other lot, to see if they bite. A Trojan Toyota with tinted glasses and room inside for at least a hundred drivers that'll dwarf its civilian model! An all-out attack climbing the fortress's walls will just have to do! Stores in the shopping centers riddled with bullet holes, with roofs caved in and windows smashed and the jagged edges in the corners only reminding the populace of the devastation. Widowed wives and house-moms and house-dads who now will have to provide for the children when this storm passes. And the children, ahhh the children, staring blankly into the cameras, neighboring suburbs watching with heavy hearts. Perhaps they will place empty fishbowls with the picture of orphaned Whootonites on the cover, asking for donations for these poor, drooling, hungry and miserable souls. The food court at the mall all but a semblance of its busy and hopping self. The cubicles and work areas nothing but a ghost-town of the modern era, for their inhabitants are off now, hiding in secret places, plotting against one another, not engaging in some metaphoric corporate war to win the boss's favor, but literally. Now is the chance: to kill one another and tear each other's eyes and hearts out and eat each other's children—again, *literally*. Devastated roadways and streets and alleys and cul-de-sacs. Abandoned strollers on sidewalks and in the stands around the high school football field. Baseball fields' grasses grown too tall, a sad sign of neglect and decrepitude.

Incredibly, all-you-can-eat sushi joints are still providing their fare, but fish that's obviously not too fresh, patrons beware. In front of the 7-Eleven, the usual crowd hangs, waxing nostalgic and existential, downing brews, with their earrings and mohawks and baggy clothes, laughing at the adults who gave them advice, the poor fools! Devastation and ruin all around, a grayness enveloping the burbs, a dreary and dreadful dawn of a new age. Fire… Fire and the wind and the earth in unbalance in the throes of the flames of unseen trolls. A world awash, in ruin, a wrath, a world in ruin…

Except… Except that not much of Whooton was in flames. In fact, ninety-nine point nine nine percent of the population *still* had no idea what was going on, starting with The Abductions, The Takeover, The Overturn attempts by isolated bands, The Undertaking by the Coalition, The Turnaround in the leaders' futures, or The Turning of the Tide. Most never bothered to read the announcements posted on any of the bulletin boards, and the fate of flyers left under doors has for centuries been known. The door to door stuff too, had, pardon my French again, gone in one ear and come out the other. In other words, there were few gunshots, no fire, no dead bodies paving the streets, no buildings in ruins, and little in the way of traumatic experiences by most citizens. There were no food shortages, no curfews, no accidental shootings. There were no job losses (due to the non-war, that is), and no new industries sprouting and cashing in on the dire circumstances. No bombed-out or ruinous alleys, for, indeed, in these wide-open spaces that were neither rural nor urban, and not even something in-between, but just an uncomfortable, unnatural wide-openness with traffic flowing, there were, actually, no alleys, light or dark. Nothing was amiss, could not be, never would happen, not in *these* suburbs, not in *any* suburb, come to think of it, never, we all know that, of course…

What did occur was this: in a masterly executed plan devised by none other than the newest hero, Rey Irani, several forces wearing berets barged into the Old Pancake House, Poppy's and Daddy's Fried simultaneously, proceeded to immediately execute the guards, cut them into pieces and put the pieces into sacks. They liberated the prisoners (eight total: six at Poppy's, two at Daddy's) all of whom seemed to have been treated well enough and in accordance with the General Accords in Treatment of Prisoners. All, also, seemed utterly clueless as to why they had been captured and dragged to the locales. No explanations were given, and they seemed fine. Thanked their liberators and basically made their way home.

At the Old Pancake House, upon the coalition members' entry, they realized that no one had been marked for execution, but that did not save Nicksha Bakhtari (NC). An old comrade of Rey's, he was still captured and held until the new leader (he was growing more and more into the role) actually made his entrance with a platoon of bodyguards. Pushed down to his knees by two guards holding him by the hair, Bakhtari pleaded before Rey to spare his life, that he'd had no choice in joining Mappolo, remember the exit ramps how we used to jump and yell, that was what he was told to do, that he'd even attempted once to contact him ('Your sister picked up and I told her to tell you to call me back, she's a fox dude, sexy voice too'), remember how—Rey cut him off abruptly: 'Enough!' he said. He looked at Tonya next to him and whispered in her ear before turning around and walking towards the door. Tonya walked up to Bakhtari and plunged her dagger straight into the latter's heart, and walked out.

Others had broken and entered the dwellings of Applbottum, Kruyss (NC) and other unsuspecting players. All had been shackled and brought to and held, ironically enough, at Poppy's, where new guards were keeping watch. All, under fierce questioning, had confirmed that Mappolo was home, had not changed residences, not even his phone number, it was true.

A squadron has now encircled the house whose basement Mappolo calls home. Rey Irani after a slight delay has gone to the scene of the encircling of Mappolo's dwelling with all the other bigwigs, namely, Sanjip Ray, Dolores Delectable and Apeltchiks. The troops tell him that the entire house is safely surrounded, and that there is no way, no chance, no sir, of escape. 'Great,' Irani says. 'We're dealing with quite a cruel dude and we can't let him get away.' He next raises a loudspeaker to his mouth, recounts the day's events to Mappolo, tells of the current circumstances, the imprisonment of his closest advisors, the chopped-off guards, the freed prisoners, and, of course, his own situation.

'It's over Mappolo,' Rey says calmly. 'You're better off surrendering.'

No signs from the house. No opening of doors or windows, no shouts. No screams.

'Mappolo Rei!' Rey Irani yells again with a bit more official, less sadistic tone. "The house is surrounded. Your allies have all been captured. All your prisoners have been freed. The Coalition has taken over. The True Revolution will now rule. You must surrender.' He then pauses, brings the loudspeaker down, gestures to several members of the troupe who in turn gesture to the others, brings back the loudspeaker and says: 'Hail Suburbia!'

In perfect synchrony and with passion and gusto, all of Irani's troops in one voice repeat: 'Hail Suburbia!'

And stand there and wait and stare at the shabby door.

12

M a p p o l o Rei in his bunker alone, before him
passing visions of the end (although you never know), unable
to bear the chant of his tormentors outside, covers his ears and
lets out a screech that echoes and echoes and actually breaks a
glass. Never, he's thinking, I will never surrender! Somehow, in
his mind, tender images of the recent past appear: his conversation with the waitress who set him up at Joe's (he forgets her
name, Katie, Cathy, something like that), Joe himself, who allowed him all the flexibility in the world and basically let him
run his own show (albeit with the occasional disagreements),
his many lovers along the way, from Bernadette to Chuck to
Eddy *and* Eddie (yup!) and Jenny (yes, the same), the grand
noches de baile and the festivities and the drunken orgies,
not to mention the countless thighs he feasted on up to and
through The Takeover, and certainly, after. So much so that his
mood changes and memories of the beauteous times prompt
the appearance of an actual smile on his face, which is quickly
erased from his panicked visage by the chant he hears again
on the outside, the screams of the evil ones, the traitors, the
collection of all Benedict Arnolds in the history of the known
universe. Never, he murmurs again, I shall never surrender…

He walks up to the window wondering whether he should
open one and holler to the traitors his thoughts. Thinks better
than to let his pride stand in the way though, and quickly

turns attention to more clever solutions, to potentially cruder recourses to ruses. Could it be, he's asking, that all my troops are down? What about the populace—are they about to allow this assault on the autonomy of their government? He goes to the phone and picks it up. No dial tone. Bastards, he whispers. And slams the phone back down. (Cell phones not yet in widespread use at time of writing—editors.) Isolated. Encircled. Defeated? Last hours of Mappolo Rei? What will happen, what is Mappolo Rei really all about? What kind of person is he? Is he going to step up to the plate? Is he going to suck it up and go for the bomb? Gut check time Mappolo Rei. Second wind time, Mappolo Rei. Play hurt not injured time, Mr. Rei. Just tryin'a get back to the line of scrimmage time. Is this not one of those situations that shows the mettle of a man? What he's all about? Absent all the bullshit and all the pretense? Is he going to walk out, hands up in the air waving a white sheet or piece of cloth? Is he going to set the house on fire and remain inside? Will he swallow pills, or turn his gun on himself? Will he walk out shooting like a deranged maniac and get as many as he can before falling in a hail of bullets? Will he pretend to negotiate in the hopes of a future counter-coup, to regain power and eliminate once and for all, all the vermin? Who is Mappolo Rei, really? What will he do? And will whatever he does now truly give us a better portrait as I'm claiming it will? Why, this is just another circumstance after all, and he could be led by irrational emotions and quirky decisions just like any other... Or, no?

Now, I wish I could set up a hotline, a poll of sorts, an online voting system that would allow you—the reader!—to cast your vote as to what might or should happen to our hero, or even offer a range of potential fates, all of which would be valid and lead to an ending based on whichever course you chose that he chose: with audience participation and voice in the unfurling of the account. Why not! (Unfortunately, I have reserved such narrative gymnastics both for the last chapter (where I briefly outline other endings to be considered) and for a future project that I invite you to look out for.) And plus, outside of all these considerations, a man's life—even if such a man is non-existent and an array of non-events, non-relationships and non-actions are associated with the word, his only true essence—is not a plaything, nor is his fate a malleable object to be molded as one desires. Pre-determined or not, there is one fate reserved for this bloke as for all others, and the fact that I have as of yet (meaning, of this scribbling) not decided which it should be, changes not that fact one iota. Mappolo Rei is reserved one fate, and one only, as is his privilege as a human, albeit an invented one. (Could I, or elsewho, devise a human with multiple fates? Who has lived out multiple fates, I mean? Possible? Desirable? Imaginable even?)

And now, here, this day, hunkered in his bunker, depressed, down, pissed off and procrastinating, unable to think clearly, slightly panicked yet still proud and brave, Mappolo Rei, at his desk in his room, the volumes of books on one side and manuscripts related to the revolution on the other, quietly now, contemplates.

He takes out several of his manifestoes from his drawers and reads. Damn, he utters within, I was good. But noticing that he'd actually used the past tense, he corrects himself and says, I *am* good, and as if to drive the point home, he keeps reading a passage from The Selfless Manifesto—'...all those who call for mutiny will in the end suffer the fate they weave...'—and another from his decidedly more poetic Sycamore Manifesto: '...The delusions of humans, of grandeur and of importance, are a thing to be reckoned with. When one sits by a river, by the ocean, by a body of water, one cannot but be impressed with the magnitude of all that envelops the littleness of each of us, and the unimportance of the species as a whole... O woes and misbegotten wailings, summon the armies of lucidity and relax, relax for Christ's sake, will you...' Did I write that, he wonders proudly, even though it could easily be argued that the sentimental piece was not any more impressive than a sixteen-year-old's existential rants in his or her journal. He closes the manifestoes and reads through some of his imaginary interviews, the post-victory interviews, the post-interview interviews, more specifically one he dubs the *Rencontre*, where in some small French village, to hail the new leaders of wonderfully progressive and fabulous communities, a French journalist would have spoken to him by a quiet river. He skims through his booklets of aphorisms, reads aloud a Sufi-inspired poem ('O Wine and Bread and Beauty, it's not every day I get that mighty Booty'), glances at observations and notes, and delays a bit on another poem that he had written as part of an epic for the new age.

Then, with sadness suddenly enveloping his face and his being, he begins to whisper, in a talkative tone and not so much a singing one, the cruel irony not lost on him (he had, after all, ordered the murder of the song's progenitor), he begins to murmur...

> *O teenager in the basement*
> *Sittin' around tellin' tales and gettin' high*
> *Wash out those colors in your punk hair*
> *Forget school and sports and the rest of the crazy fair*
>
> *What good will it do, Oooo Oooo*
> *What good can it do*

271

To hang in the basement
And wallow and wallow and wallow
In this predicament!

He suddenly snaps and stands to yell at the traitors on the outside intruding again on his lone sanctuary. And then launches full-throttle, except that it's inside, all inside, all bottled up inside and finding release still inside,

O teenager in the basement
O teenager in the basement
Wake up from your slumber
O teenager in the basement
Think about your predicament!

Get your chin off the pavement
Get your soul out the gutter
Get your mind off the stripper
Get up and make a statement!

I am, I am, I am—
A teenager in the basement
Sick—and tired!—of strumming my lonely guitar!
Sick—and tired!—of dad's old beat-up car!
Sick—and tired!—of staring at blank walls!
Sick and tired, sick and tired, sick and tired
Of fakin' all my higggggghhhhhhssss...
And passin' out on the
Cheap-ass
Devil-red
Old-style
Lazy-chairish

Motha-fuckin'
Beeeeeeeaaaaaaaaan baaaaaaaaaaaaaaaaaag!

He now blocks out the repeated chants by intensely con-
centrating on his potential course of action, and, with a blank
sheet and a pencil—his eternal saviors—head bent over, he
considers the various options, the advantages, the disadvan-
tages, the impact on his name, on history, on his place therein, not to mention the fate of his beloved Whooton. He jots
down, along with a consideration of the options I outlined
earlier, the following: a) sneaking out one of the back doors,
getting to one of the guards, killing him, stealing gun and/
or dagger and disappearing into the back woods; b) digging
a hole in the ground and further digging a tunnel all the way
beyond the radius of the traitorous gang—and making a run
for it; c) pretending to be ill and somehow persuading Rey and
cohorts to take him to the hospital whereupon he would plot
his escape, either on the way or at the institution, depending
on the circumstances.

Deep in thought, head bent down and hands on head,
breathing deeply, deeply worried. The deep thematic comes
up again and again as our hero makes up his deep mind, a
lifetime's worth of an oeuvre at stake, not to mention a life,
his, what to do.

Too late

Eh oui! You can take but only so much time pondering!
Only so long weighing the options! Only so long to determine
the correct path and choose the right course of action! Mappolo Rei had to go through his entire gamut of thought processes

and parameters (including the regret factor etc…). Well, too late! Doin' the right thing ain't what it's all about! It's who wins—who is clever enough, street-smart enough, to impose their will, ya know that Mappolo goddamnit! You killed your lover slash supreme commandant! And basically stole (like he accused you of doing) the revolution from him! Why the inconsistencies?!! One minute considering all options in the service of the perfect decisions, the next ignoring all thoughts, considerations, decisions and what have you! Well, too late, like the title says, too goddamn late!

Too late II

As he sits in his room, eyes closed, he hears the gang and a loud bang and an even louder yell. The front door has been knocked down and several members of the terrorist organization have barged in, yelling. Mappolo, instinctively, stands up. Arms extended fingers touching his desk. Incredibly, he calms his nerves. Resignation? Not really. Smarts is all. No need for commotion now. No need to panic. Deep breath in fact, and he sits back down. If they're gonna get me, they're gonna get me at my game, so. Sits back down, brings up his sheet before his eyes and examines, as if naught is a-happenin'. But Rey's forces are turning the furniture over, breaking plants and vases and yelling for Mappolo to surrender. Jumping around like maniacs. More noises. More have entered. The room is getting tighter. Shit, Mappolo is thinking. And then, 'Fuck 'em!' Rey Irani has entered, Mappolo hears his squeaky voice. They are in the living room, some positioned at the entrance, several outside still. There are no more options. No rooms to search. Mappolo knows that Rey knows. Mappolo hears the cautious, approaching steps.

The intruders are here. The sounds of their feet. Then there is a lull. A silence. No one moving. Barely breathing even. Mappolo is still seated, his paper now on the desk before him, his head bent over it.

Eerie silence—eerie by its totality. The first one he's ever heard, he thinks. A total silence. Never had felt one so clearly, so loudly, so lucidly. Wow! Three 'soldiers' suddenly come in, one crowding the door, the other rushing to the other side of the room and the last moving to the center of the room, behind Mappolo. No words exchanged, none necessary. The guns aimed at Mappolo. Mappolo stands, slowly, pushing back slightly his chair. Brings his hands up, slowly again, turns around and glances at potential assassins. Smile. Through the door, slowly, walk in Sanjip Ray and then Rey Irani, flanked by two guards. Irani stands face to face with Mappolo. Stares at him. Mappolo stares back, the wicked smile still on his face.

'Fuck you Rey, you motherfucker, don't think I'm gonna let you get the first word in!' (How eerie, Mappolo's utterance, and the whole scene: how they echo that episode with A. in his hour, when Mappolo not so long ago, in like fashion, brought down mighty A…)

One of Rey's flankers has taken two steps forward and hit Mappolo hard with the butt of his gun in the stomach, forcing him down to his knees—but he'd finished his sentence fast, knowing, he, Mappolo, what would come if he did what he'd done.

Writhing in pain and on one knee, the soldier stepping back, Mappolo proud, Mappolo loco (as his college friends used to call him O so long ago), manages to look up and spit in the direction of Rey.

'Fuck you,' he says again, undeterred.

'Mappolo Rei,' Rey Irani says in an official and formal tone, neutral and utterly emotionless (having wiped the spit from the right wrist where it had pathetically landed), 'you are under arrest for crimes against the revolution and the revolutionary spirit, for allowing your vengeful urges to divert the revolution, for clueless leadership, excessive celebrations, deprived and bizarre sexual conduct, zealous sports-fan syndrome, murder, wrongful arrest, treason, stupid-ass decision-making and bad management, not to mention frivolous spending, corruption, nepotism and general idiocy!'

He stops, tells one of the guards to make the kneeling man (head bowed from several un-narrated butts to the stomach) raise his chin. Then he says: 'Did I leave anything out? I mean, help me out here bud, what else?'

Mappolo tries the spit thing again and this time, amazingly, from the kneeling position at that, it reaches Irani's face, although lands, meekly, on the bottom of the right cheek. Impressive enough though, definitely.

Irani turns the cheek and says: 'Here, try another one.' He then laughs, cruelly, for Mappolo is slithering around on the ground as Irani with Sanjip to the side extends his latest invitation, what with a nasty hit over the head by one of the guards.

Rey's last syllables were uttered with heightened passion, diverging from the fact-spewing tone, and letting the audience in on his true state of being.

'Now, get the fuck up you worthless bloodsucking cocksucker, and get ready to be sliced to pieces!'

Rey Irani then smashes a vicious coup de leg right into a still writhing Mappolo. It sends him rolling again, blood churning from his ears and his nose, his left hand awkwardly driven to cover the corner of the left side of his face. He moans, coughs up blood, crawls, coughs some more and lies there, in his room, motionless.

When Applbottum and the others held at Poppy's heard of Mappolo's capture, they got to really experience that sinking feeling (Oooo, Oooo) as if the bottom had been kicked out from under them. Their facial expressions quickly revealed their newfound despair. It was a sad scene, really was: to have fought so hard, sacrificed so much, sliced so many, only to lose it all through some technicalities, through allegiances that you never really consider as much as fall into—haphazardly, unwittingly, just like life. Strange, strange indeed.

But under the weight of this disappointment that they felt, from this dejection, out of the quote unquote rubble of their defeat, huddled into a corner booth at Poppy's, the guards keeping a close eye on them, having feasted on cat food and dog food courtesy of Mr. Rey Irani's sense of irony, a magical lightness began to appear. An overcoming of sorts, not unlike the spirit that generates songs made up by the oppressed through their suffering, songs that bring lightness to their world, a dose of light to an otherwise dreary, hopeless condition. Amazingly, such a song was indeed created, right there in their midst—and it was Mehdi Ahangsa's doing. A classical guitar player in his spare time (in fact, a guitar player who'd fallen into these activities in his spare time), he began, out of despair, to hum a melody. The others were sitting, watching him, curiously listening as his gentle soft voice became ever more soothing, his resolve into solidifying the song ever more apparent, his manipulation of the notes and the words ever more confident. A certainty in his goal that became more and more defined as he carried on. His reserved humming was turning into a gentle, full-blown, and potentially legendary song. The initial hesitant stringing together of words now a perfectly executed improvisation. Inspiration in the true sense of the word. Almost as if dictated from above, or elsewhere for certain—and elsewho, no doubt.

Ohhhh he was a gentle soul, a child at heart

his humming had begun with the whole line in crescendo from an almost silent yet rising ooooh,

A cherubic face in the cold, dark night.

The gathered listened at first and were subsequently drawn in more and more as Ahangsa continued, their eyes with unperturbed attention fixated on the singer and his deft command of the unexpected tune. A song that was being conceived, literally, in their midst. A great honor, surely, a magical moment, no doubt. And indeed, the second time around, after Ahangsa had basically made up the ode on the first go-round, they accompanied him by humming along and even singing some parts—as if to reconfirm, as if to launch, for real, the Great Ode...

> *Oyo, Oyo* (added in sequel)
> *He was a gentle soul, a child at heart*
> *A cherubic face in the cold dark night*
> *Ohummm, Ohummmm*
> (a cross between the Om of the tantric humming and the aha/aha of the prancing rock 'n' roll singer)

> *He rose and fought oppression*
> *Couldn't stand our condition*
> *Without malice or ambition*
> *Risked his life for emancipation*

Oyo, Oyo
He was a gentle soul, a child at heart
A cherubic face in the cold dark night
Ohummm, Ohummmm

He cried and fought with passion
Not to fight or conquer or kill
Not to follow this fad or that fashion
But to make a better world—We Will!

Oyo, Oyo
He was a gentle soul, a child at heart
A cherubic face in the cold dark night
Ohummm, Ohummmm

Sent from above down below
No doubt—to save us from our sins
Humble, simple, quiet & without show
His one mission, to help us help our kin

Oyo, Oyo
He was a gentle soul, a child at heart
A cherubic face in the cold dark night
Ohummm, Ohummmm

He starved and he abstained and he
Basically drove himself mad
To make us know feel and see
A better life by all could be had

Oyo, Oyo
He was a gentle soul, a child at heart

A cherubic face in the cold dark night
Ohummm, Ohummmm

A hero like him our times won't see
Who gives up all pleasures and cachet
(Quite outré, we say)
Who dreams the dream that has to be
To show us the path, yes, the way

Oyo, Oyo
He was a gentle soul, a child at heart
A cherubic face in the cold dark night
Ohummm, Ohummmm

His name was Mappolo, Mappolo Rei
Never knew his daddy but that's okay
He's a saint and a savior anyway
His name is Mappolo, Mappolo Rei

When the ballad of Mappolo Rei, which we can now safely call The Ballad of Mappolo Rei, was finished, the four prisoners dejectedly looked at one another. There were no cheers, no applause, no audience or populace going wild. Only the whirr of the soda machines, the maddening light of the tungsten lamps, the breathing of the guards. All back into the quietude. The recognition of the inevitability of their fate. Morose, now, more than ever perhaps. But they'd remembered their leader. And commemorated him, best of all. Applbottum was even thinking of a way to write the ode down, for history's sake, for the record, for truth—but they had nothing: no paper, no writing material of any kind. It would have been futile to ask also, the guards delighted in psychological torture of the deprivation kind. But a look around gave a slither of hope: while they would make believe they were talking, Applbottum could carve the ode into the sidewall, slowly, painfully, with her nails. Cautiously, for they needed to ascertain that any noise made by this valiant attempt would be drowned out by the chatter. (Bravo loyal and eternally grateful Applbottum! Bravo Applbottum, for your unwavering support! Bravo Applbottum, for not succumbing to the power lust of the traitors, bravo, Applbottum, for your guts!—Applbottum heard in her head the array of voices lauding her uncompromising ways!)

It was decided and confirmed—with gestures and signs invented on the spot for the purpose—that yes, they were, for sure, going to attempt it. Nothing to lose, really. But more importantly, so that future generations would know who the true leader of the revolution was, what The Truth is, what despicable acts were committed by the victors: know that their community had been founded upon lies and murder. So that in the distant future when the eyes of an unsuspecting teenager on a Friday or Saturday evening with friends hanging out (for, surely Poppy's would be back once they were gone—O the terrible thought—or at least turned into another fast food joint) were averted to the side in the midst of the laughter and chatter and bravado, these same eyes would stumble upon the carved ballad, whereupon a silent reading would be launched, Oyo Oyo, only to turn into a full-fledged recitation, He was a gentle soul, a child at heart, and then said teenager brings hands up as if to interrupt his or her friends and says, Hold up hold up, and his or her friends would slowly stop, because of the sheer process of the mystery if not genius of the verse that the curious teen was now almost singing, A cherubic face in the cold dark night, and so on until the end whereupon he or she would ask the others, You know who they mean, and no one knows and no one cares frankly, but it's all right, it's been planted in their minds, and so one day if Truth shall be set free even though it won't, at least then they would have heard of Mappolo Rei, and wondered to themselves who was Mappolo Rei, and on their way home again uttered his name, Mappolo Rei, and asked if anyone had ever heard of Mappolo Rei... But now they had, they knew, who he was and what he'd done— despite all the lies and propaganda. They might even make up their own variation, a rock version, a rap version, a futurist version, a blues version, a solo for voice, accompanied by guitar, mezzo soprano, or an opera, in the desert, the eternal dream, for The Ballad of Mappolo Rei, would prove to be eternal, no doubt, The Ballad of Mappolo Rei would be sung for centuries to come... True that, true that...

The concrete version—body flesh and blood, liquids now oozing out of him, limbs still intact, although eyes practically shut after the beating he's taken at a makeshift prison fashioned only for him—Mappolo Rei, is hunched on a chair in a corner, practically lifeless. His fate, it appears, has not yet been determined. In an adjacent chamber, The Committee for the Righting of the Revolution is discussing the dilemma/notion of a public hanging, after a public flogging: sounded good except that nobody in Whooton still had any clue as to what was going on. A quick and easy firing squad would get rid of the shit real fast, Rey Irani thought inwardly—but that would be too easy. Or else, a taped confession, a small show trial, except for the fact that again, there was no one to really show it to, and besides, the local channels wouldn't go for it—no matter what pressure was put on them. Devote advertising dollars to put on trial a fellow no one's ever heard of? Don't think so!

Other options were debated until finally, Rey Irani, now officially the Supreme Leader, finally decided on the outcome. Quite the brutal one too, Mister Irani not holding back, after what he thought was the senseless murder of Eddie, not to mention A., now long forgotten who surely was trying to do the right thing but simply could not bring himself to eliminate Mappolo for the good of all. Well, Rey Irani thought, he was going to right all these wrongs. He was going to avenge all of these brutalities, this senseless savagery, this unacceptable lack of respect and honor for your fellow beings! He was going to end the reign of murder and corruption! Not to mention the fact that he was—finally!—going to get back at Mappolo—who'd beaten him out for the starting forward position on the varsity soccer team, among many other minor victories…

Rey Irani's vision grows. Well, not grows, just becomes clearer, more transparent, lucid. A certain inevitability about it. His parents are from that great land, Iran, after all, aren't they? That means, kind of, that so was he. His name even said so: Irani, from Iran, of Iran, Eyeranian, for god's sake! Who was he, to disagree?! In that great land with two thousand five hundred years of history, he repeated to himself, the mythological mantra of all the exiled and non-exiled and even religious Iranians he'd gotten to (superficially) know over the years: they swore by it, they lived by it, gave them a great sense of accomplishment, importance, supremacy, two thousand five hundred years of history, they'd repeat, The Empire, The Persian Empire, as if something to be proud of, something grandiose, a trophy of some sort. But then again, he wondered within, who was he, to disagree: this was his lineage, his peoples (he chuckles), but hey, there for the taking, appropriate and make it yours! He was born to conquer and lead into the next century, lo, the next millennium, why not, with each passing moment his delusions of grandeur increasing by worrisome, exponential degrees. In his blood. In his veins.

Behold Rey Irani, the great conqueror, emperor to be, with a whole bunch of history. Yes, with his peoples behind him, he shall march on, triumphantly, holding scepter and sword, in uniform down Connecticut Avenue with the soldiers in line atten-shun! He'll shake hands and pin some medals even, on some officers' chests, his duty, his calling! He will salute and he will command and he will make sure there are posters of him on all the walls and on all the desks. There will be statues and busts of the man in every public square. Boulevards and streets and alleys and even cul-de-sacs named after him. He will command the troops and get the money from the lobbyists and occupy the nicest office in the complex. His clothes will be imported always from France and his shoes will shine, unlike now. He will order executions and he will imprison and he will torture and he will get away with it all, giddily. His name will be sung, and his story will be told. School children will line up and sing praises and odes and paeans to the great leader of the revolution, of liberty, of independence, of the whatever else it is he ushered in. He will be invited to all the banquets and all the events and even the premiers. He will be honored by institutions and praised in the media and folks will beg to kiss his feet and his hands and even his underpants, if he doesn't mind. He will be streetified, schoolified, boulevardized, buildinguized, airportized, stampified. Museums will fight to have his belongings, will kill to place his furniture and his holdings within their vaults. March on, march on, O great Rey, you have conquered and you have won—fair and square, because unfair and unsquare is the name of this game, and this does indeed constitute its own opposite. O Great Great Rey,

O higher than the highest Rey, O Excellent be thy name, thy visage Rey, O gone and come back Rey, O O, O O, O Great Emperor Rey, your time has come, do not be fooled by lonely loserish naysayers, put them in their place where they belong, where they deserve to be, you are the new leader of this revolution, steal it, what the heck, revolutions are made to be stolen, like everything else. March on and don't give a hoot about nothin', it'll be all yours, although you're still wondering how it all kind of just fell in your lap! You're due, buddy. Your peoples are due, look it at that way. Fuck the Italians and the Irish and the Puerto-Ricans. Fuck the Germans and the French even more and certainly the new Hispanics! And for sure the Ay-rabs!! It's the Eyeranians' time! Think of it that way and feel no guilt. Who better than you?! With the name and all. Go Rey, it's all yours man, all yours dude, go and march down that avenue and hold the parades and have crowns and whatever other headgear you want on your head and all sorts of splashy junk on your vestments and keep going and keep going and buy a Mercedes even at some point and ride in it and wave to your adoring public. Go Rey go. Come now people, let's all chant, a one, a two, and:

Go—Rey!

Go—Rey!

Go—Rey!

He brings the news to Mappolo himself. Flanked by other members of the committee, he walks into the chamber where Mappolo was hunched over on his chair, his hands tied behind his back. He walks to Mappolo, bends down, puts his finger under Mappolo's chin and raises slightly his head, looks into his half-open eyes.

'Open your eyes, Mappolo,' he says, laughing.

The other members of the committee also find this funny, so they in turn crack a smile and let out a little giggle.

'So here's what we've decided we're gonna do with you, buddy. You ready?'

O so cruelly, Rey Irani himself moves Mappolo's head up and down in the gesture of the affirmative.

'We thought: why—we always first kill the folks, then slice 'em and cook 'em and eat 'em. But who said that was the way ey, Mapman? We like to experiment, we like to, how shall I say, shift paradigms, and shift even the paradigm of paradigm-shifting! Dig? Or no, I'm not being clear enough?'

Rey then shakes Mappolo's head sideways (the negative headshake) and suddenly lets it go as he stands (Mappolo's head fully back down), paces about, comes back and stands in front of Mappolo.

'We're theoretical, Mappolo, you see, that's what I'm trying to say. We're thinking: why not cut you off piece by piece, and cook the pieces right in front of you mind you. I even told Todd Toodlesworth already, he'll bring the tables and what have you. Quite the show ey Mapman? Wine, champagne, nice tables—fancy sitting here and enjoying the show… Wouldn't even have to cook everything really. Could do some raw parts. As in Mappolo Sushi—now there's an idea! Isn't it great Map, to see, to know, that people love and appreciate you so! Isn't that nice of us?'

Mappolo, almost lifeless, does not react.

'Then the big question was raised by all,' Irani says. 'That is, the question of where we begin. What about the ears, Apeltchiks said in our meeting, you remember her don't you Mappolo, you fucked her brother then threw him out in the street? Well, that's what she said. Dolores said no, we oughta start with a hand, I love the way Dolores says 'ought', you know what I'm talking about, don't you, how she goes 'ought', that haughty tone, that voice coming from deep within her throat... Anyway, she said we oughta start with a hand, some fingers in honey barbecue sauce, hmmm fingerlickin' good. And that wasn't all either Mappolo. Everybody had an idea, you know how it works, feet, more pieces of ass, somebody even suggested your balls—what do you think of that Mappolo?! Who do you think said that? Who, Mappolo, who? Don't know? Was it señorita Vonya? Remember her Map, you had the hots for her. Maybe it was Gol Dol. You could see him making such suggestions no, for what you did to A.? Or Donman (NC), he's always had it in for you. I bet he'd delight, absolutely delight, in slicing that penis of yours transversally, like a nice piece of sausage ey? Applbottum? Ah, Mappolo, you'd be happy to know that Ms. Applbottum is now awaiting her own cunt-cutting. She didn't desert you, see Mapman. Not everyone deserted you! Or maybe, maybe it was Lala (NC)! Don't act all surprised Mappolo, you knew she'd come around. All she ever wanted was a Big One! And now, she's got the best! I'll impregnate her and then, well... How's that? Hello Mappolo... I'm not getting any younger doing this babe. You gotta try it at least, wild guess even if that's what it gets to. Come on, Mappolo, who would propose that we start with your balls ey? Who?' Irani pauses, then launches again: 'Should we play 20 questions? What do you think? You ask and I answer, okay? Ready? Go... I said go... Hey... Hello, Mappolo? Can't hear Youuuuuuuu... Okay I'll start you off all right? Ready? Here goes: 1. Is it a human? Yes, yes it is. Bravo. Now, question number 2. Is it someone I know? You bet it is! Good going Mappolo, come on now, you can do it. You can do it, hello, let's go... Hello, Mappolo! Can't help you out forever here, buddy, come on. Okay one more. 3. Do I like him or despise him? Mappo, you know better than that now, just yes or no questions ey? Okay, let's try again, 3. Do I like him? No, and 4. Do I despise him? Yes, probably... Okay that's it... Your turn now, serious... Can't help you out anymore... Mappolo! Hello? Mappolo?! Mister Rei, yoo-hoo, hello, can you hear me? Mappolo! Hey, shithead, I asked you if you could hear me! Don't you have any manners? Didn't mommy teach you to answer when someone asks you a question?! Answer me Mappolo Rei, who said let's cut off his balls first? Answer! What would you like to see cut and cooked and consumed before your very eyes?! Come, speak up! Don't be shy! Buns, testicles, fingers, ears? Eyes? We can do one eye then the other eye if you like. Hello! Hello, Mappolo... Mappolo... Mappolo Rei... Hey! Austin to Mappolo Rei, can you hear me, Mappolo Rei, can you hear me? Hello, hello, Mappolo Rei, can you hear me?'

13

The traffic light is flashing, alone against the backdrop of the white-blue sky. A car going to the intersection slows down, the driver looks left and right as he approaches, puts the breaks on lightly until again he presses on the gas pedal and drives through, across the divide. The automobiles drive up, slow down, drive off again, one after another, drive up, slow down, a pause, a break, the drivers look straight again, nostalgia on the faces, fatigue on the faces, aloneness on the faces, an elbow on the windowsill, a hand on the wheel, the long drives to drop off or pick up, station wagon mom with the soccer balls in the back, migrant dad working hard, the emptiness on the face, the wonderings, the questionings, the wonderings why, the endless heres and theres, memories of walks by bridges of forgotten worlds, of otherworlds now in the name of heroes with other names, as if choreographed this perfectly synchronized play of the traffic light, the automobile and the slightly grainy face of the driver through the window cautiously, obediently, like a good citizen, looking left, looking right, almost as if the whole domestic scene of wife and son and daughter in the living room of the townhouse in front of the television or the argument in the kitchen in front of the kids or in sweeter times the family packing and going down to the lake in the park with kids riding their bikes, the death of dad's father, almost as if all of the scenes of their lives could be glanced at in that moment, in that movement, that subtle turn, right and left, right and left, to make sure that it's safe, to cross, to drive on, to drive on, to go on.

A gentle quietude, an absence of noise, an absence of shouts and screams, an absence of boomboxes and car radios and lively debates the wayfarer hears in the city, the peopled streets of the city, the folks in front of the stoops gossiping, the domino-playing men in the corners in front of bodegas or delis, the teenagers hanging out (just a bunch of homies huddled up in groups engaged in a variety of activities), an absence of lights and flashes, an absence of silhouettes and shadows on illuminated walls, an absence of hurried steps and swift dashes and sudden jerks and sprints and rushes. Absence, it feels like, of absence even. A shopping center is in the distance, visible from my perch, at least the signs of the stores, the outlines of the folks walking in and out of the stores, couples walking, mothers holding the hands of little sons and little daughters, the group of three or four teenage girls on a relaxed outing, nothing extravagant this evening, just hang out at the ice-cream parlor and grab some food at a Chinese restaurant or buy some shirts on sale. Or sneakers even. Or maybe some CDs and then to the pizza joint. A slice or two, sodas, love those booths where you sit two on one side and two on the other and you sip through your straw, a weird kind of security you feel, with your buddies, almost protected, infallible, unharmed. Then you walk out feeling the cheese in your teeth and the taste of the soda and the red peppers on your tongue and you're happy somehow, happiness right there, in that stroll from the pizza place with the red and white square tablecloth and the booths with the container of garlic and red pepper and regular pepper and salt and oregano right there with the napkins, to the car, in the parking lot, opening the doors with the remote and all together still, opening the door and standing there a minute and closing door and driving off and dropping off the buddies—somehow, happiness right there.

There is a man with a gut jogging slowly on the narrow sidewalk. He looks awkward, his face is contorted, pink, his shirt drenched. He continues to jog and turns at the gate separating the high school football field from the boulevard. There is a small gate there, which he opens while continuing to jog in place, skipping up and down, looking immeasurably ridiculous, refusing to pause! He opens and crosses and makes sure to close the gates behind and begins to jog on the asphalt track of the high school, still the same asphalt of so many years ago, or at least it looks like it, even if redone, with small rocks scattered throughout, could not be too good for your knees, if you think about it. The same soccer goalposts, without nets now, since we're not in season. There is no one on the fields. No one practicing on the main field or the adjacent fields, no one on the basketball court above, not even a pick-up game. No boys' or girls' soccer teams, no field hockey or football guys or gals, no cheerleader practice, I remember the cheerleading, from eight, nine years ago. There is no one, and yet they have all passed, so many field hockey players in their shorts and the young football players giving all they had, grunts and noises, the sitting and sprinting and sweating, the oversized and overmuscled and under too, young folks dreaming the dreams, daring, daring to dream of stardom. No one there, except for the short, baldish, chubby fellow sweating off some of the booze, and a lean fellow too, moving at a much better pace, who was already running when the younger urban professional joined in on the track. A migrant walks off in the distance, on the grass, head bent. Two high school girl soccer players walk in feeling important, in front of the shopping center, and soon I see them back, one driving, the other in the passenger seat of what else, a Toyota of some sort. A leotard-wearing just-back-from-workouts soccer-mom slash well-to-do consultant-woman walks by. Little branch of a bank situated awkwardly as if a cabin in an outpost in the middle of the parking lot to facilitate drive-through banking. Another shopping center across. Starbucks outlet. Humongous shoe warehouse. Enterprise Rent-A-Car around the corner and a Morgan Stanley Dean Witter and a Citibank and a Village Eye Center and a pizza place a video place a Hamburger Hamlet Beer and Wine Georgetown Square Washington Sports tanning computers hallmarkpizzasalonanothersalonanotherpizzaandnailsandgourmetandicecreamhairandjewelsandgiftsand, and, and… and: a meticulously kept parking lot.

And the cars almost noiselessly carry on in front of these stores, this convenience is all their owners really want, put bags in trunk or in the back of hatchback, carrying shopping bags, putting shopping bags in cars, sitting behind wheel with seatbelt on and both hands on wheel and carry on and carry on some more, with the cars, the cars, the beloved cars, parked in the parking lot, back in or front in, ah destroyed sonnet, why not adhere, you too, to the absolute lowest common denominator!

> *Beige Dodge Sonoma pickup, front*
> *Jeep Minivan Grand Cherokee, back*
> *Blue Mercury, back*
> *Black VW Jetta, front*
>
> *Black Lexus LX 470, back*
> *Red Hondo Accord, front*
> *Gray Mazda coupe, front*
> *White Chevrolet minivan, back*

White BMW 528i minivan, front
Anonymous four-door hatchback, front
Red Toyota Camry, back

Dark green Buick, front
Cyan Chevrolet, front
Gray Saab 9000CSE, back.

A one-way sign planted above the yield sign next to the sign of the gas station by the entrance to the gas station before the traffic light with the cars parked behind one another rises now, the sign and the arrow rising from the anointed place, twisting about in the air hovering above the cars passing thinking where to, pondering where to, wondering where to, go up twisting in the air, floating in the air pirouettes in the air, above the cars, the arrow freed from the sign turns and directs its tip at once out of nowhere, for no apparent reason shoots down into the roof of a car respectfully stopped behind another in the lineup at the traffic light, laughing shoots back up twisting twirls and shoots back down piercing the roof of same car, then shoots back up laughing and shoots back down again all the way through the roof of the car and back out again floating, picks another car and shoots down again piercing and back up again floating, colleagues join up, a yield sign now floats in the air and a stop sign too from afar has come to join and one shoots down into the roof of a car then another shoots down and back up and the tumult goes on and all around now traffic signs float and shoot down into the roofs of cars and back up all around now all around the landscape dotted with signs big and small and red and black and blue and white and combos there-

293

of too rising signs shooting down into roofs with patient motorists unmoved unmoving perhaps simply continue to respect the laws no matter what, no one dares pondering maybe no one scared not a soul comes out to warn or to wonder, just sit back behind wheel one hand two hands on wheel chest a yard away from wheel holding firmly wheel seatbelt on turning occasionally the wheel, obeying the light going green slowing yellow waiting on red, all around the signs raining down and back up and floating and twirling and twisting all the way up above the traffic lights some too get in the act swaying along the lines back and forth their lights in disorder rapidly going green red yellow green yellow red green yellow red yellow green, cars stopping going breaking new lines going pausing stopping rushing yielding watching thump go thump go obediently hands on wheels eyes ahead straight the traffic lights on their rods like swings go to and fro and to and fro now another swings out a baby from the back of the SUV and throws up the baby caught on the swaying traffic light like a swing back and forth, baby laughing baby smiling baby doesn't care, all around the signs shooting down and back up all around the concert of babies and traffic lights swing alike swing along in the air drivers stop going stop yielding go stop going not holler hoot obeying only the signs and the light swinging back and forth, sky all blue still with white clouds no tempest or storm ahead or anywhere in sight just a swirling set of signs now as far as the eye can see all around in the air the damn signs with babies on strollers and babies in cars and little boys and girls jumping up reaching the traffic lights swinging back and swinging forth with the joggers on the sidewalks jogging faster, now the fast food workers in their uniforms and paper hats lined up curtsying a Broadway show of sorts, if not that what, but that, no doubt, except for the fact that it's no show, 'tis true, trust me folks, I've been honest with you all along, been pointing out all the tricks and the points of the artifice, so, but, here, it's true, it's real, really, all about on sidewalks on the ramps in the entrances on roofs of cars dodging the traffic signs some even on the hoods front and back raising paper hats kicking legs the fast food workers, imagine, picture the cars swaying trying to avoid yet stopping, lining up in one lane and not bothering to use the other because everyone is in that one and the traffic lights and the arrows and the no parking signs shooting down, launch up and back, and babies taken from mommies by the silhouettes on the signs coming to life, and the fast food workers all with their paper hats on kicking up legs rhythmic rockettes with the roofs of homes changing colors and the walls too in harmony red green yellow cyan blue, lights from homes and facades, then back and quickly green again blue again red again green the concert of lights and colors, O how they rebel, O how they go, Whooton in black and white now for real, not much difference now movement all around and sounds of the babies and kids screaming swaying on the traffic lines, from the walls of each and every store in the mall around it the center of the shopping center all the hues all the melodies of yesteryears and today and tomorrow too all the stars of all time in a cacophony of concoctions that somehow coalesce into a harmony, all around all the cars in the parking lots all the cars passing and dancing and going and coming and straying and staying, in their anointed places, so immobile, so majestically, so poetically, immobile, all these cars in the parking lot, the parking lots, parked front and back, with colors and makes and models, parked, so splashingly parked, in the lots, back and front, a gray Volvo back, a white Toyota Camry front, a dark green Lexus minivan LX 450 front, a beige Acura Minivan front, a black Mercedes Benz back, a white Land Rover back, a gray Honda Civic back, a black coupe Sebring LX back, all these wondrous engines and immaculate machines, at rest, while their brethren pass, a dreamdaze as I have made abundantly clear, a freeflow of imagery, they pass and pass and pass, O traffic flow of my dreams, how you keep me off the streets, metaphorically speaking, and on, literally, O traffic flow, O traffic flow, how they pass, the Toyota Camry and another Toyota Camry and a Honda Civic hatchback from two years ago and a Volvo a Lexus and another Lexus and an Audi and a big green Ford an Accura a Honda minivan Toyota Corolla red Volvo Toyota Tercel Audi Mitsubishi green Honda black Explorer gray Odyssey, with so few passengers I must say, all makes and models and colors, but not too many folks too bad, could be more efficient as a society but fuck that and I apologize I mean, sheez, I'm just thankful for you traffic flow, really am, traffic flow, drowned in your salvationary powers traffic flow, baptized, finally, in your sacred waters (once again with total number of passengers following the descriptions), O passing cars, O traffic flow, O Toyota Camry with one passenger inside, minivan with one passenger, sedan with one, another sedan with one, minivan 1 plus 2 seniors, Alliance sedan 2, Chevy truck 1, sedan 1, Honda minivan 1, Honda sedan 1, minivan 1, sedan 1, green minivan 1, black sedan 1, red Subaru 1, red classic 1, black Benz 1, black Nissan minivan 2, black Chevy truck 2, red Toyota 2, now a whole gosh darn show it seems check it out, cars honking and making music and other cars even rebelling it seems their drivers struggling for control, right here on the highways and the roadways, putting on a show, cars in parking lots clapping, metaphoric the stage granted but who knows it could easily become real, the music of the cars and trucks and SUVs and sedans and sporty vehicles and classics of long ago, damn,

this is what a carapalooza is all about, and no limited numbers
either, just everyone go and enjoy, wow wow wow what a show,
honks and screeches and scratches and rhythms and rhymes,
eat your hearts out rock 'n' roll guitarist and hip-hop arteest,
you ain't got nothing on the bad old engines in this unbeatable
carapalooza, not a thing, for there they are the cars in the parking lot now taking the show to another level in a dance, one
lunge forward one back, shall they, one step one back, shall
they, one left one right also one front one back, shall they, also,
rebel: or is it just a dance in which they take particular pleasure, my beloved Hondas and Toyotas and Beamers and Benz-
es and Lexuses, or is it, Lexi: O beloved cars o'mine in parking
lots putting on a show right along with the carapalooza, O
Dodges and old Chevys, O how boils my blood for you all,
bring it to me built tough Ford, give it to me cute Escort, let
me roll with you roll on these majestic highways and swoon
with your cool and your charm in the parking lots, go to other
parking lots similar to ones I just got off of, on these lots, and
you shake, your booty how you slide how you glide, back,
yield, front, pause, press, turn, swerve, pause, one coming
from the left sudden stop, and off again, slow, you never know,
if someone is passing or no, in and out, better for it, right between, with nice symmetry and a little nudge back and right
back in, round and round at times, so coolly without panic
and pause, another just coming, press again and push, slowly,
look left look right, and there yes, oh no, gotta go, press again
pause again go, swerve and two left and swoon again, left and
go, slow, there, there is, blinders on stop, wait, your counterpart drearily, excruciatingly slow, pulling out, its behind
swerves and pause and go, forward while you turn left, happy,
happy my beloved Honda, you're happy, between your own
private, white, lines! We'll hold you aloft one day we will, this

dance of yours will not go unnoticed, not your fault that no one yet recognizes your genius, O parking lot, O parking lot, O O parking lot of my dreams, smack dab in the middle of roadways and highways and alleys and houses, O parking lots enchanting us with the variety of your sizes and shapes, if not necessarily with your designs, that's okay, O parking lots allowing for sleepful nights when no one else would let me in, knowing I, we, that you are there, for us, with us, so that we won't have to drive around forever! O parking lot, an ode to you one day I will write and to the fabulous automobiles that populate your space, that dance and sing (in their own way, granted) and move and swoon in a grand spectacle, poetry I say, pure poetry, not poetry in motion, because this motion, is what poetry IS, you see, and you know and I know, but who else is brave enough, to construct a temple, a pyramid, the greatest wonder of the world, in your name, lo, in your image, you, are, the ninth wonder, or the tenth, or whatever, O magnanimous, majestic, parking lot, an ode to you one day like no other I will write, consider this just an overture of sorts, an aria, a ditty if you will, because you deserve a grand opera goddamnit, what am I talking about ode, forget ode, no ode, forget ode, a tribute to you, O parking lot, shall be like no other, no other, no other, for all I see now are backs and fronts and colors and not even makes or models anymore so mesmerized I am, so, so distraught, so blind to the ugliness in the world and yes granted the other beauties and bounties but heck, you're enough, all I see is you, all I want is you, O panoramic view, O colorful view, O O O, let me allow you to come out of your shell, let me allow you to bloom, bloom baby bloom, now that I have no more qualms, nothing to hide, this whole damn book is about you, bloom baby bloom, parked in back, parked in front, back out, back out, front out, back, back, back, front, back, back, back, back, front, black Toyota Tercel back, black Ford back, beige Infinity back, white Mercury front, beige Toyota back, green BMW back, white Mercedes minivan back, beige Toyota Camry back, white minivan front, red BMW back, blue sedan front, red Honda back, gray Mazda Protégé back, gray Maxima sedan back, green Honda back, white minivan back, blue sedan back, blue sedan back, back (green Porsche), back (white Honda Jeep), back (red sedan), back (red Ford minivan), and all around and all around, gray sedan back gray sedan front gray sedan front, black sedan back, gray sedan back, black sedan back, gray sedan back, gray sedan back, blue sedan back, black minitruck back, red sedan back gray sedan back beige sedan back black minitruck back, black sedan back gray sedan back, beige sedan back, back, back, back, back, front, front, front, front, back, front, front, back, front, back, back, back, back, back, back, back, back, back, back, back, back, front, back, back, back, back, back, front, back, back, back, back, back, back, front, back, back, front, back, back, back, back, back, back, back, back, back, back, back, back, front, front, front, front, back, maroon, black, red, black, white, gray, gray, maroon, green, white, black, white, green, beige, beige gray white red gray blue gray maroon maroon gray gray gray blue blue beige beige gray red white green gray white whitemaroonblueblackblackgraywhitewhiteredgraygraygrayredgraygraygreengraybluegrayblueredbluegreenbluebluebeigebluebeigebeigewhitegray, O great traffic flow and the parking lots merging into one, merging into a dreamer's delight, ahhh so wondrous, O traffic flow and parking lots no, don't do this to me please, please, traffic flow and parking lots, no, I'm saying, stop, go on, don't, not, go ahead stop, no no I mean it, not, traffic flow and parking lot into one, no, no, no no no no no no, don't call me to you, I'll come,

no, don't, I'll come, don't, I'm coming traffic flow and parking
lots, I'm coming, stop, I mean it, not, stop, don't, let go, I'm
coming, I'll come, I'm coming I'm, coming I'm, coming I'm,
coming I'm coming I'm coming, no, no, no, noooooooooooo
ooooooooooooooooooooooooooooooooooooooooooooooooo
ooooooooooooooooooooooooooooooooooooooooooooooooo
ooooooooooooooooooooooooooooooooooooooooooooooooo
ooooooooooooooooooooooooooooooooooooooooooooooooo
ooooooooooooooooooohhhhhhhhhhhhhhhhhhhhhhhhhhhhh-
hh!!!!!!…………

The signs are down, the arrows and the traffic flow and the
posters even and the lights, they're holding aloft a walker they
found, they're marching on the boulevard laughing, cars are
honking they're swerving, the highway signs and the exits,
numbers marching, like a demented horde during a demonstration holding aloft the casket of a great revolutionary hero
they are holding aloft the walker, the lone walker of this day, Al
Rahboro again, aloft, and throwing him up even one two three
four who's the walker of the city, walk and chant and laugh and
the cars going and the arrows still at times shooting down the
roofs, now names of shops and names of buildings join in the
act and then the letters too! Saying to hell with it, we ain't gonna take it no more! No freedom, no words! They detach, one
by one, the letters, of the names, of the signs, the 'h', the 'a', the
'l', of the Hallmark store, yes, I witnesseth, the 'k' and the 'i'
and the 'm' of the laundry joint too, flying away, just like that,
floating in the sky, with the shoppers noticing suddenly with
their bags how letters and drawings are just floating above, in
the air, what, is that, not a, no, not even, well, just the letters
of the alphabet, in effect giving the finger to the signs and

now the billboards and now even the bulletin boards of the su-permarket and even the papers flying around more paper and more letters even the ones off the marquee of the movie house and off the boards in the grass of the church and all the letters of the alphabet telling them to go to hell, no way to treat us, we precious tools, no way to treat the letters of the alphabet and so the papers joining in I see it all floating about, coolly, comfortably, just not going to take it any more, just being free, the letters and the papers and even pens I now see, and then the words, how can that be! Telling to hell with it, you can't use me, gratuitously! O cashier O neighbor just can't say, Hi may I help you, and mean nothing, what the hell is that! I swear I see the cashier begin to say, Hi may I h—, and then 'help' just rebelled, just detached itself from her lips and ut-tered under breath, Fuck you, and flew away, liberated with its brethren chanting, I'm free, I'm free, O cashier, can't use me, so gratuitously, and the poor girl as if her lips had been sewn or invaded by aliens, just no words coming out, nothing, one by one rebelling, no more no more chanting, folks emitting monstrous noises then running out crying, seeing all around the parking lot the cashier of the coffee shop and the woman in the gourmet store and the waiter in the burger joint and another and another and the shoppers even running about, hands on mouths unbelieving, what the letters and the words and the papers are doing and now even some pens I see float-ing above locking arms and in a line, a chorus line, up above, the parking lot, swinging their bods, shaking their booty, we're free, we're free, O cashier O real estate agent O anchormanor-woman on TV, we're free, can't use us, so gratuitously, and the folks running trying to scream but not even the scream is cooperating, just hanging out, under a tree, laughing, not for him the chorus line but he's in with the union, solidarity of sorts, no, not even the scream, just the letters floating above the parking lots and the words out of the mouths of all the cliché-spewing creatures ruling our goddamn lives, and the signs and the arrows shooting down at the cars into their roofs the terrorized citizens running out of their cars in-between, cars enjoying themselves, going forward pause, backward pause, left pause, swerve low, slow, right pause, go, gone, in the parking lot, like kids in the playground, climbing descending left right back forth, pause and go, the chorus floating in the sky, O mister anchorman, O cable guy, O nonprofit director and company heads and headhunters, shut up, shut the hey up ey, the words and exclamations and the screams and the onomatopoeia, all in revolt, floating, alone singing happily can't use me, so gratuitously, I'm free, I'm free, the football players and the cheerleaders now on the sidewalk joining in if you can't beat 'em join 'em kind of on the street they tried the high school cheer but the words laughing at them said uh-uh no way not here not today, only one chant, this day, and then they laughed and so the cheerleaders and the grunting football players and the coaches and the screaming parents living vicariously through the kids and the football and basketball and baseball and soccer and field hockey assistants all, men's and women's, itching to scream or grunt or make some sort of noise, acquiesce, on the sidewalk, with the lone walker held aloft they sing, we're sorry, we're sorry, you're all free, won't use you, promise we do, so so so gratuitously, it's all a nice kind of harmony this chant, their chant, the words and the letters of the alphabet, the papers floating laughing letting go, the arms locking up again, kicking, say their lines and pause and the cheerleaders and the players and the coaches on the sidewalk in harmony kicking up their legs, their arms, doing their lines while the arrows still shoot up and down into the cars' roofs and the shoppers and the passersby holding hands in front of mouths scurrying about as if, and the signs and the billboards and the silhouettes holding aloft the lone walker throw him up in the air and catch him and hey ho right back up and down, the cheerleaders sing the messed-up songs, all the songs of this book now in revolt, all the songs of the book all scrambled and scattered, O Teenager in the Cubicle, eat your movies in the Mall, and now again they line up the cheerleaders of a cheerless world, leg up leg down, chanting now chanting wow, what the hell is going on, yes it seems like all the songs of the book, all the odes of the book also in revolt, all over the place, out of control, this verse and that strophe, this line and that rhyme,

O food court at the cubicle
O food court at the cubicle
The cars are parked in your testicle
O teenagers in the cubicle

Wallow not in your cineplex
Eat some shrimp and have some sex
O teenager at the food court
Hit on some chick and buy her some Tex-Mex!

They chant, they weave, they sing and laugh, their legs go high, high in the air, and then wow, all together now,

O teenager in the parking lot
Watching the cars and all their might
Check out the Mazdas and the Toyotas
You wish you were a trust fund mutt
O teenager in the food court
Eat your basement in the cubicle!

And... And thus the words out of order, it's all crumbling it's all crumbling, teenager in the car parking cock, stop the cubicle from the basement shock, O my lord shouting the cute cheerleader, O my god the male holder of the pyramid, O Jesus O Jesus what the hey, where are the words, where is the rhyme, where is the reason, where is the rhyme again, makes no sense, what are my lips uttering, what are my hips swaying to, where, who, what, am I, am I, am I, O teenager in the testicle, and the cars in the parking lots back and pause and left and go and stop and go and right and swerve and see and go and check this out now, it seems, yep, they're all banding, with the traffic signs and the cars now setting up, that's what it is, a passion play, a historical enactment of sorts, and whaddaya know, it's a passion play about the events of this book! There's a Honda and a Toyota and a traffic sign, and others, taking roles of Mappolo and A. and Rey and secondary associates even and Steve too, the deadest of heroes of books, a passion play with folks walking down the street beating chests and wailing, cars in a long line mourning, black overcoats, beating hoods, signs coming down crashing on roofs, becoming a spectacle of sorts, humming The Ballad of Mappolo Rei, re-enacting the initial abduction of Steve, the one that launched it all, *Ostrich in a Cadillac Ostrich in a Cadillac*, they chant and wail, *There there*, they chant, repeating the legendary words of A., *An Ostrich in a Cadillac*, and they march the cars do, and the signs accompany them in the air and on the ground and what not, *Are you sure, are you sure*, goes up the chant as did Steve's not so long ago and the wailing again commences and the beating of hoods and doors, *Yes yes there is an ostrich in that Cadillac an ostrich I tell you*, and they go again re-enacting the ritualistic legend, the myth already wow, so soon, there they go the wailing begins and the cars beating their hoods and their windows, quite an accurate depiction I must say of the beginnings of the new era, even though most of the times the stories get embellished but no not here, quite accurate the words and the sequences, I must say. TVs are out now, and the VCR and the fax machines decided to go out for a stroll, plus they've got some interesting stuff going on, leashes they've got around the folks, wow, that looks fun, the dishwasher and the fridge too, the computers and the ovens, they're all on the streets, decided to join in, go for a stroll it's no sin, maybe some bizzaro sexual deviance, or appliances without prurience, we're not gonna take it no more type chant, better things to do than rave and rant, gosh darn it we ain't gonna take it no more, out in the streets with humans on leashes—for sure! On the sidewalks with the adults and children, the TV sets and computer screens dominate. More forgiving are the faxes and the phones, carrying their masters them too, but it just seems like they're less upset than the television sets. The drivers without words, hands on mouths, spitting out nothing, not even blood or teeth (this is a different type of torture, the words and letters shout, you can't talk, and you're not even sick), running askance, traumatized, terrorized, not knowing what the heck to do. Hondas abandoned and Toyotas too and Beamers and SUVs, they're fine with it they're having a hoot, cheering on the televisions and the computer towers and monitors and laptops showing up, they all hang out, they honk, on their own, honk honk bravo, honk honk bravo, way to go, TVs and computers yo, make them suffer, those insufferable hoes! And a whole family now with mom and dad and grandpa who lives upstairs and the teenager out of the basement they place them there, in the yard, and hack off their hands or cut off their feet, and place them in the yard and put prices on them and then stand, the fridge and the TV and the fax machine and now all, y, a, r, d, all together now, a yard, a yard, a yard sale. And they laugh and they sing the Yard Sale Song along the lines of the YMCA Song, The Village People's version now sung by The Burb Appliances, a human Yard Sale, Y, A, R, D, flagging down the cars showing them the way, a used grandpa for sale, a cut up teenager, sliced up soccer mom, all for sale in the Y, A, R, D, all for sale, applause and chants and cheers and the arrows still shooting down all in fun with the letters and the words and the papers flying around the cars parked go ahead into each other bump and clank and bump and clank and a Honda goes smashing through into the rear of a beamer and bumps into a Ford SUV in front and bang, *métissage* of races, multiracial cars, mulattos, a multiethnic vehicle, knew it would come to this, what beauty, bravo, folks on the other side see this, and all the cars now bumping into each other and sliding into each other and penetrating, and even taking bites out of each other, they're learning from their makers and riders, a little *carribalistic* urge here and there, munching on each other's parts, why not, pretty delicious it seems, miam miam miam, munching and merging, merging and becoming one, what an osmosis of makes and models, I knew the traffic flow would end up creating a whole new way of life, I knew the traffic flow would provide the opportunity for phantasmagoric forms of liberty, O beauteous parking lot, O magnanimous traffic flow, go, go, and give the world what it deserves, a multicultural population of mulatto cars, changing the shapes of our society, color-blind, make-blind, model-blind, O parking lot and traffic flow, you great agents of democracy and muted purveyors of equality, breaking all lines, all barriers of color, make, model, year, shape, breaking even concrete things such as electricity poles and poles of all kinds and wires now all entangled, like a spiderweb of sorts, tree trunks and wooden poles and metal poles and basketball ones and their wires and fences all bent out of shape, all down at a whole array of angles, a canvas now the earth and the air, a three-dimensional artist's palette in dreams like a spiderweb, a futuristic bubble, a world unknown, with letters and papers and pens floating, playing with the wires and the fences and the TVs carrying on leashes the men and the women of their households and the children too, without mercy they are, TV listings now appearing on the walls and the sky even since all the TVs are out and seeing as to how urgent the listings can be, not wanting to miss any shows like, you know, especially since the VCRs are out too and, what the, what's this, yeah it is, shopping carts let loose now too they're mowing people down, a revenge of sorts, and the cars still foolin' around into each other, and the letters and the words are still floating and the signs and the arrows shooting in all directions except now getting caught in the entangled web of electrical cords and fences and wires and letters of the alphabet, laughter rising out of all the appliances without a whimper out of a human, thank god, they're all still running about like crazed automatons, hands on mouths or hands on heads, sad to see, truly, really sad to see, on leashes and some on knees crying, with the letters of the alphabet and the words and the papers and the pens all floating about, in the air, in the air, floating about in the air, with the cars bumping and laughing and the TVs holding their household hoes on their leashes and the arrows still shooting down and the wires and fences and ropes and pens all intertwined, dancing around, under the sun, the rain, the sky, today, Y, A, R, D, yard yard yard, saaaaaaaaaaaaaalllle, it's a yard sale, it's a yard sale, and all the other songs again, teenager in the cubicle, what's growing on your testicle, O Chinese food at the court mall, may I please have another small, better this than the motionful yard sale song, try it again though here we go, here we go now, Y, A, R, D, why it's a, Y, A, R, D, sale, and all now in chaos, in total disarray, rhymes in disarray, lines in disarray, lives in disarray, Suburbiana run amok, Suburbiana in disarray, Suburbiana in decline, the fall of Suburbiana, the end of Suburbiana, the Fall of the Great Suburbiana, the Fall of the Suburban Empire, O what a day, O what a day O, the words and the lines and the letters are free, they're free, floating about, sky canvas of the poet's pen, can't take them anymore, so gratuitously, so so gratuitously, so gratuitouslyyyyyyyyyyyyyyyyyyyyyyyyyyyyyyyyyyyyyyyyy yyyyyyyyyyyyyyyy...

Three possible endings from which the reader shall choose only one, and this after, I repeat, after reading all three, only fair: this way, an equal opportunity is given to each of the potential/actual endings, even though in the present non-hypertextual format, one actually ends the book, thus undermining in a fabulously double meta-deconstructionist sort of way the very debate between intertext and hypertext and not only that, but the very relevance of the hypertextual model and its potential masonry. Here we go.

The first ending's summary

Another séance of cannibalism (in this version, Rey throws a party much like Mappolo's and they all feast). But the resistance to the resistance is strengthened and agents of order surround the condo. It's actually now police officers and the real forces of law in Whooton. Word was out that a whole bunch of folks were creating a raucous and basically that they were pushing it and getting way, waaaaaaayyyy too loud, and so the authorities said enough is enough already and then arrested them all and told them to behave and let them back out. Refusal to surrender or back down until P.O. Schoorztet grabs Irani by the collar and says, 'Listen bud, simmer down all right,' upon which the coward Irani acquiesces and pretty much says, 'All right, yes sir, definitely sir.' And then, within this potential ending number 1, three possible endings to the ending: a) Irani goes home and really gives up the whole charade; b) Irani goes home and cusses out P.O. Schoorztet and takes rifle and goes after him and makes it personal; c) Irani goes home and gathers troops and they swarm the streets (with the ending of this ending still to be developed).

Summary of second potential ending

'Damn it dude,' Irani shouts at Sanjip Ray, concerning the failure of the troops to detect the presence of spirits, as in other-worldly spirits, at their big gatherings. This precipitates the debilitating weakening of the forces. Later, they find out that the ghosts of all the murdered motorists had come back and were taking revenge the only way they could. And so, the fabella becomes a veritable ghost story of sorts, a mystery novel. Real corny and awful. Which could mean big sales. And translations into many many languages. Great. And so endeth The Short Reign of Reza Irani The First. Too bad.

And, last but not least, offered in similar linguistic-representational format, for better or for worse (or—):

Ending number three

14

Come and see! Come and see! Come and see the great spoils of victory! Come and see the lies and the deception! Come and see the tortured ones and the ripped-up ones and the traumatized children of town in burnt-out homes! Come and see the joy in the heart of the victors! Come and see the SUVs rolling down the freeways! Come and see the parking lots full, full of fuel-consuming fools! Come and see the sway of the great cars, O great and fantastic and fabulous automobiles riding down the freeways. Come and see the breathtaking sight of lines and lines of cars zooming by, shooting by, in the day in synchrony and at night lights that shoot through the darkness like stars in the sky! Come and see, come and see, the marvels of parking lots and traffic flows, the beauty and the glory of parking lots, the mesmerizing beats of traffic flows, the splendor of the traffic flow, come and see, the great stillness, the great quietude, the majesty, of the parking lots, come and see the wonders of the traffic flow!

Tercet number two, verse number three, O patient and perceptive reader. Unnecessary to brace yourself. No evocation onto the supernatural upcoming, no dramatic opening onto fantastical realms through a last, enigmatic passage. Just a deep breath. And your eyes wide open now and another deep breath… There you go… A quick glance at all that preceded

and swift intake of this the last gasp, where we end: in the ex-
pectation of The Great Divan...

It appears (coming back to our tale) as though Rey Irani's crude measures were indeed carried out, with even more
aplomb, more probity, more ferocity than one could have
imagined. In a sense, the players involved 'got into it' a lot
more than they might have thought, even those who had nothing to do with Mappolo before.

The delights they took in the suffering of The Great Traitor
of the Revolution! In the slow torture of The Beast! A little
finger cut here, one inch at a time, a piece of skin, one slab at
a time.

'Come on, scream louder!' yells one señor Rodriguez (NC),
a monstrous dude who'd just come into the fold, completely
clueless about the history of the struggle or Mappolo's place in
it, and simply allowing his own frustrations and primal murderous urges to be met through the rationalized justification
of a need for torturers, not to mention the fact that the times
a-needed torturers, and so he'd gotten a job, simple as that,
with status and future remuneration at that. (El señor Rodriguez on his ukulele strumming fast the strings: *Ayayayay, yo
soy quien manda, ayayayay, tú eres quien grita, ayayayay, en este
mundo no todos somos poetas, ayayayay...*) All brutes have their
day, it must be said (not true for: _____; fill in the blank, because frankly, there are quite a few monsters out there who
have not had their day!), and so el señor Rodriguez should
watch his back...

Thus did Rodriguez do Rey Irani the favor of heating the
saucepan, throwing olive oil in it, and offering seasoned finger
bits of Mappolo. Rey Irani ate them before Mappolo's eyes,
grimacing, the latter, even though the hurt had passed him by,
physically speaking.

'Hmmm,' Rey is reported to have uttered, or so the legend goes, 'fingerlickin' good—pun intended!' He had then unleashed such a thunderous laughter that the entire building had shaken, not to mention the furniture and other assortments of household items.

Further, in an arrangement with the Superhuge Supermarket, a festival was arranged by the new leader. A wide corridor in front of the parking lot at the Bestest Shopping Center was cordoned off, separated with a stylish curtain, courtesy of World Draperies. In other words, an exciting extravaganza awaited the populace, first chance last dance sort of deal, don't miss out kind of shebang, The Mappolo Maiming, right here in Whooton, the cutting into pieces of a Revolutionary Traitor. Global Kitchenworks even donated their New! Innovative! Total! Cooking Machine!, and their top of the line non-stick saucepan series for the event. Something was brewing all right, a whole lot of festivities.

'Not since The French Revolution has any public been privy to such a magnanimous carriage of Justice!' the official ad campaign presented the multimedia multiday multicultural multiaffair. 'And even then! Not even The French Revolution could claim to have The Leading Blasphemer, The Foremost Treason Fellow in the gallows. Come and treat yourself to an unparalleled Spectacle. Come and see The Great Traitor Suffer Vile Tortures and Abominable Treatment. Come and see your Leaders inflict Savage Punishment on a Traitorous Worm wriggling before your very eyes. Come and see The Miscreant beg for Mercy, scream, squeal, and cry his eyes out as The Brave Soldiers of Freedom and The Righteous Path cut off his limbs and all sorts of body parts, slowly, oh so slowly! A once-in-a-lifetime opportunity to witness the squirming of The Highest Enemy of the State, this or any other state for that matter, of the rendering of Justice in unparalleled fashion! Tuesday through Saturday only! Lawn chairs provided for public cutting ceremony, doors open at 5. Refreshments provided. First hundred guaranteed Cut-of-the-Day's seasoned body part delicacies, courtesy of Myomye Videos. Kids under twelve eat free with accompanying adult.'

The Mappolo Maiming, as the event came to be called in its popular, water-downed version (the official, legal, political, historical, written-down-in-the-books version, dictated by the next and last Rey, was: 'The Trial, Torture, Maiming and Eating of the Devious and Blasphemous Traitor, Mappolo Rei, Guilty of the Highest Crime Against Whooton and the Citizens Thereof'), lasted one day more than the advertisement had promised, a fact no one complained about, seeing as to how it proved to be quite exciting, productive and even profitable for all concerned. Superhuge Supermarket didn't complain, what with the boost in circulation they got as curiosity-seekers as well as extended families of citizens dropped in and frequented the show under the tent and, as oft occurs, ambled into the actual supermarket before (not for nothing that the doors to the tent opened at 5) and after (if kids got bored; if spectacle wasn't all that was promised; if neither torturer nor victim lived up to expectations in their roles). Monti too, the fellow who wants to be a real estate broker who wants to be a famous TV anchor, made sure to drop by, after having abandoned, with all due apologies, any actual involvement in the planning, and after telling his bosses that he had to take the day off. He couldn't believe his colleagues from the office weren't going, what with the magnitude of the event. Forgetting for a moment that food was also going to be provided, he had even stopped by a drive-through window, no time to waste, and bought a couple of big macs on the way, which he'd chowed down on as he'd driven, what with traffic backed up, what with so many people going, what with the rock star and the rock concert atmosphere, what with the hullabaloo associated with the event. And he was not the only one who was motivated. Whole families with picnic baskets and sheets and other amenities had made their way, made the pilgrimage one might say, and many of them also had stopped at the drive-through, or at any number of fast food joints to make sure they would be well-fed and to make sure they got there in the right condition.

Mappolo Rei, of course, our dear dear old friend, our unforgettable and unforgettably crude and bound-to-be-forgotten hero, did indeed get a variety of limbs and body parts cut off, sliced, chopped and eaten in front of his own eyes. (Even now, as I write of his grotesque demise, his swift descent into historical footnoteness and irrelevance, his physical deactivation and possible decapitation, I cannot but recall fondly the days stocking the shelves religiously (how far they seem) while plotting his masterpiece the revolution, his crazy vagabondage between unrecognizable violence and almost saintly assistance, between delirious self-aggrandizement and humility, between exuberant extravagance and just as exuberant ascetism. Ahhh that sweet smile, that devilish charm with which he seduced friend and foe alike, that can't-put-your-finger-on-it-type charisma that led him to the justified elimination of A., wherefrom, Justice, that punishes thus the genii of our times, reserved for him, the architect of perhaps the grandest of revolutions, the most ignominious of fates! Will he at least get his wish on his tombstone, the dream of a life he never had, the game he never played, his line for immortality, box score, Super bowl, fourth quarter,

Johnson three pass from Rei, Kiriakos field goal? Will he? Will they grant him that? Oh, I doubt it I do, really doubt it, Oyo, Oyo, he was a child at heart... Enough, enough, my aching, nostalgic wrist!) No joke. His fingers first, as Rey Irani had promised (the pinky on the right hand and the same on the left had already been consumed by Irani and Rodriguez), the index on the left and then on the right, then the thumb on the right and the left, plus the last one on both, leaving only the middle finger (O cruel destinies, is this how?...) of each hand. A 'Salade de doigt' was offered as a delicacy on the second day at The Mappolo Maiming, with a spicy vodka cream and béarnaise sauce, served on a bed of linguini. Several cuts off his buns came next (day two also, leftovers offered on day three as 'Ass Haché' in a mild red wine sauce), followed by one ear (left), and three random toes on each foot with audience participation (the twist) as children and parents were invited to step on Mappolo's toes (and upper foot—could not realistically be avoided) as a first step in literally squishing and breaking them, only then to be passed on to the official medical authority (the torturer was bypassed in this exercise) who would proceed to cut off the limp useless limbs. The atmosphere at the 'toe-steppin' session' was quite joyful and merry: imagine, if you will, young kids jumping out of control in those bubbles at schools' year-end field days, ponies riding on the grass, jump ropes, water-gun fights, the sack races with one leg each of a couple in the sack while they tumble and fumble and fall trying to reach their destined mark, the water-jug-filling teens, the spoon races, the face-painting bonanzas, the relays, the jump ropes, the hoop shots. Quite the carnavalesque atmosphere! And picture now same nine-year-olds jumping not on the trampoline or in the space bubble but on Mappolo's feet, him tied and bound, unable to move, push off, or fend off, the invading hordes.

Subsequent to the cutting off of the toes, and the meticulous preparation of 'Toasted Toes' by Grand Chef Joe Lecoupeur, who was invited to prepare the extraordinary delicacy, the audience consumed heartily the magnificent dish. For comic relief and the pleasure of Grand and Eternal Leader of the People's Revolution, and to appropriately remember the descent of a wannabe into disrepute, a charlatan who will be known as the greatest footnote in history, perhaps the only true Footnote (with a capital F), a country/western band was hired for some high-steppin' and toe-kickin' session with some kick-ass tunes!

Soon, the other torturer (the new lad's name was Edwin Pizzaro (NC), thirty-eight years old, 6'8" tall and with a humongous belly, shaved head, a jungle of hair on his back and a round face but no facial hair—spoke four languages though, and despite appearances, chosen profession, alliances and allegiances, history of brutality and voting history, was apparently not such a bad guy after all, volunteered to read at a local non-profit to both pre-k kids and the elderly, and was even rumored to have worked with the blind, something he did not readily advertise for fear of the disintegration of his bad-guy image) and the medical examiner collaborated on hacking off Mappolo's right foot, then prevented any future bleeding and complications with some bandaging, then forcefully and forcibly opened wide Mappolo's mouth and shoved the foot, toes missing and front first, into it, then shut back the mouth and sewed the lips in such a way that Mappolo could not change the appearance (and could breathe only through the nose), leaving him there literally with his foot in his mouth.

At the end of this process, the delighted audience stood and applauded like never before, recognizing the genius of, what is it, this punful coming-to-life of an obviously tropological (if not topical) expression. To such an extent that a standing ovation was prompted by aficionados for such great avant-garde performance art, upon which a bit of name-calling ensued between audience members, what with class and status coming to the fore, the upper members deriding the still-sitting 'hicks' whose children were just running around unaware of the magnitude of the accomplishment, of the unique, glorious, unequaled, unparalleled artistic accomplishment. Between, basically, those who were treating it all as a day in the park, and those who with utmost seriousness were present to think and appreciate the profound contribution to civilization (not to mention the arts) of the spectacle. But so be it. Such misunderstandings and differences are to be expected at such events. Part of the game. Comes with the territory.

Anyway, after the foot came the balls and the penis (shoved down his own asshole) making of poor Mappolo a eunuch with his foot in his mouth, his dick in his ass, and his middle fingers up. Next came some skin (off his back), followed by a hair cut, subsequent to which his shaved head was painted in red. A leg, at last, making him stand on only one. By request of Irani, a huge rock was ordered (courtesy of Road Chicken Portable Rocks) and also a Hard Place (courtesy of Places in the Heart), the first placed on Mappolo's left—and close to his body—the other on his right. For comic effect, one of his arms was tied behind his back, the other left bound to the cross. His eyes were left wide open.

Thus was Mappolo Rei left standing: on one leg, between a rock and a hard place, with his foot in his mouth and some skin off his back, his head shaved and painted, one arm tied behind, his middle finger up, and his dick up his own *hachéd* ass.

For several days, Mappolo was left outside for public viewing, with the audience invited to stroll by (lawn chairs were removed) to 'get a last glimpse of the tortured soul.'

The last day, one of Mappolo's eyes was to be taken out and cooked as the ultimate delicacy. VIPs and celebrities were invited, from judges to local actors, journalists, wannabe filmmakers, the high school drama teacher and young struggling painters. Finally, in a last conclusive act, all were invited to witness the medieval miracle: Mappolo's brain would be removed (him still standing in the same position, with cranes and ladders steadying the specialists who were to perform the operation), placed on a central table, to be smashed to pieces in a free-for-all—hammers and sickles provided. Rey Irani had made a point of not wanting to cook the brain, to emphasize that this (the whole shebang) was not about money, but justice. (All fees were duly waived.) Finally, the nose and flesh from the still technically able body would be mixed to create a most unique potage, with a variety of vegetables, herbs, spices and nose hair, to be cooked in a giant *marmite* (pot), provided courtesy of Marmites Online. This last spicy addition to the festivities proved to be quite the success. The limos drove up dropping off the VIPs, they rolled the red carpet, and an unabashed good time was had by all. The last day truly brought all the folks together. Soup was eaten, bread was broken, and folks even brought their own (from wine and soda to salad and fried chicken) in an impromptu BYOW (whatever) extravaganza. The rest of the rest of Mappolo's body was left to rot, subsequent to which it was all cut up and fed to the wild dogs at Annie's. Superhuge reported a 40% increase in sales daily during The Mappolo Maiming. The event and its aftermath, in other words, had been quite the unparalleled triumph. Bravo, Rey Irani (and publicists).

And, of course, there was the matter of the head, what with Mappolo's constituting nothing less than an absolute symbol of the victory of Truth over Falsehood, Justice over Injustice, Righteousness over Wickedness. Not only that, but a spoil of war, and a symbolic reminder to anyone interested enough, curious enough, to find out what might await them if they even thought about challenging Irani's reign. Furthermore, our Man in Suburbia had gutted out Mappolo's apartment (it goes without saying), and put on display his monstrous deeds, but also had taken care to preserve and have transported his quite exquisitely assembled and admittedly impressive Head Case with the many heads of the victims. Many were exhibited (not all could be included of course), a selection from those he had taken particular delight in thus exposing (even if for minor and ancient reasons). Irani then, rather than have the Head Case brought to his and his sister's abode, had it installed at Poppy's, which he was secretly planning to turn into a shrine, an arch of triumph of sorts, since Poppy's—privately owned by James 'Poppy' McGrath, sixty-five years old, old army vet— had managed to get its own arches installed in an underhanded blow to the more famous yellow arches sprouting all over the globe. (Poppy himself gained employ within Irani's security detail.) Mappolo's head, with his foot eternally in his mouth, would be placed in the middle as the centerpiece of a permanent exhibition highlighting the struggle for freedom, justice and the new Whootonian way.

The fate of the final four held at Poppy's was just as expediently determined. They were kept alive and force-fed leftovers from Mappolo's members' parts. Soon after Mappolo's remains were fed to the dogs, the remaining associates were summarily executed and also fed to the same decidedly well-fed and fat dogs, their meat judged excessively *haram* to be consumed by any of the new leadership's members. Also, no one else in Whooton had demonstrated much of a real appetite for the sort of cannibalism our good leader had used to get into power. Although they had indeed enjoyed the ears and feet and fingers, not to mention that sumptuous Ass Haché, they were not, one could say, really into doing it every day. Although, perhaps, it's just an acquired taste… Hey, to each his own. And Rey Irani agreed. Let Annie's dogs have their fill—when else are they gonna get five bodies in one week! Let 'em enjoy the day as much as we!

Irani's vision appears again. He is on a float before the adoring crowds. He waves his hands and smiles. The clueless fans and groupies and loyalists scream and shout his name. Confetti drops from the skyscrapers he has helped build in Reyville with top architects whose works have graced the New York skyline. From balconies and windows and fire escapes they wave. He waves back. His entourage is a bit worried about the open-air celebration and tries to protect him but he says, Easy fellas, relax. (Doesn't he watch the history channel, thinks his head securities detail guy, Ray Bocincelli, doesn't he know he's ripe for assassination, isn't he in on the coup rumors!) He is enjoying the moment in the sun. Literally. He will be invited to celebrity-studded events. He will be keynote speaker and guest lecturer and honorary award receiver at countless functions. He will be revered and even roasted—at the comedy club of course. Children in elementary schools and even teenagers in high school will work on projects dissecting and chronicling his achievements. They will put those projects on the walls of their schools and online and soon the authorities will catch up and stamps will be

*issued bearing a portraitist's likeness of him. Boulevards and hous-
ing projects in the city will bear his name, as they always do the
great heroes of entire nations. Mothers will name their children
after him and the ladies will ask husbands and lovers to get his
haircut, or wear his style of clothes, or just, just, try to be like him.
Bracelets will appear bearing the initials, WWRD—What Would
Reza Do. He will unleash the suicides of countless jealous husbands, and the suicides of countless young women who want him
but can't have him and unfortunately, the murder of wives whose
husbands cannot bear the thought of their companions dreaming
dreams with the master of the universe, him. Architects will plead
with him, beg him, to allow them to build palaces that do justice
to his stature in the community, in the world, but in humility and
to make sure he keeps his modesty, he will say no, and continue to
say no, and keep to his humble ways, and direct the money to public works and projects. Until a few hours later when he gives up,
even though he doesn't want to, and tells them to go ahead with the
palaces, if that's what the people want, 'Fine, fine!' he acquiesces.
'Build me a palace!' Soon he will be worshipped as the sun god.
There will be a monument bearing his statue on the to-be built
(first on his list) gates of the city. Foreign emissaries (or even those
nincompoops from neighboring Pebbleville) will all first have to
stop and kneel there and pay their respects when on official visits.
His legend will grow and in a thousand years or so, folks will beat
their chests or heads or some other body part with some object, and
they'll sing his name and wail and cry and shout some more. If he
could he'd start his own religion. But who's got time for that! Well,
maybe... We'll see... Ahhh, how clear it all seems. How obvious.
How inevitable, how beauteous and wondrous indeed...*

*Rey Irani on a float now with his head mistress, the Eternal
Queen, with whom he planned to create the purest of lineages and
all the future leaders of this and all other 'burbs, rides atop and*

waves to the throng of Whootonites crowding the sidewalks: they stand tall and the parade goes on, with other floats, commemorating another year, whatever year it was, why not start a new calendar since they were at it, but it was not to be forgotten that they, Rey Irani and future bride, tall, tan and tantalizing future bride, were to be the centerpiece of the whole spectacle. (Plus, no more homecoming games, or in a deal brokered at the last minute, no homecoming queen, for there would be only one, only one queen, Rey, Rey Irani's queen.)

One week later, Irani decided that the event indeed shall take place, now that the earth had been cleansed of Mappolo Rei, now that all order was back (even though it had never gone), now that monotony, banality and odious (O so odious) tranquility was back in full force: now was the time to have the parade and crown the next King of Kings (for Irani had the real illusion that he would become a demagogic all-powerful king of the suburbs), forever and ever and ever The One Down Below Sign of Him Up Above, The Delegate, The Man, in other words, a Bigwig for Life! Rey Irani and who?

Who did you say?
Who do you think?

Suzy, who'd come out and enjoyed Mappolo's flesh?
(Not quite.)

The girl A. met at the 7-Eleven
from whom the reader never heard again?
(Nice try, better luck next time.)
(And oh, by the way, did, or not, anyone

ever give her a call?! Perhaps the matter shall be
resolved in a sequel, since, upon the arrest and
punishment of Mappolo, the number was,
yes, was, found by Irani, who did, indeed,
think about it, intrigued as hell about the possibilities.)

The leggy, busty, and plenty-assed Bernadette Bunns,
back for more fun?
(Way to go—not!)

Could it be...
Don't tell me...
Seems like it—
Yes it is, 'tis indeedy!

Reyna Irani, his SISTER!
His lover, his sin and his soul,
his demon and his whore,
devouring flesh (and blood),
his bride-to-be!

Rey and Reyna on a float high above waving to the hundreds of thousands of hundreds of thousands gathered in the parking lots adjoining the grand boulevard, arm in arm, the ghost of Eddie Perez driving the car, a Camaro floating above the 'burbs, and through the 'burbs rushing through the streets and the boulevards and the parking lots, wide-angle shots and zooms and long takes, in and out of focus: the little girl crying in the parking lot, the gas station attendant with his downward eyes, in and out of focus the scenes through the shopping mall and the food court where an old Spanish-speaking woman sweeping floors asks two gentlemen eating bad

Chinese food at their table 'Sorry?' since she's sweeping and there's a spill under their table, and on and through with a construction worker with his hard hat, a night-watchman at the local store lost in his dreamdaze, wide-angle shots in and out of focus, in the parking lot the slumped businessman with his loosened tie coming out of the strip joint unmarked in the long row of stores in the shopping center, an ice-cream truck with the jingle calling the kids who run, in unison all shouting and screaming and laughing too, a swimming pool with the cool lifeguards on the seats high above checking out the action, unmoving, twirling the whistles in their hands, in and out of focus, the soccer team on the practice field with the insane moms and dads running along the sideline yelling with other parents clueless about the game yelling kick it kick it, kick it kick it, top of their lungs, screaming, way to go, way to go, kick it kick it, to no one nowhere and getting mad at the refs even, for a foul on a little child of theirs, in and out of focus their lost dreams and their pathetic vicarious channelings, in this far-flung suburb, their toiling away the weeks and their kids like so running about, their ambitions and child-like desires, go with it, go with it, the screams, sitting in rows of nylon chairs holding cups of coffee talking on phones chatting about work or stalking the sidelines, screaming, kick it kick it, way to go way to go, but no mo' no, no rooting for you, no yelling or supporting your kid, no running along with the kid on the sideline, no more free cheering, no more cheering, just shut up, shut up soccer mom and soccer dad, shut the fuck up and go get the water bottles from the portable coolers and hold them so that when the kids pass they just grab 'em, go, go do your duty and stop cheering, in and out of focus the tales, the pictures, have I said it all or have I forgotten things, it's a portrait and a story, a tale, of woe—a picture fo' sho'—the friendly attendants at the stores, the driving to work and driving to school and driving to lunch and driving all around that makes everyone fat, how it's been quantified suburban tools, you're all fatter you are, six pounds fatter on average, admit it and live with it and worry not, suburban sprawl makes folks fat, should read your headlines, in and out of focus the fat ones and their cars and the sidewalk loners and all these blokes begging in the streets of the urban chaos not so far away, begging, just crying and saying he's short a dime for his coffee, O how po'! In and out of focus the group gathering in the parking lot, the young teens putting in the trunk their newly acquired toys from the super-electronics stores, there is no raggedy unshaven cane-holding vagrant/bum/ex-philosopher hanging outside the coffee shops because here, all is pure, all is clean, all must be perfectly drawn and manicured, in and out of focus the teenagers, the teenager, in a basement, holding his guitar, strumming badly, pounding his head, a teenager, in a basement, somewhere, in anguish, in despair, lost, long lost, and his cries, and his despair, O teenager in the basement, O teenager in the basement, take your warts and all, you'll think back one day with utter disappointment, just 'cause you had this temperament, all this you'll look back on and laugh, the drug-induced daze and the lovers' quarrels, musical dreams, rebels' inklings, enjoy it while it lasts 'cause one day you'll go: plaf! O teenager in the basement, in and out of focus the whole of their lives, and time itself, slung on the shoulder of a bearded man, the sky, the clouds, Steve appearing smiling now, is that him, could it be, nahhh, the tale, a tale, stories, and songs, all up and about, floating, floating in the air with mister Rey Irani and his bride-to-be, about to launch the very first dynasty, right down here in Maryland, for those wondering, confetti raining down indeed, just like his vision, even though this is still another vision, deafening the cheers, deafening the roars, a poem sung by the poet laureate of Rey's court, generals and colonels and men of the cloth making sure they're in the picture, spoiling it all almost but Rey will not let that happen, won't let that bother him, he's come too far, he holds high the hands of his bride, his sister his soul, high above, checking her out with her big boobs and great legs, looking hot, they shall conquer it all one day, own it all, it will be all theirs, and passed down, one child to another, this dynasty will never die, we'll make sure of that, smiles, thunders at the adoring crowd, dreaming big dreams, more schools, more opportunity although not too much so they don't get in over their heads, and we'll build more parking lots, more parking lots and more roads leading to parking lots and more shops to park in front of and more highways and roadways for more traffic flow, traffic flow and parking lots, traffic flow and parking lots, O Rey, O Rey Rey, deliver us to the promised land, hail Emperor Rey, hail Rey Rey hail, hail Rey Rey hail, the kings are all dead, hail Rey, and his bride-to-be, hail the Reys!

(Should I now write: the curtain is pulled, one by one they appear, Mappolo and A., Steve and Rey, and the waitress and Joe and Applbottum and everyone else. And then write: they hold hands, stand a moment and peer into the distance, smiling, sweating. And then write: and in one full swoop, and not necessarily in perfect synchrony, seeing as to how exhausted they all must be, take a bow. And then add: then the curtain is closed, we stare at the still-flapping curtain, the applause is nonstop, a few even stand, in the front, prompting (shaming?) everyone else, one here, another there to the left, and then a pocket to the right and another, popping up like plants in a cartoon, to stand also and launch a full-fledged standing ovation along with some hollers and hoots. And then write: and the curtain is pulled again, and Mappolo says, 'Shout out to my homies in the 'hood (III), peace!' And then write that the emcee says, 'True that, true that,' and they bow again. Should I? Or should I go back to 'hail the Reys', eliminate this paragraph and continue? Yes: Pick it up after 'hail the Reys'—rewind noise please—back to 'hail'...)

Hail Rey Rey hail, hail Rey Rey hail, it's a glorious day and it is not, it's a heck of a non-eventful day and it is not, it's a good story and some might say, it is not: once upon a time,

under the big blue sky,

a man, young, impressionable, is walking up a flight of stairs. He turns, then turns again and walks all the way to the fourth floor of a garden apartment without a garden, as always. He stands in front of a door and knocks, once, knocks again, three times, then says, singingly, Happy days are here agaaaa-in, stops, then says, in same whisperish singing tone, I'm a loooooooser, then stops and says, Knock, knock, who's there. The sign, password of sorts, this string of expressions—and the door at which he is standing, opens...

Three young men and a slightly older gentleman are gathered around a TV that's on but on mute, with fast-changing images of a cartoon on the screen, it seems like. The older gentleman is shouting out directions and encouragement, definitely concocting something, and not wholly holy, if I may, brewing some sort of trouble, if I may again... (I think I've seen him before too... Here in fact, within the confines of this tale... I do believe I might actually have made him up here and referred to him... Or not...)

'Good good!' you hear him say. 'Great, let's keep it going!'

And the three men standing jump up and down and repeat

an idiotic exclamatory phrase, waving arms and exhibiting great panic on their faces.

'That's it boys, that's it!' he shouts. (Yes! I do remember him: it's E.! E. from chapter... That's right, I was gonna include him in chapter twelve and then just sort of brushed it to the side... He'd joined in with Mappolo against A. and then switched allegiances to Rey after Eddie's assassination and consumption—but I wish I'd never dreamt him up and now... And now! What nerve! Invading the space of the tale! Tryin' to... Could it... Could it really be that... Seems like...)

'Thinking they can pull one over our eyes like that, the bastards!' he quips. The three younger men smile and acknowledge E.'s anger, his wrath. 'They don't know who they're messing with!' he goes on. 'They just don't know now, do they?!'

And he lets out a weird laugh, a kind of evil laugh, come to think of it, which he ends abruptly to say, sternly, to his troops, 'Let's go boys, one more time, one last time, to make sure we got it right. One last time!'

Up stand the three young men, and on three, and a one, and a two, and a—: arms start waving frantically, facial expressions turn panicky, a desire, a lust, a need, revolution come, again, carry on:

'Woodpecker in a Volkswagen!' goes up the chant. 'Woodpecker in a Volkswagen!'

Louder, and louder, jumping up and down, all three, in perfect dis/harmony (the slash for keeping up with scholarly/ academic fashion and practices of my time, reader, perhaps not anymore yours):

'Woodpecker in a Volkswagen! Woodpecker in a Volkswagen!'

'Bravo!' E. says. 'Bravo—perfect!'

The congratulatory acknowledgment does not prevent one of the three men, after the 'at ease' command, to raise his hand

and ask, after permission was granted by E.: 'Do you really think that'll work, E., I mean, not a bit long, Woodpecker in a Volkswagen?'

E. looks at his young protégé with visible annoyance, but with an attempt at cooling his senses too, for the man is young, after all, needs some guidance, is all...

'You don't worry about that,' E. says. 'All right? You leave that to me!'

He then turns to the whole group, extends his arm, grabs the remote, and turns off the TV—accent on first syllable: heightened, awkward, as in *tee*vee.

(This way then, the end? Should I? With *tee*vee?! Really?! Or... And since I've always wanted to end a book with an 'or', what better than to do it now, and in an open parenthesis at that: write, or:

ABOUT AMIR PARSA

Amir Parsa was born in Tehran in 1968 and moved to the Washington, D.C. suburbs when he was ten. He went to French International schools both in Iran and the U.S., attended Princeton and Columbia universities, and currently lives in New York City with his wife and daughter. An internationally acclaimed writer, poet, translator and newformist, he is the author of seventeen literary works, including *Kobolierrot*, *Feu L'encre/Fable*, *Drive-by Cannibalism in the Baroque Tradition*, *Erre*, and *L'opéra minora*, a 440-page multilingual book that is in the MoMA Library Artists' Books collection and in the Rare Books collection of the Bibliothèque Nationale de France. An uncategorizable body of work, his oeuvre—written directly in English, French, Farsi, Spanish and various hybrids—constitutes a radical polyphonic enterprise that puts into question national, cultural and aesthetic attachments while fashioning innovative genres, discursive endeavors and species of literary artifacts. His writings in both English and French have been anthologized, and he has contributed to a number of print and online publications, including *Fiction International*, *Textpiece*, *Guernica*, *Armenian Poetry Project* and a mash-up issue of *Madhatters' Review* and *Bunk Magazine*. His translations include Bruno Durocher's *And They Were Writing Their History*, and the first two books of Nadia Tueni, which appeared under the title *The Blond Texts & The Age of Embers*. Since 2007, pieces from Parsa's ongoing *The New Definitely Post/Transnational and Mostly Portable Open Epic as Rendered by the Elastic Circus of the Revolution* have been featured at the Bowery Poetry Club, the Uncomun Festival, the Engendered Festival, the Dumbo Arts Festival in New York, and at the Baroquissimo Festival in Puebla, Mexico, among other venues. This literary work is comprised of cantos and fragments constituting an evolving plurilingual epic that unfolds over time on various platforms, in multiple arenas and spaces (private and public), and through various scriptural strategies—from the traditional (handwritten sheets, bound collections) to the new (electronic, web). In June 2010 at the Paris en Toutes Lettres Festival and in conjunction with the publication of his book-length poem *Fragment du cirque élastique de la révolution*, he put into action *The American in Paris is an Iranian in New York*, a ten-hour multiplatformal 'scriptage' taking place throughout Paris, with texts and images simultaneously projected at the Northern Manhattan Arts

Alliance during the Artstroll Festival. The *Skizzi Ska* ensemble and *Ifs & Co*—dubbed ALEA for Alternative Literary Experiences and Adventures—constitute single-edition literary compositions and were completed in 2005 and 2007 respectively. Launched in 2015 with *Le Chaise (Yes, Le)*, a newer species is made up of the 'clandies', officially classified as Folios of the Clandestine Diffusion (FoCD), works characterized by their clandestine dissemination. The next clandie, slated to appear in 2016, is entitled *One Day Soon I Will Be the New Emperor of the New Persian Empire Just You Wait and See (And We Will All Live Happily Ever After I Promise)*. Parsa has instigated his unique encantations, readations and bassadigas, and conducted more traditional lectures, workshops and playshops on avant-garde poetics, literary/artistic innovation, critical education praxis and cultural design at museums and organizations across the world, including Norway, Mexico, Italy, France, Brazil, India and Spain. His curatorial interjections, conceptual pieces and interventions, artistic and performative fusions and subversions, along with photographic, participatory and exhibition-based projects have taken place in a host of galleries, public spaces, organizations and environments. As a Lecturer and Educator at The Museum of Modern Art, he directed the landmark Alzheimer's Project and developed programs, curricula, and learning experiences for a wide range of audiences, including the community partnerships, Wider Angles, Double Exposures and the Singular Educational Experience (SEE) entitled *1913: That Year This Time*—a multidisciplinary course that took place over twelve hours in MoMA's galleries and classrooms. He also conceptualized and created the ongoing PinG (Poets in the Galleries) program at the Queens Museum in 2007, the Rooftop Roars & Riverside Revolutions in uptown Manhattan, and the overall RiDE (Risk/Dare/Experiment) episodes at Pratt Institute in Brooklyn. He is currently at work on several series, including *La Pentalogia del Delirio*, *The Micro-Epic Decalogy* and the unfolding *¡O What a Revolution!*, an 11-piece suite exploring and analyzing the Iranian revolution of 1979 through various mediums, languages, strategies and discourses. He has taught at Columbia, the University of Girona in Spain, and the University of Maccerata in Italy. After serving as Chairperson and Acting Associate Dean, he continues to teach at Pratt Institute, where he is an Associate Professor and directs trans/post/neodisciplinary initiatives.

Meet Me
(2009, The Museum of Modern Art; with F. Rosenberg,
L. Humble, C. McGee)

Fragment du cirque élastique de la révolution
(2010, Ed. Caractères)

The Blond Texts & The Age of Embers
(2012, UpSet Press; translation of Nadia Tueni's 'Les textes blonds'
and 'L'âge d'écume')

*The New Definitely Post/Transnational and
Mostly Portable Open Epic as Rendered by the
Elastic Circus of the Revolution*
(2007-ongoing; multi-lingual, multi-mediatic,
multi-plat/formal literary epic)

Le Chaise (Yes, Le)
(2015, FoCD: Folios of the Clandestine Diffusion,
limited edition and distribution)

Tractatüus Philosophiká-Poeticüus
(2000, Ed. Caractères; 2015, UpSet Press)